RANKS OF THE BLOOD SERVICE

A SCI-FI ACTION ADVENTURE

THE CAPITAL ADVENTURES
BOOK 2

ALLEN IVERS

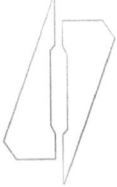

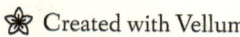

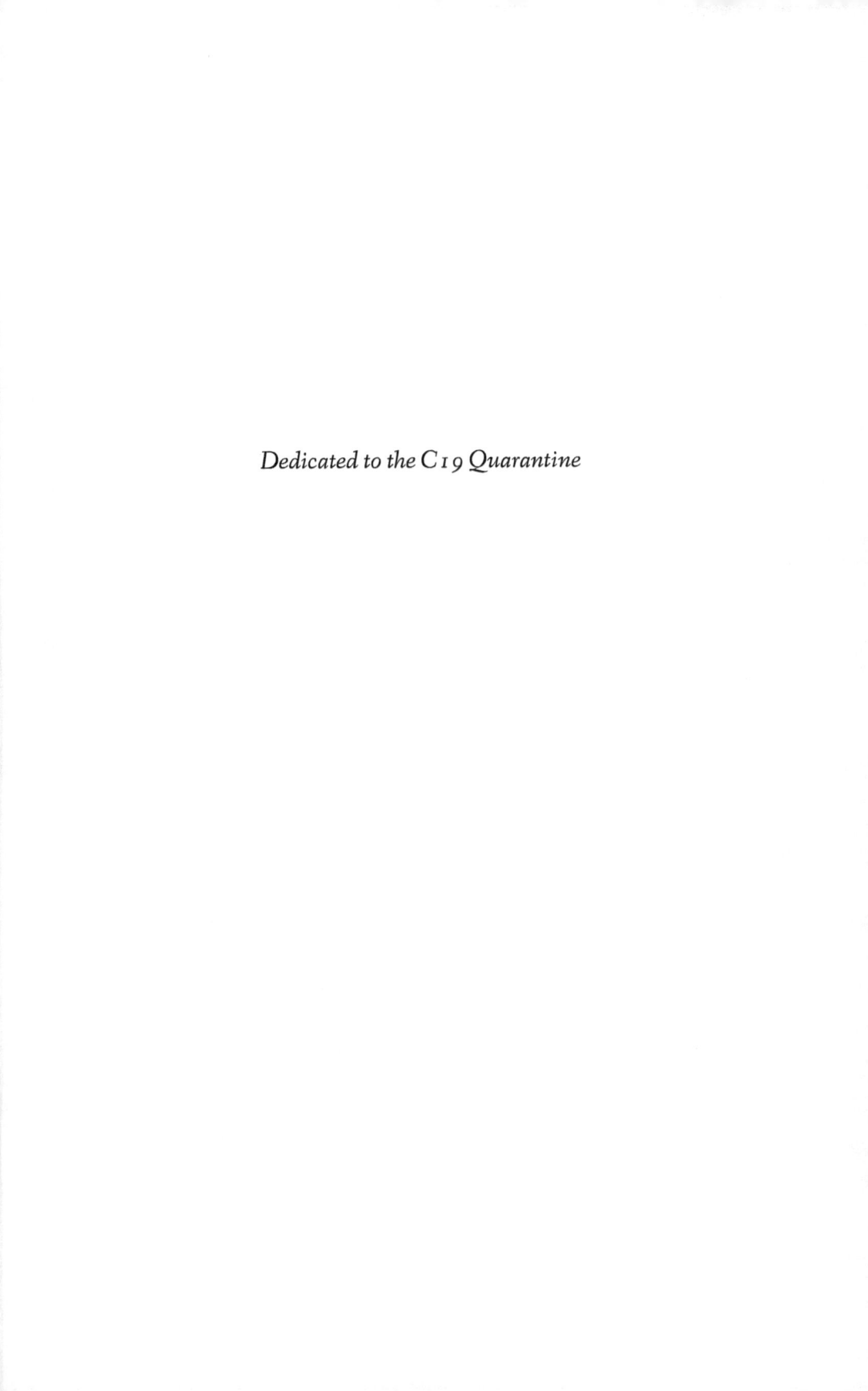

Dedicated to the C19 Quarantine

FOREWORD

Welcome to Book Two of the Blood Service, a series in the Capital Adventures. If you haven't seen the beginning of Aaron's story, check out *The Blood Service*.

This book contains the following content matter:

- *Graphic Violence & Traumatic Injuries*
  - *Many people are shot, stabbed, and torn apart in war-like environments.*
  - *Several deaths from energy weapons boiling and charring flesh.*
  - *A trauma ward with gruesome injuries and subsequent treatments.*
  - *Several characters are 'mulched' under different contexts.*
- *Frequent Foul Language*
  - *People swear under these conditions*
- *Sexual Activity*
  - *Fade-To Black intimacy*

We're here to have a good time with characters we love. If any of this material distresses you, it's okay to grab another book instead.

Hope you enjoy!

CONTENTS

PART FOUR
LEGATUS

MAP & CHRONOLOGY

The Solar Imperium, also called the Gnostic Empire by the more faithful citizenry, stretches over a fifth of the Milky Way Galaxy. This map features the primary locations featured in the series thus far.

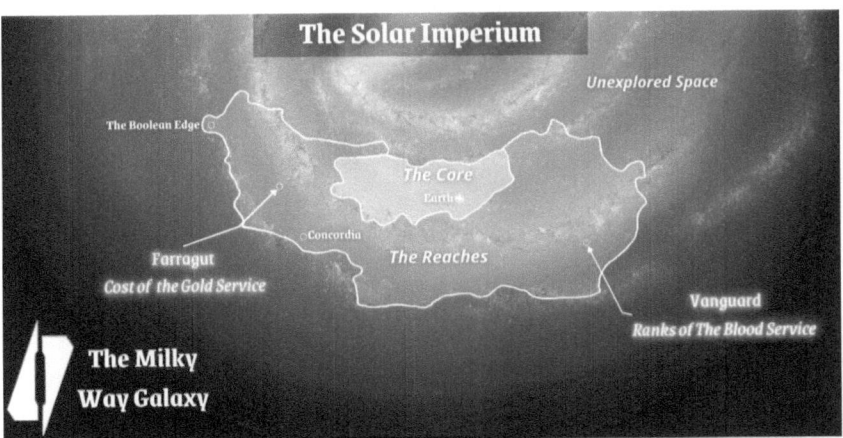

| Map of Solar Imperium controlled space, 2241 CE

The events of the Capital Adventures occur entirely within these borders. Events from one book may be mentioned in another, or characters may cross over from one trilogy to another. Think of it as a shared universe, with the individual stories having unique tones and flair, while building an overarching plot.

You may enjoy each trilogy independent of the others—and I've meticulously built them so that your enjoyment is not contingent on having read the others! But if you want the full experience of the Capital Adventures, I do encourage you to pick up the other books to get a full sense of the Imperium's reach. The official reading order would be to read the trilogies starting with The Blood Service, then The Gold Service, and finishing out with the upcoming Iron Service.

If you're like me, however, and you were looking to read the novels in chronological order, the events of all nine books are as follows:

———

1) The Gold Service
2) The Blood Service
3) The Iron Service

4) Ranks of the Blood Service
5) Cost of the Gold Service
6) Swords of the Iron Service (Coming soon)

7) Command of the Blood Service
8) Shards of the Iron Service (Coming soon)
9) Powers of the Gold Service

With even More to Come...

PROLOGUE

CALDWELL

HE HAD SERVED with distinction for over thirty years. He had been awarded the Order of Sapphire for his service. He had weathered fire and poison, illness and deception. He had even been shot on two separate occasions. His knee still ached every morning, and whenever the weather turned. He could tell you if it was going to rain in exactly three hours and forty-four minutes. But, in point of fact, it was more likely to be rain than sunshine these days. It would put the most positive man in a foul mood, aching constantly like that. And Minister Alvin Caldwell was not a particularly joyful man to begin with.

In all his years, he had never seen such a miraculous display of pure incompetence. He scratched at his arm, picking at something under his sleeve. There might've been a dry patch of skin, or an old scab flaking. The crusty edges of it, the slight pull on the skin. It felt more biting than it had the night before, with a touch of stiffness underneath. But it consumed his attention, as he followed his aides to the SCIF that morning.

The two young boys kept to their vows, silent as the grave. But even they were on edge, a hum under their feet and into their flesh.

They might have been positively bursting underneath it all, giggles and nerves. However, they held to their training.

Thirteen years old would've been a tragic age to be expelled from the Academie Bellator. What would they do with themselves now if the Navy refused them?

Even the ground underfoot held its tongue, refusing to report their footfalls. The hallway seemed to go on forever, beige carpets stained and furrowed by a thousand feet. The walls were wallpapered flat colors, an earthen brown low and a faded blue high, divided by a faux dark wood molding.

If there was a Hell, Caldwell liked to think he was long since deep within its clutches. Fire and brimstone might've sounded like a just torture during simpler bygone eras, but to make pain last for an eternity? No. Pain numbed eventually; but banality only deepened with each successive day. Caldwell was thankful for this break from Court intrigue and ceremony.

Finally. Something interesting.

The SCIF may have been the most important room in the Ministry, but it looked like any other. No ornamentation, no signage or garish elegance. A simple guard stood posted next to the brushed metal door frame and scuffed carpet.

The two aides stopped, one on either side. Caldwell extended a hand and grabbed the doorknob. Scanners embedded in the brass read his fingerprints, the signature of his pulse, looking for the unique heart murmur he'd been diagnosed with as a child. A microphone in the frame matched the unique rattle of his lungs and crack of his bones.

The human body made plenty of unique ambient noises that not even a clone could replicate—they were the signature of a life lived. If kept up to date, these biometrics could keep your own ghost locked out of your secrets.

The latches clicked free, not even interrupting Caldwell's stride.

The inside of the SCIF might've been more dramatic, with dim lighting and dark wood, as befits a meeting of secret shadow cabals and their secret shadow work. But the Ministry of Defense kept their budgets simple—a long conference table with projectors at each end occupied the narrow room. The most uncomfortable chairs he'd ever known were crammed along the edges, no cushion for old bones and plenty of cold metal. Bright clinical lights painted the space a ghastly pale hue, as if trying to paint what the living might look like once they'd been dead a few hours.

A half dozen of the seated uniforms and businessmen jumped backward in sync. The military officers and political appointees in attendance had heard the door crack and leapt up to their feet in a self-gratifying race to display their deference.

He doubted he had any of their actual respect, but they wanted to posture for their colleagues, to illustrate how superior their patriotism was. As though it could be measured with a stopwatch.

"Our brothers in the Ministry of Internal Affairs are shirking their duties, are they not?" Caldwell said, loud enough to hear the echo off the back wall. A few dared to chuckle, and Caldwell made a mental note of the offenders. Strife between Ministers wasn't uncommon, but the exceptional ones kept it under the table. Flaunting rivalry only invited response. "Though our Service is to each other."

"For we are the Shield. Good morning, sir," said one sub-cabinet Minister in a fine paisley suit, his smooth baritone voice, rich and full like toffee. He was trying to hide the blood draining from his face and the shake in his hand. "How is your son?"

Pure flattery and false pretense.

"My *daughter*," Caldwell corrected, letting the man swallow his tongue, "has nothing unusual in her life. She had a concert at the Kennedy Center two nights past. First chair! She played a wonderful new piece by a Saturnian composer that very nearly brought me to tears. My wife and I sat front row-center. And *your* seats...were curiously empty. But she's fine, thank you for asking."

The man sunk into the thin cushions at his back, wishing that he had kept his mouth shut. His spine turned to gruel and his one desire in that moment was to melt into the insulated foam walls.

Lesser men than him had long since done so, becoming so unremarkable to the human eye that they were indeed never seen or heard from again. Caldwell liked to think they'd been ground down to a paste and now served the Consul as mortar for his foundations.

They were frightened. Every one of them. Unsure of how to break the news. And who would have to do it. The longer they waited, the more it delighted him.

Caldwell took his seat at the table, dropping next to the rank-and-file officers. The Consul's seat at the head was never occupied in his absence and the daily briefings rarely found him in attendance. Just as well—Caldwell didn't want the young monarch present today.

The Colonel at his left looked to the Major, who looked to his two attending Lieutenants. Caldwell could swear the teenagers played a quick slap game under the table for the right to stay seated. The younger of the two, a woman with radiant blue hair, winced in defeat.

She waved her hand, dimming the lights and keying up the nearside projector. A map of the Milky Way galaxy leapt into the air. It spun as though on string, pulling in tightly on the painted blue & white flag of the Solar Imperium.

It looked positively garish, but young officers do so like to show off their talents. Perhaps she'd been top of her class in graphic design, looking for a transfer to a Recruitment brigade.

The young officer took a breath, as if it was going to help. "Concordia...um, there are mass protests in Concordia and in Londinium. Local commanders are requesting additional munitions but they're not reporting any security concerns."

"Concordia, isn't that Kaneda's territory?" Caldwell asked.

The lieutenant nodded. "He's been silent for the last few cycles. The Governor believes he's lost the good will of the people."

"Sounds like a perfect time to have him removed from the equation entirely," Caldwell said, looking toward the burly minister across from him. "What does Holkstad say?"

The ogre of a man shifted in his seat as he considered the

4

proposal. In truth, the Imperial Spymaster looked more like a butcher, with arms bigger than some small children. But he was not known for blending in; he was the Duke of Favors, and favor bought many words. "The Academy has a few choice students it can commit. Provided they have a target."

Caldwell smiled at the young colonel at the table. "Arrange for Kaneda's immediate liquidation." Time for the big moment. "Lieutenant, were you not briefed on the situation on HR-2056?"

The young girl stumbled, consulting her notes. "HR-20...?"

"Vanguard." Caldwell could swear he heard the Major choke on his own spirit as it tried to escape his body, the room, and Earth's gravity well. "Something of an uprising? You know, a bit more relevant than a 'mass protest?'"

A suited man leaned forward over the table, injecting himself and his moneyed hands into the debate. He propped himself on his elbows like a teacher preparing to scold. "Minister Caldwell...we're still gathering the available intelligence—"

"Nazeem, I need *you* to take a long walk off the end of a balcony."

"Sir?"

"My intelligence is coming off of my home Entiglas. If the Sunday evening news knows more than you do, I don't even think you know tomorrow's weather."

The man swallowed hard on his pride. "The situation in Vanguard—"

"Silence!" Caldwell barked, setting the sentient set of cufflinks rocking back into his chair like a knife had been set to his throat. "...is all I need from you at this time."

He let the air hang heavy with the implicit threat. No one dared challenge it, content to keep their vocal chords exactly where they were.

"Colonel Marcus Riley, a naval officer and commander, has been murdered by his Colonial charges."

"By his own hubris, Minister," the Spymaster corrected. "He trained, armed, and deployed Capital criminals as a front-line force."

"You suggest we let it go unanswered, Philippe?" Caldwell asked.

"I suggested nothing of the sort. But Holkstad remembers its students, and the Colonel was a subpar graduate intoxicated by the sound of his own voice." The Spymaster arched a crooked eyebrow, like a bow now strung with a poison-tipped arrow. "I'm impressed he didn't end up on the blades of his own men."

Caldwell had suffered through graciously infrequent commu-nique with the deceased commander. Riley believed himself a dragon, but such a lizard is merely a snake when amongst genuine titans.

Yet the Spymaster wasn't known to speak without prompting. He had a point and simply refused to get to it.

"So," Caldwell fished, "you're merely making an observation about a former student?"

The Spymaster cocked his head. "Riley ruled with an iron fist, murdered the colonial Governor, and disbanded the Statesmen. His troops were thugs, his tactics blunt, and his approach...counterpro-ductive."

"So you're willing to step up and take responsibility for his fail-ure?" Caldwell implied.

Philippe sat still, an obelisk of patriotic stone. He moved so soft and with such purpose, that his salt and pepper hair might as well have been sculpted granite. "Everyone at this table—and at many tables beyond—owns responsibility, Minister. Situations such as these do not arise because of one careless boot, but of a poorly charted road."

Of course he wasn't taking responsibility. Riley might have been his student, but he would have had such a poor student relegated to guard duty on Luna, not commanding troops in theater.

But legacy has a funny way of pressing with its weight on aging joints, even on the Duke of Favors. When the impotent and disap-pointing son of a powerful father is presented for assignment, one must do their best to not insult while preserving the quality of the Service.

And this Favor ended up having some bite to it.

The young presenting lieutenant tried to mask a cough. Caldwell leered at her. "Something to add?"

Her throat turned into razor wire and she coughed again. "M-Minister, ah...there is a lot of...conversation amongst the roster. There appears to be a small but measurable movement of deployed Regulars...leaving their posts."

Riley had done more damage than initially thought. Caldwell turned back to the Spymaster. "Philippe?"

The man pursed his lips. "Riley didn't blow up his command very quietly. My count has the number at a sympathetic few... hundred. Some Infantry, a few pilots, but mostly logistics and support staff. They're commandeering civilian vessels and rallying to Vanguard's defense."

That would be more than a single police vessel could wrangle. And the symbol of it all was a rather haunting image—soldiers deserting their posts to stand with criminals in defiance of Imperial authority.

Everyone at the table knew what came next. It just had to be made official.

"Corporate?" Caldwell asked.

The suit—Nazeem—sat up and squared his shoulders. The pop of the loose vertebrae in his neck was heard all around the table. "The Board declared Vanguard a total loss months ago. But then again, we *are* prepared to salvage from wreckage."

That was about as close to an affirmative as Caldwell was likely to get. Suits always wanted to know where the profit was to be found, not the benefit. The profit margin and the debt ceiling was all that concerned their fingers. Patriotism, for the consumer class, had a price tag. For them, the colony was simply red in the ledger.

For an Empire, the price could be quite a bit more tangible.

"Well, with the Boolean brought to heel..." Caldwell started, "how long till the Third Fleet can make sky fall on Vanguard?"

The Major spoke up. "Six months. Three, if they forego dry dock."

"So ordered," Caldwell declared. "Tell Admiral Tiberiet he is to break mooring and depart immediately with all haste. Black out their Comm access, and detain any and all vessels bound for the planet. Let it be heard far and wide: ally yourself with the Capitals, and you will find yourself among them. This is the Consul's word."

"Blessed be his steps," the room intoned, a dissonant mantra that had grown hollow from certain corners of the room.

"Minister?"

Caldwell sighed, feeling his body tighten in knots at the Spymaster's voice. "Yes, Philippe?"

"Shall we announce our coming or simply arrive at their doorstep, torch in hand?"

Caldwell's eyes narrowed. He forgot Philippe had such a talent for theater. Spycraft was as much about showing information as withholding. Of course, the colony had to know the Empire wouldn't simply let them be. But strength didn't always need direct application.

Caldwell pointed to the lieutenant. "Last thing through the CommNet before blackout, message follows: 'You will surrender, or you will burn.'"

Philippe smiled, appreciating the simplicity. "You can gussy that up however you like. Then...darken their skies."

PART ONE
CASTLES

CHAPTER
ONE
KEEPER

VANGUARD WAS about what he expected it to be. Spires of glass and metal stood tall over a wasteland, glittering in the daylight as if to sprinkle blessings on all the little people below. A train loop ran the perimeter, a platinum crown encircling a silvered head. It ushered people and goods from every end of the small city.

And just as suddenly, the city stopped. Nothing but flat plains, rolling hills, and dry grass, like humanity simply halted its advance out of tribal fear. They had enough to subsist on. Beyond their borders, the ground was cursed.

Instead of growing out, they chose to grow upward.

Even from his window seat in the shuttle, the colony's border Wall looked like it was painted, watercolor on the horizon. And beyond it, the Hammer Fields filled with small tufts of some alien grain. Great mountains shot up into the sky wrapping around the entire basin—it all felt like he was sitting in a volcanic caldera or a meteor crater, like thousands of years ago something catastrophic had happened here, on the very dirt under his feet.

Just six short months ago, something equally tectonic had occurred.

Conrad 'Keeper' Eskell adjusted his rucksack, his bottle of

Kevalky poking him between the shoulder blades. Flight standards advised against anything over a liter. But he wasn't about to respect something as trite as a poster on a terminal wall, stained with grime and faded with age, when he was joining a rebellious campaign to undermine every oath he'd ever sworn.

Not only did he not have to stand for the anthem any longer, he had seen that a man could live through that choice. An entire colony raised up their voices in defiance.

Maybe that was why he was a little surprised to see the protesters. They filled the dockets below the harbor, a few even spilling into the streets. From behind the barricades, they waved homemade signs, scrawled by angry and hasty hands. More than a few waved the Imperial flag, blue and white with a resplendent orchid at the center.

Their words were far less delicate. 'Killer. Monster. Traitor.'

He couldn't help but crack a smile.

"Get a load of the locals!" Aisling, his favorite plughead, plopped her bag down next to him, chewing on her ration bar. Somewhere behind the locks of red hair and her broad reflective sunglasses, her red metallic eye implant scanned the crowd.

Augments weren't so common on the Rim; few could afford them, let alone ones as sleek as hers. Most Dusters that could afford the operation ended up looking like a block of metal had metastasized out of their flesh. Aisling's looked like a ruby had been set into her skull and encased in marble.

It was actually a polycarbonate shell she'd had to replace twice already. And it itched like Hell.

Aisling swallowed her protein mash, cracking her neck. "They've got some rhythm."

He tried not to snort, listening to the call-and-response insults being coordinated by organizers, making for a discordant choir of middle-aged voices. It was all very preschool.

"Show us what community looks like!"

"*This* is what community looks like!"

Throw in the requisite 'traitor' and the occasional *'gulaw s'ivan'*, and you had a charming border world protest shouting at uniformed soldiers. Core world media pundits would've sold their stakes for just ten seconds of B-roll. They'd own the news cycle for two whole hours, make their careers on it.

"Rhythm," Keeper conceded, "and spunk."

Aisling stuck her tongue out at the crowd. "They shout loud enough, maybe the Empire decides to leave 'em alone."

Keeper might have been smiling, but his sigh gave away his opinion on that matter. "Yeah, I know I always pulled out when I saw the Dusters had arts and crafts."

Aisling pulled her sunglasses off, revealing the metal orb that had replaced her eye. The red iris tracked the crowd independently of her squishy green one. She gave them a good roll in opposite directions. Some nearby protestors gasped.

"What's the matter?" Keeper shouted. "Never seen a combat veteran before?"

"Leave 'em alone," Aisling murmured.

"Why?" was his one-word answer.

She leered at the crowd. "Because there's like three hundred of them and two of us, blue eyes."

His heart always went all a-flutter when she called him that. She had said his eyes looked like bright sky. His sister had always said they looked like a computer had errored out somewhere in his skull.

"We can take 'em. You'll see 'em coming."

She kicked his bag up on to his boots, as she proceeded down the gangway. They had places to be right now, and playing with the locals wasn't even in the top ten.

The billet had been almost refreshingly vague. The formatting had even looked like every other deployment order he'd received: all capital letters, training in, and subsequent combat deployment in support craft for an undefined tour. Absent the Ministry of Defense letterhead and the Navy regulations, it would've passed for the real deal.

He'd have thought that going AWOL would've meant he didn't have to read these anymore.

At the base of the gangway stood a checkpoint. A mix of Regulars and bog-standard volunteer brutes—the kind that would not go amiss at a weekly bar brawl—were scanning baggage and people, issuing badges and the usual spiel. 'Welcome to here. Your station is over there. Your favorite activity is actually illegal here, so don't do it while here.'

The Regular on enforcement duty waved his baton in the air, windmilling it like a turnstile. "Step through, step through."

Aisling handed off her rucksack to the civilians on the detail and raised her arms, stepping up for her scan. The enforcer paused as he tried to sort which eye to look at, before giving up.

A scrawny Regular, tall and thin with a crooked brow, stepped up to her, tapping a few commands into the computer mounted on his bracer. An amber beam leapt from the device and danced across Aisling's face and down her body.

"Name?" the thin Regular asked.

"Aisling Danahy, First Lieutenant, Naval Number YT-1300FD64."

"Not anymore, you're not," the grunt said. "Gunny's seeing to the new arrivals. He'll be at the end of the concourse. Welcome to the Hellmouth."

"Hellmouth?" she asked.

The guy smiled. This was not the first time he got to explain this one. "Rolls off the tongue a bit better than HR-2056."

"So does a shot of whiskey, but I don't call it Satan's Playroom," Keeper snarked.

The goon sneered, bare teeth out of one side of his mouth. "You didn't jump reservation and come all this way for cupcakes and massages."

"I did not," Keeper said with a nod. "But I will not refuse one either. Just go slow, I'm young and supple."

14

Big boy spun his baton again, urging Aisling off the gangway and Keeper on through to the scanner. "Step through."

"Conrad Eskell, First Lieutenant, Naval Number—"

"I do not care," tall and skinny said, as he handed over a badge. "Gunny is who you want. End of the concourse. Follow your friend, jockey."

"Touchy?" Keeper asked.

"Hungry," the knuckle dragger grunted in response.

In a single word, Keeper's smug exterior broke. Were they *that* strapped for supplies? His shuttle had been laden with more cargo than people, but there wasn't a colony's worth of food on board.

Aisling reached the same conclusion at roughly the same time. "There's rationing?"

Thin man shook his head, more to shush her than deny it. "Step on through. There are people waiting."

Keeper glanced at the man's chest, reading a name tag. "Kipling, right?" He extended a hand to the guard. "They call me Keeper."

The man's eyes narrowed, instantly suspicious, intrigued, then suspicious again. "Keeping what exactly?"

In retrospect, it was probably ill-advised to share his callsign with a harbor security team. "The peace, mostly."

"Nice save," Kipling mocked with a curled lip.

Keeper's face sank. "Is it really that bad here?"

Kipling shook his head. "It's been worse. But it's not good."

"Step. Through!"

Keeper spun around. "Do you think that saying it slower and with greater emphasis is going to cause something special to happen?"

Aisling took his ruck from security and grabbed him with her other hand. "Thank you for your time, gentlemen, but we must away."

He didn't fight her. She pulled him down the gangway until their boots hit dirt. They were here. AWOL. In the Hellmouth, whatever that meant.

"Step through, step through," he mumbled, absolutely not out of ear shot. "I sure hope that guy is kept away from sharp objects."

"Wishing you'd stayed on the *Esteban*?"

"No," he said, "but I am wishing I packed a sandwich."

Keeper ran his badge through his own wrist-mounted computer, offloading the assignment data to the Personal Manager. The computer hummed to life, then indicated a direction, pointing down the concourse.

They walked in silence, shared reverence at the sight of it all. The city's spires were even more impressive from the ground, the curving talons bending up and away into the sky. It made them seem taller than they actually were, and their solid glass resembled cut opals, solid blue with glimmers of the rainbow catching in the sun.

The ambient hum was all too familiar. Every footfall had power, every package had urgency. Nothing was slow but neither was it rushed. They moved with purpose. But it was all accented with something else, that metallic acid right before a combat launch.

Fear: it kindled something in his gut, and he couldn't help but grin like an idiot child.

Aisling felt it too, nudging his arm. "Feels good, right?"

He nodded. "Soak it in, Aisling. We're rebels now."

His smile only made her smile wider. Her eyes flashed with excitement, unblinking, digging into his own. He matched her stare, daring her.

Their faces both suddenly cracked into stupid snorting laughter. Passersby stared, some sneering in disgust, but they could stuff it. They'd clearly had all fun and joy leeched out of them. It was fitting that they stand in sharp relief. Maybe they'd teach 'em all to be happy once in a while, remind them all how it felt.

Were they just afraid to die? What can death do to you? Kill you? Way to blow your wad early. Kill me, sure, but then what else you got? Nothing. Death has exactly one trick in its bag and nothing else on offer. If you let that paint every day until it happens, then you're pretty much already dead.

Everyone was power-walking, clutching their cases and shoulders hunched. They sped from silver steel tower to tower, as though they were vulnerable to the elements in between.

Which made the surprise pastel color mural smeared onto the concrete a joyful—literal—surprise.

Someone had brushed paint onto a wall with their fingertips, a basic portrait. No tools, sprayers, or imprints, just hands and a bit of imagination. They were talented, captured the likeness well: a dark-skinned man, with bright eyes, looking up and away into some happier future. His defined jawline and high cheekbones were hard to keep out of your head. He looked like an athlete fresh and sweaty from the last game of the season and now leaning hard into his advertising face, or some bright young politician imagining the worlds we could build together.

But this wasn't just some street art. Candles had been set into a semi-circle. Fresh and crisp greens grown from someone's garden. Even a bouquet of roses.

Even worse, the candles had been tossed, the glass shattered, and the greens scattered by errant kicks. A shrine, but one that had been desecrated.

A number drawn onto the chest pocket of the subject's gray jumpsuit—626.

"Three guesses," Aisling said, "but you're only going to need one."

Keeper made a show of rubbing his jaw, feeling stubble grating under his fingers. He knew full well who it was: Aaron Havenes, convicted Capital, and Hero of Vanguard. The Legatus himself, who single-handedly tamed the native Jergad beasts and defeated the tyrannical Marcus Riley.

He didn't doubt the guy was impressive, but that all seemed a bit much. One particularly wide-eyed kid said that Aaron had actually ridden one of the big roaches into battle. What did he do, rig up a saddle in his foxhole? People talk. Legends rarely live up to the hype.

"Hm. A distant cousin of the Consul, a Dunsweir brat and—I'm

17

going with—a Ballistic Silver medalist in the thousand-yard last year?"

Aisling clapped Keeper on the back hard enough to send him on to his toes. She then came in with the other hand, smacking him hard on his ass.

"Hey!" he yelped, waggling a finger at her with a mock serious face.

She placed a coy hand over her mouth. "Or what? You're going to do what, Lieutenant?"

"Conrad and Aisling!"

They jumped, both falling into attention: chin up, chest out, arms at sides. And Keeper swallowed hard.

Until he recognized the perfectly coiffed graying beard approaching them. A dozen yards away, the old man strolled over with a bounce in his step. His soft grey-blue eyes pierced out from under his cap. The shaking of his head said disapproving father, but the thin smile said big brother. The faded blue jumpsuit, fraying at the cuffs and creased at the shoulders, hung formlessly off him like he was wearing a pillowcase. But his panther stance betrayed that advanced age had not slowed him one bit.

He crossed his arms, and spoke with a deep and tender voice, lilting operatic tones and soft consonants. "Dynamic duo. You two are continuously an embarrassment to the uniform and those that have worn it."

Keeper's jaw dropped, like he'd heard the discordant chimes of an ice cream truck. "Prophet?!"

Keeper threw his ruck at Aisling's feet and nearly leapt into the silver fox's arms, feet dangling as he draped around the broad shoulders. Prophet always smelled like sawdust and today was no different, like the inside of a workshop behind the house.

Prophet peeled him off, holding him at arm's length to inspect. "You've gotten taller! What are you, sixteen now?"

"No, you've just gotten shorter, old man," Keeper said, grabbing Prophet about the shoulders. "What are you, five hundred?"

Prophet shoved him off. "Alright, alright, Conrad, easy." He paused, reading the name hand-stitched on to Keeper's jumpsuit. "'Keeper?' I don't suppose that's because you keep a secret or keep to a code of honor?"

"No, sir." He eagerly dug into his pack and fished out the bottle of Kevalky. The clear liquid had a greenish hue in the light, and the label had been rubbed mostly bare.

Prophet pursed his lips. "No, it's because you're 'keeping' something for someone?"

"Always."

"For me?" the captain asked.

"Maybe."

Aisling lifted Keeper's ruck and pressed it into his chest, giving Prophet a nod. "Captain."

"Lieutenant," Prophet acknowledged. "Staying out of trouble?"

A coy little smile. "I think my file speaks for itself."

"The demerits certainly do."

Prophet's smile faded as his eyes caught the mural—and the mess beneath it. Something in him swelled up. He nudged one of the candles back to standing with his foot.

Keeper shoved the bottle back into his rucksack. "What in the Hell brings you out to Vanguard, old man?"

"Not a lot of people available with flight time logged on the Howler," Prophet said. "Your new CO reached out."

"You're going to be the flight instructor?" Aisling asked, pleased with that discovery.

"And your flight lead." Prophet gave a mocking bow of his head. "Just like old times, right?"

"This time 'round, less spontaneous combustion," Keeper quipped.

"Ah-ten-SHUN!"

That voice was far less jovial. Keeper and Aisling snapped back into stance. Prophet didn't move, and Keeper found himself worrying that the Captain was going to catch fresh Hell. But the

ALLEN IVERS

grizzled veteran that stomped past him barely registered Prophet's presence.

He was short, barely clearing Prophet's shoulder. A spattering of shrapnel scars dotted his sneering face. His uniform was tan-and-brown—Regular Army grunt—but the chest candy on his shoulder clammed Keeper up real quick. He had enough metal dangling there to forge a decent cleaver. This was the soldier they drew the crucible of, minted new ones hoping for. He was hard tack made flesh. His voice sounded so rough, it had to have been ripped out and put back in.

But the worst part was his stare. Those eyes could send monsters running back under the bed.

"I am Gunnery Sergeant Thomas Bray. My superiors call me Gunny or Sergeant. To you, my name is 'Sir, yes sir!' I want to hear that in a crisp happy tune every single time I speak." He waited for a moment, before shrugging. "I see we have some trouble with basic instructions."

Keeper and Aisling almost coughed out the mantra. "Sir, yes sir."

Bray waggled a finger in Keeper's face, so close he felt it graze his nose. "That was no surprise, son. I have read your file. Indecent exposure, drunk 'n disorderly, and four separate demerits for striking a fellow officer. You get demotions almost as fast as you get promoted again. This is, what, your fourth time bouncing off the butterbar? Tell me, 'Keeper', who did you have to *kill* to keep your uniform?"

Keeper was well trained. He had crawled through sand and muck in the midnight air; he had been exposed to vacuum; he had drilled high altitude free-fall; he had done close-air maneuvers; he had lost comrades, but never lost a wingman.

And he was a smartass. "Sir, I technically outrank you, sir."

Bray got quiet and very close. "You're not in the Navy anymore, butterbar. You're in *my* world now. There are Capitals that walk these streets. They are killers, thieves, and worse. Your attitude may just get you shanked behind a dumpster and I cannot afford that. You three jockeys are quite literally the only pilots I get. There is no

20

backup, no relief. You're the thin red line, kid, and I am not comfortable with that."

This wasn't Keeper's first scare-greeting. Every local CO liked to fry up the new kids with how rough this station would be. It was never as bad as they made it out to be. "Sir, yes, sir."

Bray's eyes narrowed, but he passed the baton. "Prophet?"

Prophet stepped forward, arms folded behind him. All business. "Report to your barracks. Intake is at 0700."

AWOL wasn't turning out to be that different than his station.

CHAPTER
TWO

AARON

IT HAD BEEN Riley's office. And from this ten-by-twenty-foot room, a seventeen-year old Orbital officer had conducted a campaign of terror on fifty-two thousand civilians below. Maybe he thought he was doing the right thing—nobody sets out to be evil.

But it was hard for Aaron to shake the sight of those city streets from his mind. Six months ago, innocent people dried their tears hiding in their homes. The soldiers they had trusted to protect them... were laughing, posing for pictures, looting and pillaging as the city burned.

And Aaron Havenes was the criminal? That's a laugh.

Riley's office, already a monument to minimalism, had been scraped bare with a belt sander and an almost religious devotion. If Talania'd had her way, Riley would've been etched out of memory with an acid wash, and his office condemned to lay empty, a cursed memorial accumulating dust and neglect.

Aaron claimed it four days into their little revolution. He needed somewhere quiet, and the computer still worked.

It wasn't very quiet right now. Three of his old allies had come by for what had become a weekly occurrence.

"How does it work?" Nora asked, staring into the display of the brand-new replicator. Tension in her small frame from end to end. She looked like a frightened cat: eyes wide, back arched, and gingerly reaching for the polished metal box. The former bartender might've been in awe, her jaw tight and her eyes wide, but Aaron knew the apprehension in her stance.

She was gazing upon heresy.

Talania sat in her seat, draping a long leg over the arm. Given her long build, it was probably the only way she could get comfortable in the tiny office chair. "It's recombining carbon molecules into a pre-programmed matrix. It's making the exact same recipe over and over again. Literally." She noticed the horror dawning on Nora's face. "Don't overthink it. Bread is bread."

"Yeah..." Nora paused, her hand hovering over the control panel. "I heard these things make you sick."

"How many do we have now?" Aaron asked.

"Sixty-five," Talania reported, reading off a stack of papers clipped to a piece of fiberboard—Aaron had tried to sell her on the benefits of the microprocessor, but she preferred to live in a darker age. Something about the feel and smell.

Eh, it's her life.

She pointed one bony finger at a statistic inked into the page. "Twelve came out of the crates busted."

"Did we get a warranty on those?" Eden asked, her wry smirk reflected in the office's one tiny window. The tiny woman was up on her toes to get a view of the city outside. She tried to feign casual, leaning on the wall with a bent arm. Her messy hair was tied back into a ponytail, matted and oily, but at least out of her face. She peered out to the metropolis six floors below them, daydreaming about being somewhere other than this weekly meeting.

Talania crossed her arms, letting her clipboard rest on her knee. A pointed wit needed a riposte. "Y'know, I meant to, but then I figured, I was boosting them from the manufacturer's convoy, so..." She mimed a scale with her hands, weighing the invisible options. On the one hand, yes—but on the other hand, no.

"They'll take any carbon and just...print food?" Aaron asked. Talania grunted an affirmative. He smiled. "That's great. That's terrific. We can recycle damn near anything. So when can we lift the ration ceiling?"

Talania leered at him. "Was kinda hoping you'd tell me."

Why him? What did he know about the statistics of colonial food consumption? He was a former court clerk, a Capital criminal convicted of murder, sentenced to hard labor, drafted into military service, and who found himself to be an unlikely friction point with a local sociopathic despot. He wasn't, at last recording, a city planner.

Talania picked up on his hesitation, scratching something off of her paper. "I'll figure it out."

"Thanks." He nodded, turning to Eden. "How's Medical doing?"

Eden tore her eyes from the window, rocking back onto her heels. Talania might've been taller while sitting down than the little doctor was at full height. "We're low on basically everything but talent. Doctors, nurses, and techs—that, I've got aplenty. What I don't have is bandages, antiseptic—"

"We got a shipment last—what was it?" Aaron looked to Talania for help. "Month back, right?"

"Yeah," Eden said. "And only half of the stuff made it to the hospitals. The rest went into market stalls!"

Aaron's brow furrowed. "Talania?"

"Four separate AutoDocs not enough?" Talania ignored Aaron's annoyance and directed her response right at Eden.

And Eden was not about to be steamrolled. "What do you think makes up all those stitches and skin grafts?"

Talania swung her leg off the arm of her chair, ready to square up, but Aaron cut her off. "Don't start fights."

"She started it."

Nora shook her head. "She really didn't."

"Talania, it's a serious thing," Aaron said. "Work with her on an inventory and then maybe get a collection together?"

"A *collection*?" Talania asked, incredulous. "Aaron, fifty-two thousand people aren't going to pass a plate around. We'll be here till next winter."

"I meant—"

"I know what you meant, I'm just mocking you." Talania turned to Eden. "Come see me after class?"

Eden rolled her eyes, hiding an insult under her breath.

"I heard that," Talania sniped without looking up.

Impressive, because all Aaron heard was Eden murmuring in an acidic tone. Or maybe that's all she heard too, and she just got the gist of it.

Side effect of politics. Nobody said anything directly to your face, because they always wanted something from you. It made Talania something of a rarity among the Statesmen—her blunt approach and frank delivery had won her many allies during her term as Governor, but it offended the traditional sensibilities of lifetime politicians that resented the legacy.

She'd won the election fair and square. She was a very visible member of the uprising, her father's tragic death fresh on people's minds. But some saw it as the daughter inheriting the crown, symbolic of the very Empire they were rebelling against. Others simply didn't care for rebels, loyal Imperials to the core.

Rebellion—Aaron had tried to stop a war, not start one. But that didn't stop hundreds of miscreants and revolutionaries from imprinting their radicalism on Aaron's survival instinct.

"Keira wants five minutes." Eden broke the silence.

"No," Talania dismissed that.

Aaron's brow furrowed. "What's that about?"

Eden started to say something, but Talania drowned her out. "She wants to send a scout ship through the Jump, get outside the blackout."

Aaron scoffed too, leering back at Eden. "She thinks we can get more support?"

Eden's glare at Talania didn't change tone when it drifted over to Aaron. "She's got a *particular* person she wants to call."

Keira had many friends. She was sentenced to Capital service over a train of bank robberies. All of her friends were going to be... unsavory. But if she had to call just one? Aaron knew who that meant.

"No." Aaron joined Talania in her rebuttal.

"Why?"

"Because being Keira Ladd's cellmate doesn't make them a good person."

"I'm with shortstack on this one," Nora chimed in. "The last thing we need is a bunch of crime lords rockin' around here. Need I remind you, a bunch of us have criminal histories?"

"Making us a fiefdom without a king," Talania said.

"Fiona McCorty isn't a crime lord," Eden countered.

"No, she's a pirate," Aaron said, "and one dumb enough to pick a fight with the Empire in the Boolean Edge—which, by the way, *started* all this mess! She doesn't do that...there's no withdrawal, no draft, Riley doesn't go crazy."

Talania chuckled. "Oh, he was always going to do that. Don't kid yourself."

Aaron didn't let her break his flow. "If Fiona had kept to herself we'd still be chewing dirt in the Copper mines."

"Not sure if what we got was an upgrade or not," Nora chirped.

"But it also means she's got the same axe to grind we do," Eden said. "She hates the Empire, and we're fighting the Empire. She's one call away."

"I don't care if she did your baptism," Talania said. "She won't respect Colonial authority. That's the end of the conversation."

Eden threw Aaron a look. She wasn't done, but she was more than ready to move on. "Nora," Aaron said with the loud intent of shifting gears. "Any Capitals making noise?"

Nora tapped a button on the replicator, toggling through screens of its functions—pastries, refreshments, deserts. "Five recommitted last night."

"Violent?" Aaron asked.

26

"Do you even need to ask?" Eden chided him.

Lovely. "Are there any labor jobs we can set them to?"

Talania ground her teeth. "Two of these men assaulted an old man coming back from work. Broke his back. I'm not sentencing them to building a public park."

"Fair enough," Aaron conceded. "But I kinda...blew up the prison?"

Nora pushed a button and the replicator chirped at her. "What did I do?!"

"You've given us all radiation poisoning," Talania said, and Aaron couldn't help but smirk. She had a very dry humor.

Nora glowered at the Governor. "Why even joke about that?"

The replicator dinged and a breakfast pastry rose up, like a gladiator to the arena, steaming up the office with its glorious smell. Talania didn't say a word, just reached over and took a big ugly bite of it. She chewed, staring Nora down.

Nora's eyes narrowed and Talania just kept on chewing.

"Talania," Aaron cautioned, with a raised eyebrow.

"My meeting, Aaron," she said through the mouthful.

"Well, if you don't need me, then can you move the meeting to *your* office?"

Eden and Nora shared a look. And there was a soft pause. Had they all tried to include him in their little flailing government?

If there was a plan, Talania didn't let the silence rest long. "What do you even do? Up here in *his* office, all day?"

Aaron's eyes darted up to the door frame, where the Orbital Creed could still be made out in the scoured paint. They had tried three separate times to burn it away before Aaron made them move on. Besides, the sentiment itself wasn't so bad.

Service To The People, For They Are The Kings.

He could still see Riley's face, his Orbital implants glowing in the acid fog, burning lights under his skin. Eyes flashing with hate as he drove the knife into Jensen's chest—

Aaron cleared his throat. "You'd prefer I stand a post?"

"I want a vegetarian meal that doesn't taste like a chemistry set," she quipped. "I need you to do a bit of your...Legatus thing."

He rolled his eyes. "I had a conversation!"

"And the Pilgrim jus' went on walkabout!" Nora mocked. "You spoke to an alien Hive mind and stopped a war single-handed. That was *some* conversation!"

"You're the face of this thing," Talania said. "You should show your face once in a while."

He sighed. Big names and titles, responsibilities. He wasn't anybody. He wasn't worthy of all this. "Can...one of you be the face for a little bit?"

Nora counted the people in the room on one hand. "I mean, he's got a point. He might be the ugliest one in the room," she teased.

"You've broken your face so many times, your skull is no longer symmetrical," Eden shot back from behind Aaron.

"Scars are just a story, and I've got good stories."

Talania wasn't ready to let this one lie though. "I'm serious, Aaron."

"So was I," he said. "You were the one on the broadcasts, trading fire with Riley, face to face with him—for a whole year! But I'm supposed to be the poster boy? I'm just sayin', why?"

Talania cocked her head. "I play the hand I'm dealt, Capital."

Her eyes flashed blue, a solid, pupil-less gaze—the eyes of the Jergad race. And in a blink of an eye, they were her deep green again. Well, that was nice and creepy. The Queen was telling him something, showing him something.

Why now? The Jergad had been silent, dormant for months, rebuilding and healing. He had almost forgotten the migraines that accompanied the Queen's influence. But there it was, one stabbing him right above the eyeball.

Aaron squinted at Talania, furrowing his brow. Maybe it would happen again if he studied close.

She squinted right back at him, taking offense. "*What*, Aaron?"

28

It was quick, simple, but it wasn't nothing. The Queen never spoke without purpose. "Something's happened," he said.

A spike. Hard. He nearly tossed his lunch onto the table right there. His eyes crossed and he found himself gripping the table. Why now?

"Damp cloth, right now," Eden snapped at Nora, as she grabbed his shoulder. "Talk to me, shortstack."

The headache subsided, but he could still feel the pain in his teeth and behind his eyes. "Somebody's a little grumpy from their nap."

Talania sat up in her chair. Her eyes went wide, and her breath hitched. With good reason. The aliens had hounded colonial defenses for almost a decade. They had raided farmsteads and butchered soldiers with alarming ferocity. And, as of this moment, the only defense they had was trust that the aliens wanted to stop fighting. If the Jergad had regained their former strength, changed their collective mind...

It'd be over by nightfall.

But Aaron didn't feel their hostility. Instead, he felt his eyes drawn up to the ceiling. The blank steel panels and the dull round rivets stared back at him.

She knew. The Queen had sensed their arrival.

"Battle carrier group," he said. "Three ships: a dreadnought, with two support craft. Five thousand people aboard. They just exited the Jump point."

Eden and Nora's heads craned up, trying to see what he was seeing. But Talania exhaled hard, leaning over to tap a button on Riley's—Aaron's—desk. She spoke up to the other end of the line. "I need to see the Statesmen in my office in one hour. Tell Stefan Whitby he's going to want to be there for this one."

Eden crouched down next to Aaron's chair, taking his clammy hand in her own. "How do you know? Five thousand?"

It was a pretty exact number, even if it was roughly off by a few hundred here or there. He swallowed the dry lump that was trying to block his windpipe. "Because *she* knows. She can feel them."

"Jump point, military impulse power..." Nora was doing math in her head. "They're two weeks from sky fall. And they out-number us ten to one."

"What?" Aaron said, gasping like he'd just run a marathon. "You expected them to fight fair?"

A melodic chime came from his desk, a happy note, like a bird song. A panel of the desk's surface shimmered with bright light, a single square of pleasant white rising and falling like full and heavy breaths.

Aaron had stacked a couple of old dinner plates on the spot. He swept them aside, and pushed down on the panel. It sprang up, revealing a monitor...and a face.

Old eyes, tired and weary, but hardened. Crow's feet that blended in with the scar tissue. Underneath a Naval cap was a shaved head, but the sugar dusting of white hair growing could be made out along the edges and around his ears. His jaw was broad and his chin held high, like he was looking down his narrow nose at those lesser.

His eyes darted left and right, taking in the room and the trio that assembled behind Aaron. "I had been hoping to catch you in private, Aaron Havenes, but I suppose I should be glad you answered at all."

"Who are you?" Aaron demanded, like he was in any position.

"I'm Admiral Deckard Tiberiet," the old man said. "And you're in my chair."

Aaron's lips tightened. "You don't want this chair. It has terrible back support."

"Talania Dedria." Deckard gave the Governor a nod of the head. "I'm glad to see you remain unharmed."

"Admiral," was her one-word diplomatic acknowledgement.

Deckard smiled, a polite greeting, before his eyes tracked back to Aaron. "They're calling you 'Legatus'—the Diplomat."

Aaron shrugged. "I think it's a little ostentatious, but everybody else seems quite taken with it."

Talania smirked. "I still call you a jerk."

Aaron mockingly held up a hand to the screen, as though he could have any privacy right now. "Can we not do this in front of the Imperial Admiral? It just scares the Hell out of him."

The Admiral might have scoffed, but Aaron knew when he got a laugh. The old man reset himself in his chair. "You've decommissioned your Thor's Hammer strike satellites. You're going to make me come all the way over there to do it personally?"

"Well, I had to come up with a reason to see you. I mean, you never call, you don't write."

The Admiral finally cracked, and couldn't hide his smirk, but his face quickly soured. "I feel it appropriate at this time to demand your immediate and unconditional surrender. I should note that this is a one-time offer."

He looked up to Talania to find her looking back at him, expectant green eyes urging him on. He looked left, and both Eden and Nora were doing the same thing. Why did they always look to him?!

"...How would it work?" He felt their disapproval fill the room.

"You'll be charged with treason and sedition," the Admiral drawled, "you'll be returned to the Core worlds for your trial. All co-conspirators will face charges of their own, but cooperation at this juncture is the only way to purchase leniency from the Ministry."

"Yeah," Nora huffed. "Two life sentences, down to one and a half. Sweet package."

The Admiral didn't so much as a flinch. "It's not your lives you'd be saving. You've left the fold. Come back."

Aaron quietly noted that the Admiral hadn't even blinked once. That wasn't an augment; that was sheer will. That wasn't a man crafted with steel, but made of it.

Should he surrender? He'd been a criminal once, had a good run. He'd bought his freedom, perhaps, but done so with more crimes.

More murder. Say 'yes' now and they might yet spare the others. Spare the colony. Spare everyone.

"I have to...more specifically, with the others and—"

"As I said," the Admiral cut him off, "unconditional. What I do with a colony full of seditionists is entirely my prerogative. You may feel free to speak on their behalf. Right now, their fates are in your hands."

Liar. They were in *his*. And he was trying to bury Aaron under the guilt of a choice already made.

He felt both Nora and Talania tense at his shoulder. But they both knew that speaking now would be worse. It wasn't just their own lives they were handling today. But it was Eden that he felt the most, as her stance slackened and her knee shook. She'd lost too many times.

They always knew this day would come. They had six months of freedom, moments they wouldn't have had without...

He slid his hand over to Eden's, wrapping her fingers in his. He squeezed, trying to pull some strength. Her brown eyes glinted in the light from the monitor.

Don't do it, she seemed to say. We can fight this. We can do this.

"I understand your hesitation," Deckard said, with a surprising softness. "It's not easy, what I'm asking...the right thing to do is often the hardest thing. But you will be saving fifty-two thousand lives. Is that not *why* you started all of this?"

The right thing to do...

Aaron glanced up at that inscription again. Service, People, Kings...

"He used to say that, y'know," Aaron said. "The whole 'right thing' speech. And then he gave the order to blast this city to kingdom come. Just like you just did. 'Save fifty-thousand lives?' You're the one pulling the trigger. Men like you twist yourselves into knots justifying what you do."

"Marcus Riley...was half a man," Deckard said with icy stillness, "drunk on his own legacy. You're not facing a child anymore. You're

32

facing the Empire's legions. I will plow your little dirt farmers back into the earth. If you take shelter, I will uproot you. If you stand, I will cleave you. I cannot be moved, and I cannot be beaten." He leered at Talania. "I am asking for just one man. Is that not a fair—?"

"Tell me, Admiral," Aaron cut him off, "when you're burning a city of the Empire's citizens from orbit...do you feel like a patriot? Or do you do it that way because it's 'right?'" Aaron leaned into the screen. "I have a history of being announced dead. It doesn't tend to stick. You want me? You'll have to come down here and shoot me yourself, because that's the only way you're going to know I'm really gone. I'll see you in two weeks."

He pushed the monitor closed and the light dimmed under his hand.

Nora gaped at him, a curve to her lip and a light in her eyes. "*That's* why you're the guy, Aaron." A shiver ran up her spine and she enjoyed every bristling nerve, rolling out her shoulders with a fire newly lit in her tank. "Let's go! We've got shit to do!"

CHAPTER
THREE
DECKARD

THE SCREEN WENT DARK. He couldn't say he expected anything less.

Deckard Tiberiet had seen a great many renegades fall to the sword, revolutionaries and radicals holding their own heads so high they practically presented their necks for the headsman. Aaron Havenes was no different than the hundreds that had come before. They were all so self-assured of their divinity, that simply being convinced of their principles was the sole requirement of victory. Londinium had believed so, the Boolean had believed so—and Vanguard would be no different.

The Jump Deck of the *Tartarus* hummed with energy. The crewmen marked their checklists with diligence and care, a few Ensigns marching across the small space so as to appear maximally busy for his watchful eye.

Deckard swiped his flat cap off and ran his calloused hand across the crown of his head, feeling the velvet soft hairs under his fingertips. He made sure to shave his dome close for trips back to the Core —regulations had strict discipline for those that eluded the dress code. But out in the Rim, the world was the ship—and it was his ship. And he only cared if hair got in the eyes of the navigator.

His flag lieutenant, Ulrich Wolcott, raised an amused eyebrow. The young man took well to the uniform, the crisp boxy shape clinging to his natural hard shoulders and plump frame. He looked like he had been pressed and dried along with his slate gray tunic. "He said 'No?'"

Deckard crossed his arms over his broad chest. "Lieutenant, if he had said 'No', the call would have been far more interesting."

He did what every rebel does. He pontificated and bloviated.

Deckard never understood these Dusters. In fairness, he himself had a penchant for the dramatic. He enjoyed taking a play at the Kennedy Center during shore leave. But these colonists didn't have the stage or the legs to buoy their words. Whatever possessed a man with nothing but a trowel and wet dirt to raise a clenched fist in anger towards a man in power armor? That was not the action of a reasonable person.

But a good soldier never wasted an opportunity to learn new tricks. And each new enemy was a new opportunity. Maybe Aaron had something to teach him yet.

"Well," Wolcott scoffed with a small smirk, "looks like we'll be home before the Holidays." He raised his right hand, a holographic display appearing at his fingertips. He tapped in his personal code, granting him access to the ship's PA system. "Condition Two throughout the fleet. Gunnery control, achieve firing solution. Target: the Aurora facility, HR-2056."

Deckard raised his own hand, really just two fingers, into the air. Wolcott felt the movement. "Stand by, Saubert."

The flag lieutenant had his own read on the situation, to be certain. The young man was apprenticing to command. Let's see if he could work it out.

Deckard tented his fingers under his chin. "Do you believe that orbital bombardment to be the appropriate action?"

Wolcott opened his mouth, but hesitated. He could feel the warrant officers gauge the exchange. Deckard had been a field commander for thirty years. He had helmed landing craft and bomber fleets, and had done so since he was Wolcott's age.

Wolcott still had the smell of Holkstad about him—the disinfectant they used in the showers had a citric hint to it. He shined his shoes like the instructors were watching. He stood tall and shaved his cheek and he never spoke out of turn.

"Sir, the Minister gave rather specific instruction..." Wolcott said, his voice trailing off in an indecisive disappointment.

Leaders didn't follow direction—they gave it.

"Yes, he did, but that was not an answer to my question."

"Is this theoretical?"

"For the moment," Deckard said. "Let's run the exercise. We've got two whole weeks!"

Wolcott smiled. "Could always roll out a deck of cards."

"Then we play for money." Deckard popped out of his chair, stretching out his stiff knees. "Bombardment from orbit: it's an absolutist approach."

Wolcott folded his arms across his chest, sighing as he thought out the event. "It's also cataclysmic. Sends echoes out that we're not to be trifled with."

The boy wanted to send a message across the Empire, broadcast their superiority. Fuck not with the Imperial Navy. Hard to argue with its simplicity. But simplicity was what made this so easy. A single city with a plurality of political support, and meager defenses? Bombing a site meant it was no longer valuable.

And life, particularly innocent life, always had value.

"You get into a lot of fights in your boarding school, Wolcott?" Deckard asked.

Wolcott shrugged. "I was on the rugby team."

"That's contact sport! Now, a fight—a schoolyard bully strikes his victim, but he mustn't strike so hard that he galvanizes those that witness it. He needs to strike hard enough to get what he needs without provoking a group response. Because the entire class would, quite simply, overwhelm him."

"You're talking about governing from fear," the lieutenant said.

"It's not my attack plan. It's yours." Deckard noticed the hesitancy. "Don't feel shame from that. It's a perfectly manageable tact. But there are *other* approaches you can take."

Wolcott bit his lip, trying to avoid glancing around the room. The Navigation crew was bringing the fleet into formation, while Engineering completed their Jump checklists and Combat coordinated the launch of an Air Patrol. And yet, they were all watching the sixteen-year-old actively pickling in the air—this, their commander-to-be.

If he couldn't handle the pressure, he shouldn't command them. They were going to be looking at him with a great deal more desperation when the room was losing cabin pressure and their companions were screaming in pain on a half dozen open channels.

"Compare and contrast with our operations in the Boolean," Deckard offered.

"That action was responsive to the loss of a military carrier and crew."

"And here, an Orbital commander was slain in a civilian revolt led by a Capital convict," Deckard said. "You believe them so different?"

"I do."

"Why?"

"Centralization," the lieutenant offered. "The Boolean was scattered asteroids, pockets of resistance and ambushes. This is a single urban center."

"You're so close to getting it, you'll trip on it."

Wolcott took a breath, his eyes scanning through the hundreds of files that school had uploaded into his wee little head. "Perhaps a gas strike? Preserve the infrastructure?"

Deckard's head bobbed on his shoulders. He heard his neck crack, but he wasn't going to let that interrupt his point. "Both are adequate tactical choices. But do you believe it to be the *appropriate* action?"

"You're not speaking...tactically, are you, sir?"

"Wars are fought one battle at a time," Deckard said, "but wars can be *avoided* with just one battle." He waved at Combat's station to his right—a half-moon shaped console with the brazen officer standing at the ready. "Saubert here can certainly reduce those structures to glowing heaps at the push of a button. He's proven his accuracy. But *should* he?"

Wolcott's jaw dropped. "You mean to take Aaron Havenes alive? Admiral..."

"I'm a crazy old man," Deckard said, bushy eyebrows bouncing playfully.

The lieutenant was about to exercise some educational insubordination. It always made Deckard smile the way Wolcott would couch his defiance in some platitude, turn his chest away and slide forward a few steps. It always made him look like a lounge singer hitting on a waitress.

"Forgive me," Wolcott crooned, "wouldn't that be in defiance of our directives?"

Deckard's lips drew tight, clamping down on the laugh. Wolcott looked around the deck, settling on Officer Saubert. "What'd I do?"

Saubert, ever the professional, fought the smile pulling at the corners of his lips. But he kept his tone even. "Sir, you...you did the slide thing again."

"Dammit."

Deckard coughed past his laughter. "How much has Vanguard taken in munitions, manpower, and supply?"

Wolcott scanned his memory bank again. My, they programmed the boy well. They had taken a human being and made a tin toy soldier. "A few hundred naval deserters, a convoy of fuel and medical supplies, a shipment of replicators—"

"All of which," Deckard cut him off, "are of great universal value, are they not?"

"Sir?"

"Now, how many colonies would claim to have *the* Aaron

Havenes, smuggled off world and now hiding in their cellars, if it meant receiving donations of bullets, band-aids, and beans?" Deckard let that inference hang. "You blast him to molten slag, and his ghost will be in half a dozen systems by week's end. You'll only kill the man. We have to kill the idea."

Wolcott's eyes went wide. "Disfavor is that ingrained in the Reaches?"

Deckard turned heel-toe and marched toward the lift. "Rebellions are like weeds, Lieutenant. Pull them up from the root, or they'll simply sprout again."

"And the Minister?" Wolcott called after him.

Deckard tabbed the lift's call button and the door opened promptly. "Is that a formal complaint, lieutenant?"

"Trying to understand, sir."

Of course, it was a formal complaint. And the Minister would be on his call sheet by the time they reached periapsis.

Deckard sighed. "You find fault with my approach." It wasn't a question.

The aide shifted on the balls of his feet. He was antsy, nervous. These Grade-A students were always so worried about bucking regulation. "It's just—the Minister's orders...."

"You said that already. Minister Caldwell wants a result," Deckard said. "He is not here. You are. Examine your surroundings, gather intelligence, and make the most informed decision to achieve the most positive end with the fewest casualties." Deckard stepped into the lift. "The colonists *will* surrender Aaron Havenes. We're going to make that happen. You have the conn, lieutenant."

"Yes, sir," the boy snapped back in crisp form. It might have been a reflexive affirmative, but the aide clearly disagreed. Too risky, too much chance for blood and embarrassment. Better to simply scorch the earth.

He had much to learn, chief among which was that he did not know everything.

CHAPTER
FOUR
EDEN

"NO."

It was probably Talania's tenth 'no' of the call. She sat in the Howler's gunner seat, humoring the man in the projection.

Aaron laid his head back on the craft's storage shelf, arms folded across his chest like a blanket. He was just tall enough to recline his head back onto it and take a tidy little nap, his hands grasping the dangling drop cables for added security. Those dangling cables, like vines in a dense forest curled around his forearms, would rock him off to sleep. All the while, a tiny sadistic smile grew on his face as he listened to the lullaby of Talania's political torture.

Eden couldn't take that nap. Aaron might have been short enough for that shelf, but Eden wasn't tall enough, the corner cutting into the back of her head. So instead, she got to watch public access television happen right in front of her.

Talania sat prim and proper, hands folded in her lap. She had pulled her hair back into a fierce ponytail just shy of the crown of her head. It draped across her neck like black silk, occasionally even reflecting the light. Maybe she had some treatment to it, some off-world oil?

While Talania's posture and presence might have been delicate, her delivery certainly was not.

"Mr. Whitby, my door is always open. Your lack of attendance cannot be accounted to me or my staff."

The stern face on the projection bristled at the insinuation. Perfect pepper gray hair coiffed without a strand out of place, and glistening white teeth that were likely artificial veneers. Stefan Whitby looked like someone had grown an evil, ambitious politician in a vat—or simply grabbed the first man who looked the part, because he had all the same qualifications as Johnny Everyman might. He was handsome, charismatic, and spoke in that infuriating tone with a rising action, even if there was no point to drive to.

The political golem's sharp cheeks and large jaw barely moved when he spoke, some tension buried in his neck. "Governor, a summit of any kind without the Statesmen is a violation of Colonial Code—"

"And if you showed up to the meeting, Mr. Whitby," Talania barked back, "we might've had a quorum and been able to bring you along. But, such as it is..."

"I will not participate in a sham government! You're protecting a wanted fugitive, a traitor to the Consul—and a murderer!"

"Aaron Havenes has been nothing but compliant with my requests. I would be a very poor friend to toss him into the cold."

The craft jostled, causing the projector on Talania's wrist to lose its tracking. The image on the hull stuttered as Whitby's lip quivered, freezing on a rather unappealing face, before resuming. "Capitals... are not our friends."

Aaron smiled, eyes closed and contented. He whispered to the cabin, just loud enough. "The more things change..."

Whitby absolutely heard that, his nostrils flaring with a hard intake. "Ms. Dedria—"

"Governor."

"Whatever you choose to call yourself," Whitby spat, "the Imperium has issued instructions. If you were a patriot like your father, you would abide by it!"

Like your father. That was a land mine right there, and one he had driven over deliberately.

Patriotism got her father killed.

Talania took a breath, quelling the fire that kindled behind her eyes. She looked like a python coiling about her prey's legs before surging up to squeeze tight on its carotid. "Mr. Whitby, you have a passionate base of support. I assume when you stood on a podium next to Marcus Riley..." She paused, trying to keep her composure from shattering. "The day he had me arrested, you were very pleased. It must've been heart-breaking not to receive the nomination—after your close friend *murdered* my father. But it takes a unique brand of delusion after all that to *still* believe the Empire means you well."

The hate in Whitby's eyes could've poisoned water. "You cannot so easily bestow yourself a crown, Ms. Dedria."

Talania flickered now, her eyes fluttering at that phrase, her head cocking.

Stop mucking about. Time for a kill shot.

"I mean, you had such a hard time anointing yourself. It must be scary, seeing me make it look easy."

As Whitby exploded, Talania waved her hand at the screen and closed out the call. Eden couldn't stop her face from cracking into laughter.

Talania wasn't amused however, taking a solid drink from her thermos, before extending it to the others. "Pompous jackass. Coffee?"

Eden plucked it from Talania's hands and took a stiff pull. She wished she hadn't. It tasted like fire, acid, and bleach had an unfortunate mutant offspring.

"A bit early for hair of the dog, eh?" Eden coughed out through the pain.

Talania shook her head. "Coffee's not complete without a little bump."

"A little?! This is whiskey in a thermos that once upon a time was shown a *picture* of coffee grounds!"

Aaron chuckled. "You see how I didn't grab it?"

———

The Hive—the last time she had seen this place, she had come under cover of secrecy. Among a dozen or so armed humans, not a word had been spoken. They had marched deep into the recesses of the mountain, in search of its heart. They couldn't have known what they would find.

It was here she watched Aaron 'die' for the first time. She still remembered the Howler door sliding shut, cutting her off, holding her back from reaching out or calling his name. He had been left behind to the claws of an alien horde. Or simply at the uncaring whims of the elements.

But the aliens had other plans for him.

She had seen the beasts at work, both as enemies and allies. Their blades—some kind of creatine composite—were strong enough to punch through three solid inches of steel, and she'd seen one of the critters charge right through a concrete barricade without breaking stride. They kept going despite fatal injuries, unstoppable and relentless.

They were quiet too, capable of burrowing under your feet and surging up from the ground. She'd often wondered if they dug with those claws or if there was some other method.

Aaron reported them as omnivores, largely subsisting on moss paddies they grew in the Hive—but short of a protein diet, she had no idea how the creatures could support their mass and be as aggressive as they were. They must have consumed metric tons of the stuff, or it was more nutrient rich than she thought. She made a mental note to take a sample for study.

If they allowed her to.

They were not to bring weapons of any kind. They were to leave rigs and packs on the surface. They were not to use visors or goggles or torches—no technology.

Fair enough. The last time humans had come this way, there had been quite an impact. But it didn't make the experience any less harrowing.

Aaron treated the slow walk down the mountain tunnel like a nature hike, almost meditative, his hand tracing the edges of the wall. The darkness didn't seem to bother him.

Without an implant or augment, she couldn't see her own hand in front of her face. Talania had to be led, one hand on his shoulder. If he got too far ahead of her, the darkness of the tunnel would swallow him whole and she'd be left alone to ponder the mysteries of the universe.

Eden dragged one hand against the wall of the tunnel, feeling out the air pockets in the wall. Some were small, simply a rough texture under her fingers. Some were large enough she could shove her whole arm inside.

They had fought the Jergad for so long, she wasn't sure there were any other natural organisms on the planet. In a nightmarish strike of realization, she thought, might there be some predator—big or small—that lived down here out of sight that would love to snack on her willowy wrists?

She tucked her hand in her jacket pocket for the rest of the journey, fingers wrapped tight into a ball so she could confirm they were all still there.

Eden had tried to strike up a conversation with Aaron, but only got one-word answers in response. Her thoughts were going to be her lone companion. After nearly a half an hour in absolute darkness, she saw a glowing amber light at the end of the tunnel.

Framed in the entrance to the Hive, stood a Jergad drone.

Eden got to enjoy Talania nearly shitting clean through her expensive pantsuit. She had seen pictures, video—possibly even witnessed an autopsy of a dead drone. But it was an entirely different experience seeing the creatures alive and kicking.

The Jergad drone stood a full ten feet tall when upright. A massive skull crest swept back like a tower shield, thick leathery plates serving as a banded mail, a bifurcated jaw full of flat crushing teeth, and twin scythes in place of hands—one great single bladed finger.

Aaron claimed the articulated reapers served as climbing axes and digging spades, but were also gentle enough to carry. Eden had no desire to test that.

The Jergad's solid blue eyes were still creepifying. They looked like bird's eggs set into their skull. How it could see without a pupil to gather light was always a fascination of hers. Were they seeing in other spectrums? Or was it not sight at all, really? Did they have any other senses, as yet unknown?

This one had a scar across one socket, the eye crushed, and notches in its leathery hide where a blade's cross guard had dug in. Eden knew this particular beast well—the Capitals had fought beside it during Riley's siege.

The beast's mark was the result of a close encounter with Aaron; and Aaron had more than a few ugly scars he'd earned back for his trouble. The two had something of a unique bond that way.

Not that this one had any individuality of its own. All Jergad were one. And Aaron had come to hold court with the brains of the outfit.

Aaron glanced back at Eden. "You can go back up if you want."

She glanced at the darkened tunnel behind her, like a black curtain drawn across her sight. Her voice cracked as she spoke. "I really can't, so let's do this."

Scar led them into the cavern. She remembered the place well enough—it had been burned into her memory—but it still took her breath away. The former magma chamber was easily a thousand feet high. Three giant spires had been built up, the Jergad's secreted resin along with natural stone shaped into a putty-like cement. The structures reached high, up and up, almost all the way to the ceiling. Pockets along the cavern walls and in the sides of the towers contained tiny nests.

On the ground floor, pools of glowing amber ooze—the source of the amber light that filled the whole area. The moss paddies floating on the surface must have a bioluminescent event with the water, a byproduct of whatever exothermic reaction was occurring.

She could still make out the scorch marks and dented stone from where Ilern had thrown his grenade. He'd set fire to their fields.

"Eden," Aaron reminded her gently to keep moving. She had begun to linger, and the Jergad nearby were growing agitated.

With good reason. She remembered how well that moss burned.

They stopped next to the giant central spire and Eden craned her neck to look up. It was probably six hundred feet of sheer rock climb.

Talania put her hands on her hips. "Quite a brutalist design philosophy."

"You're like the second...third human they've ever let this close," Eden said. "Try to be gracious."

"I'm gracious. I'm all kinds of gracious." Talania squinted at the top of the spire. "Just looking for a flight of stairs."

Scar bucked its head, skull crest waving in the air like a frozen mane. Aaron stepped up behind her. "Grab on," Aaron said.

Talania stared at Scar's immense proportions, the blades and powerful recurved legs. "To what?" she asked, already suspecting what he had in mind.

"Elevator."

"*Fra tow paz ki...*" Eden trailed off, but she wasn't going to be left behind now. Not with the biggest mystery yet ahead of them. She slung an arm around Scar's other shoulder, looping a hand underneath to interlock her fingers for a good hold. She braced a foot against Scar's hip, hoping for a little extra purchase.

Talania watched as Eden and Aaron flanked the big beast. Aaron nodded to her. "You going to wait for the next one?"

Talania bounced on her toes, her face pallid and a little green. "Hoo boy."

"'Fraid of heights?" Eden asked.

"Afraid of *him*."

Scar grunted, almost purring. It was like the entire beast shuddered under her fingers.

"What was all that coffee even for?" Eden teased. "Live a little."

Talania shook her head and marched over to Eden, draping her large frame over her. Eden's eyes went wide as she felt Talania's smooth hands brush her shoulder, her lithe legs lean against her own. She could feel Talania's heart against her back, tapping out an SOS.

"Thought you'd be comfortable being little spoon?" Aaron teased, seeing the panicked expression on Eden's face.

"Shut up," they both said, Talania with quite a bit more terror in her voice.

"Close your eyes," Aaron advised.

"What? Why?"

"Because this entire process is disconcerting," Aaron said, "and it's better if you close your eyes."

"I chose to come," Talania countered, more than a little regret in that statement.

Eden chuckled. "Yeah, how you feel about that now?"

Scar didn't wait for her to answer. The creature crouched low, coiling up his muscles before jumping directly at the spire. Eden stifled a scream, as they slammed into the rock face. It might have been perfectly safe for the big guy, but it still sounded like a train crash right at her elbow.

She barely felt the gravity change, as the big guy set a consistent pace, hand over hand clawing its way up the spire. It had places to be and it was taking them with.

Eden looked over at Aaron, who was squeezing his eyes shut and his grip about Scar's shoulder was iron tight. He might've been the one passing advice to Talania but it was *he* who was comically uncomfortable with the arrangement. Familiarity didn't exactly breed comfort, it seemed.

They flew up the side almost as steadily as flight. They passed other Jergad socketed into the walls, resting in cliffside aeries. She doubted this was an evolutionary preference dating back before humans—this was defensive. She'd seen how well these creatures took a vertical fall. And the look in their bodies, a tension even in rest...

These weren't homes. They were guard stations.

She turned her eyes outward from the Spire. She thought she had a good view before, but now...

She could see a nursery, a small pool of water with a kind of membrane over it. Some viscous fluid beneath it, embryonic perhaps? Small shadows flitted inside, some combination of walking and swimming with large kicking feet on each tadpole. Suppose that made them amphibian, by definition, even if they never returned to the water. Fascinating.

After all, this planet hadn't been a desert for that long—only since humans arrived, terraforming it with high-explosive ordinance.

A tear in the gelatinous fabric and a plaintive screech in the air. It might have been a creature of leather and blades, but every surface of this babe seemed softened and curved. The plates hadn't fully grown in, looking more like spots of scales, the velvet soft flesh exposed. Ready to walk and dig, maybe, but this juvenile was not capable to be on its own. It looked like the largest baby chick she'd ever seen. And it could probably still kill her with enough motivation.

Within seconds, two adults swooped in, gingerly lifting it from the goo bath. They laid it down on its two feet, holding it up at first as it quivered, knees knocking.

Of course—it's never stood up before. They might not have the bones of the inner ear but it must have some internal gyroscope. Especially so, with the magnetic field they used to maintain connection to the Queen.

The Queen...if she could be called that. It's not as though she was the big bad one laying fields of eggs. She was something...eldritch, the sum total of a million basic conscious minds swirled into one.

Scar cleared the top of the spire, a plateau of polished smooth stone. One edge connected with the cavern wall, additional support. Eden unclasped Talania's vice grip on her shoulder one finger at a

48

time, like she was gingerly picking a vault lock. Talania let out her breath, a swampy heat against Eden's cheek.

Talania almost fell off of Scar, staggering to find her balance again. She looked like she expected this whole stone plate to tip over and spill them all to the ground far below.

Aaron hopped off Scar like the battle-mount it was, giving Scar a few sweet pats to the head. The creature groaned back, pleasant acknowledgement.

Eden reached out with one foot and grazed the surface. It pushed back at her, spongey but firm. Almost like a crash pad.

She knew where they were. This had been Aaron's prison cell for months. But there was no sign of the creepy human doppelgänger Aaron had reported, or of a nightmarish horrible master brain, all claws and darkness.

The place was barren.

"Welcome back," Eden mumbled to Aaron with a bit of dry seasoning. "Our Gold star guests get the best seat in the house."

"Yeah, wait 'til you try the food," Aaron said.

Eden shrugged. "Can't be worse than rations."

"Oh, it can!"

"Gah!" Talania must've seen the thing first.

Eden had scanned left and right, no sign of the monstrosity. But then, all of a sudden, she just turned and there it was.

The Jergad were big, nearly two metric tons of blades and nightmare fuel with a face that only an entomologist could love. This was bigger still, a tanker trunk of shapeless shadow, shifting, roiling, bubbling darkness that seemed permanently out of focus. Four distinct claw arms held it to the roof of the cavern, but yet seemed to be under no load. With its enormity, Eden felt like the platform should've been snapping under its weight.

This thing wasn't actually...here. It was somewhere else. Somewhere deeper. If it actually 'was' anywhere at all.

Aaron stepped up like it was nothing. "And how are you going to help?" A pause. "Oh, no no no, don't give me that! I've got maybe a six hundred fighters. They'll have triple that, and that's not even counting all the tech!"

Eden's eyes shifted from Aaron back to the shadowy orb of madness. His eyes weren't tracking on it, however. He was looking at something eye-level. Something walking among them. He was seeing something she wasn't.

The ghost. That creepy human copy. The Queen.

If she had seen this before they fought Riley, she'd have had him sectioned and medicated. But then, looking up at the 'Queen' itself made her question her own stability.

Talania tried to flex her new mantle. "Your...Majesty?"

Aaron waved her down. "Well, no...not—don't do that."

"She can understand *you*."

"No, I mean the—the 'your Majesty' bit. She doesn't think about hierarchy. She probably couldn't *spell* the word 'etiquette.'" A pause, and he whipped his head about. "Stop."

Tee-hee. She had started to spell it.

Aaron whirled around to face the Queen, propping his hands on his hips and rolled out his neck, frustrated. "Well, excuse me! But I think we long since passed the point where you and me get to have separate problems." His voice weakened. "*You* got me into this."

"Well, no," Eden found herself saying.

Aaron slowly cranked his head over to her with a patented 'you're not helping' face.

Eden wasn't backing down. "*You* got you into this. You could've forked over everything you learned here. Instead you put your neck on the block because you wanted the fighting to stop. And we all stood up there with you—of our own free will, I might add. Talania too. Nobody's standing here right now because of somebody else."

Aaron sucked on his teeth with a dissatisfied smirk. "When you said you wanted to come along, you..." He was too annoyed to finish the hushed statement.

But it just wasn't true. The unknowable elder God sleeping in the mountain had done no such thing.

Eden pursed her lips with a shrug. "You were wrong." Simple as that. She didn't want to take his legs out or anything, but he was walking himself into a bad corner.

Aaron forced a wide smile, and sighed, turning back to whatever invisible poltergeist he was arguing with. "It's a family thing." There was a dismissive tone to his voice.

Talania arched an eyebrow. "What is?"

"The Queen's a singular consciousness for an entire species," Aaron explained, "She's never seen people disagree before."

"Good," Eden said, crossing her arms, "because that had all manner of weird places that coulda gone."

Aaron squared up on the Queen. "The Empire is coming. We got as ready as we can be. But I need your help."

"How did she know that, by the way?" Eden asked. Aaron ground his teeth, but that didn't stop her. Eden looked from him to the amorphous shadow monster and back at him. "The instant they hit the Jump Point, she was ringing alarm bells, and even had an accurate troop count. That's..."

Talania propped her hands on her hips. "I'm a little curious about that myself."

Aaron straightened up, tongue in cheek. She was telling him something and he was listening close. "She...okay, so...you're alive, right?"

Talania nodded, brow furrowed. Where was he going with this?

"Okay, so...*why* are you alive?"

Uh...

"Well..." Eden began, "Maybe we're all just in your head."

"You're not," Aaron dismissed that philosophical hurdle, "because there's an electrical current running through you, biochemical markers in your brain, and—you've got a soul. She can *see* it. We can see light, smell chemicals in the air, taste, touch. She can *see*...life. That's how she did it."

Eden leered up at the uncanny black hole of oil and darkness purporting to be the hive mind of an entire alien species. She pursed her lips. "She can see my life force?"

Aaron nodded sharply, as if trying to just move her past the enormity of that. "It's also how they were able to sneak up on us all the *gulaw* time. They don't need to see you. They *see* you."

"How did we sneak up on *them?*" Eden asked.

"How did we..." Aaron paused, then whirled right back to his meeting with an elder God. "How *did* we?"

Talania leaned in. "Five says she let you guys in."

"I mean..." Eden waved her hand at the gigantic titan wreathed in shadow. "Give me another plausible theory."

This creature had a sixth sense, could detect elements in the universe as yet undiscovered. Riley's private scientists had concluded the creatures communicated via electromagnetism—and their baby Rebellion had put that to use, disrupting Repeater cannons on the Wall to cover their advance.

But sensing...life? That's a whole new bag of tricks.

Talania stepped up to Eden's shoulder. "Is it too late to give him up to the Imperials and just hope for the best?"

"She's kidding!" Aaron called out, loud enough to also be a scolding.

"I was half-serious."

Eden cupped her hand around her mouth. "We could wrap him up all nice and pretty."

"What, like put a bow on him?"

"Or just tie him up with rope."

Aaron was now pacing the plateau, ignoring the dynamic duo and berating his imaginary friend.

All the while, the black simply hovered, permanently out of reach but still way too close for comfort. It wasn't unlike watching a holo-call with the privacy setting—one person acting all shifty and talking to air, while the other side is completely absent to any other eye.

Why did he ask them to come along, if this was all there was?

They were going to just be there third-wheeling while Aaron tried to badger an entire alien species into aiding them?

"I don't need you to fight!" Aaron snapped. "I've got thousands of innocent people. They're not fighters either. Doctors, teachers— dammit, *kids*! I've gotta get them out of harm's way. Let me bring them here..."

The shadow blob bristled at that, like a stone skipped across its surface.

Aaron shivered in kind, like it went through him too. "I know that. I hear ya. And I'm open to suggestions but..." He fizzled; maybe they were talking over him. Every time they 'spoke,' he seemed to shrivel up. Maybe that was a physiological response to the telepathy? Or maybe he was getting beat around.

"There *is* nowhere else!" he exploded. "I can't put an entire city in my back pocket."

Aaron was getting heated, throwing his arms up and flailing. He was getting angry. She didn't need to know the details. Human situation was a human problem. The Jergad had their own lives to look after, their own problems. Their own children to protect.

"Please," Eden said, her soft voice stopping Aaron cold. But she wasn't talking to him. She walked toward the shadow.

It was a curious illusion, seeming to drift away in time with her steps, always keeping the same distance. Eden gave up on that and planted her feet. "We helped you. And now we need you to help us. We put ourselves out there for *you*. My friends died for you...and in two weeks, so will everybody else."

The black rippled, edges pulling forward but vanishing before they reached the front. It was so strange to look at, like you couldn't take it in entirely, only a piece at a time, never a full picture of it. But agitation was easy to see in nearly any creature.

"Yeah," Eden conceded, "we're scared of you. And you're scared of us. Plenty o' right to be. But right here, right now...you can give us a reason not to be."

The Queen considered, twisting and curling on itself. It was almost like watching a gemstone through a kaleidoscope, never any one thing to look at. But in this case, there was little that was dazzling and plenty that would stain the mind, an inky black for the evening's dreams.

Aaron sank into his shoes. "Alright then."

"Alright, what?" Eden asked. "What did they say?"

"She's worried about her people. Well, no—" He paused, rubbing his neck. "She's worried about *our* people. What they'll do. We've got a lot of scared people and scared people don't sit still, if you know what I mean."

Talania nodded. "Scared people get angry."

"Yeah. And one angry mob, plus an enemy we raised our children to fear..."

Eden finished the math on that. They were on their own.

CHAPTER
FIVE
AARON

THE SUN WAS SETTING, finally putting the long day to rest. The jewel-tone oranges of the sunset stretched high overhead. Paired with the rumbling under his seat, that he could feel more than hear, Aaron could've sworn a dragon had taken flight to burn down a small medieval village.

It was a quiet trip back from the mountains, but Aaron was pretty certain that Eden's existential crisis had more to do with alien super-powers than about the setback. The only questions she had asked him were about the Sense. Was it a visual spectrum, or more like smell and taste? What was the range on it?

Did he have the Sense too?

She had been a doctor, working on her residency. They might have given her a jumpsuit and a number, but that wouldn't rob her of an analytical mind and a natural predisposition to research.

Or maybe she was just trying to avoid thinking about what would happen when the bombardments began. So...instead, superpowers.

He hadn't really thought about any of it, to be truthful, so he just shrugged at a lot of her questions. He had just bought in to the witch-craft and moved on. Applying the scientific method to the Queen's psychic abilities wasn't something he'd had time for anyhow.

He was still trying to get her to stop calling him '*ak'thun.*' He was short. Got it. Could we move on?

Eden hadn't been pleased with his lack of answers. It felt like gravity had lightened up and she floated away from him, falling further and further out of his orbit.

But right then, in the Howler, it just felt like he had that much more oxygen, every breath somehow safer and quieter.

Talania had taken three different calls in the time since, a nonstop chatter as she took reports and dispensed orders to her aides. She kept her voice down and hushed, casting sidelong glances his way from time to time.

Great. Even she didn't trust him anymore. Although *that* was more akin to what he was used to.

The Castle rose up around them. He'd been so in his head, he hadn't seen them arrive. This particular Wall prefecture had been beefed up in the last six months—repairs made and built upon, ever since Aaron and his damnable crew of rogues had punched an eight-foot hole in the side of it. It had become as much a maintenance job as a beautification project. The site was part military installation and part famed spiritual site.

He could always tell from the air who was military and who was a civilian tour group. The tourists stood in the way of twelve-ton military vehicles with roaring engines like they were props to pose with.

Some of the new arrivals had no idea what to make of Vanguard's Wall, but they all wanted to see the site of Aaron's famed attack, where Legatus had changed the course of their local history.

A *gulaw* tourist trap, but Talania had insisted. The people couldn't be kept sidelined; they had to have this all made tangible, tactile. She wanted every single citizen to be able to reach out and touch evidence of the battle. Skeptics took it as a chance to prove Aaron's treason, pick apart the stories for inaccuracies; worse still, believers came to gawk and humble themselves at the site.

What had once stood as the single line of defense against the Jergad, now stood as the FOB and Proving Ground for Aaron's growing militia. There was a graduating class in the garrison now, close to fifty men and women in their new uniforms for the very first time.

They wore Capital Gray.

Aaron had sworn the same oath they were now taking. It was a military code twisted for the Capitals, removing the Dunsweir blessings from it—no Capital deserved their words.

Now, Civilian, Regular, and Capital alike said the oath as they formally joined the ranks: 'I Serve with distinction and honor in this time of great need. I Serve my neighbors and my friends, my commander and my subordinate. I will Serve in a manner that befits the cause.'

They used to then say how they 'served' the Consul and the Empire. Now...they just said, 'I Serve.'

Bray thought it fitting.

Aaron didn't like the chant one bit. It sounded too much like prayer.

The Capital ranks had swelled in the past six months—they might not have been all from Capital convicts anymore, with civilians and even some former Army Regulars taking the oath—but they bore the name and badge with an ironic pride. They were all convicting themselves by putting on a uniform and pledging to stand a watch against the Imperium. One morning they had said their daily pledge to the Consul and Empire, and the next they took up arms against it. Seemed appropriate that they take the name too.

And the prefecture itself had blossomed, with facilities building up on either side of the enormous brickwork line. Tents and structures had been propped up to support the increased numbers. The Thumpers had been decommissioned, the giant concrete hammers hanging off the Wall scraped down to skeletons, stripped for their parts, leaving the concrete slabs tilted, leaning against the foundations.

It was all at once beautiful and an act of vandalism, almost necromancy. Aaron would have been happier to see the whole thing deserted.

Instead, it had only grown.

The Howler set down and the door officer cracked the seal. The inside was quiet enough Aaron could've meditated, but that silence immediately flushed with machines whirring and metal scraping, boots falling in unison and platoon leaders sounding marching songs.

He couldn't describe why, but it all felt so dour, like everything was tuned to a minor key, sober and heavy.

Aaron stepped out of the Howler and three different nearby platoons all dropped their formations, whispers rippling through the crowd. This kept up, he was going to start wearing a hood in public. But then he'd be the only one in a hood and it would still be weird.

The graduating class stiffened like they were crusting with frost. They must've thought he was touring their event, arriving specifically for them. They were to be blessed.

Aaron's heart sank into his shoes.

Eden rubbed his shoulder. "Chin up, 'Legatus.'"

Chin up. They always told him to 'chin up.' Had to look good for the tourists and the worshipping public. It was exhausting.

He was allowed a moment or two to look sullen. It always looked like he was bowing his head in prayer.

Hands were pointed in his direction, hushed whispers, and a few sneers. Though none were brave enough to taunt. Not here, in the very heart of Aaron's power.

A tour guide and military escort had been leading a group through the area, detailing the site of the Capitals' attack on the Wall. Some took it as a chance to see any family that were deployed. But a majority were just on holiday, sightseeing. Glowing amber displays popped up from almost every arm, as they recorded their close encounter with *the* Aaron Havenes, Legatus, Hero of Rimpau and Champion of Vanguard.

One body pushed through the crowd, uniform crumpled and face wrinkled. Gunnery Sergeant Bray had been a brusque and direct man when he had trained Aaron. He had only grown surlier now that he had to babysit the occasional civilian through boot camp.

"Alright, alright! Move 'em back. This ain't a pep rally."

Most tourists listened, but one sneaky teenager thought he could hide his recorder inside a jacket sleeve. Bray grabbed the kid by the offending wrist. "You realize that thing *glows*, right?"

The boy's mother immediately leapt in, with some combination of 'how dare you' and 'give me your name.'

Bray wasn't having it. "This is a working military base. I am not your camp counselor. Move it along."

Aaron sighed like he was wrapped in a warm blanket. Ah, that voice. Music to his ears.

The tour group moved along, and despite the offended mother-son combo, the rest were hushed whispers and gaping eyes. They'd just been accosted by *the* Sergeant Thomas Bray, demigod. How cool was that!?

Aaron recalled the early days, having similar bumps on the streets. It never felt *that* magical to him, but the recipient always acted like he'd blessed the dirt under their fingernails.

Bray didn't take any heed of it, stalking right up to Aaron like *he* was the one in trouble. There was almost a wind Aaron could feel blasting off the stocky man. Aaron had to take a deep breath and a trip down memory lane just to remember he was actually the one giving orders now.

"Havenes," Bray greeted him, surly. "Don't say it."

'Be nice.' Heh.

"Then I won't," Aaron said, with a forced smile. "...but uh, can I get some advice?"

"You can ask, but I can't promise I got any."

Aaron nodded after the tour group. "How do you deal with it?"

The old man glanced after the retreating horde of jabbering tourists. "You know that old phrase, what was it...never meet your heroes?"

"So you're just a colossal dick until they stop asking you for pictures?" Eden said.

"You stopped, didn't ya?"

"Bray, I'm pretty sure if I did take a picture, my hard drive would find its way into a compactor."

Bray raised an eyebrow at Aaron. "You look like you need some rack time."

"I'll sleep when I'm dead."

"Okay. You want old dog wisdom?" Bray said. "Sleep, eat, and play whenever you can. Don't know when you'll get another shot to."

Talania swung herself out of the Howler, her wrist still glowing from the last call. "Exactly what do you mean by 'play', Gunny?"

"I've been shootin' and drinkin' for longer than you've been walkin', so why don't you use that potent imagination you're so famous for?"

Talania shook her head and clamped her jaw tight. "No, I don't think I will, Gunny. It's better for both of us that way."

Bray didn't smile. Not with his face anyway. But somewhere behind that old leathery face, a demon piloting his skinsuit cackled to itself. "Six hundred triggers, strong and armed."

"Ready for combat?" Aaron asked.

"Better than you were," Bray said, "but that may not be saying much. The real trick is getting 'em organized."

To be expected. This was exactly what Riley tried to avoid by drafting Capitals in the first place. This was a colonial militia: a mealy dough of civilian volunteers that were undisciplined, out of shape, and dreaming of grandeur. Mix in some career infantry and the seasoned Capitals themselves? Well...they were not going to play nice with each other, even with their collective heads on the metaphorical block.

"Have a sit down with some of the more tactically talented minds," Aaron said. "We're going to need some options for the next few weeks."

"You'll be there?" Bray prompted. Talania leered at Aaron, curious.

What did he have to offer? Moral support? He was a bureaucrat and an alien translator. He wasn't a strategist. He wasn't even very good at chess. "...Yeah, just give me the time and place."

"0600 tomorrow, right here."

Oh goodie.

Aaron turned to Talania. "You'll head back and spread our good word?"

She nodded, dangling off the handrail on the Howler's door. "Yeah, Whitby's going to *love* me."

"Don't kid yourself," Eden said. "Nobody likes you."

Talania clucked her tongue at the little woman as she took a swig of her coffee.

That's when it hit, knocking the thermos right out of her hands.

He felt the pressure wave first, like a pair of hands clapped hard over his ears, a light shove on his back. Then he heard it, a deafening drum that seemed to come from everywhere. The wind swept over them, as displaced air tossed the dirt and billowed Eden's oily hair.

Then shrapnel, bits of steel and stone cascading around them like heavy rain. A chunk embedded itself into the Howler's hull.

Had the Admiral really started firing orbital kinetics all the way from the Jump Point? They might've fired right away and it just took this long for the strike to arrive. No—they'd have heard the supersonic strike breach the atmosphere. This came from the ground.

A bomb.

Bray and Eden had Aaron on the ground, shielding him with their bodies. Gunny stretched one hand out at the Howler, shouting at the pilot. "Get that bird in the air *now*! Off the deck!"

"Kilo Six-Two, breaking off!" The pilot put in on the radio.

Aaron caught one glimpse of Talania before the door shut. Her eyes were cast up, back behind them toward the barracks, as she took in the nightmare.

There was no fire, just a crater. A large explosive device had atomized a building and blew an entire chunk off the Wall and into the field, pieces of it still raining down. Cinderblocks the size of steel crates buried themselves in the dirt and into other buildings like a meteor shower.

Worse still, tiny metal shrapnel had shot outward. Entire platoons lay scattered on the ground. Through the hanging dust, Aaron could make out the bloody chunks of what had once been a person.

The graduation.

So many screams. The confused, the injured, the frightened. The dispersed cloud of ash and debris grew and grew, like a sandstorm filling the air. A fog of war.

Aaron heaved his protectors off of him, and the old Gunny immediately spouted instructions into his radio. "Lockdown! Nobody gets in or out of the Castle. I want triage teams and security at their posts! Now! And get me a damage report!"

Eden grabbed Aaron's wrist. "Are you hurt?"

He shook his head. "You?"

"I'm solid!"

"Get with medical," Aaron shouted, "they're going to need every hand we've got." He paused. "Where's that tour group?"

Everyone was running. Nothing but silhouettes in the growing cloud of dust. Huddled, fearful for the next explosion to come.

One person walking, upright and urgent. Headed for the Wall.

"Hey!" Eden called out.

That was the spark they needed. The figure broke into a sprint, vanishing into a door at the base of the Wall. They shouldered in the door so hard it bounced off the inside and banged shut behind them.

Aaron jumped after them, slipping out of Eden's fingers. "Aaron, don't—!"

He didn't hear what was said. A bomb had gone off and this fleeing person had been far too nonchalant about that fact.

His radio crackled as Bray issued commands. "Kilo Six, we have a runner on the Wall interior, east bound. Provide overwatch!"

"Kilo Six, affirm. Coming around."

The Howler passed overhead like a twelve-ton ghost, its shadow passing over the cloud of ash. Aaron pulled his shirt up over his chin, trying to filter at least some of the horrible building materials that were now aerosolized for everybody to breathe.

He kicked the door in—and immediately ducked back, as a pair of tungsten slugs etched lines along the doorframe.

Up the stairs to the left, happy fwumps from a Gaussian sidearm. Everything they had was still chemical burn bang-sticks. That was Off-world tech. That was an Imperial saboteur alright.

How they got through border check would be an interesting conversation.

Had they really tried to assassinate him? No. His location wasn't exactly a secret. And he *had* come back from the excursion early, off schedule. This was meant to happen while he was away—bomb used as a distraction, shock and awe at the graduation. Then steal whatever they could, and get away.

He knew the op well enough. It was the same op Riley had run on the Jergad. Recon a sensitive spot, hit it hard, and escape in the confusion.

Aaron listened for the retreating feet. The bomber wasn't holding that doorway, just trying to dissuade pursuit. But Aaron was acclimatized these days to being shot at. He peeked the corner and then broke back into a run.

Aaron had been posted on the Wall a few times in his Capital days, but he hardly knew his way around. Every prefecture might have looked the same outside, but they were all different. Steel panels over concrete bracing, with reinforcements dropped deep into the ground—to block Jergad burrowers.

But the interiors were cramped and narrow; hollow spaces were weaknesses. Inside, you were just supposed to move to your next post. So the hallways were mostly shoulder-to-shoulder affairs. Each tower was a parapet and armory, with a posting of four troopers. Outside the cover of the parapet, was the body of the Wall—like a vertical raised trench, allowing dozens, if not hundreds, of shooters to take a line and fire down at an invading Jergad force.

These prefectures were little more than elevated foxholes, with plenty of notches to rest rifles and canteens.

Sunlight. Aaron emerged from the stairwell to see two dead Capitals, red painting their gray uniforms and the steel walls, their rifles still slung. They hadn't even had a chance to draw before matching holes were carved in their chests.

One Capital wore a necklace, cheaply made of wrapped copper wire: a dog tag with the numbers '626' hand-hammered into the tin.

But no sign of the shooter, here or along the Wall.

The next Prefecture was over two hundred yards away. There was only one kind of person he knew that was *that* fast.

Aaron keyed his wrist computer. "Bray! I've lost them!"

"Kilo Six, anything?"

The pilot mumbled something, but then cleared his throat. "I've got uh...activity Northeast of the Castle. Tracer fire on the Wall."

Aaron took off running. If they had an Oskie to deal with, they were going to need every gun available.

Riley had been Orbital Strike Command. Riley had killed Jensen, Carmona, and dozens of others. He was heartless, vicious, and his augments made him faster than a bolt of lightning.

A platoon of Capitals armed to the teeth would be cut down like grass. They wouldn't know how to fight Orbital, how to wear them down and overwhelm them. How Orbital's God-tier subdermal implants would overheat under duress. This wasn't an enemy to fight carefully, take cover, and conserve ammo.

This was an enemy you killed with a cloud of bullets.

Aaron listened for the violence, hearing cracks of gunfire and battle shouts from the next Prefecture over. Aaron snatched a weapon from one of the fallen, and a few magazines. He checked the action, dropped the safety, and slammed a round into battery.

Well, that muscle memory was still ripe.

He grabbed the handrails and slid down onto the Wall proper, sprinting along its length. The sun glared in his eyes and the harsh floor battered at his feet. Had he twisted his ankle back there? Maybe there was something to all of Bray's draconian drills, because Aaron had clearly lost a step.

It wasn't a long distance between Prefectures, but this was the actual residence of most stationed to the Wall. Bedrolls were laid out for those on rack while the on-cycle took up positions facing the Wild. Rickety three-legged tables were laid out every so often, barely off the ground. They were useful for field stripping a rifle or eating a quick meal or a quick game of cards, so long as the commander didn't see.

Now, it was deserted. No reason to post anyone up here anymore. So what was the bomber after?

He jumped tables like they were hurdles on a track. He had to get there while there was anybody left to help.

Movement at the Prefecture ahead. Friendly? Hard to say. Aaron had a bad history with shadows moving ominously.

It was a shooter. Gun up. At him.

Another movement, striking the figure hard. The electromagnetically propelled fifty caliber tungsten slug meant for Aaron's head instead drilled into the concrete on his left, boring an ugly crater half a foot deep into the fortification and pelting Aaron with chunks of stone. He fell backward, tilting away from the shot and dropping into a slide. His back had some objections, as the rough ground tore at the stiff backplate under his shirt.

It was probably already over, whoever hit that shooter. Broken neck or spine, a knife slipped through their ribs. Hell, an Oskie could move fast enough, Aaron wouldn't be surprised to see them rip a still-beating heart from a person's chest. The people who attacked an Oskie in hand-to-hand and lived to tell about it included other Oskies and...well, he had to include Solomon now, he supposed. Had managed to get the Oskie to throw himself onto a quick knife in a brilliant use of the bad guy's own speed against him.

Get up. They need you. They can't do this without you.

Aaron pressed himself up and shouldered his rifle, ready to re-engage should the bomber poke his head up again. He would have to lay down nearly the entire magazine just to keep the Oskie occupied. But if he could do that, swap in a fresh magazine, get a little help and a lot lucky...they could do this.

But nobody appeared. No more screaming, no more shouting, no grunts or bangs or noise of any kind.

Aaron crept forward. His arms burned. His neck dripped—probably blood from the bad slide. His back creaked. And his ears wouldn't stop ringing.

Go. If he didn't do this, the bomber would get away.

Aaron lifted one cinderblock foot and then the next, stepping up into the prefecture. He tracked to the right, down towards where the bomber was tackled.

Brass casings everywhere. Three Capitals dropped like they'd been kissed by the Reaper, laying themselves and their burdens down wherever they were at his passing.

He saw the boots first, two pairs. A woman was splayed out on the ground, a knife buried in her abdomen to the hilt. She had stopped breathing, most of her blood drained on to the pavers. She wore simple civilian clothes, a loose tunic and pants—a holster in the small of her back. Bright orange lines still glowed on her cheek where the augments cooked hot.

The Oskie saboteur—Dead? But who killed her?

The second set of boots, a man standing tall. His clothes were not his own, ill-fitting and hanging heavy, with sleeves covering most of his blood-drenched hands. His wide thin lips, too wide for his face, might have been crooked into a smile, but no pleasure was behind that face. A lock of raven hair dangled in front of his left eye, bobbing with his breath. And his hawkish eyes tracked Aaron, waiting for the moment of discovery.

That tell-tale yellow flash in the iris. *Another* Oskie?

Aaron didn't lower his gun. "You Imperial?"

"I suppose. If we're getting technical." He nudged the dead woman with his boot. "But she's your bomber."

His voice was like jazz, seductive and lyrical, almost playful. That wide smile cracked even wider, like it might split his face in two. Aaron couldn't shake the idea that he was some kind of fae, a trickster or illusionist.

"And what are you?" Aaron asked. "Doin' charity work?"

"Something like that. You got yourselves a little insurrection. Where's the sign-in sheet?"

CHAPTER
SIX
EDEN

WHILE EVERYONE else couldn't wait to shout—at each other, at the prisoner, at the ceiling—Eden just stared through the monitor. The amiable Oskie stood in his manacles and chains like he was in a bank queue, bouncing idly on the balls of his feet and chewing on his cheek. He had patiently allowed the Capitals to detain him, cuff him, and seal him away. At no point did he resist his new hosts.

The former warehouse had been converted into a brig—interrogation rooms, holding cells for the lawmen.

But as former inmates, the Capitals had some notes. They had installed a proper mess hall, gymnasium, even a library. An in-house therapist was there on a volunteer basis, both to provide care to inmates and to advise the guards on how to segregate the populations. The last thing they wanted was hardened monsters teaching each other, making a bad situation worse.

Aaron had called them all to talk about the newest addition to the roster. Many held the opinion that the Oskie should not be jailed at all, in point of fact.

"We should put a bullet in the back of his head." Solomon was positively vibrating. Eden was sure they could use the pit viper's shaking to generate power for a small town.

It wasn't bad advice, per se. Perhaps overzealous. Reactionary. But not *bad*.

Never far from Solomon's arm, Keira might have been far calmer than Solomon, but she was firmly in the camp of swift execution. "Then we cut him up and melt the scrap. Just to be sure."

"Salt the ground he walked on," Nora added, arms crossed. This was a done deal as far as she was concerned. She'd already moved on to other things in her head.

"He's an Imperial officer, an Orbital Strike commando." Talania was *not* issuing a defense. Rather, that was her prime indictment. "He's loaded down with cybernetic augmentations and a decade of training and conditioning. He's a threat to everybody here."

They had Aaron circled in the small antechamber, pressuring him to take the obvious road. Anyone sporting a Blue & White flag on their lapel was the enemy.

But Aaron was not so easily swayed. "So let's talk about his evil plan then."

"Let's make evil plans of our own," Solomon said, practically blood crazy.

"No—you say he's a bad guy. So let's assume he is. He links up with the dead lady, plots to bomb the Castle and the graduation. Right? Use that fire to cover an escape." Aaron paused, waiting for everyone to pick up on the obvious gaping flaw. "Why are they doing that *at all?*"

Eden narrowed her eyes, peering at the man in the monitor. Not handsome, but not repulsive either. Young enough, early to mid-twenties and with no recognizable features or marks, no cartoonishly obvious traits. He was like beige wallpaper became sentient—completely unremarkable.

By design. He could blend in, vanish in a crowd, equally welcome at a blue collar barbecue and a white collar soiree. This was no soldier.

Eden chewed on that observation, the same one that Aaron had thrown out and no one else had picked up.

"You don't need to show your work, Capital," Talania sighed. "Spit it out."

"He's not a soldier. He's a spy," Eden said, musing to herself. "Why do you spy on something you plan to atomize?"

Aaron pointed at Eden while tapping on his nose. "Tell her what she's won."

"He's not from the Imperials. He's got his own agenda."

Talania's eyes turned to the screen. "Two-man sabotage and disruption. Hits our morale, hits supply. And if he's caught, it's an acceptable loss."

"Okay—a two-man team inserts. And when caught, he just offs his partner and gives himself up?" Nora pieced together that scenario with an incredulous shake of her head. "It really *doesn't* make sense."

"You didn't see it." Aaron turned to Talania. "I don't think they were together. See, his 'partner?' She set the bomb. And she was going to blast my head into mashed potato. He stopped her. Why protect me? I'm *the* high value target. That could've been an exceptional assassination mission—even if they didn't get out alive!" Aaron pointed at the screen. "So maybe they came together. Maybe he was here all along. Maybe...something else. And you're not at all curious?"

The room was quiet for a moment, until Solomon raised one bony hand. "I'm curious how squishy he is."

Keira reached up and pushed his hand back down to his waist, swallowing hard. "...You're right, it doesn't square up."

"It doesn't need to," Talania objected. "He's an Imperial officer. The risk outweighs everything else. Full stop."

"He gives an answer I don't like," Aaron assured her, "you can be first in line."

"Second in line," was Nora's rebuttal to that.

Aaron pointed at Eden and Talania, gesturing for the rest to stay behind. Aaron and Talania led the way with purpose and gumption. One was out to save a life and the other one eager to pass sentence.

She never understood how Talania was always so ready to act, so ready to just leap without regard for what was below her. But she also remembered the Governor in that isolation cell, when Eden first met her—matted hair and shivering shoulders, ragged breathing. She had been sniffing back a cold, or some other respiratory infection. Her knees and elbows scuffed to a red shine, and then left to dull into scaly scabs. She had been kicked, dragged, and abandoned, left alive only because it wasn't prudent to kill her.

And she had crumbled.

It was Aaron that brought her back around, breathed a bit of fire back into her. Now, she had caught that flame and done wonders with it. But Eden found herself shaking her head at Talania's retreating back. She was so ready to dole out penalties, even when she had reaped the benefits of unsolicited kindness.

The woman was almost elven, tall and lithe and just so harsh. Eden herself stood somewhere at Talania's bicep, having to crane her neck up whenever Talania decided to stop slouching. Sometimes she wondered if they were even the same species.

The 'shortstack,' Aaron, barely came up to Talania's shoulder, but stood with all the same power she did. He was walking with a bounce in his step, rolling from heel to toe so hard his boots snapped against the ground.

"Ease up," Eden said, pawing at his arm to slow down. "He's not going anywhere."

Aaron nodded quickly, but didn't say anything. He had been so sulky, so quiet before. It was almost heart-warming to see him kicking again.

Aaron slung the hefty door open—it was only then that Eden realized it was a meat locker, just no longer powered. A musty and rotten smell hit her nostrils, blended with a burning bleach. They had done their best to clean it out, but after a while that smell just gets into the walls. A single light set into the ceiling projected down on to him, like it too was pushing onto his shoulders. The other lights were kept off, leaving shadowy corners to lurk in.

Was this where Riley had brought Aaron? Or did Keira and Solomon design this creepy little nook?

The prisoner stirred a bit, stiffening up and looking their way. Eden was alarmed how intoxicating his stare was—not from an attraction or a charisma, but more of a depth, like the colors in his eyes seemed to spiral and the pupils were bottomless pits. Alluring but disconcerting, like her feet were poised on the edge of a cliff and the little voice said to jump.

The uncanny valley, something just slightly off about his face. Maybe it was because of the surgical scars, neatly hidden, tucked under the jaw and behind his ears. She could make out the incision along his hairline, thin and fine like a tattoo needle.

A graduate of Holkstad Academy, a real horror-show draped in patriotism. Only a third of the applicants graduate; another third don't survive. These gossamer threads were the fingerprints of master surgeons, whose steady hands had been tested on thousands of teenage boys.

It took a certain kind of broken to cut on children day in and day out. It took a whole other level of broken to be fully aware of that statistic, and lay yourself on to the gurney anyway. They were all, doctor and patient, warped zealots.

The prisoner looked her up and down, more of a predator sizing up a threat than assessing prey. Or maybe, he was committing her image to an Imperial memory bank of known dissidents.

"I don't suppose you're going to thank me and spoon feed a hot meal?" the prisoner quipped, his eyes sliding about the room, drinking in each of his guests.

Talania dragged a chair across the floor, setting it just to the edge of the light. She settled into it, crossing her legs. "Name, rank, mission."

"Graccus Ontarim," he said, "formerly Captain, Orbital Strike Command. Emphasis on the former."

"Oskies don't just up and quit."

"Yeah, well, most citizens don't just up and kill one of us either," he said with a pointed look in Aaron's direction. "You've done it twice in your life now. First time, you were just a kid in a market stall dealing with a drunk bully. Then Riley? You guys are something special."

"Way I saw it," Aaron said, "most recent dead Oskie was *your* handiwork."

"You're welcome, by the way."

"You make a habit out of killing your kin?"

Graccus shrugged. "In my experience, a person can be quite surprising if they've got enough reason."

"So I take it you won't be sharing yours?"

Another shrug. "Give me some time and I might."

"Your mission," Talania pressed him. "Talk."

Graccus shifted in his bindings. "Don't have one."

"Very good." Talania stood up, projecting her voice. "Ventilate him, dump him in the Hammer Fields. I think the Jergad will appreciate some fresh meat."

Talania was halfway to the door. Aaron was lingering, but being drawn away by her raw gravitational force. If she was bluffing, they had to commit to the bit for it to work. But Eden knew that she was absolutely serious.

So did Graccus. "What's the plan, right now?"

Talania stopped in the doorway. "Yeah...*you're* the prisoner. This is a one-way exchange."

"That's a terrible way to start a friendship," Graccus said, extending one hand to her as far as his clanking bonds would allow. "I've got the Imperial playbook and you're going to frog march me to a firing squad? How are *you* the one in charge?"

"You're speaking to the Governor of Vanguard," Talania

snapped. "And the only person in this room who gets to decide what happens to you. I'd watch your tone."

Graccus threw a glance at Aaron, eyes hungry. "Admiral Tiberiet has two full and fresh battalions of infantry, a complement of Orbital with Warcom, and about two dozen armored assault vehicles, supported by heavy armor and artillery. That's not even counting an Eisenclad dreadnought, two frigates, unmanned Combat Air Patrol, and a squadron of Bearcats. He could win this fight five times over without even breaking a sweat." Graccus smiled. "You've got *me*."

"One Oskie?" Aaron asked, incredulous.

"And a turncoat, at that." Talania pointed out.

"Well, that was the plan anyway," Graccus confessed. "Going about as well as I thought it would, but not as well as I'd hoped, if I'm being honest."

Talania took a breath, trying to hide the shiver in her shoulders. "And what benefit could one man possibly be—"

"Ask Aaron," Graccus said with a smirk. "He's just one person. Did quite a bit."

Aaron tensed up, but Talania didn't let him cut in. "I've got enough testosterone around me, thank you very much."

"They'll take your skies first," Graccus said, darkness instantly in his eyes. "Seed it with hydro-munitions. They call it 'the Blindfold.' The sudden and spontaneous cloud cover will mask their descent from thermal and LADAR. From there, they'll drop Oskies through the artificial storm to hit your critical subsystems: take power, communications, munitions dumps; anything you actually *like*, really. They're picking their targets right now. After that...that's when the troop landings will start. Anyone stupid enough to be outside for that will be blasted into a fine fleshy caramel."

The blood drained from everyone in the room.

Graccus was not impressed. "Consider that your first tip of many."

"You know how to fight back?" Aaron asked, his voice cracking. Not the strongest position being put forward there.

"They spend an entire semester at Holkstad learning how to put down little uprisings like yours. Yeah, I know how to fight back."

"And why help little ol' Dusters like us?" Talania just went right for the heart of the matter.

"Because." Was his only answer.

Eden couldn't shake how casual he was being. She had no idea how augmented Orbital commandoes were—or even if there was a standardized method. Maybe they were each unique little snowflakes, upgrades hand-selected for their combat role.

But she was fairly certain he could break those bonds and kill two out of the three before they could so much as scream for help—if he wanted to. They might as well have stuck him in a dog crate, for all the good it would do them. And yet, he was tolerating their comical restraints on him.

Or Graccus was genuinely at their mercy and that cavalier attitude was just his personal quirk.

He glanced her way, giving her a nod. "You believe me." It wasn't a question.

"How do you figure?"

"Your heart rate fluttered," Graccus said, "body temp spiked half a degree. Your diaphragm contracted. And those just now? Those were your first words to me. The Governor came here to tell me something. You came in to listen."

"*Gulaw paz ki lomar...*" she cursed under her breath. He took her vitals by eyesight. His ability far outstretched anyone in the room.

If Graccus wanted to kill them, they'd already be dead.

Aaron stepped up to her shoulder. "What *do* you think?" he whispered.

"Why do you want to know what *I* think?"

"Because I don't really know what to think, and I trust you!" he hissed back.

Eden studied Graccus. She didn't doubt that he could show her whatever he wanted to, down to the pores in his skin. A man like this had complete, almost psychopathic, control of his body. He wouldn't have ticks or tells or twitches. And yet...

"Do you have any injuries?" Eden asked.

Aaron's face scrunched up, looking from her to Graccus and back again.

Graccus smiled. "Be more specific?"

"Self-inflicted injuries?"

The smile widened, a toothy grin. "Intercostal space, third floating rib, my left."

"What are you talking about?" Talania was demanding, not asking.

Eden stepped forward and lifted Graccus's shirt. More thread-thin scars in broad sweeping lines over his immaculately sculpted stomach. But, indeed, exactly where he'd indicated: he had shaved his body hair away and a half-inch incision was still healing.

"You did this yourself?" Eden asked.

Graccus pursed his lips and nodded. "It's at a funky angle for me, but..."

"Your needle was too big."

"Eh, well, I used what I had."

"Tell me you heated it, at least."

"I had a hot engine coil."

"Your implants, if you don't mind me asking." Eden was on a roll now. "How do you trigger them? Is it some kind of biohacking? Or conditional programming?"

Graccus shrugged. "How do your legs work? You got a joystick for 'em?"

Fair enough. He was hardly the surgeon, or the designer.

Talania windmilled her hands in the air. "I'm sorry, I have a question still waiting on an answer. What did he do now?"

Eden stepped aside to Talania, pulling Aaron with her. "Oskies aren't just specialized combat and intelligence operatives."

"They're expensive." Aaron connected the dots. "They had a tracker on him?"

"He removed it," Eden said. "And he knew exactly where to go get it. So he's either *deep* undercover trying to get in our ranks..."

"Which doesn't make any sense," Aaron said. "It's not like they need a subtle approach."

Talania rubbed her forehead, trying to massage the mounting headache away. "Or he's telling the truth."

The triumvirate locked eyes, taking a silent vote. Talania didn't like this one bit. If she'd had her way, they'd have killed him already. Eden wasn't a hundred percent certain that was something they could pull off.

"What would you do?" Eden asked, turning back to Graccus. "If we let you out?"

Talania set her death stare upon him. "He's going to shoot us all and take a few pictures for the news feeds. That's what!"

"What would you do?" Eden repeated.

Graccus considered the question before answering, "Your troops responded to a bombing by screaming and running. They're armed, sure. They're brave even. But they're not soldiers. You're not fighting animals anymore. You're fighting a not insubstantial portion of the greatest military force mankind has ever assembled. More than weapons, more than troops, more than anything else on this little dustball...you need intelligence. You need an inside man, somebody with the entire playbook willing to play ball." If he could've given himself two thumbs up, he would've. "Lady...*you're* the one that needs the spy."

Aaron's eyes narrowed, and he shook his head. "What is the Oskie creed?"

Graccus looked like he suppressed a hiccup, like his brain skipped a beat. "What difference does it make?"

"It's something you say at the beginning of every day, every night when you go to sleep. It's a religious chant, a mantra that binds Navy to the Empire, and the Empire to you. You've done that song and dance since you were six years old. And we're supposed to believe you just got up one morning...and saw the light?"

"You'd know all about social programming," Graccus countered. "They had you good and subservient for years, *Capital*."

"You're nothing like me."

Aaron was the last one out of the room, turning off the lights and locking the door behind them. But Eden couldn't shake the thought— if Graccus wanted to be out, he'd get out.

He was just very patient.

CHAPTER
SEVEN
KEEPER

GOOD GOD ALMIGHTY, the *Howler* was ugly as sin. Aisling had told him all about it—but what he saw was a root vegetable with struts and a paint job. It looked like some elementary school art project that a team of highly trained engineers had to turn into a workable aircraft.

This wasn't a troop transport; it was a crime against his eyes.

The air field was positively humming. Security was tight and Keeper had his badge scanned at four different checkpoints between zipping into his pressure suit and the tarmac.

But he was never late, not for air time. No sir.

He beat both Prophet and Aisling to the landing pads. And he had been left to stare at the DH-55, a lump of coal that had wished for a pair of wings and a military contract.

Keeper pointed at the mutant black turtle on the cradle. "*That's* our super ship?"

"That's the one," Prophet said, the proud father walking up to his baby. "Little over a thousand meters per second in the Basin. With a five-hundred-kilometer mission radius and a 10,000 kilogram usable load."

Keeper pointed at the ship, like a schoolyard brat who just saw someone eat a bug. "It's a baked potato."

"It's your new ride," Prophet corrected.

"It's my new ride. And it's a potato!"

"Lieutenant Eskell." That was a new voice.

Keeper swung himself about and into attention, chewing on his lip and dreading what he was going to see.

On the launchpad above them, three people. At the front, a woman who looked like she could break his back across her knee. And oddly, he kinda wanted her to do it. A short woman, lean, with raggedy blonde hair she'd buzzed short under one side. A nasty scar could be seen peeking out from the hairline. A small, crooked nose and a hard stare was all he got from her.

It made him tingle in his fingers and toes.

Flanking her to the left was Sergeant Bray, the veins in his neck and forehead popping with the fire he was holding back.

But what stopped Keeper's heart was the third, standing to Blondie's right.

Aaron Havenes. *The* Aaron Havenes. Hero of Rimpau, the Legatus himself, Slayer and Tamer, the Dead Man Walking. *The* Capital.

Aaron drew a heavy sigh, two fingers hiding his eyes. Face palming? Embarrassed? Was he tired? Oh no, did Keeper call *him* a potato?!

"Son, pick your jaw up from the floor before I break it off!" Bray barked.

Keeper stiffened in his stance. Prophet and Aisling fell in beside him. Aisling shared the same nervous electricity as he did, like she might touch off a spark on anything metal nearby.

Blondie must've been a Capital too, one of Aaron's troops. She stared down at the pilots from behind mirrored goggles. "You like breathing air, do ya, Lieutenant Eskell?"

"Yes ma'am." He didn't know if she held a rank or was anybody of note, but right now, he was not going to screw with command structure.

Blondie looked back at the Howler. "My ride not sexy enough for you, jockey?" Before Keeper could answer, Blondie was spouting off again. "Good! She's not supposed to be sexy. She's supposed to keep a couple dozen grunts in your bay from being drained of their vital fluids. She's grumpy, she's heavy, and she's got a door gun suckin' enough juice, it'll make your instruments flicker."

Blondie squatted down on the edge of the pad, looming over Keeper in particular. "And you, ol' blue eyes, are going to teach her how to dance. In a little less than one week, the Imperial Navy is going to be knockin'. Repeaters from Wall Prefectures will provide air cover, Infantry will defend the ground. You...will be how those happy little grunts move from target to target." She pointed back at Bray. "You listen to this man, you listen to your flight lead. And after all that, you listen to your gut. And *maybe*...I let you fly in my skies."

Her skies, huh? Who the hell does she think she is?

Blondie must've noticed his criminally bad poker face, because she smirked wide. Whatever critique she had to follow up with, she kept to herself though.

She marched over to Aaron, and squared up with him. "Ready to watch these guys drive around in circles?"

He said one chilling word, almost playful. "Behave."

His voice wasn't trumpets from the hills or a silky violin or high like a flute. It had a mild gravel to it, a lilt in the middle, and he slurred the last syllable. He might as well have been any other Duster or some kid from a Lower Wards on Sol. He was just...there.

Keeper expected something a bit more impressive.

Blondie, Capital, casual with a legend. That must be Nora Silva, a bit of a minor hero in her own right. She had a proclivity for collecting injuries and doling them out tenfold. Anywhere Aaron had been, she'd been too.

And Nora didn't seem to have the same holy reservations for

Aaron. She just rolled her entire head, sighing dramatically, like Legatus was her annoying brother she was being forced to sit next to. "Jus' saying. We're watching seasoned combat jockeys drive around with training wheels."

Bray hushed her. "Right now, we're doing deck drills."

She gave a sweeping mocking salute to the Sergeant's back. "Well, you don't need me for that. Buh-bye!"

She turned to leave, cool kid with places to be. And the Gunny stepped in front of her, palm to her chest. He had no words, just a blockade made up of stocky shoulders and a stained uniform.

She looked him up and down. "If I can hit you in the crotch, will you let me leave?"

"If you can hit me in the crotch, Goldilocks, you can do whatever you like." That wasn't a challenge; it was a statement of fact.

Nora looked back at Aaron, waiting for his tacit approval. But it didn't come. Aaron was staring at the floor about ten yards in front of him, just waiting for this all to be over.

———

It was like being back in Flight School. They spent the morning familiarizing themselves with controls and power management. The potato was surprisingly ergonomic. The controls felt nice in the hands, comfy seats, and no switches were going to cause him neck strain reaching for.

The Bearcat's shield generator was tucked up and left of the throttle, requiring him to roll his wrist in a really unpleasant manner. Now his left wrist popped all the time. But everything in the Howler was exactly where it should be. He'd never have thought the Bearcat was the newer of the two ships.

That afternoon they took to the skies for the first time.

Aaron was watching from Air Control, shuffling his feet and crossing his arms, his eyes sliding around to focus on anything but. It wasn't disapproval so much as disconnection—he wanted to be anywhere else right now.

He supposed, being charitable, Aaron's experience was in mining equipment and infantry combat, in that order. Combat aerial maneuvers might've held a passing interest, but not an entire day's worth. And these touch-and-go drills were hardly theatrical.

"Coming over target site Alpha Sierra," Prophet said over the radio. "Dropping cables in three."

Three, two, one.

Keeper flicked the switch. He could hear the floor drop out behind him, and a dragon's roar of wind filled the air. The Howler slowed as he pulled back on the throttle, just enough to lazily drag the cables along the dirt. Anybody below could grab ahold and clamp their harnesses in.

Keeper counted in his head, as both Prophet and Bray counted out loud on the radio. Five seconds. That's what infantry was being drilled on. They'd have five seconds to hook in.

Before Keeper pulled up and the Howler swung away into the sky.

"Keeper, watch your roll," Prophet scolded. "You just swung your cables across my path."

"And killed the six guys attached," Bray added.

Nora had something to say there. "But he didn't hit anything." Thank you! Somebody thought he was doing fine.

"No, he just brought a half dozen people locked, loaded, and injured around like a bullwhip," Bray offered. "Run it again. This time, pretend you like the people back there."

That just wasn't true. They didn't need G-suits to survive a turn like that. Sure, they might lose their lunch, but Keeper was trying to extract them alive, not comfortable. Capital Infantry was going to prefer his speed wagon over the first-class care and comfort of Prophet's leisure cruise.

But Keeper could feel his stomach turning over. He had done

zero-G inverted dives into dense stormy atmo; he'd pulled hard turns that should have turned his ankles into jelly; he'd ejected from his fighter in the middle of a pitched dogfight. But he had never felt more physically uncomfortable than right there.

Somewhere down below, Aaron Havenes watched and judged his movements. All the while, Aisling flew silently alongside him and Prophet graded him like he was still a child on his first Air Patrol. If he had forgotten his pants and his teeth fell out, this would have been a proper nightmare.

The flying potato shook under his butt and through the controls, eerily not making a single sound as it did, not even as metal parts meshed and scraped together. It was a cramped space in the pilot seat of the Howler, with switches and toggles on every surface. They tried to sit the pilots right about center of mass—it helped prevent blacking out, having the pilot be the one holding a whip, rather than on the end of it.

Okay, so maybe Gunny had a point about the people on the end of the cables.

A single hatch led back to the cabin and the bays. The damn hole was small enough only a child could comfortably fit through it. Keeper had considered taking his gear off to prevent damaging it. How Prophet and his suit fit through this without a grease bath was a mystery.

It could be flown without the suit, but Prophet had insisted. Safety first. Deadly G-force maneuvers don't schedule themselves.

The one and only smooth bulkhead in the cabin was drop-dead in front of the pilot's face, a projector painting the outside view with all of the relevant data he'd ever need pasted up there with it: altitude, air speed, even targeting data. The vast desert and the mountains beyond all painted up with every random factoid he'd ever want.

"Single line, children," Prophet ordered on the radio. "And watch your spacing."

That was aimed at him. He was drifting out of formation.

On the reset, they were to fly out over the Hammer Fields,

between the Wall and the Jergad-occupied Mountains. They'd perform a drag-brake left and then right, following it up with an Immelman turn and one barrel roll just for fun before returning to base for the touch-and-go. It was as much for the Howlers, as it was for the pilots. Get a sense of how the machine moves—and to make sure it still does.

The mountains loomed up before him. They'd seemed small from the Castle, but Keeper could make out at least three different climates in the altitudes. The foothills were lush with fresh grass and undisturbed by conflict; the midlands were bare rock, like angry steel. And finally, the peaks held a dusting of snow deposited by the meager clouds.

It was the only weather he'd observed in four days on the planet. The clouds came and went around the mountains, while the basin had nothing but sunlight. Never any rain. One day had been as windy as back home, but for the most part, Vanguard had proven to be a tame and boring experience.

Out here, however, that weather looked ominous, threatening. Up there was no kind soft rain. It looked as though something hid behind that curtain.

And he knew that something absolutely did.

"Break on my mark," Prophet said. "Three, two, one, mark."

The entire formation turned as one, a synchronized turn.

This was as much for the observers on the ground, testing these professional pilots and the rocket-powered boulder they were flying.

"Kilo One-Three lagged on the Immelman turn."

What? Keeper hadn't lagged. "I went when he said!"

"I believe you," Bray lied. "Note for the gear heads on One-Three: limber up those control surfaces."

"Control surfaces, copy."

Keeper strained to hear, hoping he'd pick up a thought, a word of Aaron's take on it. But Legatus hadn't so much as grunted. Maybe he could elicit a response.

The hard deck for the mission was set at four hundred meters—

anything below that was a simulated 'crash' for training purposes. The Howler ran off jet intakes, after all. Any debris or dirt kicked into them would be disastrous.

But how low could it go? He tilted the nose of the Howler down.

Aisling noticed. "One-Three, switch to secure channel."

Yes, darling? Keeper smirked to himself. "Go for channel 103.9."

Two toggles later. "Don't do it," Aisling warned.

"Do what?"

"Don't lie to me. We're workin' right now."

"I really don't know what you're talkin' about, Aisling."

"Get back in formation, Keeper," Aisling said, forceful.

Prophet cut in. "We're under the microscope today, Keeper. Whatever you're doing, I don't want to hear it. Form up. Now."

"Sorry, Prophet, I did not copy. Say again all after—" And Keeper closed the channel with a flick of the toggle.

Let's see what this potato had under the hood. He settled his hand on the throttle, cranking it forward.

It threw him into his chair and he felt the waves of foam ripple in his suit, compressing and absorbing the G-forces. His craft ripped away from the formation like he'd been shot from a cannon.

He expected the super sonic boom, the vapor cone of compressed gases to flash around his hull as he broke this planet's sound barrier. But it didn't happen, as the fat beast got faster and faster. The frame was absorbing the air burst, keeping him fast and quiet.

Neat.

"Keeper, return to formation. That's an order."

They wanted to test the machines, so let's test 'em.

He got lower and lower, watching as the ground became nothing but a whirling color palette of tan and brown. He could vaguely make out the ghost of a rock as it reached up from the ground before whipping past his shoulder.

The altimeter whined and a display pointed out that he was at a mere one hundred feet.

Go lower.

"Break off, Keeper. Now."

The Wall was coming up. He'd have to tilt up to avoid it. Or...

Keeper rolled the Howler onto its side and pulled up hard. He climbed and climbed, the ground whipping past his shoulder as the Wall raced up to meet him. It was getting closer very, very fast.

Was he going to clear it? So many warnings. Altitude, craft orientation, air speed, even hull temperature were all banging on.

"Hoo!" Keeper involuntarily grunted, feeling the intense G-force of the maneuver.

The Wall paused at his belly—and he heard the Howler scrape against the metal and concrete. But nothing more than an angry racket.

He'd made that turn and given the Wall a haircut while he was at it. Keeper let out some combined version of a laugh and a gasp and a cough. Before realizing he was speeding toward the broadside of a Thumper at Mach 1.4.

"Whoa!" Keeper tilted the Howler, tumbling it off the Wall and away from the obstacle. It danced at his touch like a ballerina.

This machine might have had a fat ass, but at least fifty percent of it was rocket-flavored testosterone. It was an ugly muscle car hand-built for performance. It was a dragon and he was its rider. This was a mythical fusion.

He loved this thing.

But the ground team was less amused. Bray had some specific things regarding Keeper's anatomy he wanted to discuss. So the pilots were all ordered to RTB ASAP.

———

Keeper was barely out of his craft when he saw that Nora and Bray were angrier at each other than him.

"He risked one of only *three* Howlers we have! I want his wings, his ass, and his head!" Bray's face was so red and sweaty, Keeper thought he was going to melt.

But Nora was giggling. "He showed you what those Howlers can do while you were having him fly in circles! He kicked this into gear."

Keeper never saw it coming, as Aisling punched him in the shoulder. "Let me ask you something, jockey. Do you do all your thinking with your little head?"

"I mean, he gets a vote," Keeper said. "That's only fair, right?"

"We've been here four days, and you almost get yourself killed mowing the lawn."

Keeper glanced at his Howler—scuffed underbelly, one landing strut snapped off, and sparks coming from something that shouldn't be sparking. Two technicians were already examining the damage, and pulling what little was left of their hair right out of their heads. The dirt was still settling around his intakes.

Prophet walked through his sight, dragging out a death glare, as he marched over to the ready room for a debrief and shower.

"He doesn't get a ship," Bray barked with finality for everyone to hear. "He doesn't get a particularly heavy *rock*. He gets to sit."

"You didn't want to give us rocks," Nora countered, hands on her hips and still recovering from a laughing fit, "and we did just fine."

Bray crossed his arms. "Oh! That went *just fine*, did it?"

The duo parted like grass before the wind. Aaron would have bowled them over if they hadn't, his hands gripped tight at his sides and eyes sharp. Keeper froze as Aaron stalked right up to him, stopping only a few feet below the landing pad. "You think you're untouchable?"

That voice, a gravelly saxophone, baritone but bereaved. He wasn't angry or disappointed, but rather touched with sadness. That was a genuine question.

Keeper didn't quite know what to do with that.

"Do you?" Aaron asked, a bit more forcefully.

"No...sir?"

"You think nothing bad happens, ever? Not to *you*? You're special?"

Aisling leaned forward, then backed away. She wanted to defend him, step up like she had dozens of times before. But something froze her to the spot, leaving Keeper out to twist.

Aaron sighed, the weight of something flashing across his eyes. "You're not immortal, kid. If you die...you take other people with you. Act like it."

CHAPTER
EIGHT
EDEN

"HE DID *WHAT?*" She'd never seen Talania turn that particular shade of red. She looked like a chili pepper fresh on the bush, a bright red pushing past the dull yellow hue of her natural tone. It made her face look like decorated porcelain.

The Governor's office had been once upon a time at the height of the Aurora tower, overlooking the colony sprawled out below. It had glass paneled windows wrapping two-thirds of the perimeter, with displays and shelving to support the many knickknacks and kitsch a politician accumulated during a career.

Talania—and her father before her—had selected a more modest approach. The Governor needed privacy, but not a fiefdom. Her office was on the main deck, with plastic walls and frosted glass. And Talania's exaggerated proportions meant her ponytail brushed the light fixtures hanging overhead, and she could just about touch each opposing wall with her hands outstretched.

A heavy desk of fake wood and pot metal had been screwed to the floor with lag bolts. The chairs were a little too small or a little too big, and always creaking. Eden couldn't put a finger on it but it made the whole thing seem...leased? Like Talania had a nice and booming operation here on Vanguard, but still had rent to pay.

Right now, Talania looked like she was going to set the building on fire.

Eden raised a cautionary hand. "They took care of it. Aaron gave the boy a dressing down. And you know how Bray likes to spout off."

"He's lucky Bray didn't rip his lungs out through his throat and put 'em on display," Talania muttered. "Nobody was hurt?"

Eden shook her head. "Some egos and the belly plate of the Howler, but those are going to see some abuse in their lifetime."

Talania flopped into her seat, draping one willowy leg over the arm of her chair. She traced a circle in the air with her toes as she rolled out the tension in her ankle. "So...Bray seeking approval for something he's already gone ahead and done?"

"They settled on latrine duty," Eden said. "And some PT for the whole wing to...inspire cohesion."

"I'm sold," Talania said with a wave of her hand. She really didn't want anything more to do with this or other military matters, but after Riley, it was decided that a civilian had to have a bigger hand in things—even if she rubber stamped anything Bray sent her way.

Talania took a pull from her thermos of coffee. Eden raised an eyebrow. "You want to be alone for a bit?"

"No." Talania was quick with that. "I really don't." She stared at the wall, counting the imperfections in the flecked paint.

Eden kept forgetting that Talania was only nineteen, and had already made Governor. She was far too young to be this tired.

"How many drinks do you have a week?"

"You my physician now?"

Eden shrugged. "For today."

"Not many."

"Got a numerical answer for me?"

Talania scowled at her. "I might die in a week and it isn't going to be the whiskey that kills me."

"True enough," Eden mused, "but it's not going to help you sleep the way you think it does."

That stopped Talania mid-swig. She swallowed hard, like the

drink had suddenly hardened into paste. She gingerly balanced the thermos on the edge of her desk, letting her fingers dance along the lid. "Did I ask you?"

"Even modest consumption can affect the quality of your sleep. You'll knock out faster, sure, but you'll still be tired the next morning. Like right now."

"I've been tired for a lot longer than I've known you."

"Do you have a hard time sleeping?"

"If you're sleeping well right now, you're not paying attention." Talania was quick with her rebuttals. She was so very quick.

"You're the Governor of the Colony," Eden stated. "Consider me a concerned citizen. Lay off the juice for a few days?"

Talania's eyes meandered across Eden. At first, she was scanning Eden for something she could use for a comeback, but then she just was looking. Eden waited for her to finish whatever thought she was constructing in her head.

But nothing else came. Talania checked the time on her display. "You're rolling into my three o'clock."

"Who's three o'clock?"

"Talania!" someone outside the glass shouted.

Talania just pointed at the door. "Stick around. I may need a witness." She cracked her neck and sat up straight, running her fingers along her lapel to straighten the folding edges.

The door flung open and the middle-aged suit that stomped inside had such blinders for Talania, he didn't even acknowledge Eden sitting right underneath his line of attack.

"Y'know, I knew nepotism was a force stronger than electromagnetism but this is a whole other level of incompetent!" Salt and pepper hair, sculpted jaw, and a familiar incendiary stare: Statesman Stefan Whitby. The spit that this silver-spooned elite was flinging dropped somewhere into Eden's oily hair. And still, he paid her no mind.

"I have a pretty full schedule today, Stefan," Talania said. "Skip the theater and get right to the emotional terrorism."

His eyes flared, keying up a picture of the Castle bombing on his bracer. The image flashed onto the wall of her office, the frosted glass catching and reflecting, filling the whole room with an amber glow. "Interesting choice of words. When were you going to brief the Statesmen about an act of *terrorism* inside our borders?"

"Oh, I figured it would leak its way back into the zeitgeist all by itself."

"One of your Capital zealots?" Whitby asked. "Or do you even have a suspect?"

"An Imperial officer," Eden offered up. Whitby jumped, twisting at the torso like he might turn and run, before cementing himself back into the ground. Eden pursed her lips to avoid smiling. "They're in custody."

"Where?" Whitby demanded. "I want to speak with them."

"That's going to be complicated," Talania said, "seeing as how responding security forces shot and killed them."

Eden caught Talania's eye. If she didn't mention the Oskie in lock up, Eden sure as Hell wasn't going to. She looked back up at Whitby. "We've got pretty good training."

Whitby spared Eden a single look, a mixture of disdain, pity, and outright hatred. Perhaps it was her mop of greasy hair, her slight stature, or the uniform she wore, but he didn't care for her one bit.

He directed his answer back to Talania, looking for a fight more worthy of his time. "Well, that's convenient for you, isn't it?"

"Seventeen people injured, and another eleven dead? 'Convenient' isn't exactly where I leapt to, no."

"What are we doing about this?" Whitby asked with crossed arms.

Talania's eyes narrowed. "Forgive me, I know I'm drunk and disorderly, but you're *not* on the Security Committee, are you?"

"Security of the Colony during an armed insurrection against the Empire is the concern of every Imperial citizen."

"What Committee are you on again?" Talania pressed. "It's Transportation, right? You're the *Chair*."

"I don't follow."

Eden did. "Our bomber wasn't catalogued. So either they landed on the outside of our borders and walked in…"

"An area of land controlled by vicious territorial monsters," Talania pointed out.

"Or…" Eden paused, letting the pressure build. "Someone landed at the Port without being logged in."

Whitby's eyes darted between the two women. "You can't be serious."

Talania shook her head. "Don't be absurd, Stefan. But I was hoping you'd use your considerable influence to investigate this breach of security. A soldier and a weapon of no small power were delivered through our checkpoints without being so much as questioned. I don't like ghosts. Do you?"

The implicit threat was there and message was received. Whether the fierce loyalist was responsible for the delivery of a brick of explosive and its owner, or whether he was simply in charge when it happened…he was going to be the person holding the proverbial bag.

"Man to Ma—Governor," he paused, inserting her title instead of what his reflex had been, "an appearance of standing up for principle is not a *bad* political tact—in theory. But when are we going to order the arrest?" He threw a look down to the Capital in the room.

Talania stood to her full height, her ponytail actually squishing against the roof of the office. "When I find out who the *spy* is in this colony, they'll be brought to whatever justice the Clerk of the Court determines will best serve the Colony. Of course." She smiled, big and wide like the spoiled brat she was.

That wasn't what he meant. He meant arresting Aaron, Eden, and the rest of the seditionists. Talania had twisted it back in his face. She had an alluring amount of confidence, some cocktail of delusion and arrogance that made Eden's heart skip.

Whitby's face hardened, muttering under his breath loud enough for both to hear. "Can't believe I made an *appointment* to have my loyalty questioned!"

"I didn't think it was in question. You've made it pretty clear where your loyalties are."

"I'm not without a heart, Ms. Dedria. I'm just not a lunatic."

"That so? Because I thought you were a sycophant," she said. Then quickly added, "Of course, I guess my boots don't taste as good as others on offer. Now, if you don't mind, the power-crazed and the criminal cabal have a colony to pilfer and plunder."

Whitby smiled, tapping a button on his wrist. "Can I offer a bit of advice, Ms. Dedria, as a seasoned political officer in the Statehouse?"

Talania smiled. "You're free to do as you wish, Mr. Whitby."

He tapped another button, and Eden's face paled as the recorded voice repeated the words. "...The power-crazed and the criminal cabal have a colony to pilfer and plunder."

Talania winced, biting her lower lip in regret. Whitby grinned wide, a hungry cat presented with fresh blood. "Sarcasm doesn't play in sound bite. I'll see you at the surprise press conference you're going to be having in about two hours."

He spun on his heels and practically skipped out of her office.

Eden's jaw dropped. "He can just secretly record us?!"

"No..." Talania groaned. "And I could have him arrested, which is what he wants me to do."

Eden coughed at that absurd idea. "Why would he want that?"

Her voice was cold, like iron dipped into an acid bath. "Because it's what I wanted Riley to do for six solid months. Right up until he did it." Talania considered the retreating Whitby and the smug bounce in his step. "I'm not who he wants me to be."

"Proud of that?"

"If a little annoyed by it."

Eden studied the Governor, as her eyes darted to-and-fro. She was replaying some old event, some scene playing out beat for beat in the back of her skull. It was tinged with pain, wistful sadness, the hindsight that only comes with experience and scars.

If she had only stood up to Riley sooner...

Eden looked after Whitby. "Want me to take care of it?"

Talania's eyes locked onto her, dark and serious. "Don't ever ask that question in this office, even as a joke."

There was a gravity to her voice. Not a strength, but a mass, something deeper and more potent. A wad of pain that had been spun and woven into willpower. Eden knew that look all too well.

It was Aaron's tone.

"So while we're in the fight for our lives," Eden asked, "he gets to just wander around making it harder?"

"Yes. Because a mountain doesn't give a damn about the wind." Talania took a pull from her thermos. Based on her wince, it was mostly whiskey.

Eden pursed her lips. "Doesn't a mountain get worn down by wind and water over time?"

"If you're going to shatter every metaphor I've got..."

CHAPTER
NINE
KEEPER

IT HADN'T STARTED as a bacchanal, but he had a certain influence on the course of events. First thing: people were nervous—easy enough, there was a war coming with a possible end to all of their lives. Second thing: people decided to alleviate stress; they played games, chattered and gossiped—and they wanted a drink.

And so the third thing happened: they came to the man who keeps. Keeper didn't have his callsign for no reason, after all.

It started with a bottle of fine whiskey—not so fine in the grand scheme, but fine enough for warzone shine. Then others threw into the pot: a case of home-brewed ale, some dregs of a gin bottle, an empty steel barrel, a lot of juice. This was all well and good...

Until someone produced a replicator. It had recipes for grain alcohol. And all Hell broke loose.

Everyone might die tomorrow—so they lived a little today.

The Castle sounded like a night club on Ilum. Music thrummed in the air, and the lights were turned down low.

Even the Governor had joined in. While people danced and drank and frolicked in the quad, she sat on an over-turned barrel. Her long legs were splayed out, almost circling around Eden, who had plopped cross-legged on the ground in front of her.

Talania ran a broad-toothed comb through Eden's hair. In between quiet, happy moans, the much smaller woman interjected with some half-formed rant. Her voice was kinetic, bouncing from sentence to sentence, and more than a little slurred. "I don't need to pick up after them! I don't! I did it in Detroit, I did it in the Pits—I think I've done that enough, right?"

"Yes, you have," Talania assured her, nice and patronizing. "You *should* relax more."

"I should!"

Keeper couldn't help but smile. He balanced the bottle off his forearm, refilling Eden's empty cup like a high-class waiter. Talania gave him a two-finger salute in thanks. Keeper returned the gesture with a mock curtsy of his own.

"How's latrine duty?" Eden sniped, making the reflexive association off Keeper's face.

The smell would be in his clothes for days. He sniffed at his shoulder, shrugged. "Worth it."

Eden grunted out some derisive sound, unintelligible to anyone but her. Talania shook her head, continuing to comb out the rat's nest Eden hosted on her head.

"For you, Governor?" Keeper offered the bottle.

But she tapped her thermos. "I keep my own, jockey."

"Smart woman."

"Damn right!" Eden called out.

Keeper leaned into Talania, whispering. "How drunk is she?"

"Shush. She needs this."

"H'okay."

Keeper resumed his party patrol, to see if anybody else needed a refill or a pep-up. Every party had that one mess, that person who needed the release and ended up releasing more than just their inhibitions.

He scanned the perimeter of the festivities. On-duty Regulars— the archons of discipline and unit cohesion—stood on the fringe, like riot guards just there to make sure the party-goers didn't set anything on fire. They looked like clay statues in the dark, illuminated by the occasional beam of light that managed to reach out to them.

They had corralled the fun, fenced it in. All fine by Keeper's standards. Let the fire burn itself out. It might even be good for the environment.

Two of them stood awfully close together, Capital drab gray uniforms tucked and belted tight around them. But their stances were softer, more relaxed. They occasionally snickered to one another. A tall burly woman and a slender snake of a man, pale as bone. She looked like a warrior; he looked like a man who slept in graveyards.

Ripe for the corrupting influence.

Keeper sauntered up to them, bottle in hand, offering it up. The big woman smirked but shook her head.

"It's Kevalky," Keeper said, sing-song while dangling it in the air, feeling the weight of the hazel ambrosia slosh around inside.

"Why's it green?" the slender snake asked.

"I'm glad you said something!" Keeper said, uncorking it. "It's because of the wood its aged in, a *kyrwood* on Londinium. Even though the tree has been felled, it's still alive and growing. Puts all kinds of..." Dramatic pause and tented fingers. "...*illuminating* qualities to the liquor."

"Interesting..." The snake reached.

But the big woman scolded, "Solomon."

Keeper nearly swallowed his tongue. "Solom...Solomon Lipkin?" His eyes slid over to her. "That makes you...Keira Ladd?"

She tilted her head in firm acknowledgement. "Look at that Solomon: he knows who you are."

Keeper could swear Solomon hissed like a happy viper. "We're famous?"

Solomon and Keira, the deadly duet, a duo of destruction. Both had served as Capitals against the Jergad. Keira Ladd had a kill count longer than Keeper's arm. His eyes slid back over to Solomon: the only other Capital alive with a recorded Oskie kill.

And he was certifiable *before* that, too.

Solomon flashed a toothy snarl. "Want an autograph?"

"Want a drink?" Keeper offered, dumb and fast.

"We're workin'," was all Keira said.

Something in Keeper was quite happy to leave them on duty. Their kind of party would likely involve less debauchery and more fight club. Or maybe equal parts.

"Well then, you two have a lovely evening," Keeper said, as he started to back away.

"Don't be a stranger," Keira called out to him all too cheerfully. The two leaned into each other, and Solomon laid his head on her shoulder, like a bear trainer and his grizzly. Her arm draped around him, squeezing him in tight.

She giggled and there was something romantic...even necro-mantic to it. It was like listening to two super villains find each other —and thus, retire. They were fine just where they were, outcasts on the outskirts.

But happy nonetheless.

Still, it was a nice gesture to go over and include them, even just for a second.

"Oy, blue eyes!" Aisling ran up to him. She planted a big wet kiss on his cheek. Her single red eye illuminated her round face, giving her an alluring demonic quality. "You ran off!"

"Just trying to be a good host." He gestured back at Solomon and Keira.

Aisling threw a look over his shoulder at the Capitals, and her eye went wide—night vision seeing *everything*. Her voice lilted with suggestive poetry. "Looks like they chose the edge of light for a reason."

Keeper blinked, processing the only conceivable reason. They liked an audience, but not a crowd. "Just public *enough*?"

He'd turned his back for all of ten seconds. What were they— nope. He did not want to know.

"H'okay, let's walk fast now."

"Why?" Aisling asked, lingering as he tugged on her shoulder.

"'Cause if we watch, they're going to make us play along."

Aisling laughed, as much amused as teasing him. He yanked her back to the safety of the gathering. "Never known you to be the blushing bride!" she jeered.

Keeper spun her into him, sliding one leg between hers. Her eyes fluttered, but she otherwise held her poker face. He cocked his head. "It ain't bashfulness, Aisling. I just know when I'm in crosshairs."

"You really don't."

"Yes, I do. And I break contact—unless they're in my crosses too."

"Oh, then you just outshoot 'em?"

"That's right."

She reached back, grabbing a fistful of his hair and pulling him hard into a kiss. He closed his eyes and fell into her embrace, her fingers running along the back of his skull. Before he knew it, she pulled away, sending him off-balance and staggering forward.

She raised an eyebrow, a thousand pleasurable ideas reflected in her metallic eye. "Top of the Wall?"

"Great view of the stars," he conspired.

"If I'm looking at the sky tonight, you screwed up."

"Interesting choice of words!"

He followed her like she had him on a leash. She strolled toward the Castle's main prefecture, her hips giving him a preview of her own active imagination.

"Hey now, this used to be a family establishment!" Keeper swung about, looking for the guffaws and sneering. Two Regulars— tall & thin and short & stocky—were just shy of pointing and laughing.

They were the Regulars from the Port, when he first arrived!

Tall & thin had more to add, leaning down to his friend. "Anatoly, you have to understand something about young men of his caliber. They are creatures of impulse—"

"Kipling, right?" Keeper shouted back, throwing his hands up. "Call me dumb, call me arrogant; but I'm the one following the redhead to a dark romance."

Anatoly cheered that, a drunken huzzah. Kipling doffed an invisible cap in a mocking salute.

"Have fun tonight, boys!" Keeper waved goodbye.

Anatoly threw a thick timber of an arm around Kipling's skeletal shoulder. "We *are* the fun! Ha-hah!"

Aisling laid a hand on Keeper's shoulder. "All good?"

"Oh, yeah. They're already drunk."

Keeper followed Aisling toward the base of the prefecture. The helical towers were set into the Wall every hundred meters or so—firing positions down into the Hammer Fields beyond. There'd be plenty of dark corners in the building itself, but he had his heart set on the Wall line—a battlement not unlike old Medieval castles. He could lay out a bedroll on the cold stone, hold her close, and stare up at the night and its glittering curtain.

At the base of the tower, a small electric lantern threw several shadows up onto the stonework, like a campfire at night silhouetting those that huddled near. Three figures sat close to the light, their arms flailing in the air, causing the shadows to trace elaborate sweeps behind them. It looked as though some ghoulish phantoms had taken haunt. Enough blood had been spilled here—why not?

But as they got closer, Keeper recognized the three shapes.

"Jergad claw," Bray said, pulling down his collar. "First tour. Drove it down and shattered my clavicle."

Prophet whistled. "How long were you down?"

"Two weeks, plus some physical," Bray said, tapping his head. "It missed the important bit."

"That's nothin'." Nora stood up, lifting her shirt almost too high, revealing a nasty scar on her ribcage. It looked more like a brand seared on her skin than a cut or slash.

"Where'd you get *that?*" Prophet asked.

"Broken bottle, Southside Mars," Nora teased. She mimed the action, driving a bottle in and twisting. "Like they were going ice fishin' in my side. These two ribs are Silksteel now."

"See?" Prophet said, taking a swig from a bottle. "She beat you—and it wasn't even a combat scar."

Keeper decided to add his voice. "Show us one of yours, Prophet!"

Prophet extended their usual greeting, a polite middle finger thrown blindly in his general direction. Nora and Bray laughed, waving to the passing duo.

"Don't break him, Aisling!" Bray shouted.

"No! Break him!" Nora countered. "You want a *real* battle scar..."

Aisling cocked her head, winking her glowing red eye so as to be maximally obvious. "You want to help?"

Wait—what? Keeper almost broke his neck turning to see if Aisling was serious. The crazed look in her eye said absolutely.

And Nora started to get up—before Bray pushed her back into her seat. "Can something in this world happen without you jumping in with both feet?"

"No," Nora said, lifting her shirt again. "How do you think I got this scar?"

Aisling pushed Keeper into the Prefecture door, maybe because he was lingering too much, to see how that might progress. She all but drove him up the switchback stairs—

But he spun about, pinning her against the wall of the stairwell. The cold stone sapped the warmth from his hand, and she craned her back to avoid it. He kissed along her neck, working his way up to her ear. She shivered under him, either from the cold stone or his touch, or both.

He loved the feel of her skin under his fingers, the way her hip fit into his. She was the perfect height and the two of them pressed into each other like it was meant to be. He pawed at her uniform, popping clasps to reveal her undershirt.

"What happened to stargazing?" she moaned, biting her lip.

"We can do that too."

"A-hem."

They both froze, turning to see Aaron Havenes standing at the top of the stairs.

For a long. Awkward. Moment.

"Keeper. Aisling." Legatus said, with a polite nod to each.

"Hi..." Aisling gulped. She was either having a dream come true or a nightmare, and he wasn't entirely certain which. Keeper threw her a quizzical look, trying to parse it out. Based on the panicked expression on her face, even she didn't know.

Aaron trudged down the stairs, averting his gaze and lips pulled tight. His feet sounded heavy, hitting each step with all the grace of a hammer on an anvil.

He paused at their level, coughing. "It's a beautiful night..."

Keeper chewed on those four words, before coming to the other half of Aaron's thought. "Take her outside?"

"Yes." Aaron nodded a little too quickly.

Aisling slipped out from under Keeper and darted up the stairs to the Wall battlements above. Keeper moved to follow, but stopped when he saw Aaron's eyes tracking him. He'd been scolded by authority figures before, nothing new, but there was a distance in Aaron's eyes. A kind of sadness.

Keeper couldn't keep quiet. "They're having a lot of fun in the Quad. You should join 'em."

Aaron nodded absentmindedly, but said nothing.

"Sir?"

"Don't...Don't call me 'sir,'" Aaron said, hardening up. He said it again, more forcefully. "Don't call me 'sir!'"

"...What should I call you?'

"Call me—I don't know. I don't—Do what you want." He sounded so hollow.

Keeper tilted his head. "You alright?"

Aaron rubbed his cheeks with both hands, massaging out the stress in his head. "Yeah. Yeah—I'm fine, really."

"Big day tomorrow?"

Aaron's breath hitched in his chest. His eyes sank to the floor, lost in memory. He was there for a long moment before forcing a smile. "Don't keep her waiting."

"Yes, sir." It was reflex, and Aaron winced at it again, but he didn't respond. Aaron patted him on the shoulder and marched down the stairs.

Something told Keeper he wasn't going to grab a pint with the others.

———

They laid out on the stone battlement, their clothes tucked under their heads as pillows. He could still feel the cold stone through their combined bedrolls. Warmth radiated off of her, wrapping him in comfort.

"What do you see?" Aisling propped herself up on her elbow, casting the hologram off of her bracer up for them both to inspect: a chart of constellations.

Some local artist had worked with a few astronomers to mark their night skies.

Keeper consulted the drawings before looking back up to the glittering stars above. "The Maestro there. And the Canids."

"Philippa behind the mountains. She'll be up by midnight."

"You're cheating. You see them in your implant."

She giggled. "Jus' because I can, doesn't I mean I am. Sometimes it's nice to just look at the stars."

These little people on this little world, they had built something out of nothing, and brought with them what they couldn't. And little traditions, patterns in the sky—it was something that they couldn't leave behind.

Made for a good analog navigation tool.

"What made you jump reservation?"

"You did," she said, quick to humor.

"I'm serious."

"Me too."

He nudged her. "Come on!"

Her lip curled in that seductive devil way it always did. "I have my plans."

"What?" he mocked. "Aisling the Farmer? You goin' to open a little shop somewhere? Sell knickknacks to kids?"

"Better to be dusting crops than dusting people."

Hard to argue that.

He pulled her close to him, and she lowered her head onto his shoulder. "What's your plan?" she asked.

"Don't got one," he lied, as he held her tight.

PART TWO
SIEGES

CHAPTER
TEN
DECKARD

THEY HAD DISCUSSED strategy in his office for the better part of that week: whether to bombard the outer reaches and fence in the cattle, or surgically excise hostile elements with controlled incursions. Even to simply blockade the system and wait for rebel supplies to wane. Wolcott had strongly urged the ring of fire approach, raining devastation and pausing only to listen for their whimpering pleas for mercy.

It was a sound enough plan, brutal and theatrical, demonstrative to any other would-be dissidents as much as punishing to the ones present. It had a lovely decimation flavor to it—line up all the men in the village and start counting. Squeeze the trigger on every tenth person.

Indiscriminately fair. The Minister would approve.

The Minister might as well have been vampiric for all the blood he lusted for. He held dearly this arcane belief that obedience was commanded. Terror campaigns were aptly named, but terror is not loyalty. Heads should bow out of supremacy, not fear.

Deckard preferred the all-powerful hand that dispassionately dispensed just and equitable violence only when forced by an irrational hatred. 'It's just such a shame they have to die,' he might say. The will of the Empire should not be wielded from tumultuous emotion, but be more akin to a natural disaster. Speak ill of the Gods and the ground simply dries up.

Tactically, Deckard could not lose, so why appear so gleeful in victory? No, better to appear resentful of the blade than amorous. Even other dissidents will shake their heads in mutual agreement. Such a shame—if they had only bent, they would not have broken.

The strategy was simple. Cover their advance, strike at tactically critical centers of supply and transport, and cripple any ability to counter-attack. Once the Rebels refused to surrender—which they would as a matter of course—that's when the fist would tighten.

The deck officers were in launch prep, a flurry of holographic keys hammering away on data entry. The Officer of the Deck—a young gentleman named Trevor Lindell. His regulation-defying beard was the stuff of shipboard legend. The man could grow a deployment scarf in about four days.

Lindell marked the work of his subordinates from his multi-field displays, flipping from each station like he was leafing through a magazine for the good bits.

He called out to the room one at a time: "Combat?"

"Check."

"Point Defense?"

"Check."

"CAT-C?"

"Check."

It was the overture to any deployment of weapons in theater. And Deckard never liked it. As coordinated and drilled and efficient as it was, it bore an unhappy signature. In order to play this song, something was terribly wrong.

Wolcott took quite differently to it. He was almost humming along to the song, resisting the urge to bounce on the balls of his feet. He'd been a runner at University, Deckard could tell. The young

Lieutenant had all the airs of a horse in the gates, chomping at the proverbial bit.

At this stage, the pieces had their orders and an Admiral's role was to observe and correct. But Wolcott wanted to be at a station with a toggle that ended lives.

There'd come a day when he'd regret that enthusiasm.

"Damage Control?"

"Check."

"Orbital Control?"

"Check."

"Reactor Control?"

"Check."

Wolcott almost skipped forward at the completion of the checklist, taking two confident strides towards the view screen. Not that there was anything for him to do but block the projector, creating a Wolcott-shaped silhouette, like a cartoon punch out of a wall. Regardless, all the deck officers turned to him, the movement drawing eyes from every corner. "Let's get these Dusters back into line, shall we? Saubert? Clearance granted. Drop the curtain."

The Gunnery officer nodded and palmed his glowing display.

An Eisenclad dreadnought was a fleet unto itself, but 230,000 tons of steel didn't move easily. They were quiet beasts by definition. If an Eisenclad was making noise, then there was a dragon slayer about. That first barrage from the ventral cannons had enough kinetic muzzle energy to snap a lesser ship in two.

Deckard's mighty mount barely shuddered.

But this was no conventional ordinance. The cartridges were altitude-calibrated to detonate and spread ice in the upper atmosphere. This shot of temperature and water would cause sudden collection of clouds. Soon, friction would take over and the atmosphere would ionize—

Deckard hadn't just created cloud cover directly over Vanguard's city center; he'd made a storm front. And this planet hadn't known weather like this for a thousand years.

He watched through the view screen, as the rounds started popping in the upper atmosphere. The clouds swirled at first, a mist of gossamer threads weaving into a gray tapestry. Layer upon layer of clouds gathered, omens of what was to come. They rose up, an anvil head, a pillar to support the heavens themselves.

It was with no small amount of irony, Deckard thought, that some of the Colonists below had never seen a thunderhead before. They might be so naive as to think they had done something immoral, that their God had decided to purge their stain from his world.

The Loyalists must have been so disappointed. Perhaps their Faith had been too thin. Perhaps they deserved this.

Psychological warfare was so much more effective than blood. A man will take up arms because he believes himself in the right. Now, you can take his life for that insolence. Or you can take his will to fight.

Deckard took a steeling breath as the ship groaned underneath him. His eyes drifted over to the Sergeant-at-Arms, a woman built out of cinderblocks, her eyes locked forward on the view screen, watching the show.

"Mayfield, isn't it?"

"Sir?" she asked, almost concerned. Did he need something?

"Would you do me a favor, Mayfield?" Deckard asked. "Say a prayer with me?"

The woman considered for a moment, before fishing in her tunic, pulling out a pendant with a white orchid on it. And she began to murmur.

He joined her chant. "Bless our burdens, for they weigh on our shoulders. Bless our feet, for our Road is long. Bless our hands, for our work is hard. And Bless our souls, for the day is dark."

"Orbital Control, you have a green light," Wolcott said. "Happy hunting."

Deckard sighed, the words light and lyrical on the young lieutenant's lips. His eyes fell to the floor underneath them and the planet below. "For the day is dark..." he whispered.

Radio chatter: "Copy, *Tartarus* Control. Commencing drop."

"Icarus is deployed. You are manual control."

"Copy, manual control. Boosters on, cluster up."

The Icarus drop pods—despite having the most ironic name of the Ministry's Greco-Roman obsession—were a personal favorite of Deckard's. Gigantic steel eggs, little more than heat-shields with control surfaces, helped the occupant to 'glide' into target with precision down to a square meter. A single Oskie with Warcom could be dropped behind enemy lines to cause all manner of havoc. They could destroy infrastructure, break fortifications, or even sow terror in a civilian resistance.

Deckard would never cram himself into a coffin designed to slam into the ground at terminal velocity and he had no idea how these sixteen-year-old death knights did it. But they did so with aplomb, like it was just a trip down the water slide.

An officer's holographic display lit up a crimson red, to catch the eye of his superiors. It was the Officer of the Deck, Lindell.

"What is it, Lindell?" Deckard called out.

"Anti-aircraft Repeaters are coming online and tracking on the Icarus pods," Lindell reported with a suitably booming voice. "They'll be in their engagement range in...five minutes."

Wolcott grimaced, feeling Deckard's amusement fill the room. "Don't worry, Lieutenant. I'll collect your debt at a more appropriate time."

The Jump Deck chuckled, sharing in the levity. Wolcott worked his jaw, miming outrage, but he wasn't really all that upset, the humor of the moment soon making him shake his head and smile.

They'd seen the Repeaters from orbit, but turning them skyward was something Wolcott had scoffed at. 'Colonials are not tactically creative,' had been his defense. He'd bet his week's salary on it.

Deckard just took the poor lad's lunch money. He'd have to thank the colonists for being so supportive.

GA-102 Repeaters, about four dozen of them. Hundred-and-twenty-millimeter mag-pulse retrofitted to serve as cans of bug spray.

They had been effective at breaking Jergad charges on the Colony Wall.

Now *this* was what they were actually made for: ship-to-ship combat. And they'd serve as adequate enough flak. They'd have to be silenced before proper landings could be conducted. They might even snag a pod or two.

But really, it was just another sign of defiance. They had prepared for this.

Deckard threw a look up to the embarrassed Wolcott. "Proper battlefield Intelligence means you're never surprised by anything."

"'A good soldier wins first, and then goes to war,'" Wolcott quoted, with a nod. "Your source is loyal."

"Loyal is a very loose term," Deckard admitted. "Lindell, take us to Respond Protocol."

The Warrant Officer keyed his radio. "Icarus teams, ROE adjustment. Do not fire unless fired upon. We have friendlies in your theater."

"Copy all, *Tartarus* Combat. We are Respond Protocol."

The spy had performed admirably. It'd be a shame to lose them in crossfire.

More radio chatter: "Icarus 3-5, taking ground fire. Adjusting trajectory."

"Break formation and proceed to targets."

"Copy 4-1. Break on my mark. Three, two..."

"This could've been so quiet," Wolcott said with a sigh. "Shall we give those Repeaters a little firmware update?"

Lindell smirked, rolling out his wrists. "Yes sir. Uploading now."

Of course the Dusters hadn't taken the Repeaters off of Imperial Extranet. To them, a shovel was a shovel, even if it had sixty-two million microprocessors inside it. Resistance cells were rarely that surprising.

Pirates, insurgents, dissidents—they all had the same patterns, in the end. Their world was so simple and their tools obedient. They never thought that when they decided to revolt, those same tools would not share the same politics.

There were three large spires in the center of Vanguard, glittering glass obelisks to Colonial ingenuity. Deckard would take those from them first.

CHAPTER
ELEVEN
AARON

AARON WATCHED as the storm had swallowed the tips of the skyscrapers, three glassy fingers dipping into a murky pond over their heads. Most everyone in the Colony knew the supersonic boom of atmospheric reentries happening overhead, but now they couldn't see. It blanketed the colony center in a violet artificial night.

Aaron had given the order two days before, as a safety measure. Any citizen not taking up arms were to retreat to their emergency bunkers. They were designed to protect the citizens from a Jergad incursion, more well-hidden than they were protective shelters. But then, there wasn't a structure built that could withstand a kinetic dropped from low orbit.

Physics would always kill more people than any monster.

The Castle fortifications were at the edge of the cloud line, and there were more than a few places where one could stand in sunlight and in the shade at the same time.

Aaron had liked how sunny it was here. Now...

It was a simple defense—Repeaters shoot down enemy aircraft and Infantry mops up whatever makes it to the ground. Howlers were on station to move pieces wherever they needed to be.

Tiny burning darts sliced through the cloud cover. The falling stars were clumped together, tandem groups of four or five.

"Weapons free!" Bray spoke into his radio. "Don't let 'em get to ground!"

The Repeaters on the Wall took aim, crews inputting tracking data and monitoring firing solutions. Heavy gears bit into each other, whining as they cranked the giant cannons into position. No amount of love or care were going to make these beasts agile. They were a full fifty feet overhead but he knew they might as well have been right next to him for how loud they were about to be.

Aaron mashed a crusty gelatin over his ears. The sealant provided a solid enough protection against the concussion wave about to wash over the entire quad. But he couldn't tear his eyes off of the tracers left behind as the pods streaked to ground.

"What are they, Gunny?!" Aaron shouted to be heard.

"Why do you think they're called 'Orbital Strike Command?'?" Bray responded calmly, his voice muffled by Aaron's ear protection. "For the jackets?"

Each one had an Oskie? Each with a specific mission and top-flight gear to complete it? My God...there had to be two dozen of them.

Aaron peered at the Sergeant. "Shouldn't you get your ears on?"

"Son, I have had tinnitus since my—"

The Repeater smothered whatever else he had to say, issuing a declarative spit of fire and a concussive blast that he felt in his boots. It was joined by its neighbors down the line, the entire circle of Wall-mounted Repeaters, over forty miles wide, shooting up towards the spiraling pods. They shot a fresh flame every second, thumping the ground like a battle drum.

The falling pods suddenly broke for their formation, like petals off a flower cast to the wind. Not soon enough, as a few caught fire in the sky. Lightning speed, cold calculation, and years of war college couldn't help anybody once they'd been thrown out a window at altitude. This was the one and only time they'd be vulnerable.

First one, then another. They'd laid down a harsh grid of interlocking fire. It would be tough for the Oskies to slip that net.

His radio lit up. "Pod dropping in the Market."

Aaron grabbed it. "Kilo One-One, this is Red Haven. We've got positive contact. Market Square."

"Roger, Red Haven," the voice confirmed. "Moving to deploy."

Somewhere in that city below the firing line, the three Howlers were hovering. The infantry in their gullets were led by Keira and Solomon. They knew what to do with Oskies.

Son of a Bitch, this might actually work.

But then the Repeater over their heads stopped firing. Bray noticed the hiccup in rhythm and turned to scold. "Quit touching yourselves and—"

He stopped, causing Aaron to turn and see what had caused a combat-seasoned Army Regular to freeze up. The Repeater was lowering its barrel down, down, down...

To the City.

"SHUT IT DOWN!" Bray screamed.

Too late.

The Repeater went off, and a cough of compressed gas erupted from the barrel, rippled through the air. A canister of liquid copper the size of a person streaked through the sky. Aaron was able to watch its burning tail, as it lanced toward the City—and pierced two of the glass spires.

He didn't hear the explosion at first, but he saw the plume of fire, the light glittering as thousands of shards of glass caught the light and reflected it around the entire basin.

Dozens of other shots, from across the line slammed into the center building, an artillery barrage on a civilian structure.

Aaron hoped everyone was in their bunkers—but quietly he knew that wasn't the case. Some loyalists had defied the order and went about their day, absolutely convinced that either the Capitals were lying or were overreacting. They were Loyal Imperial citizens, entitled to their lives. The Imperium would strike down only those that stepped out of line.

Of the three main skyscrapers, the central Barnes-Lennox Monolith held fourteen hundred offices and was staffed by thousands. Not to mention the damage that would be suffered when it fell...

Bray and Aaron took off running, racing for the Repeater station. It was a stair climb to get there, tight hallways and switchbacks. The Repeater was set into the Wall, with gunnery operation seated inside the Wall itself. Four operators could select targets and provide maintenance to the automated dragon.

They arrived to find the four Capital operators in a panic.

"What's wrong?!" Bray shouted.

"We don't know!" a whimpering Capital blathered. "It just started on its own!"

Two Capitals were trying to disconnect the Repeater from its ammo feed with a set of wrenches. That would expose the firing chamber when it—

"No, no don't—!" It was all Aaron got off.

The feed fell open—and the Repeater fired anyway! The back pressure from the shot spat gases through the opening and into the room, knocking Aaron off his feet. The two unlucky bastards who had been so industrious had found their ingenuity rewarded: they had been flayed into stew meat.

But, disconnected from its feed, it did indeed stop firing.

"*Gulaw zu*...Gunny!?" Aaron called out over the gonging sound in his ears.

"I'm here, kid," Bray responded, dusting himself off.

Somebody crying, screaming in pain. Aaron pulled himself over to the wounded Capital—everything below the right shoulder was gone, dangling shreds of meat were all that remained. Based on the red cloud in the air, Aaron didn't think it impossible that they were breathing what used to be his arm right now.

"What happened?"

Gunny clambered over to the command console, inspecting the characters streaming across it. "Some code got patched in."

"They *hacked* our guns?!"

"They were never really ours to begin with." Bray grabbed his radio. "Repeater stations: shut down. Say again, shut down!"

"Take 'em manual?" Aaron asked.

"At this range? You'd just be putting on a light show, and these crews aren't artillerists. They'll just hit more buildings."

"Argh!" Aaron fumed, spinning the wheel of random ideas in his head. "No anti-air...."

Bray nodded. "Which means they'll land, take the city, and be home in time for supper."

"Well, we knew it could go like this," Aaron said with a shrug.

"Square up? You and me may be the only ones who did."

A voice from the courtyard below. "Watch out!"

A steel pod streaked down, landing hard in the center of the quad. Metal panels ejected on impact, hurling outward and crushing one poor bastard that happened to be in the way.

What was birthed from that egg was an unholy fusion of gun and more gun—a single man strapped into a steel roll cage with stilts and gloves, like the deadliest roller coaster ride. At every joint and appendage of the skeleton, a new open barrel for some awful weapon of war.

Warcom—a super soldier needs a super suit.

The man at the center lifted his head, his eyes flashing yellow, the heads-up display projected into his skull. Two vicious scars cupped along his throat and up to his cheek, thick and ragged, almost like burns.

He scanned the threats available, and smiled.

A Capital stepped up with his service rifle, emptying the entire magazine into the side. The star-pattern muzzle flash kicked up dirt around him, like a billowing cloak, and the Capital battle cry could have been etched into a heroic sculpture.

Here depicted, a warrior battling a steel ogre.

But with each shot at the Warcom, a shimmering rainbow appeared, like a soap bubble. And the Oskie inside looked positively charmed by it.

He lifted one hand up, pointing a thick Silksteel finger at the attacker—lining him up with the wrist-mounted cannon, a steel bore a full two inches across.

Ka-CHUG!

Whatever the Oskie shot him with, about a third of the Capital's chest simply ceased to be, spraying its contents across the yard behind him like some kind of impressionistic art.

"Come on!" Bray tugged at Aaron's shoulder, but Aaron wouldn't move.

The Oskie scanned left, right...and up. He locked eyes, no expression, as if commanding Aaron to watch closely now.

Every surface on the Warcom lit up, spouting tracers and beams of light, gouts of flame, whorls of vapor leaving tracks of frost. One Capital tried to flee, but found a tongue of lightning reach out from a coil on the power armor. It snapped to him like a bullwhip. The poor man was instantly ablaze from head to toe.

All of the elements of nature had been mastered and brought to bear as tools of war.

Aaron heard the spoon of a grenade kick free, an almost gleeful sound amongst the chaos. Bray and two others hurled their incendiaries into the courtyard, hoping to burn the Oskie out.

The canisters never hit the ground—the lightning node snapped the three grenades out of the air, splitting each in turn. The contents caught flame in pitiful little puddles on the ground.

"What do we do?!" somebody wailed

And Aaron felt a bit of himself wither. He had no idea. Aaron had enough trouble with a naked Oskie. He had no experience fighting anything like this.

But he knew who did...

"With me!" Aaron called out, rushing for the stairwell.

They ran into the belly of the Castle, Bray hot behind him. The few in their wake were confused, alarmed. Maybe they thought their fearless leader was running away.

But Bray had already figured it out. "Can we trust him?

"You didn't trust me," Aaron said, stopping in front of the jail cell door.

"No, I did not," Bray affirmed. "And I'm beginning to wonder about that instinct."

"Me too."

And Aaron hurled the door open.

Graccus Ontarim hung off his restraints. His lips pursed as an explosion rocked the compound, sending bits of cement tinkling from the ceiling.

"What do we do?" Aaron asked.

Graccus didn't hesitate. "Warcom units will strike at important infrastructure, try to sow chaos and division, break down fortifications, clearing the way for the bulk of the Army to swoop in and crush you."

"So what do we *do*?"

Graccus shrugged. "You do what you should've done a week ago. You run. Get the fighting out of the city, away from innocent people."

"We give up Vanguard, the Wall," Bray said, shaking his head. "We give up our one advantage."

"I know you Regulars love your last stands, but this is hardly your one and only advantage."

"And what would you do, Oskie?" Bray demanded.

Graccus's face darkened. "I took an oath once. I feel like I'm the only one in my unit that remembered what it was."

"Service to the People?" Aaron asked.

"For They are the Kings," Graccus finished.

It was a phrase that had meant so much pain and anguish for Vanguard and for Aaron. Those were words used to justify senseless tyranny and violence. Those words had killed Carmona, killed Jensen.

They sounded different coming from this man.

"Let him out," Aaron ordered.

Before anybody could move, Graccus was at Aaron's side—his chains swinging like pendulums. Everyone snapped their guns up at the turncoat, but Aaron knew better.

Graccus could've stepped out of that door whenever he liked. That was, in itself, a sign of trust.

"Thanks for coming around," Graccus remarked, rubbing his wrists. "It was getting musty in here."

"Give the order, Bray," Aaron said. "Evacuate."

Graccus pivoted in close to the Sergeant. "Start with the high-profile targets, anybody the Imperials would want to execute on sight."

"She's not going to want to go."

"When does she ever?" Aaron said. "The Statesmen too."

"All teams," Bray called into his radio, "we're at Firesale. All troops fall back to hold points and wait for extraction."

Graccus stripped off his bulky tunic, revealing a tight-fitted undershirt, as he pulled Aaron to one side. "You'll never get out of here with that Warcom on the deck."

"You got any ideas about that?" Aaron asked.

Graccus smiled. It positively sent chills down Aaron's spine. "Keep him distracted."

And Graccus melted into the air, like he was never properly solid.

Of course—he was an Intelligence operative. His augments were probably more of the stealth variety. Speed, active camouflage, padding in his feet. He would be at his most deadly with the least amount of gear. It's not like he needed to be perfectly invisible when he could move as fast as Oskies did.

"You heard him, Gunny," Aaron said, shouldering his rifle. "Let's distract the God of War."

"I've only got so much blood in me," Bray grumbled.

"Will the Repeater still fire?"

123

Bray thought for a long moment. They had cut the auto-feed but..."Technically?"

"That's all I need," Aaron said. "Let's move!"

They ran back down the corridors, down the stairs and back up again. There might as well have been a hurricane outside, all kinds of howling and screaming. Concussions battered the fortifications and the cement was cracking under the duress. Aaron's feet ached as his boots slapped the ground. His arms complained and his chest burned.

Come on, don't quit now. The night's only just getting started.

And suddenly, all of the sounds were not muted anymore, and something hot flashed across the back of his neck, accompanied by the timpani of crumbling stone.

Bray cried out in surprise, and Aaron instinctively dropped to a knee, looking back—to see a gaping hole in the Wall clean through left to right. The layers of concrete, rebar, and steel had meant nothing to the Oskie's reactor-powered energy weapons. Judging by the scoring on the stonework, Aaron doubted that there was a building built by man that ever would.

"Go!" Bray waved at him, as he slunk behind what was left of the wall.

"What're you going to do? Scold him?!"

"I said, GO!" Bray stuck his rifle through the brand-new gun port and sprayed a salvo down at the Oskie.

He didn't think he could do any harm, but he could probably draw focus. If the Oskie shut down the Repeater, they'd lose the Castle here and now. Bray had to keep his eyes elsewhere.

"Stay alive," Aaron ordered.

"Sure," Bray wheezed, trying to not cough up the half a gallon of cement powder in his lungs.

Aaron took off running again, the sounds of battle falling away like a distant ocean's waves. Soon, all he could hear was his own heavy breathing.

Something hit his head, light and damp. Then again and again. Rain. He might ponder that minor miracle of a cloud burst on a desert planet, but he had more pressing concerns: like the demigod in power armor down below.

He took the stairs two at a time, coming back up to the Repeater housing, where the burnt-up bodies of the operators remained. They died fighting because he—

No. Not right now. Grieve them later.

The Repeater still hummed, waiting for a live round to reach the chamber—and back blast the housing again. It might not have been an internal combustion chamber spitting an explosive out into his face, but air pressure from a magnetically accelerated round was still enough to turn Aaron into a fine red mist.

First things first. Six months ago, Capitals and Imperial Regulars had separated the targeting computers and aimed the behemoths manually when trying to murder Aaron and his friends. Now how had they gone about doing that?

Well, the computer had a nice convenient plug it could remove. Thanks for that.

"Aaron, if you could move it along—" Bray's radio cut out before he could finish.

No computer tracking. Okay.

The beast was mounted on ratchets, two great big ones driven by metal wheels. He felt like he was driving just the most advanced pirate ship.

Aaron spun one wheel, feeling the clicks of the gigantic ratchets underneath. Normally, a minor change was all that would be needed, altering the point of aim by hundreds of yards over the distances it was rated for.

But he was aiming...*very* close by.

He cranked and cranked, and the muzzle of the Repeater dropped down. Soon, Aaron could see the courtyard through the slit in the housing—

And the Oskie Warcom craning his neck up at the threat. Curiosity. Wasn't that big gun on *his* side?

Aaron dashed over to the feed line, heaving one of the cartridges out. It felt like he was hugging a copper bucket the size of his torso. How *did* people use to do this?

Right. They got machines to do it.

Aaron dumped it into the chamber, looking about for some way to seal the open breach. The gun hummed to life.

No time. Just run.

Aaron threw himself down the stairwell—and the concussion wave blew down after him. Followed by an equally deafening crunch as the gigantic shell bit into the ground, tossing five hundred pounds of dirt high into the sky.

The foundations of the Castle shuddered, as if it had to reset its feet.

Aaron went to stand, his hand slipping out from under him, giving his chin a good morning crack on the stonework. His teeth tingled to match the hum in his ears, his whole head one giant tuning fork.

He worked his way to his feet, stumbling outside of the tower and bouncing off the walls as he went. He made his way over to the parapet to look down at his work. His fingers found a nice notch to grip, a fracture in the stone. That shot might've done more harm than good.

The dust was still settling and the edges of the crater were plainly visible. Nestled deep within, silhouetted in the smoke was...no...

"How in the..." Aaron murmured.

He'd hit the thing, maybe a foot or two off-center but guns like this didn't need to be pinpoint—s'why they made the bullet so big.

But there it sat, as fresh as when it hatched. The Warcom suit was frozen in place, the Oskie inside glowering up at him. Clearly very pissed off.

Uh-oh.

The Oskie's hands flashed about his chest rig, undoing his harness. Curious—the Warcom must've spent its entire reactor charge on its shield to soak that hit. Now it was just a very expensive lawn ornament, with a very angry man inside.

Aaron lurched back away from the wall—and the Oskie practically ran up the brickwork, vaulting up over the edge, and snagging the collar of Aaron's shirt.

He was a young man, in his prime, with a square jaw and pristine shaved head. He looked like he'd been minted from a foundry, his Oskie surgical scars the only blemish on his otherwise perfect skin. It was jarring. Did he molt like a snake to get that pristine look?

The Oskie's eyes flickered yellow and a satisfied sneer dawned. His voice came out like sandpaper and acid, gloating. "And how exactly did you expect that to go...Legatus?"

A shimmer behind him.

The Oskie reacted immediately, whipping his free hand around, grabbing onto thin air. The ghost trapped in his clutches kicked and scraped, dangling in the air. The Oskie might as well have been holding onto groceries for all the strain it was giving his shoulder.

Under his fingers, the stealth camouflage melted away, unable to correct. Graccus grimaced, clutching at the fingers biting into his throat.

The Imperial's smile dropped to a flat robotic face. "Graccus Ontarim," the Oskie said with an air of awe. "Never thought I'd see the day."

Graccus went lax, relaxing into the hold. "That's because you lack imagination, Callum."

He opened both palms—and a light flashed and strobed from them.

Oh, how Aaron wanted to be anywhere else. It wasn't just blinding or disorienting. It wasn't a regular pattern. In the half second Aaron saw, he could swear he'd seen the origins of man and its destruction and his own grave marker and his own birth. It was borderline hallucinatory.

The Oskie—Callum—must've felt the same, dropping Aaron to the stone. Aaron scrambled away, but it was all over before he'd gotten three feet. His eyes flared, his ears thundering, his hands numb.

He shook his head and both men were gone.

Aaron yanked himself up to the edge, scanning the ground below. The Warcom sat unattended, as Capitals emerged from their pillboxes.

"Graccus!" he called out.

If Aaron had picked up anything, it was that Graccus had a penchant for the dramatic.

"What're you looking at?"

Aaron jumped, turning to see Graccus standing beside him, peering down at the crater below. His implants glowed a fierce orange, etching magma lines under his skin. The man was positively glow-in-the-dark, the rain snapping and sizzling against his glowing skin.

On top of that, he had a swollen eye, blood leaking from his left ear and a hand clutched at his ribs. He'd had a bit of a fight.

Aaron tried to swallow his heart back into his chest. "Did ya get him?"

Graccus shook his head with tight lips. "I got a bit of him. He... got a bit of me."

Aaron pointed at the mint condition exosuit abandoned in the quad. "I hit that thing with a—"

"Yeah," Graccus drawled, "Warcoms are pretty elite. Microfusion reactor powering a deflector shield, gauss cannons, energy weapons—looks like that sucker's even got a Tesla coil! But in emergencies, or when under intense fire, they can dump the entire reactor into shields to protect it from intense heat and force. The suit can't run without power anymore, but...at least you survived the whatever, ya know?"

Aaron shook his head, not really following that marketing rundown.

Graccus's smile widened. "It means we've got a suit of power armor—if we can figure out how to power it up again. Come on, Legatus. We got a planet to save."

CHAPTER
TWELVE
EDEN

THEY HAD MADE landings throughout the City, perfectly dispersed to prevent any one focused counter-offensive. It wasn't unlike battling an infection. The troops would push back on the Market only to lose the Harbor.

Eden had grown to hate the sucking gasps of the Howler's circling in for a landing. The hammer strike of their struts grinding into the deck was louder than their engines, but she could always hear the screaming wounded tucked in their bellies.

There weren't enough beds for their work. Casualties starting to pile up in the hallways. It was difficult enough working in the dark— for their safety, they had cut off all the lights in the Hospital, to prevent the Imperials from finding them. But now the orderlies were tripping over patients awaiting care.

They were cycling patients in front of Eden like she was a short order cook. She hadn't sat down in hours, and her left foot was going numb.

"Code Red!" the nurse shouted. "Multiple fractures, a broken spine, and TBI. Swelling in the neck and jaw, possible JVD."

"Multiple GSW, chest and stomach, through and through!"

"Eden!" She perked up at her name.

Julius, an orderly with the hospital, approached with a patient bed. The big man was over twice her age, gray starting to fleck his large beard and the jovial twinkle to his eye now drained by exhaustion. He'd been a hematech and then an anesthesiologist—today, he was her third hand.

His voice had gone raspy from yelling. "He's alive, but I don't know how."

Eden glanced at the patient on the bed—then averted her eyes to his chart. The man was hamburger. She recognized the Capital uniform and little else. Something had sprayed him with shrapnel, a great deal of it still buried in his flesh, like ugly metal sutures.

A good chunk of his jaw was simply missing.

"Was he in the Gagarin Tower?" It had collapsed an hour before.

"No," Julius said. "He's got a bunch of metal in him, and more abrasions than I care to count."

"Well, that's not really your department," Eden said, pulling the AutoDoc console to her side of the bed. The AutoDoc panned a laser across him, highlighting in green thirteen different pieces of metal jutting from his torso. Eden cursed. "He's going to take up this whole unit for the next four hours. Spread the word, we're going to have to start treating patients directly."

"I'm sorry?"

"They went to med school; they'll know what that means."

"Ma'am, they diagnose and program. Most haven't handled a scalpel in years."

"Well, they can lodge a complaint at one of my four customer service windows." She entered the last command. The AutoDoc deployed a grey surgical veil across the patient, as a dozen tiny arms lunged in, launching into their grisly tasks. "They're not pharmacists. They're doctors."

"Have you ever seen stuff like this?" Julius asked, his voice almost distant.

Eden spared another glance at the butcher block masquerading as her patient. "I've seen a lot. Nothing like this."

Julius swept away the patient, as a new poor sod was wheeled in front of her. He looked like a bloody sack of potatoes.

He didn't rightly have a face anymore.

"Do we have an AutoDoc open?!"

The nurse ran over to a recovery station, murmuring an apology to the patient as she cut the computer free from him. She wheeled the heavy machine over to the hamburger that Eden was treating and hooked it on to the bed.

Eden studied the injuries presented. Cheeks swollen from blunt force trauma, both eyes swollen shut, nose completely crushed. Bruising of the neck, red and swollen flesh as blood pooled under the skin and spread into other tissues. His jaw hung loose, dislocated, but the man was graciously unconscious.

This was Orbital handiwork—they could've just killed him, but they knew that the living sent messages better than the dead. So they broke his back against the street curb, and beat him until someone else drew their cruel attentions.

The nurse was midway through rattling off his vitals when he started convulsing.

"Hold him!" Eden held a hand across his forehead, as the nurse strapped him down. She pawed gingerly at his neck.

He was choking.

"Clear his airway! Now!"

The nurse punched in the commands on her computer, and the AutoDoc swung into action. Crane arms leaned in with precision lasers, cutting and cauterizing cleaner and faster than any human hand—they sliced open his nose and removed the offending tissue; they intubated him with an insect-like proboscis slipping through the gash; they smeared gel on the open wounds to disinfect and staunch the bleeding.

The patient thrashed, breaking one of his restraints.

"Julius!" Eden called for the orderly. "We need you!"

Slender hands snuck in, binding the patient's spasming arm and forcing it down with no amount of kindness. Eden looked up to see

Talania, stained with ash and grimacing from a gash to her forehead.

"We've got this," Eden assured her.

"Doesn't look like you do."

"You need treatment yourself. Sit down—"

"Save him and you can yell at me all you want!"

A gasp from the patient, his body arching as the twin lines from the AutoDoc reached his lungs and inflated them. But the diaphragm didn't budge, his breaths shallow. She palmed his stomach, feeling the muscle contract inward as the lungs inhaled.

One set of ribs was broken free from the chest wall, and his breathing was expanding *that* way rather than down.

"Flail chest," Eden noted, grim.

"Talk to me," Talania said.

"Turn him over!"

The nurse typed and the AutoDoc rotated the bed, gently revealing their patient's back. The musculature more resembled a rocky road, lumps and discoloration throughout. They'd shattered his left scapula, leaving a half dozen ridges poking out of the skin.

But that was the least of her problems. He looked like he was smuggling a fruit at the base of his neck.

"I've got fluid pooling between C3 & 4."

"How do you know?" Talania asked, almost accusing.

"Because I do!" Eden snapped. "Imaging!"

A light panned over the patient's neck and a holographic image popped up, a multi-colored cross-section of the patient. Sure enough, a ball of blood, pus, and cerebrospinal was choking out the vertebrae.

"Add C2 to that list. And we've got cracks along the entire cervical zone."

"This guy jump off a building?" Talania gasped.

"He might've been thrown off one," Eden noted gravely. "Drain the site, clear and burn. Mark."

"Mark!" The nurse typed in the codes, and the AutoDoc started its work. The bed floated off with its attending nurse, sounds of carving meat echoing back up the hall.

Eden passed her hands through a disinfecting spray and hosed off the blood. Talania watched, frozen in her boots. Eden threw her a glance. "Thank you, but you probably gave him a nice case of sepsis."

"I'm sorry?"

"You're not scrubbed."

"It's a war zone," Talania said that like Eden was unaware.

"And you helped keep him alive," Eden said with a nod. "The post-op infection is tomorrow's problem. I'll take every hand you've got but *if* you want to help: scrub up. It'll do a lot of good."

Her mouth said shock, that no one had ever talked to her like this —no woman anyway. But her eyes wrinkled at the corners. It was like she wanted to smile, but was too shocked to fully commit to the facial expression.

She took half a step away before pivoting back. "Where do I do that?"

Howlers, circling in with a new batch of patients. Eden raised a hand, shushing Talania. She didn't hear any screaming, signs of the wounded. Had they died on the way?

"Julius? Get the Governor scrubbed in!" Eden called to her orderly as she jogged for the front office.

The soldiers that greeted her were upright at least, and she recognized the two infantry goons instantly—her former prison guards. "Anatoly, Kipling."

Tall and thin, short and stout greeted her with murmured hellos and grim faces. They bore superficial scrapes and burns. Kipling favored his right knee, only able to tap his toe on the deck—hamstring injury of some kind.

The third was one of the pilots, a short and fiery attitude in his jog. She couldn't make out his face past his helmet and visor. The jumpsuit had six letters hand-stitched into the chest pocket: Keeper.

"You'll be fine, boys," Eden said to the Capitals. "We'll get you cleaned up and brushed up, but it'll be a little wait."

"They're not here for a new coat of paint," Keeper said.

The words hung. They weren't here for treatment. They were here for her.

"I'm not going," Eden said.

Keeper shrugged. "Not my call, ma'am. Orders were to collect the HVTs and get the Hell outta here."

"Eden..." Anatoly appealed to her. "It's gettin' awful bad out there."

"I'm well aware." Eden pointed at the long hallway, lined with the crippled and the dying like some kind of morbid dust collecting in the corners. "They *need* me! I'm not going."

"Ma'am, I brought some nice men with guns, because this isn't something we *discuss*," Keeper said. "Get on the Howler. Now."

"Did you just threaten the good doctor?" Talania stepped up to Eden's side, her pale arms exposed and sleeves rolled up. She might've just come from the hardest scrub wash of her life, but she looked ready to throw punches in a bar brawl.

"You're going to find your new hosts to be a lot less house-warming than I am, I promise you that, *Governor*."

Eden looked over at Talania. At nineteen years old, hard edges to her: deep eyes and a sharp jaw, sunken cheeks. As much as it was genetics, it was also trauma. She had seen the inside of a prison for her beliefs once already.

And she was ready to risk it again.

"All aboard."

Talania snapped her head around, looking for who said that, before she realized it came from the stout little doctor at her side. "What?"

"You're the Governor of Vanguard," Eden said. "They'll *kill* you."

"I can help—"

"And you will. But this is my thing. Let me do what I do."

Keeper cocked his head as he listened to his radio. He started to back toward the Hospital doors, bouncing on his heels, urgency in his steps. "Get your tickets ready 'cause the window is closing."

Talania gritted her teeth and settled her feet. Keeper cocked his head at Eden. She wasn't going to leave without some assistance.

She remembered what Talania looked like in that cell—her eyes had gone glassy, her voice distant and strained. That would be the best-case scenario. She could hope that Talania would live; she could hope that they'd kill her quickly, even if publicly.

The worst-case scenario was far more...deliberate.

"If we're going to fight, let's get started," Talania growled, rolling out her neck, "but I hope you brought more than these two."

Eden nodded to Keeper. And he nodded to the soldiers.

"Sorry, miss."

Talania was not ready for Kipling to step forward, and grapple her about the waist. She might've been a giant, but she was no soldier. He had the lower center of gravity and slung her over his broad shoulder like she was so much laundry. She folded in half over his short stature, toes and hands almost touching the ground.

"Put. Me. Down."

"Deepest apologies!"

Keeper jerked his head at Eden. "You too!"

"You're going to have to drag me."

And he wasn't going to. He shook his head. "Do whatever you're going to do and be ready in one hour. We'll be back!"

"Copy that."

Eden watched as the soldiers receded with Talania, pulled away by the gravity to the Howler waiting on the steps. Eden watched as the soldiers took up their flanking positions, helping the Governor into the beast. The Howler's engines spun up, a moment's dragon roar, before choking back into a low hum.

Someone shouted. "Contact!"

Something struck the Howler's side, a piercing ballista—its arrowhead opening to grip the metal. A cable strung back into the darkness beyond.

135

A tether.

The Howler lifted up and reared back, nearly clipping its tail against the pavement. But it was tied down now, a fish on a line.

The oblong craft backflipped off the stairway—narrowly avoiding the shot meant for its broadside. The air rippled with its passing, a pressure wave cast off the passing arrow shaft.

It slammed into the Hospital roof over her head—showering the air with plaster and wood. It carved a wound channel in the side of the Ward, and from the screams, it took some people with it.

A platoon of Imperial Regulars—green uniforms covered by plated vests, form-fitted helmets. Ghostly steel plates covered their faces, like each soldier had the same features fresh from the factory. The eyes were glassy panels, likely full of tactical information.

Seeing the tethered bird, the whole group raised their weapons for the Howler. Streaks of gunfire lanced upward, magnetic shots plinking and skipping off the hull of the Howler.

Sparks ripped off the engines.

"NO!" Eden shouted.

Two Regulars leveled their weapons at her. They didn't care about the red cross on her arm. She was Colonial, Capital.

Enemy.

Eden slammed the Hospital doors shut—and their shots ripped two-inch diameter holes in the plastic, skipping the copper slugs down the hallways.

A bullet snapped by her head, like a walnut shell cracking inside her own skull: the supersonic boom of a tiny object waving as it slid past. A bullet hitting flesh was a lot quieter than the movies made it out to be. Beneath the crack of the bullet in flight and the boom coming from the muzzle of the weapon, she could hear the slightest wet sound, like somebody spilled stew on to the floor. Wet, but with a little bit of solid bass.

First, she heard that. Then she heard the screams wash over her, as a hundred injured and innocent realized what was happening.

These were her patients, already injured, conducted to safe harbor. And they were getting shot at again.

They would down the Howler. They would kill Talania...

But what could she do? She didn't have a weapon. She was trapped like all the rest, in the dark...

Yes. It was very dark out there, wasn't it? What if it very suddenly wasn't? They'd turned off the lights to hide the Hospital—but that advantage was now lost. Might as well lean in.

Eden crouch-walked over to the Hospital front desk, reaching over to paw for the controls.

She grabbed the toggle and her world came aglow. Through the windows, she could see the entire platoon of soldiers—and they suddenly dropped to the ground. They might not have needed the light, but they had been sheltered by the dark. Now, they were exposed, with nothing to hide behind.

The Howler drifted back overhead, looking for the owner of its tether. The door gun slid open, and licks of green plasma streaked out, kicking up a barrier of dust ten feet high. It was a gun meant to drop a Jergad drone in full gallop. The recoil alone was known to sprain shoulders.

The Imperials were tossed like rag dolls. And soon, the shooter found his mark, snapping the line. Talania and the Howler streaked off into the skyline.

Nobody was quick to get up. Moans and crying were all she could hear. That gun had done its job.

Now, she had her job to do.

"Julius!" Eden called out. "Let's get them inside!"

CHAPTER
THIRTEEN
KEEPER

RECRUITMENT BANNERS all had the same look to 'em: noble-looking multicultural folk looking off to a brighter future, the blue and white Imperial flag fluttering in a patriotic breeze, while three Bearcats flew in an echelon formation at some distant spot overhead, often accompanied by the silhouette of an *Alleghieri* fleet carrier. It was meant to inspire strength, faith in the institutions, and stability with unity.

This looked like the polar opposite.

Prophet's Howler drifted up into the formation, all three departing the combat zone at top speed. The clouds had begun to swirl around the city, a cyclone stirred up by the falling drop pods. Fires dotted the skyline, underlighting the clouds with brushstrokes of red. Flashes and tracer fire reached up into the sky, as if to make vain and futile strikes at the yawning maw above them.

"Aaron?!" Someone had given the Governor a radio. "You son of a bitch! I'm going to come over there and peel your ears right off your head!"

"You're welcome," came the taciturn response.

"Kilo, let's keep it low and hot," Prophet ordered. "It's not our sky anymore."

"You *left* her!" Keeper felt a fist pop his shoulder. His controls bounced and the ship lilted to-and-fro, like a boat on the water.

"Will someone please restrain the passionate leader of the people," Keeper asked, "before she crashes and kills us?"

Anatoly got a hand on Talania and pulled her back into the bay. They sat her right next to the forty-pound expanding tip of the ballista still stuck in the side of the ship. Good, she could contemplate what that would have meant for her had they not shown up when they did.

The Howlers streaked over the countryside, zipping over the Wall and the Castle. The mountain range loomed up in front of them—a wall a hundred times more impressive than the manmade thing. In tight formation, the Howlers peeled up the surface and headed for the designated LZ—a plateau at about two kilometers altitude.

Anatoly strapped a drop harness around Talania. "Make sure you're nice and loose, or the drop cable will break your neck."

Talania went white as a sheet and stiff as a board. "Why not just land?"

"Because you're not the only one we're rescuing today," Keeper remarked. "Drop safety?"

"Drop safely!" Kipling shouted back.

"What does that mean?" Talania asked.

"It means this is your stop." And Keeper flicked the switch, opening the Howler's belly. He heard her shriek for a hot second, before it was swallowed by the wind shear. Kipling and Anatoly clung to their gunnery stations, both craning their necks to watch her go down. The cable whirred behind them, as it spooled out her line, snapping to a crawl as it gently laid her on to the stone below.

A few others were already on the plateau, and rushed to her clearly traumatized side.

"Kilo One-One, pieces are on the board."

"Form up on my wing for combat re-deploy," Prophet ordered. "We've got another shipment of heroes to collect."

"Heads up!" Aisling called out over the radio. "Four LCs. Coming down on the cardinal corners."

He could see them on his scopes. Landing craft emerging from the storm over the city, four rectangular bricks the size of a city block with retroboosters firing. They were descending on the outskirts of the city, ready to box the rebellion in. Each would contain two hundred infantry, small arms, anti-material, and a complement of robotic harassment units.

They'd own the city in a matter of hours.

"Prime the plasma!" Keeper called back into his cabin. "We're going duck hunting."

Anatoly grinned, kicking the spent capacitor out from the base of the gun, and kneeing a fresh one into place. The gun and operator stood on a swivel arm that would pitch out a foot or so from the side of the Howler. Kipling took his station by the door panel, ready to cue it open for him.

Keeper plied the throttle, zipping out of formation.

"*Fra tow ki*—Keeper, back into formation now!"

"If those LCs make the deck, we lose the City."

"We do not have air superiority. Fall back into formation!"

Keeper could've kept that argument going for another few minutes, but Aisling had broken formation too, streaking after him. Her heat signature read toasty warm, guns primed.

Prophet cursed, ordering his own door gunners to spin up.

The Howler had no hardpoints—so Keeper would have to make do with Anatoly's marksmanship. Beyond that, all he could do was give the fat guy a clear line.

Keeper gave the nearest LC a quick scan, pulling the hologram close to his face. It really was just a falling brick, ten times his size. They were never going to conventionally destroy it. The only hope they had was for gravity to do their work.

He tapped a few spots on the underbelly before chucking it over his shoulder—Anatoly's gear would 'grab' the data he just sent their way and upload it for view. "Anatoly, targeting spec. Drop the engine block and it'll fall like pig iron."

"Affirm, jockey." Keeper heard the plasma launcher prime.

The door guns weren't shooting energy blasts, nor were they strictly ballistic. Ionized gases were supercharged and hurled out of the cannon's muzzle with alarming accuracy and range. The material neutralized fairly quickly, but anything it did come into contact with would find free electrons ripped away.

In short, they were spewing gobs of electrified acid at a couple hundred feet per second. They'd chew through any plating or protection that LC had.

They zipped over the Wall—they'd be on the City in less than a minute. Keeper eased up on the throttle, letting Aisling close up on his tail.

"I'll strafe the engine cluster," Keeper said. "You take down any countermeasures looking for my neck."

"Keep it fast, keep it hard!" she confirmed.

"You know how I do." He looked back at his gunners, "Strapped in?"

Kipling just finished rigging himself up—six-point field harness. "Strapped in!"

Edge of the City, the gigantic landing craft right ahead of them. He could already see the automated flak turrets tilting his way. "Hold on to your breakfast!"

Keeper throttled up and rolled the Howler on its side, flying directly underneath the falling LC. Explosions lit the sky around them. Those cannons lobbed carefully metered rounds that would detonate in the air, throwing shrapnel and concussions in a broad field. When one cannon had to hit multiple targets, there was no better way to lay a protective blanket of death around your very expensive ship.

But the Howler wasn't many targets. It was just one.

A round went off nearby, gonging off the Howler's hull. Damage alerts flashed on his screen, one battery of his sensors going dark. The image vanished, revealing the raw bulkhead. He'd lost the sensors covering the high left of his craft—if indeed that part of the ship was still attached at all.

But the ship slipped through the field, and he could see the flaring whites of the thrusters above.

"Guns, guns, guns!"

Kipling threw the door open and a cackling Anatoly spooled out into space, wind whipping through his hair. The green clouds leapt from his barrel.

They were under the ship for a grand total of 1.2 seconds. And those engines kept cooking like they hadn't been there at all. If they had done any harm, it hadn't registered.

Yet.

"No joy!" Keeper said. "Aisling, bring some heat. Strafe the bastard until he drops."

"Swing back and cover my approach."

Keeper looked behind him, and he could vaguely see on his visor that Aisling was scraping some of the turrets off, popping them like little balloons.

"Focus on the aft exchange." The indicated thruster flashed on his display, as Aisling sent him the targeting data. "That one's looking the saddest."

"Solid copy. Comin' around," he said. "Boys! Throw some hate on that flak."

All he got was a cackle in response. If he didn't know any better, he'd think these two were waiting their whole lives for a day like this.

Keeper's Howler zipped across the LC's midsection, far too close for the anti-air to effectively engage. Anatoly's cannon swept it like an acid whip, popping more of the anti-air cannons.

Aisling made a pass underneath the LC, now considerably less pressure on her. The enormous engine cluster sputtered, but kept its fire.

Keeper drifted their ship back underneath. "Do it! Do it!"

"Bring it down, Anatoly!" Kipling shouted encouragement.

The little troll of a man gave a shrill battle-cry as he laid his weight on the trigger, spraying a final layer of green plasma to the underside of the LC.

It was like the engine lit up twice as bright, a sun's collapse, before winking out of existence. The Howler slipped out the far side, as the LC began to fall. They were on the outskirts; nothing was underneath it.

As it slammed into the ground! Anyone caught underneath would be flattened out of existence. Keeper swore, somewhere in that crash of metal and burning fuel, he heard the thing squelch, a collective notice of the people that had been inside.

Anatoly cheered at the fireworks, the implications of the explosion missing him completely. Kipling didn't miss it; his face soured in an instant. They had just killed a conservative two hundred people.

Welcome to the War.

Keeper cued up a radio channel. "Check-check, Kilo One-One. LC Alpha has been destroyed."

A pause before Prophet's voice came through, sour but grumbling affirmation. "Solid copy on that. Good kill, Three-One. Our forces will retreat down that open line. Provide top cover until further notice."

Until further notice. That meant at some point they were going to be recalled. Anyone left in the field when that happened...well, they'd have a very bad day.

"Stall that celebration, Kilo!" Prophet said. "CAP's on the way."

Combat Air Patrol.

Without the Wall's cannons and no air response of their own, the Imperials were free to take the skies. Bearcats weren't suited for atmospheric flight—far too large and few control surfaces.

These nimble little jackrabbits: the DH-301 Havoc was a triple-tandem multi-role aircraft, broad canards ahead of swept wings and vectored-thrust engines. Focused energy weapon systems were tucked back into the hull when not in use, to provide minimum drag and protection during re-entry.

They were also unmanned, making them numerous, small, and perfect for air density tactics. They'd get together and pull the Howlers apart like cotton candy.

"Break, break, break!" Keeper shouted.

A laser beam punched through Keeper's cockpit, searing a two-and-a-half-inch diameter hole through the roof and down through his floorboard. He had no doubt that half a dozen others lined the cabin behind him.

He hoped that Anatoly and Kipling were okay and hanging on, because he sent the Howler into a three-axis tumble, diving straight for the collapsed LC.

Think, goddammit. There was no way that those two Regulars back there were going to swat these bugs out of the sky. What could he do that they couldn't?!

The Howler was a potato. It was ugly, brutish. Fast but fragile. It was a troop carrier, not a dogfighter.

It could stop on a dime. They couldn't.

"For what it's worth, I'm sorry!"

The Regulars didn't have a chance to ask him what he meant. They were almost certainly tasting the contents of their stomachs, as Keeper barrel rolled the Howler, trying to shake the pursuers on his way down.

If he could get low and then stop, he could shake them off.

But before he got too low, the shooting suddenly stopped. He glanced backward, his HUD showing the Havoc all peel off from their pursuit.

"Aisling!" he called out. "They have a hard deck at eight hundred feet. They can't chase you down here."

"That low, and we'll take ground fire!"

"I'll take ground fire over getting shredded."

"Kilo squadron, form up on the Barnes-Lennox tower," Prophet ordered, exhaustion in his voice. "Friendlies pinned down by multiple Oskies. Requesting air support."

"Those LCs make landfall," Keeper said, "and everything else is just spent casings."

"That is an order, Three-One. Get your ass in gear."

He could be in the airspace in less than forty seconds, get himself and his gunners into a pitched fight with an elite shocktrooper that lived for duck hunting. And those LCs were going to be safely down almost as fast.

This battle was going to be won or lost in the next ten minutes, and Prophet had him sweeping up chaff.

Aaron had orders to retreat at Rimpau. He dove into the fray and saved his friends. Keeper could save a few now and blame Prophet for the call. Or he could save a lot and get blamed for insubordination.

He knew which one would help him sleep. Keeper banked his Howler toward the next descending LC.

"Goddammit, Keeper!"

He couldn't stop himself from grinning at Prophet's frustration. "Anatoly, ready for Round Two?"

No response. He scrunched up his face, looking back to see Anatoly draped against the back wall with a burn scar etched up his flank—his left arm seared off.

He'd been hit.

The big guy was woozy, eyes blinking rapidly. A Havoc shot had caught him, punching through the floor of the Howler and slagging his shoulder in its passing. Kipling struggled with his six-point rig, trying to get to his first aid kit.

No time.

"Kipling, on the gun! We're on approach!"

"But—"

Lasers streamed past as the Havoc fighters formed up on his ass. *"Right now, Kipling!"*

Kipling said goodbye to his friend with a plaintive look and darted over to the gun, hooking in. His friend's charred flesh was still spattered on the barrel.

"Keeper, you have no cover!" Aisling shouted over the radio. "Break off!"

No time.

The flak started, lighting up the skies around them, and the Havoc fighters circled away.

Interesting. They didn't want to get close to the flak. If he could get inside the flak field, too close to the LC for the turrets to safely engage—and where the Havoc CAP couldn't follow.

Keeper pushed through, sliding the big gunship left and right, doing what he could to dodge the worst of the flak. He could hear the shrap tinkling off the sides of the hull.

Behind him, Anatoly was muttering advice. "Bend your legs...and lean into it."

"Not sure I can do this, 'Toly!"

"Yes, you can. You *can!*"

He was going to have to.

A flak charge exploded directly in front of him, and a full two thirds of his vision blacked out, sensors destroyed. Keeper could no longer see directly in front of him.

"Gyah!" Keeper shouted. "Kilo One-One, I'm in the blind."

No answer. Did he even have his radio anymore?

He could still see out of the side of the ship, the only slice of his hull that hadn't been scored. He didn't want to think about how ugly his potato was now—he'd get to see it on the landing pad and wonder how the Hell he had landed the son of a bitch.

The engine cluster was directly in front of Kipling.

"Guns, guns—" The third word was buffeted behind the blare of the weapon spitting its green death. Keeper counted the seconds of sustained fire. And Kipling's face seemed to glow, the golden hue of the barrel illuminating him in the night.

He was going to melt the barrel.

"Kipling, bursts! Short bursts!"

"I've got it!" Kipling snapped back.

And just as soon as he'd said it, the engine cluster popped. Keeper felt it in his chest.

And the brick began to fall.

"Hang on!" Keeper pointed the Howler straight down, glancing out to his only live camera to get a vague idea of where he was going. He had to get them out from under the LC. And he was going to have no idea what was in front of him.

Kipling's scream was not helping anyone's confidence. Bits of the crippled LC cascaded around them. Keeper counted, trying to guesstimate where the ground was.

He had enough separation now or he was going to nose-dive them into the ground.

Keeper pulled up, and jetted them forward. The LC flopped on to the ground behind them.

"Gah!" Keeper exhaled, the tension slipping out of his frame. "Kilo-One-One, LC Delta is down."

No response.

"Um, jockey..." Kipling began. "Light a fire under that kiester, because we've got company!"

The CAP, a swirling vortex of Havoc response craft. They looked like they were one great creature, a leviathan come to swallow him whole or burn him clean with a fiery breath.

Something hit them first—a lance of cloudy green plasma—as Prophet's Howler came streaking up to his side. Several fighters detonated in the air, with the volume of them veering off.

"Keeper!" He had never heard Prophet's voice hit that register before, a shrill scolding tone with a soupçon of panic. It plucked at something within him, and he just wanted nothing more than to apologize, but the old man wouldn't let him have the moment. "You are RTB. Get yourself to the ground while you still can."

He wanted to thank the old man. He wanted to cheer him. He wanted to say something.

He didn't get a chance to. No sooner than Prophet had finished his sentence, a red laser blew through the heart of his Howler, right through where he'd have been sitting. It looked like someone had driven a crimson lance through him.

It robbed all breath from Keeper's chest.

There was no more life in that bird, and the Howler drifted down and out of view, to collapse onto the corpse of the landing craft below.

CHAPTER
FOURTEEN
AARON

"KILO ONE-ONE, respond. Kilo One-One, what's your status?!"

"Prophet, sitrep?"

"He's *gone!*"

"Two-One, this is Red Haven," Aaron's voice croaked. "You're the lead now. You understand me?"

A long pause before Aisling spoke up. "Solid copy, sir. Keeper, on my wing."

Aaron thought being in battle was hard. But there was something so paralyzing about listening to it. Chatter of coordinating ground forces, electric calls for violence and screams of pain and fear. And he could do nothing at all.

It hadn't taken the survivors long to set up an Operations point inside the Hive, spooling cables to the surface to grant radio contact, generators to power lights and consoles, even some cots for the worst wounded. The floodlights blanketing the trauma ward were now merely the backdrop to deeper agonies broadcast over the sound system.

The Jergad hadn't stopped them, hadn't turned them away. In

point of fact, the Jergad were nowhere to be seen. The entire cavern was barren, hollow. Not one sign of their passing.

Whitby stood at Aaron's elbow, like he was afraid to be more than a few feet away from the impromptu Commander. He clutched his linen jacket in his fingers like it was a safety blanket. "Where are they?" he asked for maybe the third time.

Aaron didn't answer him.

Whitby was not amused by this. "Capital—"

"I heard you."

"Oh! And so you choose to ignore a Statesman?"

"No," Aaron said, "but I have no new information since the last time you asked me that question."

"And I think you're not telling us everything, *Capital*."

Graccus materialized at the man's elbow. "Do you have something helpful you'd like to contribute?"

To his credit, Whitby didn't jump at the Oskie's sudden appearance. He masked his surprise well, his jaw tightening before he turned to address the ghost.

It occurred to Aaron then, that a traitorous Oskie might actually be more offensive to the loyalist than Aaron could ever be.

"Captain," Whitby started, "I order you to take this criminal into custody in the name of the Consul."

Graccus's eyes slid around the chamber, counting. "There's about fifty of us lawbreakers in here, you're going to have to be more specific."

Whitby pointed a manicured finger at Aaron's head, inches from his ear. "Arrest *him*! Kill him! And we can stop this madness here and now!"

"I'm busy saving your life, can you threaten me later?" Aaron groused.

"*My* life?!" Whitby said, breathlessly. "We are standing in a dank cave at the bottom of a mountain, and *that* is not because of *my* patriotism, Capital! I would be within my rights to—"

Enough of this horse shit. Did this linen shirt know *who* he was talking to?

"To do what?" Aaron spun on him, bringing the two men nose to nose. "You're going to do what, Stefan? Kill me?"

"You cannot kill something that is not alive, *Capital*."

He is alive because Whitby allows it. Is that it?

Enough of this. He was Legatus. Whitby was not. It was just that simple.

"Graccus." The Oskie stiffened at Aaron's voice. "Would you kindly escort Mr. Whitby to whatever quiet corner he would like to stand in? Maybe something poorly lit and moldy."

Graccus took Whitby by the arm. "Resist and I will pull it off."

Whitby went limp like a scruffed kitten, happy to keep his arm exactly where it was. Aaron turned back to the assorted radios. A technician was hooking up a holo-projector, so that they might have an actual view of what was going on.

Talania stepped up to his side, leering back toward the retreating Whitby.

"You have no idea how satisfying that was to watch."

Aaron sighed. "Imagine how it felt to do it."

She faked a shiver, a pale mockery of the chill that was going up Aaron's spine. He'd just ordered a Statesman of the People into a time-out. A far cry from the little mine laborer of a year ago.

"He's not alone," Talania cautioned. "Even among the Regulars, there's bound to be loyalists who'd turn you over to the Imperials for a pat on the head."

"Yeah...I think we're well and truly past the point where we cooperate for extra credit."

Talania scanned the empty cavern behind them. "It's eerie, though. Did they know we were coming?"

It was hard to disagree. The Jergad had made this place their home, and now it was an empty shell. He couldn't feel them, see them, but the Queen had a drama streak of her own—she hadn't gone far. She was just watching and waiting.

Something was eating at Talania. She was swaying from side to side, shifting her weight to-and-fro as she weighed the thought in her head.

"What is it?" Aaron asked.

"She didn't want to come."

"Who didn't want to come?"

"These two brutes, they throw me on their shoulder like I'm—"

Aaron waved his hand in the air. "Don't lose the thread, Tal. Who didn't come?"

"She's still at the hospital, Aaron."

Eden. In a snap, he felt his blood turn to acid, burning under his skin. Aaron looked up. "She wasn't on the Howler?"

Talania shook her head. "Eden stayed behind to—"

"God—*Fra tow pa ki somar!* When I say get on the bird..."

Talania's eyes went wide at the sudden outburst from Aaron. She didn't have a right to be shocked. She wanted him to get more involved; well, he was more involved now.

"Bray!" Aaron shouted.

The Gunny came jogging over, reading a report glowing from his wrist. "Landing Craft are on the ground in two sectors. They're rolling right over us."

And Eden was still in there.

Aaron had been left behind to die on a hilltop, while an enemy clawed at him from every side. He was left with no support, abandoned by his friends.

But Eden wouldn't be presumed dead. Admiral Tiberiet would go out of his way to broadcast her corpse for all to see.

"Where are the Howlers right now?"

Talania stepped in between them. "Aaron, do not do what you're thinking—"

"Where are they?"

"Over the Fields on return approach," Bray said, eying Talania. "I'm inclined to agree with the Governor on this one, Aaron. It's over."

It wasn't over, not yet.

He picked up his radio. "Two-One, this is Red Haven. How copy?"

"Aaron!" Talania objected, pulling at his shoulder.

"Two-one, how copy?" he asked, glaring at the Governor. She was really about to argue for leaving Eden behind?

Aisling's voice came over the line. "Solid copy, Red Haven. Standing by."

Bray leaned in close, whispering in his ear. "Aaron, they are out of combat. It is a goddamn wheat thresher you're about to send them back into—for *one person*."

"I'd do it for her," Aaron muttered.

"You're *not* doing it, though," Bray said. "You're not the ground pounder anymore. You're asking *someone else* to do it. That's the reality of command."

Reality of command. Why did that phrase sound so familiar? And why did it leave such a foul taste in his mouth, like an autoimmune response?

He would go back. He'd go back a thousand times. Eden was his friend. She'd saved him, risked more than her life to do so. She'd done it again and again...

He shook and shivered, barely containing six months' worth of grief. "It was supposed to me, Bray."

"What?"

"Jensen. He goes and gets himself...it was supposed to be *me*."

Bray looked off to the side, as if to see if anybody was watching. Aaron didn't care. To hell with 'em.

"Yeah, well," Bray began, "it wasn't. And if Jensen were here, he'd tell you to save who you can. Putting more people on the line... for a maybe at one?"

"I can save her."

"You *might*, but these kinds of things are like accruing debts. You always have to pay up, some day. You don't get to just have whatever you want."

"I'm not that person, Bray. I can barely decide things for myself. You want me to decide—these are my *friends*."

"Not anymore," Bray said. "Now they're your responsibility. One of many. Don't put one over the others."

Uneasy is the head that wears the crown. He was just some kid, a court clerk and staff assistant convicted of murder and sentenced to hard labor, who was drafted into the service, betrayed by his commander—he wasn't ready to be *this*.

Not his friends anymore? Eden, Nora, Keira, Solomon.... how about if he could have saved Jensen or Carmona or Quinn? They were too important to him. How could he not?

He clenched his fists and lifted the radio. "Two-one...get back to the Vanguard Hospital double-time."

Bray shook his head and stepped back.

Talania stared in disbelief. "You just killed them."

"I gave them an order. They'll follow it," Aaron corrected, though he himself wasn't that comfortable with the notion.

Bray stalked off to some other duty, but Aaron could swear the old gunny just wanted to be far away. On the other hand, Talania had grown roots, just staring at him. "You sound like *him*."

Like who?

Her eyes grew dark, a twitch to her lip: pain, anger, anguish, and despair. Her piteous stare shifted to something harder, resolved.

Aaron shook his head. "I'm not Riley."

There was a long pause before she answered. "I want her safe too."

But that wasn't an endorsement.

CHAPTER
FIFTEEN
EDEN

THE AUTODOCS WENT OFF-LINE after running solid straight for six hours, finally drained of their reserves of raw materials. They started reloading them with whatever carbon they could get their hands on: spare scrubs, shell casings—hell, they were dumping in boxes of floss! Julius rigged up a battery bank using the cells from most of the Hospital's lights, keeping the big machines cranking.

For an unhappy eternity—a mere half an hour—Eden thought she was back in Detroit's Lower Wards, pulling broken glass from legs and suturing scalps, disinfecting tools by hand.

Two patients with blood pooling in the chest cavity; another with his left hand blown completely off; one young boy needed his ribs reconstructed after being pulled from a collapsing structure. Tension pneumothorax, and coughing blood—something was shredding his lungs.

In the five seconds it took for her to scrub up from her last patient, he drowned. He was twelve years old.

Nothing to do. Next in line.

Julius pulled the next bed in front of her. The patient twisted against cloth restraints, fragments of charred skin peeling away to reveal the muscles below.

His shoulder was exposed but unmarred. She grabbed it with her hand, feeling the residual heat from the fire through her gloves. She also felt the spasms rippling up his body.

"What's his 02 level?"

Julius leered over at the monitor at the end of the patient's bed. "92 and dropping."

Hypoxemia—he wasn't getting enough oxygen. And those contractions. "Intubate him."

Julius looked up from his IV bags and needles. "Doctor?"

"He inhaled fire," Eden said. "His lungs are bleeding and collapsing. We have to drain them *now*."

He'd need a brand-new lung, but right now, they had to get him oxygen.

Julius scrambled with the plastic tubing, while Eden dropped painkiller into the patient's arm. They wouldn't be able to adequately shove a breathing line down his throat with him thrashing about.

Footfalls behind her. No. No, not now.

She threw a glance back. Keira and Solomon stood shoulder to shoulder, weapons slung. Solomon was covered from the elbow down in blood—suffice it to say, that the blood might not have started as his, but he had taken possession of it. Keira was taking deep even breaths, trails of sweat cutting through the grime on her broad forehead.

"Doctor?" Keira said it all in one word. It was time.

"I told the Jockey one hour."

"It's been three," Julius said gravely.

She sagged. He was right.

The orderly swallowed hard. "You really have to go?"

She nodded. "You can handle this."

"I really can't!" A look of panic in his eye. It's not like he had a choice. It was time for him to step up to the plate.

"Julius, you're a giving heart. You're brilliant. You know what you have to do."

"But what if I do something wrong?" he said. "What if I hurt somebody?"

156

"You want to know a dirty little secret?" she asked. "I've worked in hospitals, I've worked in slums, I've worked in war zones. That feeling? Doesn't go away. So take a breath...and then do what you have to do."

Julius nodded, looking down at the patient. They hadn't been a soldier, judging on what remained of the fine collared shirt. They had just gotten to enjoy the warm embrace of Imperial ordinance.

It was the natural hazard to hosting the party; innocent people were always the worst to suffer.

They won't shoot unarmed people. For all this to stop, the guns have to leave. And as long as Eden stayed tending to the wounded, the guns stayed and more wounded came.

Time to go.

Eden stripped off her PPE and shucked her gown. She reached for her Capital uniform but Keira stopped her. "Plain clothes."

Eden noticed that Keira and Solomon wore their civis—workman's pants and boots, with close cut t-shirts. Keira might still have had her tac rig, but Solomon's extra magazines were sticking out of his pants pockets.

They had tossed their Capital gear—didn't want to be identified on sight.

"If you're not part of the racket, you're part of the take?" Eden quoted.

Solomon smiled, a demented tilt to his lip. "We missed you out there, Eden."

"Let's just go," Eden said, pulling on her own rig and clipping it at her waist.

Keira tossed Eden her custom short-barrel rifle. The JP-36 assault rifle was a little big for her small frame. Keira had been so kind as to size down the barrel and pull off the stock, giving Eden a kind of sawed-off carbine that better suited her hands. Eden checked the chamber and thumbed the safety.

Doctor to warrior. Not the friendliest of transitions for her, but not a new one either.

Keira and Solomon led the way out of the hospital down to the steps. The Imperials Eden couldn't save still laid where Keeper had cut them down. And the thrusters from the Howler had created a fascinating blast pattern in the concrete.

The last time she had left this hospital with a gun in hand, the city had looked remarkably similar. Fires both near and far, sounds of gunfire and screaming. It felt like one continuous bad dream, that she was forced to walk endlessly through until she found the meaning of it all.

God, she wanted a drink. She wondered what Talania had in her thermos. Maybe it would take the edge off her nerves.

Eden paused. "Where's our ride?"

"On the way," Keira said. "But we need to hoof it into the boonies a little bit."

Solomon had his rifle tucked in his shoulder, his eagle eyes scanning for movement. "This isn't our neighborhood no more."

He pointed in the distance to the Aurora building. The three towers backdropping it were now glass skeletons, giant holes drilled right through them and fires cooking within, sending glittering lights all over the city. But draped across the side of the Aurora tower was a single image, projected up from somewhere below—the Blue & White orchid of the Imperium.

They were behind enemy lines right now.

Eden found herself drifting behind a planter for cover.

"Let's go," Keira whispered. "Our ride is not going to wait for us."

The trio took off running, leap frogging through the city streets. Two would take cover and look for threats while the third moved forward. The spires of the city made for nerve-racking movement—any threat wouldn't be just on the ground, but in any of the ten stories of glass and steel above them.

"Wait!" someone yelled. She knew that voice. A certain orderly was jogging after them, out of breath.

"Julius!" Eden snapped. "Keep your voice down!"

The man stopped to catch his breath, heaving panicked half-measures more likely to worsen his state than help. As if being terrified and in a war-torn city-state wasn't bad enough, he was likely power-sucking on all kinds of building materials and fumes.

"I can't do it," he gasped, "I just..."

He'd left the hospital, left the patients. "So you *ran?*"

The thought hit him but he shook his head, freeing himself of guilt. "I wasn't going to help anyone there."

"Yes, you were. Go back."

"We're going to attract attention," Keira warned.

Eden laid a hand on Julius' shoulder. "I know how you feel."

"We can't do this without you," the orderly said, near weeping.

"Keep talkin'," Solomon said, "and the Imps will make sure you're not doing much of anything at all."

Eden took Julius by the shoulder, forcing his bleary eyes to look at her. "I'm not the thing holdin' that hospital together. Y'all were doing plenty of good there well before I showed up."

"But you're..." He couldn't finish the thought, but Eden knew where he was going. She was a Capital that stood with Legatus. She was something *more*.

"Hold up!" Solomon hissed, tilting his head like he was listening to the wind.

Eden did the same, hoping to pick up whatever he was searching for. But nothing.

"What is it?" Julius asked.

"Quiet!"

Then she heard it. Buzzing.

"Get down!" Keira grabbed Eden by her rig, yanking her down and pulling Julius down with her. The three fell down behind a dumpster in an alley—and just in time, as the cloud of tiny robots streamed through the air: a swarm of metal locusts.

"What—" Julius started before Keira could slap a hand over his mouth.

The entire cloud stopped as one, turning to the sound. Julius pulled at Keira's hand, begging her to let him go. Maybe he slipped her grip—maybe she let him go—but he came free, flopping into the alley.

And the cloud descended, a thousand hungry insects. Eden saw the flash of polished steel, two-inch long scalpels at the tip of each, like stingers on a hornet.

Meat, blood, bone—they minced poor Julius into bite-sized pieces in under a second.

The cloud rose up to come back—

And Eden heard the spoon of a grenade, a metal soprano. Solomon hurled the rock down the alleyway, and it clattered its way on.

And the cloud pursued.

Keira held Eden close, as the pressure wave washed over them, the fiery blast sending licks of flame back their way. The locusts dispersed like mosquitos in autumn, before reforming and billowing away.

Solomon picked Eden up off the pavement, but Eden couldn't tear her eyes from the stew meat that had once been her friend. "Why..." Was all she could get out.

"Don't know," was Keira's disappointing response, "but they seem to like noise and movement."

"How did you know that would work?"

Solomon's eyes glittered with that psychotic satisfaction. "I didn't." But boy was he pleased with himself.

The Capitals started to move on, but Eden lingered, staring at the red patch of pavement. That would be his grave marker, a painted patch of stone.

"Eden!"

She followed her friend's call.

———

The residential district was almost disconcertingly quiet, museum pieces, like facades that weren't quite real. Their lights were off and blinds drawn. No one wanted to draw the ire of the Sky God shooting bolts of light and thunder.

The trio of Capitals creeped on through, joining in the nonchalance. Nothing to see here: just three criminals evading the authorities in your neighborhood at night with full tactical gear.

She wanted to knock on doors, make sure everyone was down in their bunkers, safe, secure. But she wasn't the neighborhood watch or a member of a volunteer fire brigade. Right now, she was a soldier.

Keira clutched the radio on her shoulder. "Kilo One-Two, this is Hammerhead. We're on approach to LZ. How copy?"

The voice on the radio was so quiet it sounded like it was crackling a whispered secret. Keira nodded and dropped to one knee, and gestured for the other two to circle up.

"What's the word?" Solomon asked.

"You like rollercoasters?"

"No," Eden flatly denied. "Why?"

"Then I don't really have a way to describe what's about to happen."

"Keira, you realize I was standing next to you all o' last year, right? Combat drops, the mountain Hive—"

"This isn't going to be like that," she said, as Solomon hooked a cable to Eden's rig. He jerked on the webbing, ensuring a solid hold—he'd hooked himself to her.

"*What*...are you doing?" Eden asked, more concerned than offended.

Keira sauntered over to Solomon, pulling from her pack a large cable encased in bunched up nylon. At the end, a carabiner hefty enough to beat someone to death. She slipped it through the drop hitch on Solomon's rig.

They were tethered together, all three. The Howler was going to grab one of them...and by extension, all of them.

Eden put the dots together all at once. "The Howler isn't even going to stop, is it?"

"It's going to slow down," Solomon said, with a diabolical look in his eye.

Oh, that's just great. She was better off in the Hospital. If the Howler whipped by too fast, no amount of elastic cable was going to fix the G-force trauma. For a brief period, they'd be dangling in space, where any number of bad things could happen. And if the Howler had to take a high-G turn—something that was entirely possible— they'd be turned into raspberry jam on the end of a fishing line.

Keira planted a stake in the street, extending out a pole with their line on it. Affixed at the end would've been an IR tracker so the Howler could see them.

The Howler would be swooping in a mere twelve feet off the ground. In the dark.

"*Fra tow ni laska*," Eden muttered. "When?"

Keira shook her head. "If I tell you, you'll just tense up."

"If you don't tell me, I'll just *be* tense."

"Tense up and you'll snap your neck," Solomon warned.

"See? This—*this* is why I never let you two plan *anything*."

It was past her before she knew it had been approaching. The silent Howler slid by overhead, the jet wash billowing her hair. A drop bar six feet wide snagged the stake-line.

And they were airborne, three people tied together like a bundle of weeds.

The bird's eye view of the City was worse than the ground. The smoke occluded vision, hid entire swaths of the devastation from sight. What had once been a gleaming city of glass towers and industrial blocks had been chipped away. The chief of the glass towers at the center of town—the Gagarin building—had been snapped at his waist, tipping over and crumbling into the city below. The severed wrist stuck in the sky, smoldering with a light glow.

Two crashed landing craft had cratered the surrounding areas, dirt piling up under their bellies to bury what structures they hadn't crushed. The hyper loop that ran the circumference of the City had snapped, the train inside having spilled out like a mechanical intestine.

Then suddenly, the belly of the Howler closed around her, sealing off the smoke and blood. And she was greeted by Nora's sweet face. Blood trickled down no less than three separate scrapes to her head. That crooked nose, that cropped hair and gregarious smile—broadened by an overbite. "You think I was going to leave *you* behind?"

Eden felt like her whole body just wanted to hug this person. She wrapped both arms around Nora and squeezed tight. "Where have you been?" Eden begged quietly into her shoulder.

"With these two maniacs, mostly," Nora said, giving Solomon a shoulder punch. "Ready to get outta here?"

Eden slackened, leaning against the wall of the Howler. "Just us?"

"Those are the orders." Something in Nora's eyes, a distance.

Aaron. He'd sent them in for her and her alone. Nobody else. Not Julius, not the civilians, or even more soldiers. Her.

"I'm going to kill him," she whispered.

"Kill him when you see him," the disgruntled voice of the pilot called back to them. The woman leaned back and Eden caught a glance at a single glowing red eye socketed in her head. "Strap in tight, we're going for the hard deck and there will be some chop. Keeper, take point. I'll walk you all the way home."

Eden hitched herself to a pick point overhead and tightened the line. Nora reached over and tied another line from the floor to Eden's belt, cinching it tight. There was just enough flex in both cables to prevent her from bouncing around the cabin, but not enough to let her move freely—the only thing that could object now was her center of gravity. Eden stooped to Nora's waist, returning the favor.

"Three, two, break-break-break!" the pilot ordered, and the Howler lurched downward. The cables stretched and everyone came off their feet—but their anchors kept them fixed at their places in the cabin.

The craft jumbled left and right. Nora peered out the portside window, watching the world whip past, but all Eden could go off of was Nora's expression. And Nora was almost too expressive to accurately read: eyebrows up, eyes wide, and jaw squeezed tight, blood vessels popping in her neck.

There were hordes of tiny robots with their rending claws; there was infantry with their tether ballistas; the air assault UAVs controlling the skies; and that's avoiding mention of the buildings themselves and any tricks the Oskies hadn't yet shown off.

The Howler was threading several needles in a row—and they only got one shot at it.

The silence was the worst part. The grunts and labored breathing were all she could hear. She'd give anything for a sign of how they were doing.

But she didn't want to give the entire portside of the ship. The whole bulkhead sheared off as a laser cut down the length. A momentary flash of fire, and Eden could see the entire battle below. They were out over the Hammer Fields—and falling fast.

"Kilo Two One: we're hit and going down!" the pilot barked into her radio.

"Keira!" Eden had never heard Solomon's voice hit that register before, as he reached out for Keira's hand.

"Oh, you're all going to hate this part," the pilot said, as she fiddled with switches.

She could feel as the Howler started to spin: thrust was coming from only one side of the craft. There was nothing their intrepid pilot could do about physics.

Suddenly the craft lurched again, as airbrakes opened on the hull. She had to slow their descent.

"Drop prep!"

...She wouldn't. In an uncontrolled spin over the open Fields, she wanted to send the Capitals hurtling out of the belly of the craft?

They could end up underneath it, or worse, just plain whipped into the ground!

She had to. Inside, they'd be crushed as the big fat bird flopped onto the deck. A cable drop wasn't a good option; but there wasn't a good option available.

"Oh, boy." Keira drew her quick knife from its sheath and dragged it across her stability line. Immediately, she came off the ground, lifted by the centrifuge they were ironically calling an aircraft. Solomon did the same.

Nora couldn't reach hers. She was on the wrong side of the spin, her arms pinned to her side.

Eden drew her quick knife—and fumbled it, the blade sailing past Keira and out into the Fields. Dammit!

Keira and Solomon looked on in a mixture of horror and elation. The two psychos were likely enjoying every second of this exhilarating tumble-dry, with only a minor understanding that they might not survive it—or perhaps, that was acceptance?

Eden reached over, and snagged Nora's quick knife from her rig, ripping it from its sheath. She slashed Nora's retention line, and nearly received her friend's boot to the face as a thank you.

Now to her own.

"Drop safe!" the pilot called out.

Eden cut the line. Just as the floor dropped out from under her. The line spooled and the horizon appeared under her boots. 'Below' them was the skyline of Vanguard, its smoky trails high in the sky and the sun just beginning to paint the side of the cloudy supercell that masked its heights. Swirls of vehicles spun around the tallest towers, like dark halos.

As the Howler spun in for the ground, they trailed out of its belly further and further. Normally, the sensors would read distance to ground and let them go just before.

Now...who knew?

The grassy field rose up to introduce itself. Hello, my name is thirty percent quartzite and seventy percent fine sandy loam.

What's your name? I don't care. I'm going to punch you in the face.

And the cable let go. For the briefest moment, Eden felt suspended on a cloud. Then the ground blurred into a palette of earthy browns and grays, a hint of golden grass. Then nothing but darkness...

But she could hear the Howler catch flame.

CHAPTER
SIXTEEN
KEEPER

HE'D WATCHED Aisling's Howler go in. He'd seen it flop onto its side, cutting a trough in the ground, burying its nose in the soft Earth. The CAP strafed its helpless frame, lancing it with red until something within went critical in a hideous fireball.

Aisling. Prophet.

His Howler was the only one that made it back, and he barely did that. He had to wait for the medics to tend to Anatoly before he could crawl out of the cockpit. The medical team took up nearly the entire troop bay, with their gurney and diagnostic gear. The doctor, old enough to remember the first human satellites, spoke to everyone but his patient, directing others with a kind of staid spoken word poetry.

It was a full five minutes before they got Anatoly onto the gurney and out of the Howler. Kipling never left his side.

Keeper swung out of his seat and into the vacated bay. Spent saline bags and tubing lay on the floor, stained with spots of blood. A smear of black against the back wall where Anatoly fell, his carbon-scored arm leaving flecks of ash behind.

Back home, they'd be measuring the big guy for an augment right now, talking up the various modifications he could select with his military health plan. Three months, maybe six, and he'd be able to bend steel or drive a cruiser with his mind.

Out here...at least he had Kipling with him. Keeper was alone now.

And why was that? Because they got orders, turn around, go back. The orders...who gave the orders around here?

Keeper barely noticed the divots and craters in his craft: most of the front end of it had been scorched, sliced, and chunked. Someone was spraying it down with fire-retardant foam. They jacked it onto a wheel bay and tugged it off the plateau under the cover of the mountain's outcropping.

"What did you *do* to her?" an engineer exclaimed, hands thrown up in despair, but a colleague threw a hand over his shoulder and guided him out of Keeper's way, lest a teenage jockey rearrange his teeth.

Whatever possession this grease monkey had over the potato, and whatever Keeper's emotional state, this was not a place to linger. The plateau was hardly a safe landing zone, fully exposed to the ire of an orbital strike, but it was also hidden in the mountain's dense cloud bank. Given enough time or enough ordinance, they could absolutely blanket the resistance stronghold, but they'd have to be looking for it.

And right now, their attention was on the City.

Keeper stomped across the plateau. Bloodthirsty. Hunting. This was all *his* fault!

"Where is he?!" Keeper roared.

Aaron gave the order. The Legatus. The self-made Messiah of a 'peaceful' revolution who selfishly sent the woman he—

"AARON!" Keeper bellowed, as he stomped around the landing pad. "Where are you?!"

The deck chief pointed to the tunnels, down into the belly of the mountain and the Jergad Hive. He was quite eager to send the angry voice away from his team. They had enough to do cutting away the damaged panels without him breathing fire down their necks.

Keeper marched into the mountain. Someone had strung work

lights down the whole length, different staging areas set up to provide refreshment and debrief for those returning. Quartermasters took inventory of crates. Medical triaged the wounded.

Everyone paused and hushed up as Keeper stalked past.

"Keeper..." A voice croaked. Anatoly reached up with his one remaining arm, pawing at Keeper's jumpsuit. Keeper paused, barely recognizing the raspy voice. He already had more tubes in him than Keeper thought possible.

Two doctors tended to the burn scar, while a third struggled with a clipboard, arranged sheets of paper. He struggled with the physical, leafing through to find something and show whatever he wrote to his colleague. The Doctor sneered. "Oh, I can't read this! Do you have a digital?"

"Get me an AutoDoc up here!"

"We only have the one and it's—"

"Of *course* it is!"

Kipling surged past Keeper and grabbed on to Anatoly's extended hand, like a drowning man in the ocean clinging to driftwood. He hushed his friend. "You got us home, soldier, all the way home. You're safe now."

But Anatoly's eyes never left Keeper: big, watery, pleading eyes. Who did he think Keeper was? Did he somehow think Keeper could help right now? He couldn't help anyone. He should be asking for Legatus—maybe he could 'cure' him of his amputation.

Aaron had sent them back in. For what? For one person? Now, they're all gone.

Anatoly had been his fault. Prophet had been his fault. But Aisling—

He paused for a second, his mind lingering on the image of Prophet's flaming wreckage collapsing into the City, of Anatoly's scored arm. His fault. If Anatoly hadn't been hurt, Prophet wouldn't have had to jump in. If Prophet hadn't been...then maybe Aisling wouldn't have been the....

No. Don't think like that. It wasn't his fault. It was Aaron. Nobody would even be here if not for him!

He picked up his pace again, ignoring the tears free-flowing down his face.

"Aaron!"

A hand reached out and pinned him against the wall, his helmet the only thing saving him from a good concussion against the basalt. He felt the porous stone compressing behind him, bits of it crumbling onto his shoulders.

Gunnery Sergeant Bray was instantly in his face, a cold whisper. "Get yourself under control, Lieutenant."

It took Keeper a half-second to recognize who was in front of him, and when he did, he hocked a big wad of spit into the Gunny's face.

This was clearly not a new experience for him, as the Sergeant didn't even flinch. "Want to give that another go, put some gusto behind it?"

"He sent her back out there!"

"Those were the orders—"

"He sent her back! And now she's gone."

Bray had a lot he wanted to say back, but he said very little. "Sometimes, that's the way it goes."

"Is that all you got?" Keeper hissed. "'Sometimes, that's the way it!—'"

"Yeah." Something in Bray's stare, a softness in his raised brow, despite the stiff grip on Keeper's shoulder. Strong and firm, almost paternal. He wasn't going to let Keeper go, but he wasn't holding him there out of spite or anger.

Keeper pushed back, but Bray's hold was iron. And like water on rock, Keeper melted, sagging against the wall of the tunnel. He shivered, sniffing away the tears. "She had plans, y'know?"

Bray looked up the tunnel, toward the retinue of grunts getting their wounds checked and tended, his eyes catching on Anatoly's shoulder cap and Kipling's unflinching devotion. "They all do. Every single one of 'em."

"You?"

"Nah," Gunny dismissed. "My plan is helpin' kids like you keep yours. And she died...trying to do the same thing: help others."

"She was ordered to."

"You've lost people before, yeah?"

Keeper's lip curled, but he couldn't deny it. He still remembered their names, though he had long forgotten their faces. Brognan went up like a cloud of vapor over Londinium during the Raids; Siobhan went down in a jungle and was never found; Chindasa took an Image Recog missile right up his tail pipe—Keeper had dusted the trigger hand that had done the deed: some pirate slaver with a taste for robotics.

Had they all had plans for after? Or had they even thought that far ahead? Aisling had.

"You can't bring 'em back," Bray said. "But you *can* help the people who are still here."

"...She had plans," Keeper said, weakly.

"You'll have to tell me about 'em some time." Bray pulled him off the wall and Keeper damn near slumped into the small man's shoulder. Bray propped him up and shoved him down the hall. "I'm buyin'."

CHAPTER
SEVENTEEN
AARON

"THEY'VE CLOSED THEIR FLANK," Graccus urged. "There's nothing more to be gained."

Bray marched up around behind him, snorting at the statement. "For the amount of hot air in you, it's a wonder you don't just combust. Three companies are trapped in there."

"And that's awful, but that's all we can do. There's nothing else. They have the air, the ground—the City and the Wall."

"*You* told us to give those up. Why don't you share your vaunted combat expertise, spook? Or do they teach nothin' but clever thinking up in that fancy academy of yours?"

Bray was always an acerbic old leather boot, but this had a bit more caustic burn in it than usual. Bray was a full foot and a half shorter than the augmented agent, but Aaron never would've guessed that if he recalled this conversation later. Gunny was bluster and power, able to break down a man twice his size with words and emotion alone. As well he should be able to, being a drill instructor at heart.

And yet, Aaron could tell there was something else itching his back today, a little extra gas in the tank. Bray wanted a fight and Graccus was obliging him.

Aaron let them have at it. Two Imperial veterans were going to have very fixed opinions of battle tactics. This was just a military edition of speed dating—they'd end up loving each other or killing each other.

Instead, Aaron was listening to the radio reports. It was like trying to decipher a riddle. People would say where they were, but not what they were doing; they would say what they were doing but not who with. He felt like a kid with a flashlight, whipping it around his bedroom late at night, looking for ominous moving shadows.

And then he saw one, a figure walking past, drifting at the edge of sight behind Bray's head. But nobody was walking. Everyone was rooted to their stations, consuming the same horror he was. Aaron first looked to see if a screen had lit up or a fixture had been bumped. But all of the light sources were static.

It was Her. It had to be. The Queen.

"I don't know how it's done up in Intelligence," Bray snarled, "but when somebody takes a swing at me—"

"You unhinge your jaw and swallow him whole?"

"Shut up," Aaron cut him off.

"What?!" Bray asked, more than ready to add another to his body count.

"I said, shut up." Aaron wasn't really in the room with them anymore, his mind wandering. If the Queen was here..."How many are trapped?"

"Three hundred and fifty." Bray might not have said it, but there was an inflected 'sir' at the end of his words, and it made Aaron's stomach do flips.

Graccus was a bit softer. "And there's nothing more we can do, not right now."

No. There might be one thing.

Aaron stepped away from the base camp set against the cavern wall, and craned his neck to look up to the pillars—the seat of the Queen high above.

She wasn't really here. She wasn't really 'anywhere.' So maybe...

"You called us, *ak'thun?*" That disconcerting multi-voice whispered into his ear.

Aaron turned towards it, only seeing more shadows retreating from his gaze. He turned again, and another shadow flitted away out of the corner of his eye. He was in full view of the base camp of technicians and strategists, Bray and Graccus, Talania and Whitby and the Statesmen.

What this had to look like...

"Where are you?" he demanded of the empty air.

Whitby cocked his head and leered at Talania, who pursed her lips. If she hadn't seen the Queen with her own two eyes, she might be considering what brand of straitjacket to fit for him.

"Where are you?" he repeated, loud enough for his words to echo and bounce back to him.

She answered, whispers echoing from distant corners. "We did not want to fight you. Your people...they are frightened."

"We didn't...I didn't want to come here, but..." He didn't have a choice. They'd die out in the Fields.

"There's always a choice, *ak'thun.*"

Aaron withered, feeling her pressure behind his eyes and on the bridge of his nose and pulling at his eyes. "I need my friends. I can't do this without them."

The shadows flickered at the edge of sight, black flames cast against the stonework. He felt some invisible hand brush against his cheek, cup his face, and let him lean into its warmth. "We see you. As you once saw us."

A shape emerged from the shadows—Jensen, but eyes a radiant solid blue. Aaron's knees nearly buckled at the sight. Tall and broad to support a thousand muscles, pristine shaved head and a smile that could light up the night.

But this wasn't him. Jensen was dead, beaten bloody, Riley's knife in his chest. And his smile, the permanent fixture with brilliant white teeth, had long since frozen.

This Jensen...did not smile at all.

The Queen lilted to one side, awkward as ever on human feet.

"You brought your people to our home," she said with Jensen's voice. "You brought them seeking refuge, sanctuary. But you bring fire and hate."

Aaron blinked away the tears at the corners of his eyes. He couldn't breathe, couldn't speak. Jensen's voice, that trumpet call, brought a thousand happy memories—all poisoned by the last of them.

Of course. She was using faces from his mind to communicate. She selected Jensen with deliberate intent. She wanted that kinship. And she wanted him on his heels.

The Queen circled him. "Now what would you ask of us?"

Now? He wasn't some debtor asking for another loan! She was the one who begged him for help!

"I've got almost four hundred people trapped," Aaron whispered. "Help me get them out."

She came back into view—quietly shifting to sport Whitby's silver-haired grimace. The stare was withering, like she was growing and he was shrinking, smaller and smaller with each passing second, driving him down into the stone. "And where does it end, *ak'thun*?"

"What do you want?"

The Queen's image shimmered, ripples on water. Disturbance. "Blood shed only sours the ground—"

"Stop...with the slam poetry reading, and tell me what you want," Aaron demanded.

She stepped away from him, considering him for a long moment. There was a wistfulness to it, like nostalgia gone sour. "We want to survive. Just as you do."

"My friends fought for you—"

"They fought for *you*—"

"What the *fuck* is the difference anymore?!" Aaron snapped. "I mean—you, me? We're not on different teams! Every second you stand aside, you prove..."

She proved Riley right. But he couldn't bring himself to say it.

He paused for a second, shaking his head. "Maybe I shouldn't have helped you. Maybe you should've killed me when you had the chance."

He heard a gasp from the assembly behind him, some middle manager or technician witnessing his messiah commit blasphemy. They could all hear him melting down at a ghost they couldn't see. Was this who they were following?

He owed these people a leader. All they had was a teenage office drone with an unnatural string of luck.

Talania leaned forward, ready to jump in. She was the only one that knew what was happening, that knew he wasn't crazy.

Aaron held his ground. "Help me. Not because of what I can do for you, but because of what I already *did*." He straightened his shoulders. "It's what family does."

The Queen considered him. He wished then he could read her alien features. Even wearing a human face, she was stilted and flat.

Whitby stood up from the edge of the cavern. "Am I the only one seeing this? We're really going to lose our homes over *this*?!"

Behind him, on the wall—a single glittering blue slit, tilting, turning in the dark. The ton and a half of leather and blades made all the sound of a pair of pants rubbing against each other, as the plates of its hide shifted and slid. Aaron almost chuckled as Scar silently eased off the wall, before snorting a blast of hot air up Whitby's back.

Whitby froze, mouth agape and finger up, ready to begin some political diatribe of the century. He dared not turn, as Scar's bifurcated mandible rested on his shoulder, a chitter coming from somewhere deep in its gullet.

Dozens of Jergad emerged from the Walls of the cavern—their mottled hides indistinguishable from the rock.

They had never left at all. They had hidden. Aaron supposed that was one way to avoid conflict.

He turned back to the queen, now sporting Jensen's big grin again. Aaron waved his finger around. "How long were they going to keep that up?"

"The real question you should ask," the Queen started with a devilish twist to the corner of her lip, "is how else this conversation could have ended?"

"You keep saying you don't have a sense of humor but..."

"Whatever do you mean?"

Aaron turned back to Bray and Graccus. Graccus couldn't hide his shifting eyes and the tension in his shoulders. He was debating if he could melt away into the shadows, or if the shadows would swallow him whole.

But Bray's grin could've cracked his face in half. He clapped a hand against Graccus's narrow shoulder. "How's that for clever thinkin', spook?" Bray grabbed the radio. "All hands, hold your positions and stand by for extract. Cavalry's comin'!"

CHAPTER
EIGHTEEN
EDEN

THE HOWLER BURNED, a scrap heap with wildfires lit around its perimeter like braziers at a memorial site. But the flames were dwarfed by the rising sun, rising up over the distant mountain peaks. The sky lit up like a watercolor painting, with streaks of red and purple stretching high overhead.

Eden shook her head, abrasive dust and dirt in every crevice. She flexed her fingers and toes—first good sign. No spinal injury. But her shoulder was another matter, burning when she tried to lift her left arm.

She had landed on it before her tumble. It was in its socket, but probably had some soft tissue damage. Great.

A flat hunk of metal laid atop her legs, pinning her down: an armor plate from the Howler that had sheared off on impact. She pushed and tugged and pulled, but it would not budge.

Nora got up, dusting herself off. Glad to see she was okay; she was one big ball of scar tissue anyway.

"Nora!" Eden croaked, surprised by how weak and dry her words sounded. Maybe she'd inhaled particulate or smoke? No, she definitely had—immediately falling into a coughing fit.

Nora darted over, inching her fingers under the debris pinning

Eden down. A quick count and some back strain later, they were able to wriggle Eden free.

"We're alive," Nora huffed with a kind of sick glee in her voice.

Eden shook her head. "We shouldn't be...after *that*? Keira! Solomon?"

"Both here!" A big meaty hand waved in the air, popping out from behind a dirt crater—Keira's fall from the Howler had carved a scar in the ground, but she seemed otherwise fine. Adrenaline was keeping her going for now. And she didn't sound alarmed, so Solomon had to be okay as well.

If Solomon had been hurt, Keira would've walked back into that city and butchered the entire battalion herself.

"The pilot get out?" Nora asked.

"I didn't see—"

A thick metal stake slammed into the ground a foot away from Eden's leg, like a three-foot tall javelin. A croquet ball on the tail end waggled in the air as the shaft flexed to-and-fro from the impact. The lawn dart cracked open along the midline of the ball, revealing a glass lens underneath.

Eden knew a weapon when she saw one.

Nora dove at Eden, pulling her down and behind the Howler's debris. The ball spat hot light, a discus of plasma at waist height, like a human weed whacker. When the energy flickered and petered out, the ball exploded—embedding superheated metal shards into their cover.

One piece stuck through next to Eden's head.

"Mortars!" Keira shouted from her foxhole.

Three more landed around the crash site, the plasma cutters flaying ugly scars in its hide and the explosions lighting brand new fires.

"Where's the pilot?" Eden asked.

Nora shook her head, her mind already two steps ahead. "You're in no condition."

"Nobody is!" Eden snapped.

Keira peeked her head up from her foxhole—and found several shots come streaking past her head. She dipped back down.

And suddenly, she punched her fist right through the side of her dirt hillock. She jammed her gun barrel through the opening and cracked off a few rounds at whatever soldiers had her pinned down.

"Go!" Keira shouted. "We got this!"

Eden pictured the inside of the Howler, the crumpled troop bay and the small hatch to get into the cockpit. The Howler was tilted on its bad side, the remaining wing reaching high in the air. The belly was still open, but on the far side of the wreck.

Nora pulled her rifle close. "You get to her, I'll cover you. On three."

Eden counted in her head, rocking back and forth. And they heaved the metal bulkhead off of them!

Nora shouldered the rifle and cracked off two choice shots. Eden didn't see what she was shooting at, didn't stop to see if they hit anything. She just ran, her bad arm cradled against her gut.

Don't look. Run. Just run. There's a patient that needs you. She's been in a crash, single vehicle, tri-axial tumble. Likely compressed spine, concussion. Her ribs might be crushed by her harness.

A bullet cracked past her ear, and she slipped to the ground. She might not have cover, but she'd be harder to hit flush against the ground. She inched along, worming towards the wreckage, picking her way around the flames.

More snaps as gunfire ripped the air around her, thudding against the loose dirt and gonging off the hull of the Howler's side. She felt flecks of metal scrape her cheek. It burned like a cattle brand.

The mortars had stopped. That meant there were people nearby they didn't want to hit by accident—the Imperial army was coming in close to inspect its kill.

She heard Keira's war cry, a bestial collection of epithets boiled down into a simple roar. It was soon dwarfed by the reports of her rifle, issuing declarations of its own.

Eden slid safely around the backside of the Howler. The drop had been the right answer—the bay was a third of its previous size, flattened against the ground. A fire blazed against the far corner, the heat billowing past her and searing her face. Had they stayed in the Howler, everyone inside would've been smashed into putty, and the ones that weren't, would've baked in their restraints.

But there was still enough room for her to wiggle inside.

She called out, "Pilot!"

No response by the crackling flames and the gunfire outside.

Don't leave. She needs a doctor.

Eden clambered inside. "Lieutenant?"

She made her way toward the cockpit, the tiny hatch compressed into an oval. Smoke burned her eyes and the heat was overwhelming, her skin aching.

She could make out a slumped shoulder through the hatch.

Eden made her way over—and the shape swung about, presenting a pistol. Blood leaked from her ocular implant and up along her scalp. The implant itself had gone dark, a black hole in her head. Her breathing was ragged and hitched.

The pistol shook in her hand.

"Save your shots," Eden said. "You only get so many and we're going to need every single one."

The pilot nodded, lowering the pistol.

The hull bonged as someone pounded on it from outside. Keira's voice: "Move it or lose it, Doc!"

Eden looked into the pilot's good eye. "What's your name?"

"...Aisling."

"Aisling," Eden murmured. "Can you walk?"

The pilot turned back to her console, checking on something. "I don't know. My back feels *really* weird."

"Pins and needles?"

Aisling shivered. "You know how it feels when you get water in your ear?"

Eden nodded. Aisling might not have broken her back, but she might yet still. She'd slipped a disc and the nerves were pinched. Any attempt to move her might cause permanent damage.

But if they stuck around, they'd all get shot or worse.

Eden reached in and plucked the pistol from Aisling's hands. Pocketing it, she went to work on Aisling's harness. It was stuck fast and she almost had to peel it off the pilot's uniform. The G-suit had done a remarkable job of keeping Aisling conscious, but it wasn't a crash kit—that harness had broken too many bones to count right now.

She dug in her kit and fished out a hypo. "You're going to hate this."

The pilot hadn't noticed the needle yet. "Really? I've been loving this day spa so far." Eden slammed the needle into Aisling's neck and dumped the entire painkiller dose in under a second. "*OW!*"

"Count to ten," Eden told her.

The pilot was skeptical. "Why?"

"Lieutenant, we're being shot at and your back is *jacked* up! Count to ten."

The pilot chuckled, the painkiller already taking effect. "I love me a woman who takes charge..."

Nora called out. "Eden, get goin' or get left."

Understood.

Eden reached into the cockpit and looped the arm under Aisling's. Aisling immediately shrieked in pain, but Eden couldn't stop now. If she thought it was bad now, she should have done this *without* the painkiller!

They emerged from the Howler's belly, to find Nora, Keira, and Solomon having followed Eden's example and taken cover under the crashed ship.

Eden couldn't see clearly, but there was a lot of movement in the shrapnel field around them.

Aisling might have been crying from the pain and delirious from the meds, but she was still alarmingly focused. "What's the plan?"

"Run until they stop chasing," Nora said as she cycled in a fresh magazine on her rifle. Eden noticed the empty pouches on Nora's vest: that was her last one.

The gunfire had settled, but the chatter could be heard as the Imperials shouted to one another. They were closing in.

Keira grabbed Solomon, pressing her forehead to his. They smiled, heavy heated breaths. Goodbye, see you on the other side, save me a drink, such feasts to be had.

They were right. No one was getting away.

Eden looked at Aisling. "I tried."

Aisling nodded. "So did I."

Eden laid the pilot down against the hull, and pressed the pistol back into her hand. "Any Imps come around the backside? One to the head, one to the heart."

Aisling smiled, a wistful want for memories she hadn't yet seen. She liked this Capital Doctor; too bad they'd met on the last day.

"Capitals, huddle up!"

Nora gathered everyone's eyes with her own, pulling them in for a big speech, but she had only a few words. "Wouldn't have it any other way. I love you guys."

Keira wrapped one big palm on the back of Nora's head, fingers gripping the short fuzz of the undercut. "The only way I'd want it."

Solomon set his empty rifle down, drawing his sidearm and quick knife. He scraped the edge along his cheek, checking the edge against his stubble. "I rode it with the best."

They all looked at Eden. What pithy words did she have, a fine summary of all the memories and the places she'd been? They greeted their inevitability with an ease, a readiness, or at least an acceptance.

She didn't have any. She wasn't ready. She had nothing.

Nora shouldered her rifle, and nodded to the others. No more words to say. They'd say them all later.

Keira took a big breath through her nose and blew it out her mouth, meditative.

And then, Solomon lunged out from behind the Howler—finding

an Imperial officer right close. He plunged his quick knife into the man's chest and tumbled with him to the ground.

Keira spun around, plugging two shots into the Imperials that were too busy trying to line up shots on Solomon. Nora swung wide, laying down fire on whatever else was beyond. Eden followed close behind.

The Imperials hadn't made the mistake of underestimating the Capitals. There were at least two dozen Regulars using the Howler's dirt scar as makeshift cover. Backing them up—an Oskie in Warcom, looming over all with his absurd complement of weapons.

They weren't just here to salvage—they were here to double-tap the dead bird.

Keira saw this as a glorious challenge, aiming straight for the Oskie—the shots glanced off the personal shield, a rainbow flickering in the morning sun. The Oskie almost seemed charmed by the attempt, by the fire in her eyes, by the distilled rage on display. He tilted his head back, looking down his nose at this cute little creature standing up to him.

Eden could see two vicious scars on his throat that dragged up to his cheek: old, possibly even from childhood. And he would delight in sharing that pain. He raised a big metal hand...

Solomon looked up from his kill just in time to see Keira cut in half by a narrow red beam, from shoulder to hip. Solomon didn't shout, he didn't cry. But whatever human light was in his eyes left him like a gasp of smoke.

Solomon lifted the dead Imperial officer as a shield, shooting out what remained of his pistol at the line of Regulars. He danced around the man's body, peeking out from different sides as the Regulars struggled to find where he'd emerge next.

One Regular had enough and simply shot center mass, punching a hole clean through the meat shield and into Solomon's gut.

Solomon didn't even blink. He palmed his quick knife and hurled it at the offending shooter, a wild and passionate throw. The blade sank into the Imperial's throat, the tip poking out the back and tilting the officer's helmet at a jaunty angle.

The Oskie pursed his lips, impressed by the throw. He kicked the gurgling man aside, lest the speared Regular fall on his exosuit and sully it with blood.

What was that demigod waiting for? It was almost a taunt, begging them to hit first so he could respond with excessive cruelty.

Out of weapons, Solomon flopped back behind his cover, both hands clutching the half inch hole in his stomach.

It was just then that Eden noticed Keira's torso, a spasm in the chest as she struggled to breathe. She was still alive, asphyxiating. Eden could only hope that shock had long since robbed Keira of awareness.

Eden felt her heart float up and out of her chest, taking with it whatever strength she had left in her feet. She collapsed, dropping behind cover next to Nora.

The spring-loaded fighter instantly noticed Eden's slackening form. "Eden! You hit?"

She couldn't answer. They should surrender. They should just give up. What was the point? They'd fight and the Imps would come back ten times as hard. The people she loved would still die.

Eden shook her head, listless and weak. "I'm sorry, Nora."

Nora instantly knew why. "Ain't nothing to be sorry for, girl. Nothin' at all."

A flush of dirt went into the air, almost six feet high. Shouts of confusion and fear. Surprise, horror, pain.

Eden's eyes narrowed. There was a collective tone in the Imperial voices that almost shot her back in time. She remembered it so clearly. Claws and teeth, reaching up from the dirt, pulling, gnashing, rending—friends disappearing into the hard earth like the world itself was hungry.

She looked at the ground, watching the pebbles dance. Rolling thunder.

"They're here."

The Jergad sprung from the ground, a horde of hateful blades and gnashing teeth. The Colonists had Thumpers to collapse tunnels, mounted Repeaters to blast the main hordes, and hovering vehicles to avoid traps.

But the Imperials brought infantry, purpose made to quash human resistance. Half of them were bloody mulch in less than five seconds.

The Oskie backpedaled away, every weapon in his arsenal sounding off—plasma cutter, flame thrower, Gauss cannons. He transferred from target to target, piling up the dead Jergad as he tried to keep the chaos in front of him.

But the beasts had figured who the real threat was on this field. Even as he cut them down like grass, they simply widened their net, circling him up. It was what they did best. Surprise, rush hard, and overwhelm a superior opponent.

"Come on!" Nora shouted, already waist deep in a Jergad tunnel. She waved both arms in the air.

Eden looked over at Solomon, bleeding from the gut. She jerked her head toward the hole in the ground. "Go!"

Solomon raised his head, fighting the weight that had been draped about his shoulders. His eyes were hollow and dark.

Eden wasn't having any of it. "You can kill more of them later. But right now, in you go!"

He bared his teeth, animalistic, rabid. But he moved for the tunnel.

Eden ran for the Howler. The wounded pilot would never escape on her own.

More mortars rained in, the spinning lasers and popping grenades stunning the Jergad assault—the Oskie had called in some indirect fire.

Eden picked her way through the airborne minefield, ducking and weaving her way to Aisling's side.

"You can't carry me," Aisling gasped.

"I've carried bigger, going farther." Eden slung the pilot over her good arm, trying her best to ignore Aisling's agonized screams. She stood up, lifting the girl into the air.

Just like her Capital qualifier. Lift someone bigger, pace yourself, and just keep going. Bray trained them for this moment—though she doubted he meant to be this literal about it.

Nora and Solomon watched helplessly from the tunnel, no more weapons or aid to offer. The Oskie might be occupied, but there was a field full of live ordinance she had to navigate with a wounded pilot draped across her own wounded shoulder.

She ran, darts falling all around her, each throwing out a few feet of focused laser hatred at waist height. A thousand shards of metal flying after each explosion.

Nora shouted encouragements from the hole. She was almost there...

A metal fragment slipped into Eden's leg. She felt the blood spit into the air. And she tumbled forward.

———

When she opened her eyes, she was in the tunnel. She either fell ten meters forward, or someone was crazy enough to come get her.

Solomon tended to Aisling, giving her a sip of water. Nora sported a fresh scratch to her pocked face, blood leaking down her nose and to the corner of her mouth. She managed to gasp out two words, "You're welcome."

CHAPTER
NINETEEN
DECKARD

HE HAD ORDERED the City taken. He had ordered passive ROE, neutralize and disarm tactics, preservation of infrastructure.

Deckard awoke to find nothing short of a massacre. Only the Oskies stuck to the rules of engagement, firing when fired upon. Once the first landing craft was shot down, the Regulars engaged without discretion and use of the Locust riot control was trusted to field commanders; they deployed the machines with glee.

They were supposed to be liberators, a judicious and swift hand swooping down to lift the problems away. The return of the generous Empire's hand. Instead...

Deckard squinted at the projection on his wall. It might have been a hologram, but it felt like someone had dropped his cabin onto the planet's surface and taken one entire wall out for his convenience.

He saw the enormous concrete palisade spanning three stories high, over a foot thick and lined with a corrosive wire fringe. Platforms mounted on a track roved the circumference, the guard towers themselves moving as needed along a track. A steel gate stood wide, two Oskies in Warcom watching as colonists and Capitals funneled inside.

A prison camp.

The warden—a man so sprightly and positive, he was likely sculpted from candy glass—bubbled through his presentation. His sunny disposition unnerved Deckard, seeing as he was chatting to a floating camera sphere about his brand-new detainment facility.

"We were operational in two hours," the warden said, quite proud of breaking a very morbid record. His voice crackled a bit with radio interference. "We were able to reinforce existing facilities and restore electric, and we're working on some sewage facilities."

Deckard swiped his hand in the air, spinning the camera sphere to look toward the tailings dam—the remnants of the mining operation that once was the center of Vanguard's industry. Capitals had once worked these Pits. Now, Imperial citizens were being shuffled off to camp next to the toxic fumes.

This was supposed to be routine. This was supposed to be a blitz, not an occupation. Deckard massaged the bridge of his nose. "Resistance?"

The warden shrugged with a dopey grin, unable to read Deckard's sour body language through the featureless drone. "Nothing unusual. Y'know, they see the walls, the fencing, the tower guard, they get understandably tense. But all in all, they've been pliant."

Pliant.

A prison camp. Barricades, deadly fumes, the Imperial Orchid flying high, a demand for bended knee at the end of a gun barrel. This was a show of force, of cruelty.

By design; just not his design.

Deckard knew a concentration camp when he saw one.

"Thank you, warden, that'll be all for now." Deckard pinched the window shut, the entire image lifting off the wall with his fingers and winking out of existence. It was like he opened a digital curtain, revealing the ship models, medals, and battle trophies on the shelves behind it. A scale model of his first command, a Naval cutter ship called the *Tempest*; a shard of rotten wood with a brass placard. Two words: '*Zu gloriam.*'

A picture of his wife and son, formal attire and soft brown eyes staring back at him with warm smiles. They had been visiting the Academie Pacem. He'd graduate by the time Deckard returned: destined for Court, or the Ministry of Justice. He always liked the idea of being a Cleric, out solving crimes and catching bad guys.

If they knew...

They'd never scold him, either way. His son hadn't said a word to him in four years. Deckard had said nothing when he should've said something, and now he was only a father legally.

"Commandant?" Deckard asked, calling up the ship's AI with a chime. "Who authorized this action?"

The pleasant and neutral voice responded with an easy grace. "Define the action in question?"

"Deployment of the Engineering Unit to Vanguard City Center."

A breath's amount of time as the AI culled the relevant data. "At this time, records show Lieutenant Wolcott was the Officer of the Deck."

Wolcott was too obedient to leap to prison camp on his own. This was the Minister's doing. He'd coerced a young officer into committing a war crime.

Deckard was going to reach down that old tyrant's throat and pull out his vocal chords to string his violin.

But first. "And where is Lieutenant Wolcott right now?"

"The lieutenant retired to his quarters for confidential memorandum."

And there was all the confirmation Deckard needed. Caldwell.

Deckard had underestimated exactly how hands-on the Minister wanted to be. But of course, the Minister would undermine Deckard through a proxy rather than come out here personally. That would mean he could still insulate himself from responsibility, moral or otherwise.

"Please inform the lieutenant I'm on my way."

Deckard rose from his chair, marching out of his cabin.

The halls of an *Eisenclad* dreadnought were wide, so wide they appeared to be shallow—they were in fact over ten feet tall, but they wanted to accommodate small vehicles like Warcom as much as they did people.

Deckard swooped over to the lift tucked against the far wall. The Commandant AI knew where he was headed, inputting the ship-board coordinates without needing a single word of further instruction.

The happy nature images projected on the walls of the lift glided in the appropriate direction, helping to facilitate the inner ear with the abuse it would otherwise take. The tube had smooth and careful glides, as it pulled Deckard out of the alcove and onto the main thoroughfare to move down the length of the ship. The *Tartarus* was far too large to get around on foot with any kind of haste, so the lifts operated as a kind of tramway. But without some visual aid to ease the nausea, the lifts needed to be frequently...sanitized.

Wolcott's quarters were a full four hundred meters aft and three decks down. Deckard arrived in less than two minutes.

The lift's door opened and the admiral strode across the hall and right on in to the lieutenant's dorm. Deckard had clearance to come and go as he pleased—perks of being an admiral. There wasn't a door onboard that wouldn't open for him.

The young lieutenant sat at his desk, shirtless and damp from a shower. He smiled wide as he sipped directly from a bottle of brandy. "Admiral! You look...necrotic. Have a drink."

"We celebrating something?" Deckard asked, eyes narrowed.

"Constantly. But yes, today is very unique."

"As I understand it, unique is a binary condition. It either is or isn't." Deckard plucked the bottle from his hands and set it aside on the desktop. He gripped it by the neck, menacingly. "A prison camp?"

Wolcott blinked. This was not taking the tone he expected. "It's...gracious."

"Oh, it is?" The words made his blood boil.

"They're traitors to the Consul and the Empire," Wolcott explained. "The law is quite clear on our authority here."

"Which law is that, lieutenant?" He asked, on the edge of explosion.

"Captain..." Wolcott stammered out. "It's captain, now."

He pointed to the jacket hung on the door, a silver flower pinned to the lapel. He looked back at Deckard, a doofy smile on his face, like he could change the direction of the conversation. He wanted Deckard to be proud, to see his achievement.

Caldwell was rewarding his new pet, plying him with prestige and shine. No matter. The boy had made his loyalties self-evident. No need to warn him where that devil's bargain was charted for.

"He's given you a ship, I take it?" Deckard asked.

"Hm?" Wolcott pursed his lips, like a cat that ate the canary with feathers still stuck to his chin. He wasn't being coy. He was just so full of his new title, he actually hadn't heard the question.

"I haven't been relieved," Deckard said. "But a *Captain* needs a ship."

"Oh, yes, uh. I'm to take command of the *Pompeii*. After losing two landing craft during planetfall, the Minister has lost faith in Captain Ilya's...creativity."

The *Pompeii* was one of the two support ships sailing with the *Tartarus*, primarily loaded with the ground assault teams, while the *Hestia* had supplied the Orbital Strike forces for the operation. Captain Ilya had served under Deckard with distinction for a decade. He had started as a Warrant Officer when he was fourteen years old.

This new prospect, sixteen years old...had just jumped the line dramatically. He was nowhere near ready.

"Captain Ilya is under my command. Why was I not informed?"

Wolcott's eyes darted left and right. "I...I assumed that the Minister was in constant contact with... doesn't matter. He's not being punished; he will still serve the Empire. The Minister said he would be transferred to another command upon return to Sol, something more...fitting for his skill level."

"Two landing craft—"

"*Half* of the assault force," Wolcott corrected. "We should have taken the city without a shot fired."

Deckard crossed his arms. "*You* wanted to start with shooting, as my ship's log recalls."

Wolcott might have been smiling, but his lip twitched at that. The 'shots fired' comment wasn't his own elegant commentary, after all, but rather quoted from the Minister's unreasonable standards.

The kid was so out of his depth. Wars weren't fought with shiny displays of expensive toys; simply showing them to your enemy was never going to be enough. Illustrative events like landings and barrages were necessary evils, and your foe was unlikely to be idle during the work. If violence was to be exchanged, as was often inevitable, then soldiers died. That was a fact.

Now the Minister was so eager to race to conflict, but then wholly repulsed by the results of it. For a man immersed in the practice of war, he seemed wholly unaware of its results. He wanted all of the glory, but none of the painful cost.

In a perfect world, a good army would stay home behind ceremonial glass: break free in case of irrational greed or unrivaled hatred. A soldier's first and most important role in a civilized society was as a tool for diplomats, used to dissuade conflict and avoid shooting. They were not to be cudgels for a despot to enforce his will. This was wrong.

The Minister wasn't here, in theater—but he insisted on ranking and rating performance of his men from behind a desk, trading in influence and handing out commendations. Insufferable prick.

Deckard kept that bit of insubordination to himself.

The admiral tapped a quick-key on his bracer and threw an image up to the wall of Wolcott's cabin. An animation of the prison camp's rapid construction, heavy lifters and engineers crawling around it like termites in reverse.

Then prisoners funneled in to the space.

The animation matched over to live footage from the air: thousands of people, packed into the area, sometimes shoulder to shoulder. People lay on top of one another to sleep. All of them desperately trying to get away from the toxic lake, but guards kept them away from the fortifications with electric coils.

"Captain," Deckard began, "why are you doing this?"

"I'm taking your advice," Wolcott said, meekly. "I examined my surroundings. And I...made the best tactical decision to achieve the most positive end."

He did what the Minister told him to do and got promoted for it. That's not the same thing.

"You're killing them."

Wolcott stood up, almost dancing over to the image on the wall. "No, I'm not. Quite clearly, I'm *detaining* them."

"Near a toxic gas cloud."

Wolcott swiped his bottle of brandy from Deckard's loose grip. "That will simply reinforce the lesson."

"Caldwell ordered this," Deckard said, eyes narrowed. "You're not this cruel."

"This isn't cruelty. This is...something else." Wolcott took a hefty swig from the bottle. His cocky veneer might have been polished to a shine, but the pause told Deckard everything. Wolcott was a puppet —and what's more, he knew it.

Caldwell was calling the shots now.

Deckard would have to be careful. He had assumed he was well beyond the Minister's hand out here on the Reach, but Aaron Havenes and his Capital rebellion had garnered more attention than he had anticipated.

The newly minted captain plopped back into his seat. "I'll be on the next shuttle to the *Pompeii* to take up my new post. It's still your fleet. I'm under your command. But it's my ground offensive, now." He raised the bottle up in a toast. "*Zu gloriam*, Admiral."

"*Zu gloriam*, Captain." Why did those words taste so foul today?

PART THREE
SCARS

PART FIVE

CHAPTER
TWENTY
EDEN

"SOLOMON, YOU ARE UNBELIEVABLY LUCKY,"
Eden said, as she smeared the last of their medigel over his gut
wound. "Half an inch to the left and you'd have bled out in minutes."

Imperial rifles and pistols both fired thirty caliber Horus—jack-
eted rounds designed for cavitation. The bullets actually shattered
inside their targets. Solomon caught a piece of the bullet that went
through his human shield, making his wound far less severe.

It had lodged in his back, trapped in the muscle fibers. She'd have
to wait to have access to a decent surgical bed to remove it, but for the
time being, the round was done moving. Solomon was stable. In
theory, he could spend the rest of his natural life with that shard in
his back, provided he didn't bleed out or get an infection.

Nora held aloft a chemical flare, lighting Eden's work. The Jergad
tunnel was a thing to behold. The critters worked as small packs,
grinding forward through compressed dirt and slate rock like a coop-
erative drill bit. With their combined strength, they had chewed
through at an impressive pace.

And yet—not one of them had come back down into their tunnel.
Solomon stared down the tunnel. "Where are they?"
They. The Jergad.

Nobody had any theories, none that they were offering. Maybe the big brutes were occupied on the surface, engaged with the Imperial Army proper. Maybe they'd gone home a different way. Or maybe they'd been summarily wiped out. Who knew?

But the lost little Capitals were on their own.

All they had was this impressive tunnel, nearly twelve feet wide and tall enough for Nora to stand at her full height.

"We shouldn't hang out," Nora said.

Aisling chuffed at that, her brow slick with sweat. "The Imps have their hands full right now."

"Yes," Nora conceded. "But they're not going to keep to the City."

"I don't know if you've noticed, skullcap," Aisling snapped, "but I can't walk, she's got a bum leg, and the *skel*'s got a hole in him big enough for a tea cup."

"I'm fine," was all Solomon said.

"See? He's fine," Nora said.

"You are *not* fine," Eden scolded, her face inches from his.

She could feel the anger radiate off of him like heat, but his body held the unnatural stillness of the dead. "Step. Away."

"We won't get five hundred feet," Aisling warned.

"We'll take shifts with you and hobble our way out. This tunnel's gotta go somewhere."

Eden stared into the black. "I hope."

"Leave me." No one was expecting those words. The pilot pushed herself up against the wall, wiping the dripping blood from her head. "You'll never stand a chance hauling me."

Nora's eyes were wide with shock. "Not happenin'."

"You have to."

"We're not!"

"I'm luggage, lady! Look at me." Aisling's voice was tinged with panic. "My orders were to get you out—"

Nora brushed that off. "We're a rebellion. We're not big on orders around here."

"Shut up." She intended that to be a bigger denouncement but she didn't have the energy. "My line of work...this is how it was always going to go."

Solomon looked around them. "In the dark, far from home?"

Aisling raised an eyebrow. He was right but not right. She expected to die in some pitched space battle, not a tunnel underground. But it was still an apt description.

The pilot knew better than most what she was asking. She'd never survive on her own. If she didn't succumb to her wounds or dehydration, the elements would get her. The tunnel might collapse on her.

Or the Imperials might find her.

She shouldn't be here, none of them should be. Keira should be alive and draped over Solomon. But they all came after her, just a Doctor. Because Aaron...

Aisling had made her request. It wouldn't be Eden's first patient to cross that particular bridge.

Eden staggered over to Aisling, plopping herself down next to the pilot. "Is that what you want?"

"It's what has to happen."

"Is it what you *want*?" Eden said, forcefully. "I need you to say it."

The pilot scoffed. "I, Aisling Danahy, of clear sound and mind?"

"Yes."

Aisling had been kidding, but she saw the serious look in Eden's eye. Her eye watered, refusing to let her barrier down. "It's what *has* to happen."

No, it doesn't.

"Nora? Pack the luggage. I'll help Solomon."

———

Their progress was slow, but then, they didn't have any metric to measure against. Had they gone half a mile or just a hundred feet?

The tunnel looked the same no matter what. It seemed to bend and flex as they went, like a frozen liquid. She'd seen the Hive, how the Jergad secreted a resin to build their towers; perhaps they used that to reinforce the tunnels?

And maybe they only dug the tunnels once, like building a highway system? Then they just ran at full speed toward their destinations, burrowing only when they must?

Eden took a big pull from her canteen. It tasted stale, musty, like it was swamp water. It had no burn, no character.

Talania had the good stuff.

Eden offered the canteen to Aisling on Nora's back, but the pilot shook her head. Eden insisted, "You need water."

"I need," she snapped, "a saddle."

"I could drop you whenever I want," Nora grunted, quickly adding, "but that would be mean."

"A nice leather saddle," Aisling mused. "I could bust out some boots, a big hat."

Nora swept a little close to the tunnel wall. She didn't bonk Aisling into anything—she wasn't as cruel as that. But she did drag the pilot's hair through the dirt.

For a woman with a broken back, Aisling was in remarkable spirits. Suppose having had a chunk of her face carved out in violent fashion gave one a certain faith in medical professionals.

Eden soured, blinking away the building stress headache. They stumbled down this dark and dreary tunnel now all because of her. No food, no gear, no idea where they were even going. And Keira...

Was this what it felt like? Behind enemy lines and presumed dead marching inexorably to a distant horizon in the hopes that someone was watching? Aaron had been presumed dead once—

Aaron: he was so cavalier, gambling with these lives like they had no value. Four people in exchange for her? How did that math square? Why was she valuable enough to risk all of them? If he had just let her continue working, they'd all be fine now.

And she'd likely be up against a wall, counting down the seconds before a firing squad.

Was she that valuable to him, or at the least, valuable enough to warrant a rescue? Maybe.

But was that his bargain—four people for just a chance at getting her home? That was a decision he was comfortable making?

And in the end, she'd probably die anyway.

Would she do the same for him? Send four people? Surprising herself, she thought, yeah...she would. But would she send Keira, Solomon, Nora—would she risk Talania to get Aaron back? No. She wouldn't. She couldn't gamble with lives she knew, so how could she then gamble with those that she didn't?

She wouldn't save him.

If she had another chance, another swipe at Aaron on that mountaintop...she'd leave him there. Never thought she'd see the day that she agreed it was right to leave him behind.

Solomon wavered, his head lilting from side to side like a reed in the breeze. Eden stepped up, trying to throw herself underneath him, but he slipped away. "I'm *fine*."

"Solomon: you are, at best, *conscious*," Eden said, sternly. "You don't even qualify as 'okay.'"

He growled back at her, the only answer he had. She turned him against the wall, lifting his shirt. The gel was slimy red, saturated with blood. She might have staunched his bleeding, but it was still a heinous injury.

The slender hand of Solomon grabbed her shoulder, a cold vise. "She didn't want to grow old, Eden."

His eyes weren't watery with tears or distant in memory. Rather they were deep, like they swallowed all light into them. There was a certainty, an embrace somewhere below the surface.

Eden shook her head. "Yeah, well...I wanted her to."

He nodded. For all the delirium plaguing his body, his eyes were steady. "She liked you."

"I'm not hard to like."

His brow furrowed and his voice went to a rasp. "I've hurt...a lot of people." He paused, choosing his words with care. "Keira...I found her. I didn't—I didn't *hurt* her. Nothing I did. Not once. Like, I *couldn't.*"

He turned his eyes up the tunnel, examining that darkness for something beyond. He couldn't dare lie down here, but he was absolutely ready to.

Anger, grief, guilt, and a touch of fear.

Solomon had been happy, perhaps for the first time in his unnatural life. He was happy, Nora was safe, Aisling could walk, and Keira...all because Aaron couldn't let Eden go.

Fuck Aaron.

CHAPTER
TWENTY-ONE

AARON

"FASCINATING." The sight of the Queen's enormity stole the breath from Graccus' chest, but certainly not his curiosity. "It has no physical form."

Graccus took a cautious step forward, measuring how the Queen's black shadow seemed to glide away from him, then glide back as he retreated. The glint in his eye seemed very prosecutorial. "You're not really *here,* are you?"

"Yeah..." Talania drawled, bored with this. "It's wild."

After Aaron's display below, Graccus had insisted on seeing the Jergad Queen himself. And given the situation, the Queen was in no position to refuse him. The humans were everywhere, practically infesting her house. She might have a mind to evict them, but for the swarm of insidious forces that battered on her walls outside.

Survivors were coming in by the dozens, overwhelming Medical. Never had Aaron been so happy to hear bad news. Four hundred people had been surrounded at dawn. Now, they were on their way to safety.

"How were your losses?" Aaron asked.

The Queen's doppelganger shimmered, matching the ripples that danced across the shadowy mass. Graccus almost giggled at the sight.

She turned to him, melting into an amalgam of human features as she constructed her own 'face.' She'd gotten better at it, had some practice. It didn't look quite so uncanny anymore. Or at least, it was less of a hodgepodge of his friends sewn together in a mockery of human life.

The Queen refused to face him, staring upward at something beyond the rock. "Does *ak'thun* really concern himself with such things?"

"I asked, didn't I?" he said, drawing a look from Talania. What were they talking about? Or perhaps she objected to the half of the conversation she was privy to.

The Queen closed her eyes. "It has gone so very quiet now. Few have returned."

More casualties. Great. He was naive to expect they would simply turn the tide of battle with nothing but surprise and a gung-ho attitude. They were, after all, a barely Stone Age Hive mind with broad shoulders, and he had asked them to engage the greatest naval armada ever assembled.

"Can she see me?" Graccus asked, like a school boy at the zoo.

"Yes," Aaron said, with Talania throwing in a patronizing "Oh, honey" for added impact.

The Queen's eyes settled on Graccus. She didn't furrow her brow and curl her lip, but there was an intensity to her, a fixation that could only be read as aggression. "*Ak'thun*, why do you trust him?"

"I don't," Aaron said.

Maybe it was the tone of his answer, but Graccus leered at him, fully aware of what question must have prompted that answer.

Human scientists had once derided the Jergad as simple beasts, using tonality and scent patterns as a communication, as though human languages were above such simple things. Right then, Aaron preferred their psychic link rather than this crude trumpeting. It was like everyone on the platform spoke different dialects of the same language, nobody on the same wavelength.

The Queen softened, feeling his envy. "Speak plainly and

honest. Do not hide behind clever wit. They will do as you will. Now...tell them, what do you need done?"

Plain and honest, huh? He took a steeling breath.

"We need an inventory of everything that made it here, personnel and material," Aaron announced. "Graccus, work with Bray on material goods. Talania, do a head count. Include any particularly strong kids."

"Excuse me?" Talania drew up to her full height. "Kids?"

"You heard me."

"I'm not drafting children!"

He hadn't asked her to distribute rifles; he wanted to know who was here. How was that objectionable? But then, she'd made a career out of moral indignation.

"We're in for the fight of our lives," Graccus cut in. "I think you'll find that plenty of them are willing."

"It's not about willing—Aaron, do you hear yourself?"

The Imperial Navy had blown over their homes, set fire to their fields, and slaughtered their neighbors—killed Eden.

"I'm not drafting anybody!" Aaron said, raising a hand to quell the rising tides. "But if people want to defend their homes, I'd like to help 'em do that."

"Children—"

"If we're being strict about it," Graccus interjected, "you both are still 'children' too."

"This *child*," Talania always met fire with three times more fire, "didn't have a choice."

Aaron's blood ran cold. "Neither did I."

Talania might have thrown him a hard look but the slump to her shoulders spoke the truth. She had spoken a little fast there without thinking of who was around. Aaron, Eden—all of the Capitals might have volunteered for military service, but many had been indentured for crimes they didn't commit, or their punishments were wildly out of step with the crime.

Okay, sure, Solomon probably deserved to be isolated from

society for everyone's safety, but Eden was a *gulaw* medical resident who eased a patient's pain; Nora had been in one too many bar brawls.

Nobody chose their circumstances. But here they were.

Aaron shrugged it off. "You wanted me involved. Well, I'm involved."

She swallowed her pride, crossing her arms. "What am I supposed to tell Whitby?"

"Blame me. He likes that." Aaron turned back to the Queen. "We can't just wait to see if the Imperials get bored and go away."

"You didn't," the Queen stated with a shrug.

"I rest my case."

Graccus started to circle the platform, walking his way through the problem. "As long as the fleet remains in orbit, Deckard remains untouchable. He can hold us in siege, await reinforcement. It would be embarrassing for him, but hardly unheard of. They'll simply outlast us."

"So we need a way to take the fight to them," Aaron concluded. "Push him right back to the Jump point. He's in our house. So how do we make him feel that way?"

"The longer we fight..."

Aaron turned on his heels. Talania had stalked over to the edge of the platform to pout. She was staring down at the decimated human colony below her, clinging to the fringes of the light with their metal and their bags, while monsters lurked at the edge of the sight, shifting shadows. A baby's cries echoed off the cavern walls.

Talania sniffed, clearing her nose. "The longer we fight, the bloodier this gets."

Graccus pursed his lips. "That *is* how fighting usually works."

Talania looked back over at Aaron. "I can't ask you to..."

She wanted him to surrender. She wanted him to give up. What? Had she lost her taste for it?

"You really think he'd stop?" Aaron sputtered. "After last night, all that? You think he slaps me in irons and this all...goes back to before?"

"I didn't sleep through it, Aaron," she said. "But I would be a piss poor governor if I put you over *them*."

She really *was* advocating for Aaron to surrender, give himself up. The Empire would simply name a new military commander— some young officer looking to make a name for himself—to enforce law and order. Riley would look like the good old days against whatever sociopathic thirteen-year-old came next.

The Queen slipped up to his ear. "She has responsibilities. As you have yours. Your positions are not opposed to one another."

The alien hive mind was right. Their positions had natural friction, but Talania was not his enemy. He sighed. "The Empire doesn't care about the people."

"And you do?" Talania countered. "Whitby isn't wrong. We're huddling in a cave surrounded by smelly renditions of our worst nightmares."

"We share the sentiment," the Queen snarked. Aaron had to bite his cheek to not chuckle at the remark.

Talania wasn't done. "You've had a miraculous experience, but picture this: you're fourteen years old. For half your life you've been told that a hulking beast with hollow eyes will carry you away if you misbehave. They took your brother last year and hacked him into pieces! Now ask him to sleep within a stone's throw of the things that did it... How long do you think that will keep?"

Graccus stepped between them, but clearly squaring off with Talania. "Governor, due respect, you can huddle in *their* cave or be tinder for an Imperial pyre. Aaron is doing what he must."

Imposing though Graccus was, he was not going to obstruct the towering woman's withering stare at Aaron. She looked right clean over the Oskie's head. And he couldn't so much as meet her gaze.

"Fine," she grunted. "Call me a ride. I'll go get started on that headcount. *Sir*."

She turned away, arms crossed. Aaron nodded to the Queen, and a drone rose up to meet her, like it had simply peeled off the tower below them. With an alarming confidence, Talania hopped on to the creature's back.

Aaron caught a glimpse of her, eyes squeezed shut in terror, before she dropped out of sight.

"She's not wrong either," Aaron said. "Somebody's going to start throwing rocks."

"There's no shortage of supply," Graccus said. The hawkish naval officer clapped a hand across Aaron's back. "Leaders aren't common, you know."

"I'm sorry?" Aaron asked with an arched brow. There were too many ways of taking those three words.

The Oskie shrugged. "Something an old instructor of mine used to say."

"Your teacher have any other ad campaigns masquerading as wisdom?"

"You can't be Aaron the Court Clerk anymore. You're a messianic figure leading an armed insurrection. You are literally not a 'common' thing, and you cannot *be* common anymore. You are something more...Legatus."

The name hung in the air. The very air seemed to hum the syllables along with him, as if the thousand voices below were all recumbent in prayer.

Graccus pointed to the people down below. "They *need* you to be above it all. If you're just some person...a simple man who challenges an entire Empire...then *they're* screwed."

"But I *am* just some guy."

"Yeah, we'll work on that," Graccus dismissed, turning back to the Queen's monstrous hulking black morass. "So is this some sort of projection or...?"

The Queen was a manifestation of a species' collective will, a personification of the web of electromagnetic connections that made up their unity; she *was* the species, but that was going to slide right over Graccus' narrow interpretations.

She wasn't a person. She was something more. At least Aaron had a model to look up to.

The Queen sidled up next to Graccus. "How do you plan to proceed?"

"Why don't you ask the 'uncommon man'?" Aaron said, gruff.

Graccus eyed the empty air to his right—the Queen's doppelgänger invisible to his eye. Maybe his Oskie enhancement picked up something? Or maybe he was just deducing what Aaron must be seeing?

"Tactically speaking, a defensive posture was never going to earn you anything but a black eye," the Oskie said.

"I'm not taking the fight to the Imperial Navy with nothing but my upbeat attitude."

"You were never going to *win* this fight."

Aaron slumped. It wasn't anything his brain hadn't told him before. He'd laid awake many a night with that refrain bouncing off the inside of his skull.

Dusters didn't stand against Empires.

Graccus folded his arms across his chest. "You *can* make them lose it."

Aaron furrowed his brow, a gear slipping in his head. "Whether they win or lose isn't all that material to me, if I also *lose*."

Graccus flicked the lock of black hair out of his face, like he was adjusting a crown. "Aaron, you're new to insurrection, but let me tell you—as an agent who spent half of his life instigating chaos across the known galaxy: the only way the little guy ever wins a fight is with his back to the wall. And when he makes the fight too bloody, too costly for his bully to even want. Too embarrassing."

Aaron shook his head, dismissive. "We put up a fight, they'll glass the planet."

"Maybe," Graccus conceded. "But a lasting symbol of their failure might actually be *worse* than letting you live."

Aaron considered that idea. "We don't have to win..."

Graccus's lips smiled wide enough to crack his face in half. "We just have to make sure they lose."

"The Admiral didn't strike me as a man of thin skin," Aaron said. "He's not Riley. He's not going to snap just 'cause someone pushed back."

"No, Deckard Tiberiet is a man of poise, honor, and station. He will not hit an unarmed man, nor will he tolerate anyone else doing so."

They could use that. Come under cover of peace; use a cloak to hide their dagger.

"Your Highness?"

The Queen responded, stepping up next to Graccus. He seemed to feel her approach, somehow, and stepped back, giving her the floor.

"You flummoxed the Repeaters with your...brain...thing six months ago. What's your range on that?"

She tilted her head, a confused dog.

"Can you feel the ships in orbit?" Aaron asked.

The Queen looked up, skyward, through the rock and toward the stars and the three obelisks trapped in an endless circular fall. They drifted in her skies, leering down on her world.

"Four thousand four hundred and thirty-nine lives," she said, reverential. "They hang in the air like clouds bearing metal rain."

Aaron popped to his feet, marching over to Graccus. "Won't hit an unarmed man? That's it."

"I don't follow."

Aaron stuck both hands in the air. "I surrender. Me, and an elite team of hand-picked badasses posing as my leadership team."

Graccus thought about it for a moment. "Duplicitous. He'll want to take you into custody..."

"We go in on the last Howler—under cover of parlay."

"Smash and dash?"

"Something like that." Aaron leaned in, conspiratorial. "They have to be running supplies to the surface, same way we were. An army marches on its stomach."

Graccus caught on immediately. "We can load the shuttle with enough detonite to snap a cruiser in two. But you'll never get through their defenses."

"Sure we will." Aaron marched over to the edge of the plateau, nodding down below. "They gave us the key."

Graccus' brow shot up. "The Warcom..."

"Can we get it juiced up again?"

"With what?" Graccus asked. "I don't think it's compatible with wishful thinking."

Aaron chewed on that, scanning the field below them. They had what at hand? Solar? What, they were going to set up a solar farm on the surface during an active siege? Bioluminescent moss was hardly a good fuel, and they couldn't convert any burn into electricity anyway.

But they had something. "The AutoDocs have a backup generator in case of Hospital outage. Or...for when they get hauled into a mountain hideout."

Graccus' eyes narrowed. "Enough of them in series might give us the kick it needs, but Aaron...you'd take easily half a dozen off-line to even try this."

Without medical, people died. Without that suit and this plan, everyone died. It was cruel, maybe, but it was easy calculus. "We give up a lot, yeah. But we make them start paying for their parking spot."

Graccus nodded. "We get the shuttle flying, we'll need air cover we can't provide." He wasn't shooting down the idea. Just another hurdle.

Aaron turned to the Queen. "What do ya say, your Highness? Can you do your voodoo and keep the shuttle safe all the way in?"

Her eyes were aglow with blue fire. "We can."

CHAPTER
TWENTY-TWO
KEEPER

PERMISSION TO BE outside the Hive was granted for exactly one purpose: observation. Word was, the Jergad would sense any attack coming, but that didn't help with whatever else was going on in the world. Only a handful were allowed out at a time—the heat plume would be visible from orbit otherwise. But they needed to track Imperial movements in the Basin.

Keeper couldn't sleep. He kept seeing that red eye staring back at him. She never said anything. He couldn't even see her face. So still and watchful, as if waiting on what he'd do next...

So he took a shift in the Crow's Nest.

It was just a small crater, a former volcanic vent, perhaps. It offered some natural cover and a convenient place for him to cool his heels, reclining backward on his stool with feet up on the edge.

They were heavily shielded by cloud cover, but an infrared scope offered him a view of everything below. He panned it left to right every so often, looking for flares of color on the monitor, as he poured himself another glass of green liquor.

The bottle was almost dry. He took a sip, savoring the warming spices, the plum aftertaste.

Kevalky was listed as a hallucinogenic drug and marked as a

Class 4 controlled substance. That was asinine, as the psychotropic component had long since been removed due to lack of supply. But Keeper liked to think that the world was more colorful after a glass.

"This seat taken?" a voice asked.

"Only one in the house," he grunted, but he paled when he saw who said it. Talania Dedria balanced a steel crate on the lip of his crater. "Governor!"

"Stand up and I will throw you off this mountain." She leaned over the side, swiping the bottle from his side. "Kevalky Medán Liquor? Someone's got expensive tastes."

It had been for her.

"Get it before it's gone," he offered, wistfully.

"I'm not supposed to," she said, hand over her heart. "Doctor's orders."

He squinted against the mid-morning sun. Her clothes were ruddy with soil, and her hair touched with ash, like she'd been forgotten in the family attic for one too many years. Her eyes were sunk into her head.

"What's in the box?"

She shrugged. "Who even knows anymore?"

"Not a whole lot of things come *out* of the mountain these days," he noted.

"If I told you, kid," Talania quipped, "I'd have to kill you."

"Well, we don't want that." He smirked. "How long's it been since you slept?"

Her head bobbed as she counted backwards to infinity. "...I don't remember."

"Me either." He toasted to that, taking another sip of the Kevalky. He could see the liquid slosh about inside the bottle, droplets clinging to the inside of the glass.

Keeper rinsed his mouth with the liquor, swirling it about his mouth, coating every surface with its flavor. He wanted that burn to set in, start to scald him.

"What brings you to this neck of the woods?" she asked, her voice a hollow refrain.

"Aisling Danahy, First Lieutenant."

Talania's eyes drifted down as she connected the dots. She might not have known the pilots, but she knew that Keeper was the only one left. "I'm sorry."

They practiced for that moment: when a civi decides to sympathize with a soldier's pain, express their gratitude for service. Somehow, to him, it just felt humiliating, like he was being called out for a body of work that simply did not deserve adulation.

But Aisling did.

"She punched our commander last year, the same man who had pinned a Copper Combat Cross on her chest and hung the Humanitas around her neck."

That second medal had only one meaning. "She saved somebody?"

The question was implicit: had she saved him?

He'd gotten himself properly dug in, like he always did. She broke formation and came after him.

"...Yeah," was all he said.

Keeper felt his eyes start to water. He told himself it was the humidity. If ever there was a time for a patriot's shower, it was now. No one would think less of him.

Talania set the bottle back down, turning away to the Basin and the camera feed, as if to give him privacy. "Our gracious guests done anything of note?"

Keeper sniffed away the tears in his sinuses, panning the camera over. "They've fortified the old Mines."

The Imperials worked fast. Those new walls were almost as impressive as the Wall Prefecture that separated Colonial lands from the wilds of the Basin.

"Can you think of any *good* reasons they'd rebuild the prison?" she asked.

"Nope."

"Maybe they're cleaning up the toxic waste?"

"That'd be a helluva thing. But you and I both know what they're doing down there."

Keeper saw her shoulders sag, as despair took hold of her. He lifted the bottle by the neck of the glass, swirling the emerald fluid inside. "You've had a very long day."

"They're only going to get longer."

"Doesn't make this day any better." He tapped her leg with the bottle.

She glanced down at the fine liquor, its allure obvious, but she shook her head. "I've had enough."

"You're smarter than I am," he said, taking a pull straight from the bottle. The cinnamon had started to burn his lips, but he didn't care.

She smirked. "That's not difficult, jockey."

Movement on the scope. Talania wasn't looking, her hand dragging the image across the fields below—but he saw it, he was sure.

He sat up, snatching the scope from her grasp. The multicolored image was solid blues. So why had he seen a plume of red heat? The eyecup almost suctioned to his face as he pressed it close, scanning back over the basin again.

"What is it?" the governor asked.

There! A plume of yellow in the field of blue. Four figures were clustered around some kind of hole in the ground.

Survivors.

His breath hitched in his chest. It was her. He knew it. He just did. She was alive.

Keeper grabbed his radio. "Chief, are you sittin' down?"

"Grabbing some chow," the voice crackled back. "What've you got?"

"Get me flight ready."

The deck crew was manic, scrambling over his potato and welding on parts as others wheeled it out onto the plateau. It's not like they could make the thing any uglier. Launch operators cranked the fuel lines off of the hull and ran them back to the cover of the mountain.

The chief threw open the side door for Keeper. "Half tanks and we stripped the gun off. Should give you a bit more *gusto!*"

Keeper clapped the man on the back. "You're the best."

"Stand down!"

Now *that* was the tone he expected from a man known around the galaxy as 'Legatus.' That voice boomed, that voice had oomph in every consonant.

Aaron stood in the tunnel's overhang, projecting his will from its dark. He didn't need to repeat himself, and he wasn't going to. The crew started to undo all of their work.

"Aaron—"

"Not one *gulaw* word out of you, kid!"

"How about many then? What are you going to do? Huh?!"

Aaron didn't move, but his eyes seemed to suddenly glow in the dark. He stepped out of the shadows, a reptilian ease to his movement. In the long walk over to the Howler, he never once blinked.

Keeper expected to get popped. If Aaron was polite, he might even give Keeper the courtesy of picking head or gut. Veterans preferred the head: a loose jaw clicked but unsticking lungs from the ribcage was a day-long task.

Aaron didn't say a thing. He grabbed Keeper's wrist and twisted it behind him into an armlock. His elbow and shoulder cried out, but there was little he could do with his thumb touching his shoulder blades.

Successfully detained, Aaron started to march Keeper back to the Hive tunnel.

"They're out there, Aaron!" he pleaded. "We can help them."

Suddenly, he snapped close to Keeper's ear, his arm compressed between them. Aaron whispered, drops of venom, "You think it's going to be a quick out and back? I lost people

216

running this particular play just last night, and I *will* *not* lose more."

"I can do it."

"Oh? Okay then. Well, following that persuasive argument, let me cross examine."

Aaron spun Keeper around and planted him into the mountain rock. Aaron stopped shy of planting a hand on the young pilot's throat.

He didn't need to. The look in his eye did it for him. "Three orbiting starships saw them *before* you did, I guarantee it. They are scrambling air defense and ground assault forces right now. You will get there..." He nodded, granting that. "But they will be dead when you do. And Hell will be waiting for you."

"They'll die!"

There was more pain in Aaron's words than Keeper expected. "Yeah, they will."

A small crowd had started to form at the mouth of the tunnel. Bray and Talania, Graccus—they all watched. But they couldn't give a damn about Keeper. They were watching Aaron, with slack-jawed horror.

Keeper's eyes darted from them back to Aaron. "Get the Jergad out there. Bring 'em back!"

Aaron looked aside, as if consulting with the little angel and demon on his shoulders. Whatever they had to add was bad news. His jaw went tight and he shook his head. "They'll never get there in time."

"But we *can!*"

Aaron leaned in close, eyes dark. "They are just as dead now as they were this morning. All we get...is the added privilege of watching them die for the second time. You were about to get your-self dead—and take my *last* Howler with you."

"Aaron," Keeper begged, "they'd do it for us."

The words were torture. Aaron slackened, letting him loose. "I know it. But we can't."

217

"So we're just going to...do nothing?"

"We're not doing nothing. We're just not doing this."

Keeper's eyes went wide. He'd served with a lot of cruel, cold men, calculating geniuses who had done the math and run the assessments. They were men that ruled from spreadsheets and acceptable losses, who entered combat with a margin of error. They were distant, removed, barely human.

Aaron was abandoning his responsibility to his people. And why? What could be more important? What were they even fighting for if not each other? That look in Aaron's eye, that was something...pitiful.

Aaron stepped away from him, calling out to the crew. "You have your orders."

This was a rebellion. Fuck the orders.

Keeper swung at him, his fist connecting with the side of Aaron's head. Aaron's balance was so off, he tumbled to the ground, slapping his jaw against the stone. He was clearly seeing stars, his eyes wide and confused.

Turns out some legends are really just folks with a commanding presence. They flop just like everybody else.

A single voice cheered from the cave mouth as Keeper hopped over the crumpled Aaron, while a shocked deck crew looked on. He clambered into his Howler, pulling his harness on and firing up the engines.

A form suddenly at his back, a hand gripping his shoulder—the Imperial, Graccus.

The Oskie squeezed, and he could feel his clavicle bend under the pressure. "Give me one good reason I shouldn't paint the inside of this bird with every bit of you."

"Because," Keeper said, "you're not strapped in."

Keeper felt the hand go to his throat and squeeze—and he yanked up on the controls, sending the Howler into a vertical spin. The Oskie flipped over, going with the gravity and walking on the roof of the cockpit like it was nothing. The big guy was surprisingly flexible and he moved with the ship like they were one.

His eyes glowed, little yellow discs somewhere in the back. "Don't do this, kid."

The grip tightened and Keeper felt his vision narrow. But pilots train for blackouts.

"Rip my throat out," Keeper growled past the fingers, "and you crash us. Unless you know how to fly one of these."

"I'm resourceful."

"Then why haven't you done it already?"

"Land this bucket right now," Graccus ordered. "You're toying with the survival of this entire colony."

"Well, then you'd better help me get back safe."

Graccus thought about his options for a moment longer than Keeper was comfortable with, running calculations.

But then his fingers loosened. "You'll never get them out without a crane operator."

Keeper sighed relief. "I was going to give it a try."

He could've sworn the Oskie actually smiled. "Let's do better than try."

CHAPTER
TWENTY-THREE

EDEN

THE TUNNEL HAD COLLAPSED SOMEWHERE HALFWAY—HARDLY surprising, it wasn't the soundest construction and the Jergad obviously didn't care. They'd simply burrow it out fresh. But four injured humans were instead forced to the surface, where Imperial ships would spy them immediately.

Aisling had scratched out some quick math for them. If the bad guys were in synchronous orbit—which she was sure they would be—they'd be at 25,000 kilometers above. That meant a kinetic weapon would take fifteen minutes to impact at target with the force of a small meteor, aided in no small part by a clean nuclear detonation. Everything within three miles would be obliterated.

And in the midst of all of that, the expendable Locust bots would be haranguing them, trying to hold them up.

The rangefinder said it was seven miles to the foot of the mountains. The Rebels would come get them—or not. And either way... they were going to be running for their lives on busted legs and broken backs.

They had packed up Aisling as well as they could. Solomon used scraps of their tac rigs to lash the pilot onto Nora's shoulders. The bartender might have had a gymnast's build, but she worked like a beast. She'd drag that pilot across the finish line if she had to.

Eden broke down two rifles and pulled the barrels free. Tearing some long strips from her pants, she lashed them to her leg like a steel splint. Whatever damage she did to herself could be fixed on the other end, but only if they got there. And she had to be able to flee on her own.

She saw what the Locust could do.

Eden gritted her teeth, staring up the pile of rocks to the exposed sky above. Solomon dusted up his hands for traction, eyes darting to-and-fro as he plotted his route.

Eden caught his eye. "Once you're good, help Nora up."

"You'll move faster without me," Aisling reiterated.

Nora reached back, slapping the girl. "Hush!"

Eden leaned in to Solomon, whispering. "We get back, we'll patch up and get right back into this."

He grimaced. Or maybe growled. She couldn't tell.

The lean and pale man had a half-inch hole in his gut, possibly a perforated bowel, but you'd never have known it seeing him vault up the rocks. He moved like gravity had no hold on him, some kind of jungle cat bounding from stone to stone.

In comparison, Nora clambered on to the first step. "Shit, we should've made him carry the cripple."

Eden clapped a hand over Aisling's mouth, halting whatever wise-crack the girl had. She grimaced at the warm, wet tongue that wiped across her fingers. She glanced at the pilot, nonplussed. Did this girl think she could gross out a medical doctor? "What are you, twelve?"

Ashamed, the pilot's jaw clicked shut.

Solomon had stopped just shy of the exit, turning back. He waited for Nora and Aisling, hauling them up to his level and then shoving them up to the surface.

That was it—fifteen minutes. Start the clock.

Eden hobbled up the rocks as best as she could manage. Her leg screeched with every swing. The torn muscle hated the bending, so she had to heave it up each step. Solomon plucked her from the last and swung her up the rest of the way.

Nora had already taken off, lumbering across the plain.

Solomon clapped her on the back. "Care to wager?"

And with that, Eden's brain had to reboot. "We might *die* out here."

He smiled, yellow dagger teeth. "Have to make it exciting somehow."

Eden rolled her eyes and took off, a halfway jog as she swung her leg wide to keep with the splint. Solomon easily overtook her, shouting as he passed. "Winner gets to beat up Aaron!"

Like he could stop her. She was going to break that boy, fix him, so she could break him again.

For some time, it felt hard to remember to run. Her leg ached, her breath ragged. And there was no sign of a threat. But every intellectual thought she had screamed danger. Somewhere above her, a lead pipe the size of a small truck was screaming through the atmosphere, tearing through like a dart of fire.

The quake it set off would be felt around the planet.

She chanced a glance over her shoulder. The Wall far behind them, with the City's broken skyline just peeking out over the top. Clouds of smoke spiraled up into the sky. At least, she hoped that was smoke—it seemed a little too animated to be part of the rest of the watercolor tableau.

Sweating and gasping, Nora had slowed to a power march, dragging one foot in front of the other but keeping a solid pace.

Eden slowed as she came up behind her. "Come on! You have to run!"

"I'm not?" Nora huffed, mildly delirious. "Sorry, coach! Jus' gotta dig in."

"Hi-ho!" Solomon called out, pointing ahead. A clear white tracer streaked down the side of the mountain. It looked like the tip of some invisible knife carving a rift through the sky.

A Howler.

"Ha-hah!" Eden cackled. "They're coming!"

"They're *coming!*" Aisling blurted, far more apocalyptic. She pointed back toward the Wall.

That smoke billowing had been more akin to a plague.

"Locust!" Nora shouted, breaking into a jog again, as fast as her feet could go with a whole other person on her back.

Something snagged Eden's foot, grabbing the tip of her boot. Maybe she didn't lift her feet enough, but it felt like the ground had trapped her shoe. She flopped to the ground hard, jamming her chin into the loose dirt. Her leg complained about being shunted but not near as much as her jaw did.

Solomon swung about, having heard her fall—but he froze at what he beheld. There was nowhere to hide, no cover to be had. A thousand flying blades descended, their daggers glittering in the sun. They fell upon Eden—

A thrust of dirt tossed into the air! A Jergad drone lurched up in front of her, and she fell into its shadow. The beast roared, deep from its gut. There was no way that one Jergad would do anything but be meat for the cleaver.

But the swarm broke off, swirling around—refusing to go near the Jergad.

The Queen—she must be interfering with them, jamming them up. It must've been like trying to fly into a squall, roiling clouds blinding the little robots' sensors. The swarm couldn't see what they were supposed to kill.

Hands grabbed her about the shoulders and heaved her up to her feet. She was pulled back into the run, fleeing as the Jergad drone vainly swatted at the swarm overhead. It chittered and growled, issuing threats only it understood and it could hardly back up. Two more popped up, creating a wall of leathery hide between her and the danger.

They could dive back into the Jergad tunnels—but the falling kinetic would almost certainly obliterate anything in the ground. Their only hope now was to get into the air.

The Howler had almost vanished inside the rippling edges of the distant mirage—but she could see the engine's flare as it approached.

A cry—and Eden looked back to see a Jergad recoiling, one bladed arm melted away. With each swipe of its great limbs, the swarm of Locust had drifted out of reach, like a strange flying liquid. But now the swarm shivered and shook. A thousand individual sensors kicked on—and they descended on the creature, pulping the mighty beast in a matter of seconds. Chunks of bone chipped into the air, viscera and gore splattered.

Eden didn't dare look a moment longer, staggering away from the horror. The Howler was swooping in, but she heard the swarm buzzing behind her, coiling up.

The Howler dropped its cables, dragging them in the dirt.

Oh good. This again. This worked so well the first time. And this time, they were going to be doing it with a knife to their neck.

She immediately regretted that metaphor.

"Hook up!" Nora shouted as she slapped the carabiner around Aisling's rig.

"What do I need to do?" Aisling asked.

"Don't throw up on me."

Eden and Solomon hooked up to the line. The three-plus-one then looked back at the swarm. It didn't loom, wind up, or wait. It simply reached for them, a bladed finger extending.

Eden had been so preoccupied the first time, she hadn't seen Keira actually do this maneuver. Nora pulled the largest carabiner she'd ever seen, the size of her whole hand. She clicked it open and threw it into the air.

The Howler slammed overhead, punching a hole through the swarm. It might've had a dozen different drop lines hanging out of the bay, but there was no way she'd actually hit one with that hook throw?

She didn't need to. Two of them were drawn in to the carabiner and locked—a magnet? Before she knew it, she was jerked into the sky. Eden could've sworn she left her bad leg behind, it hurt so much.

Aisling screamed. Nora screamed. Eden screamed. Solomon just grit his teeth, eyes wide, and lips flapping in the wind.

They sailed through the swarm, passing through the hole carved by the Howler's passing. Metal parts came cascading past them along with the occasional flash of a steel blade.

They were anti-personnel units, small and replaceable members of a whole; the Howler was a flying steel brick that could clock Mach 3. It was like hitting glass with a hammer.

The Howler paused, taking a gentle moment to wind up its passengers into its belly.

Eden looked down to see the swarm screaming up after them.

"Faster, faster! Much faster!"

The whine of gears turning, ratcheting them up to safety, even as the Howler's twin cargo doors winched shut around them, ready to pinch off someone's ankle. The timing of this was so thin, Eden quietly hoped that it was on purpose, a result of hours of ruthless practice. She knew otherwise.

The operator dragged them in, lining them up on their feet even as the deck closed under them. Dozens, if not hundreds, of the Locust slammed into the belly of the Howler, scratching and scraping. Two or three buried their blades straight through, lodging in the three-inch steel floor, the tips of the curved single-edge talons just poking through.

She almost didn't notice that one of the swarm had actually made it inside the bay!

It was small, with almost half its body being a fixed single edge hanging in the air. Above it, a tiny vectored engine and a sensor package in a single housing, rusty and stained. Its bulbous head called to mind some homicidal house fly that picked up a karambit.

Everyone pulled away, but they were still hooked together, and ended up clumping against the bulkhead—Eden popping the back of her head against the shelf.

The Locust scanned the room—the crane operator, or the Capitals. Four versus one. Math was easy.

It lunged for the Capitals.

A blur of motion and the crane operator slammed the Locust into the side of the Howler with a clenched fist, hard enough that it left a bug-shaped indent in the metal—and stuck there. It didn't so much as twitch ever again.

"Oskie?" Eden asked, a touch of horror.

It was their prisoner—Graccus—very much free and very much saving their lives. He just shrugged to her, mocking some recruitment poster from his memory, "They said 'see the Galaxy, meet interesting people: kill them.'"

Solomon bristled, hand wrapping his quick knife, but the Oskie waved him down. "Relax, spoonman. I'm on *your* team."

"Aisling!?" Keeper shouted back, frantic. "Is she with you?!"

"I'm here, blue eyes!" Aisling shouted back. "Get us outta here!"

"Alright, everybody, hang on to something!"

He didn't give them much time to actually do that, before the Howler tumbled in air and streaked off toward the mountain. Something told her that they weren't quite out of the woods yet.

Radio chatter: "Kinetic strike imminent. Brace-brace-brace!"

Nora cupped the back of Eden's neck and pulled her in close. With her other arm, she pushed against the wall of the Howler.

Thor's Hammer was a kinetic weapons platform in synchronous orbit capable of firing inert metal rods into the ground with the approximate force of a small fission device. Riley had been petulantly threatening to use its power on Vanguard.

This was a kinetic weapon too, but hardly as...inert. And it was orders of magnitude larger.

The shockwave lifted them off their feet, as the force of the explosion jostled the airborne craft. Grunts of pain, exertion. Eden flopped to the deck, almost hacking her own fingers off on one of the Locust blades.

She had her ear pressed to the hull, so she could hear exactly when something of mechanical importance ripped off. She could almost feel it leave, a screech of torn steel passing up through her palms.

"*Gulaw zu s'ivan!*" Well, cursing like that was *always* a good sign.

"Keeper?"

Aisling might've called his name, but he was deep in his headset. "Mayday, mayday—this is Kilo One Three. I've lost my port thrust. Comin' in all kinds of hot!"

Graccus overheard that, and swung down the harnesses from the roof. He separated them from each other like a magic trick and proceeded to tie each passenger high and low with elastic cable. The craft might crash, but they were safely suspended in personal spider webs.

Of course, they had been ejected last time because the belly of the Howler could collapse in—and that was still very possible.

Suddenly, Eden was on her feet, Graccus' hands about her shoulders as he lashed her in. "Close your eyes. It'll all be over in a second."

His voice was honeyed wine, something she immediately didn't want to trust. But she obeyed, squeezing her eyes shut.

The Howler struck ground, grinding and sliding. Flecks of metal and dirt spat in her face, people screamed and cried out. This was Aisling's second crash today, after all.

Her knees buckled, but Graccus held her up.

To their joy, this was far less abrupt, more like a train having hopped its rails. She felt the uneven ground under the Howler as it skipped along, bouncing and grinding against the rock.

Then it jerked to a halt—and all was quiet.

Graccus loosened his grip, his arms a comforting cage around her. He patted her on the shoulder, almost paternal, before moving to check on Aisling. "Everybody in one piece?" he asked, a tinge of anger to his voice.

"I'm good," Nora croaked. "How's the baggage?"

"Screw you."

Graccus shrugged. "She's alive." The Oskie levered the Howler's door open, the moaning steel barely slowing him down. They were a few hundred feet shy of the landing plateau, and rebel deck crews were rushing to the crash.

"We have to get out, let's go," he ordered. "They'll shell this just like they shelled the Basin."

There was a voice that hadn't spoken yet. Nora, Eden, Aisling, Graccus...Keeper was silent. Eden unhooked herself, and vaulted forward into the cockpit.

She saw the blood first. The entire front half of the Howler had caved in, splintering the metal bulkheads. Two different panels had shattered and their multiple spear tips had lanced into his chest, pinning him to his seat. His head hung loose, blood leaking from his mouth—

"Blue eyes?" Aisling had noticed Keeper's silence, and now Eden's too.

"Graccus, right?" Eden called out.

He gathered everything from her bedside tone. "What do you need?"

"A cutting torch."

CHAPTER
TWENTY-FOUR

AARON

THE KINETICS POUNDED THE MOUNTAINSIDE, reducing the wreck of the Howler back to something conceptual. Pebbles and dirt tinkled from above, an almost pleasant vibration in the floor.

This mountain was older than human hate. And it would withstand their passing.

The antechamber just before the Hive—the very same place Aaron and his friends had come to almost a year before—was now a converted triage center. Beds littered the area, while the iridescent glow of the Hive beamed in through the window, a golden hue to the air, fresh moss already lighting up.

Aaron found her there—matted hair tied up in a ponytail, bobbing in and around the much taller folk. She creaked from bed to bed, the steel brace on her leg announcing her coming.

Maybe it wasn't her? Just someone that looked like her? Everyone was so busy, dancing around Aaron like he was a just another part of the mountain.

Eden's gaze paused on him, hitched on his stillness. He let out a sigh, almost woozy. Eden stared back at him, her thin eyebrows arched and her jaw tight. Her hands went stiff at her sides.

But she was alive.

A hand looped around his shoulder, pulling him away and breaking the spell. Nora leaned in close. "You *really* don't want to talk to her right now."

Aaron swallowed, his head drifting back to catch another glimpse of her. "She needs to rest."

"So do you," she said, guiding him up the hallway. Nora was escorting him away from her.

Aaron ducked her arm, turning around. "I need to talk to her."

"And say what, shortstack?"

Nora didn't bother chasing him, knowing what she said was fish hook enough. It was a loud enough sentiment that she was drawing an audience too.

Aaron chewed on his cheek, and stalked back over to her. "Nora?"

She smiled back like a devious child. "Hi."

"You maybe want to keep your voice down?"

"No, I don't think I will. Did you take six AutoDocs offline?"

Is *that* what this was about? "I made a hard call."

Nora scoffed. "Well, I'm sorry the job is *hard*. I guess I'll tell everyone to cut you some slack."

Aaron rolled his eyes. It was always going to be a contentious decision and he knew Eden would have something to say about it, but he expected to hear it *from her*. "Are you done?"

"Oh, I could go on and on."

"Then maybe take some time to boil it down to your best five minutes." Aaron whirled away from her, setting sights on Eden.

The next thing Nora said might've taken the bones right out of his legs. "She needs a break."

He was about to respond, some carefully crafted barb he'd kept quivered for just such an occasion. But then her words sank in, twisting into his chest. And they hurt more pulling out than they had going in.

She needs a break. A break.

From him.

Nora cocked her head. "Have your attention now?"

Aaron propped himself against the wall, casting a glance down the tunnel to Eden. The good doctor didn't even spare him a look, tending to her patient. She looked frantically at the flickering screens of the nearby machines.

Aaron hung his head low. "...She ever going to talk to me again?"

Nora drew in a breath, composing the words. "Aaron, I'm your friend, so please take this in the spirit in which it's intended. You fucked up. And not just with her. You made a bad call that put her in danger and got some other people killed. And in any normal circumstance, I'd punch you in the junk, but we're kind of in the *middle* of something here." Nora jerked her thumb at the line of wounded bedded along the walls. "You...let your head take a break from thinkin'."

"I had to make a call."

"'Is she ever going to talk to me again?'" Nora mocked his facile tone. "Get your head screwed on straight, or I will take it off. You will never be this big Legatus-thing to *me*, you got that?" She stomped off back down towards Eden's station, stopping for a second. "We're going to do a memorial service tonight for everybody."

For everybody. For the wounded who didn't make it. For everybody he failed, that he chose to abandon.

For Keira.

"I'll be there."

"You better be," Nora threatened. And with that, she continued on over to Eden, posting up by the corner like some kind of guard in case Aaron decided to come sulking. Eden looked askance, unwilling to look in his direction. He couldn't hear what she said, but the melody of her voice carried up the tunnel as she consulted with a patient.

He wanted to cry, to break something, to eat, to go for a run. He wanted to shout, to throw up, to go sleep for forever. His skin felt like it was molting, every inch of him vibrating, a plucked string.

He wanted to know she was okay.

"626?" A familiar voice cut through the buzzing in his ear. He turned to see Kipling, that single strand of a man, standing an almost reverential distance away, clutching his cap in tight fingers.

"Kip. You alright?"

"I'm..." He choked on all the words he wanted to say, unable to arrange them in an order that made sense, before shaking his head. "It's not me."

Aaron looked around, a gravity suddenly pulling hard on his shoulders. "Where's 'Toly?"

Kipling's eyes started to water, openly weeping. "They took his arm, Aaron. Whole bloody thing. It was his good arm. He—he shuffled the cards with that arm. He...they *took* his bloody arm, Aaron!"

Aaron squeezed his eyes shut. These two men had been prison guards at his Capital barracks, bored and boorish. They had been hungry for action, to see something of purpose.

Now they had tasted it. And the sweet adrenaline had turned to ash in their mouths.

"Would you..." Kipling hiccupped, sniffing away his grief. "Would you come say something to him? He's pretty torn up about it."

Say what? That his sacrifice had meaning, that his bravery had inspired, or that his courage deemed worthy? Standing up against bullies might be the right thing to do, but it's going to get you hit. That's a fact.

The right thing wasn't the easy thing, even if it's easy to feel right. Now, Eden wasn't talking to him. And Anatoly, Keira...

"I just wanted to..." Aaron muttered, musing to himself.

"Sir?" Kipling asked.

Aaron's eyes wandered afield, anywhere but right there. And he saw it. Over Kipling's shoulder, attendants guided the gurney into place alongside the tunnel wall.

Keeper. Graccus stood by his side, a sculpture of a man standing watch.

"I'll be right over," Aaron murmured to Kipling, laying a hand on the man's shoulder. The grunt leaned into the touch, grabbed Aaron's hand and pinning it down. But he let Aaron slide away.

Aaron's boots scuffed against the stone as he approached Keeper's gurney. The kid was motionless. He wasn't even sure the boy was breathing. If the machines didn't chime in rhythmic confirmation, he'd never have believed it.

Graccus looked up. "Kid's a helluva pilot."

That was it? That was all he had?

Aaron drew his eyes up to the Oskie. His eyes were dry, his stance solid, but there was a lingering weight to him. He was going to stand silent vigil over this boy. Out of shame or duty?

Keeper moaned, stirring from his dream. Aaron's throat seized.

Look at him. The chunks of metal protruding from his chest, oozing blood-soaked bandages, while his breath hitched and wheezed.

They did this to him. Those honorable benefactors from Sol here to dispense happy justice. Keeper had stolen a ship, streaked out into danger to save defenseless people from horrible ends.

He didn't even have a weapon. And they did *this*.

One blue eye fluttered open, like a crystal in the light.

"Hey," Aaron stopped at that, hearing the tremor in his voice.

"Hello, sir," his voice grated, "...sorry I hit you."

"Don't be."

Another kinetic strike and the mountain shivered. Keeper strained, his lungs defying him for a moment. He pulled and pulled, unable to grab air. Aaron thought he must be choking but then, he broke through.

Sweet release.

Aaron couldn't look at him, couldn't look at those blue eyes a moment longer. He stared at the rock above his headboard, counting the air pockets in the stone. "Doc told you anything?"

"Nobody's told me nothin'," the boy said, weakly, a gurgle in the back of his throat. "Guess they've got a lot to handle, huh?"

A rivulet of blood flowed off his chest and down his ribs, staining his uniform. Aaron looked about, grabbing some loose cloth from the bedside. He gingerly laid the cloth around the wound, trying to pack it.

Keeper coughed hard. "Are they—okay? Is she..." He couldn't say it.

"Some injuries from the first crash," Aaron confessed, "Aisling's back is pretty bad. But she's stable. The others got dinged up, but... they're walkin' and talkin'. You did it."

The pilot let out a ragged breath, every ounce of air, and for a second Aaron wondered if the boy would draw another. His eyes squeezed tight, thanking unseen powers.

He couldn't tell him that it was all for naught. He'd saved four people—but now, they had no way of fighting back, no plan other than a last stand. The Imperials had them fenced in.

The kid had gone out a hero—and killed everyone.

Keeper shivered. Aaron moved to adjust his blanket, then stopped himself. He had no idea how to help this kid.

How to help anyone.

A white coat passed by, and Aaron grabbed them by the arm. He pulled them in close, whispering an aside. "Why isn't he on oxygen?"

The medic glanced at Keeper, eyes dour. "All we can do is make him comfortable."

"What are you talking about?"

"The AutoDocs are tasked to their limits, we're low on supplies. We have to prioritize—"

"I don't—I don't understand. We arranged for medical to have everything they needed!" Aaron objected, probably a little too loud. He was drawing attention now.

The doctor gingerly pulled Aaron's hand down, his voice stern. "Those resources were reassigned. Sir."

He had the technicians clear a small alcove for him, where they set up a simple uplink. Cable was run to the surface, and Aaron waited patiently for the screen to light up.

Admiral Deckard Tiberiet settled down in front of a similar screen high above him, recognition flashing across his face. "Legatus."

"Admiral, you're a bad person. I hope you don't mind me saying so."

"Granted freely," the Admiral said, shoulders slumped. "Have you reconsidered your position?"

"You make a habit of shooting people in the back when they're running away?"

A pause, to go along with the glimmer of regret in Deckard's eye. "I don't fight wars theoretically, Aaron."

"So it's not murder if you win, then?"

"It's not murder if you have power," Deckard corrected, but a faltering voice. "I think you know that by now."

Aaron's eyes narrowed. "You don't want to fight like this."

"Of course, I don't!" Deckard hissed. "But this fight is bigger than either one of us. Every day you stand in defiance of Imperial authority, more Dusters decide they don't want to pay taxes anymore; more Capitals believe they can be free if they simply kill their jailers; more people defy the Consul's will. You—right here, today—might be in the right, but you create a hundred wrongs in the galaxy tomorrow. That calculus cannot be ignored by a man in my position."

"Bullshit," Aaron countered. "You gunned down an aerial transport full of wounded. Any other century at any other place, they'd have you strung you up."

Deckard chuffed, a bitter laugh. "Military history is a bit of a blind spot for you, is it?"

Aaron sighed, leaning back to stretch out his neck.

"Aaron, you...confound expectations, do you know that?"

Aaron chuckled. He was hearing those words come in several different voices these days. "That a compliment?"

Deckard considered him, careful study of an animal behind glass. "You don't strike me as a natural renegade leader."

"Admiral, you're underselling yourself. You should retire and become a therapist."

Deckard shrugged. "I've met my share. Even killed one."

"Is it my 'devil may care' ambience? What, what was the big reveal?"

The military man's eyes softened, careful and considerate. "You don't have an axe to grind. No tragedy to avenge. You have no politics, no agenda. You're not a figure making history. You're made *by* it."

"Disappointed?"

"Not many people have assembled the support, inspired such devotion, purely by accident." Deckard cocked his head, puzzling it out. "But you have no *reason* to be fighting me."

"I like living. I like my friends living. Reason enough."

"No, it's not." Deckard's eyes fell, studying the lack of shine on his boots off-screen. "But all of those around you fight *for* something. The fall of the Consul, abolition of their Capital status, or even pure greed. You..."

He stopped, considering the young man.

Aaron took a breath, slow and heavy. "I fight...because people keep coming down here to hit me."

Deckard blinked. He never blinks. But right then, he did. "Will you surrender?"

"What do you think?"

Aaron closed the screen with a clack. He let out a ragged exhale, one step short of sobbing.

Hands slid around him, draping across his shoulders and down his chest, embracing him. He felt the warmth behind him, around him. He reached up to grab it, pull it close, but found nothing but empty air.

He looked up. Eden stood across from him—but glowing blue eyes. The Queen.

"I'm sorry," he said to that face.

She nodded, her eyes soft. "Our story enters its final chapter."

A chittering purr, as Scar sniffed and chuffed around at his elbow. The big beast nuzzled at his arm, abrasive leather pads scraping his skin. Aaron laid a hand on the big guy's hide, feeling out the pocked and porous surface.

The Queen smiled. "But it has been such a journey, *ak'thun*. We have enjoyed...having a family."

"Sir?" a timid voice asked.

Aaron blinked. And she was gone.

"Yeah?" Aaron barked, rubbing his nose on his sleeve.

An aide—maybe an orderly. They wore civilian clothes, business wear, but spackled with old blood. They'd been standing next to someone who had met a particularly unnatural end.

They couldn't be older than fifteen, fresh faced but sunken cheeks.

Aaron blinked. "What is it, kid?"

The aide swallowed hard. "You wanted to be told...the Lieutenant—"

Keeper.

"He's dead?" Aaron asked.

The kid nodded, small jerking motions. They shrunk away, afraid that Aaron might lash out.

Aaron didn't have that level of vitriol left in him, not for anyone. "Thanks. Do me a favor, can you tell—"

"Already done, sir."

Aaron nodded, waving the aide on his way.

Instead, the kid stepped forward. "Sir? Can I get you anything?"

Could he end a war and cook a good hamburger and mute all the noise of the world? No?

Aaron smiled, soft, petting Scar again. "No. But thanks for asking."

He laid his head down against the big beast, feeling for the warmest spot and waiting for the pain to fall away.

CHAPTER
TWENTY-FIVE
EDEN

EDEN RUBBED out the stress in her hands. An old colleague had taught her how to roll the wrists, and to squeeze out any tension in each individual finger. It kept her hands from cramping up after thirty-hour shifts.

Her eyes were barely focusing, dry and crispy sand at the edges. She probably couldn't spell anymore, let alone give adequate instructions.

She sauntered up to the rock face at the side of the Hive, fully prepared to curl up in a corner—not expecting the Jergad drone to step out from a shadow. As if she had enough energy to be jump-scared right now.

She stared at it, her eyes crossing, before she realized where it had stepped from.

The Jergad had carved an alcove, one of several, into the face of the rock: the beastie had made little bunks for its guests.

Eden looked up at the Jergad, her eyes watering. She mouthed a thank you, kissing the tips of two fingers and comically pressing them against the creature's side. It inspected the point of contact, as if expecting to find something she'd left there.

She slithered into the space, pulling her stubborn legs in behind her. The rocks seemed to warp to her shape, cushioning her back and head. She didn't really want to think very hard about how that was happening. The Jergad secretions were known to harden into—

See, now she was thinking about it. Gross.

She turned over, her shoulder brushing the ceiling of her little stone pocket. Behind her eyelids—

—Keira's upper half gasping for breath, her legs splayed out a few feet away.

She snapped her eyes open. They felt dry, almost crisp against the cold humid air. She turned over, trying to get comfortable. She rolled her shoulders, shifted her hips. She rocked her head to-and-fro, feeling for that natural place, that sweet spot. But every time she closed her eyes...

Keira stared back at her.

The Jergad groaned, shriveling at her discomfort. Had it done something wrong?

"Not you, *bocho*," she said, using the Colonial creole term for baby. "This is all me."

Eden sighed, draping a hand across its crusty skull fan. She could feel the hollows of its bones.

This did nothing for its spirits, as the creature nuzzled against her hand. Aaron said they could sense life. How far did that extend? Of course, it had been long established the Jergad were quite sensitive to smell—perhaps it just smelled her stress and exhaustion? The sweat and blood of her hard day had to be quite potent.

She propped up onto her elbows, matching stares with the Jergad drone. "I'm super grateful for this. It's just..." She couldn't get comfortable.

A chitter back from the beastie.

She sighed, pulling herself out of the alcove. "Walk with me, *bocho*."

The big guy sort of coughed. Something she took as a yes, because it followed on her heels. And Aaron said these things had no individuality! Or maybe it already 'knew' her from their shared experiences with Scar?

She was going to go batty trying to figure these things out.

Eden wandered out into the cavern. Most of the day's work had simmered down, people huddling in small spaces to rest and eat while a skeleton crew manned stations.

Soldiers dribbled in from the tunnel, limping their way out the impromptu Hospital ward and into circulation. They all bore the same slack-jawed awe as they took in the massive construct before them.

Eden shook her head—she'd let herself become accustomed, let the magnificence of an alien civilization become a backdrop. The big biological tank nuzzling her back had worked with hundreds of others to assemble titanic spires hundreds of feet tall. It had taken engineering, ingenuity, and no small amount of sweat.

Bocho chittered, as someone stepped up to Eden's side, marveling at the alien towers. "You think they stacked 'em up like bricks? Or did they carve out the cave around it, and knew enough architectural engineering to leave behind some supports?"

Eden's head lolled to one side, her neck far too tired to hold it up straight. The Governor, Talania, leered down at her. "You look terrible."

"That's because I'm exhausted."

Talania smiled and it was the most welcome thing, like fresh baked food or sunshine on a blue sky.

The governor looked back at Bocho. "Who's the new guy?"

Eden shrugged. "He's adopted."

"Who saved who?"

"Shut up."

Talania chuckled. She nudged Eden with her elbow, nearly bopping the much smaller woman in the ear. Eden couldn't even be irritated—she was suddenly that much lighter on her aching feet.

"Come on, Doc. Have a drink with me."

"I need to sleep."

Talania smirked, incredulous. "So you're sleepwalking out here with a guide drone?"

Eden shrugged. "I'm wandering. He's following."

"One drink," Talania said, raised finger. "You'll sleep better, I promise."

"Speak from experience?"

Talania rolled her eyes and waved for her to follow. The sylvan woman couldn't help but strut, legs too long for the rest of her frame. She was likely to have hip problems in later life.

God, could she just turn her brain off for five minutes?

"You look like hot garbage," Talania commented.

"No. That's jus' the smell."

"Your hair looks crunchy."

Eden swiped her hand across her scalp, caked in oil, gunpowder, and a not insignificant amount of blood. She reached back, pulling on the hair tie and shaking out the boggy morass of her pony tail.

It immediately fanned open in every direction, a sticky mess, frizzed and broken strands draping over her face and running down to her shoulder blades.

Talania sucked on her teeth, the amusement positively dripping from her eyes. "I have never been more attracted to another human being in my life."

What?

Before Eden could process that, Talania had walked on, leaving her standing there. Had she noticed, or had she just tossed that sentiment blindly over her shoulder?

Bocho nudged her back, urging her onward.

Near the base of the rightmost pillar, several soldiers had gathered. Lights had been strung up, pressed on to the Jergad resin. It gave the entire area a glassy refraction, like they were being lit through ice. People passed around canteens and bottles, sharing what they had in a kind of alcoholic commune.

"Your kind of people, huh?" Eden asked.

Talania didn't have to say a thing. She simply raised her hands and a polite greeting from the assembling rose to answer. As much as they were saluting her arrival, they were trying to keep their voices down.

But one guy wasn't so warm.

"Hey, whoa," one big Regular said, a recently bandaged burn wound to one cheek, "No roaches."

Bocho murmured, confused by the confrontation.

Talania didn't miss a beat. "Then what the Hell are you doin' here?"

"Governor," he grumbled in acknowledgement.

The man didn't back down, lip curled as he stared at the Jergad. Eden knew the look. She'd dealt with many an unruly patient.

She didn't recognize him. Maybe he was one of the new recruits, or maybe he was one of the Regulars from the Riley days. He was tall and broad, like someone had hewn him from the mountainside, with a square jaw. He belonged in a storybook felling huge trees and slaying evil wolves.

Talania also didn't back down. It wasn't in her nature. She cocked her head at him. "Do you have a comment you'd like to share with the whole class?"

"No ma'am." Yes he did. Men like him always did. He said it to all of his friends like he was in a loop. But now that the Governor was at hand, he was suddenly all sneers and disdain. Respect for the office, he'd say later.

He was a coward.

A hand clapped on the Regular's arm, pressing a half-empty bottle of mead into his hands.

Aisling.

The Doctors had trussed her up in a mobility aid of sorts—her gurney had a joystick, and she glided through the air on maglev, like she was sitting on a cloud. A fitting description, since she left a perfume of antiseptic fumes in her wake.

She raised an eyebrow at the guy. "We are all crashing on the same couch, so maybe try on your big boy pants, eh Parralt?"

The Regular—Parralt—sneered. "I'm not drinkin' with no roach."

"Then don't share with him," Aisling said. "He probably wouldn't appreciate your exquisite palette anyway."

Parralt took the bottle and slumped back against the rock, leering at Bocho the whole way.

Well, they weren't going to fix a generation's worth of fear and propaganda in one evening.

Talania leaned over to Eden. "Sorry about that."

"Oh, 'I'll sleep better', huh?"

"I'm a politician," she ribbed, "I might've lied a little bit."

Aisling floated back over to the side of the pillar. She had her very own alcove in the rock, where a nice supply of liquor had been pooled.

Talania pursed her lips. "Quite a haul, Lieutenant. Did you knock over a few grocers on the way in?"

"I learned from the best," she quipped, sipping off a bottle of green Kevalky liquor.

"What's the damage?" Eden asked.

Aisling wiped her lip, head craning back as she jogged her increasingly fuzzy memory. "Spinal reconstruct if we ever get back to the world."

"Slipped disc?"

Talania bumped Eden in the shoulder, scolding. "Stop working."

Aisling rolled her neck out. "Yeah, well, I don't fly with my feet anyway."

What to even say to her? Eden had lost friends before, lost them to cruel and violent men, lost them to the very creatures that now sheltered their fledgling rebellion. She never wanted to be reminded of their faces or congratulated for surviving.

Aisling and her had that in common.

"I'm sorry about Keeper," Talania said, eliciting a silent wince from Eden.

Aisling noted Talania's good will and Eden's reaction. "Thanks." But she gave Eden a knowing nod.

It hurt. It always did. But the civilians didn't know any better, did they? They meant well. That's what mattered.

Eden hunched over, peering at Aisling's implant. "Want me to take a look at that?"

Aisling shuddered, and shrugged, trying to hide the fact. "Knock yourself out."

It was a simple enough modification. Military wanted to be able to repair and upgrade easily. There'd be a plug in the back of the socket. She likely just had a bent lead.

She searched for the release, but vines of her oily hair kept drooping across her face. Eden tried to gather her hair up in the hair tie, but it had been released from its prison and refused to return without a fight. Whenever she got one bunch back up, another would slip free.

She paused, letting out an exasperated sigh. If she couldn't even get her hair in place...

She felt murky, like moving through a thick fog that held fast to her limbs.

Vision blurred. Her eyes fluttered shut—and Keira gasped, hollow and wet.

Eden shook her head, stretching out her eyes.

Talania looked at Aisling with a forced smile. "What do you have in the hundred proof area? We're going to be here a while."

All Eden could think was 'Get it out of the way.'

She snapped her quick knife off of her belt, grabbing a clump of her matted hair. Before anyone could object, Eden sawed through the morass. In a few short seconds, she had pared back the wild, leaving a dusting of black strands on the ground.

Talania peered at the disheveled doctor. "Please tell me that's not what you've done your entire adult life."

"It was in the way," Eden chirped, as she stooped over an alarmed Aisling. She inspected the implant, eyes crossing as she tried to suss out what the surgeons had done on this case.

Aisling was not comforted by the delirious woman and her knife. "Maybe you should sit down?"

"And do what?" Eden snapped. And she regretted it instantly, hearing the echo off the walls of the cavern. She couldn't sleep. She couldn't grieve. She couldn't even cut her hair.

Talania laid a hand gingerly on her shoulder, and wrapping her other hand around Eden's knife. "Aisling? Round of drinks. Eden, give me the sharp and pointy."

"Why?"

"Because we're going to do this correctly. Come here."

Talania pried the knife out of her hands, and pulled her over to the pillar. She leaned against it and guided Eden to the ground between her knees, locking her in place with a firm grip.

Before she knew what was happening, Aisling pressed a copper mug into her hands. "Take care of yourself, or there won't be a person left to care for everybody else."

"But..." Eden stopped, no real response to that. There were patients that needed to be seen. There were defenses and strategies to plan. There were people in prison back in Vanguard.

And Aaron...

And Talania...her fingers tracing along the nape of Eden's neck, assessing and touching and, and, and...

Aisling gave a solemn tap of her own cup against Eden's. "The Path is guarded by some good people."

"Yeah," Eden said, giving a weak toast back. She took a pull of the liquor—a clear numbing peppermint flavor filled her nose and burned her throat.

But at that moment, she didn't care.

Talania sniffed hard, the pungent stench hard to ignore. "Well! You broke out the good stuff."

"Nothing but the best for my Governor."

"We appreciate your support and your donation," Talania said, as she plucked the bottle from Aisling's hands. She took a strong swig of the stuff—and judging by her bulging eyes, it was more than she had prepared for.

Eden sipped her drink while Talania worked, carefully paring her hair down with the knife's edge, and combing out the clumps. She poured water from a canteen into the comb to brush it through, at least rinsing her hair of the oils that bound them up.

She took a breath and let her eyes fall closed.

Their voices were clarion, and the idle scrape of the comb's teeth against her scalp was a stinging massage, as though there were pounds of stress in her scalp that had to be buffed away. She eased into it, like reclining into hot water, Talania's fingers in her hair and the liquor in her gut.

The calm was seductive, alluring. She felt Talania's knees squeeze a bit tighter about her shoulders, holding her upright as she had slackened.

A shelter.

Aisling started up some story, but Eden drifted away, listening to the sound of her voice and the pull of Talania's fingers in her hair. She heard laughter from the soldiers around her and quiet celebrations. Lovely.

Bocho scuttled up to her feet, like he was trying to hide his arms and legs under his body, a gigantic mutant sourdough bread loaf. He nudged her boots with his head, chittering. She smiled, idly draping a hand onto the big guy's knotted hide. He was an ugly buddy, but he just wanted her to feel better.

It wasn't to last. A new voice drew her out of her reverie.

The momentary joy was sucked away by the vampiric aura of Whitby, as the statesman failed at his attempt to casually saunter up to this underground speakeasy. Hands shoved into his frayed jacket pockets, shoulders hunched up and hiking the tunic halfway out of his trousers. He trudged over to the trio like he was a child being forced to apologize.

But his tone was far more aggressive. "Governor Dedria, fancy seeing an *addict* like you at a gin joint like this."

"Stefan," Talania said with the fakest of smiles, a dagger hidden in her pleasure while she held a literal knife, "I'm actually off the clock right now, but I'm sure one of my aides can take down your threat *du jour*."

Aisling kindly extended him her middle finger.

"Charming," Whitby mused, turning to the wider crowd of boozy soldiers. "Our Governor's giving a makeover while the rest of us sit on rocks."

"You couldn't sleep either?" Eden asked.

"That's hardly my—" Whitby was going to say something else, but he took a step too close to Eden.

Bocho growled, deep threatening bass. Whitby damn near jumped out of his skin. He looked at the creature in horror as it unfolded in front of him, rising up to its full ten-foot height.

It took a moment for Whitby to find wherever his breath had run off to. "You can...you cannot bully me into silence, Governor."

"Bully you?" Aisling asked. "Buddy, you came over to *us*."

"I came over to advise the Governor as to the state of things." He didn't wait for them to contradict, but spun about to the crowd. "The Governor is complacent with her power, content to flex it as she desires and silence any who would dissent!"

"Hey!" Aisling tried to cut him off.

But Whitby just took that as fuel for his fire. "Even now! Her allies would have me shut down for my beliefs! I swore an oath, not one all that different from your own. There are people back in that city we owe our service to. Their homes, their lives—all shattered by her pride. Because she made a devil's bargain, throwing her support behind criminals and monsters."

It would've been a stirring speech, had it not dripped with self-satisfaction and salt. It was like he enjoyed the taste of his words, the soothing sound his voice made as it bounced back to him, wrapping him like a blanket. He was never more comfortable than when bloviating into open space.

Bocho flexed its broad shoulders, a threat display. It gave Whitby a moment's pause, as his active imagination illustrated the possible ends.

He had bluffed his way into an ugly scenario. If Talania really was the despot he claimed she was, there would be very little reason for the beast not to cut him down where he stood.

The soldiers around the bar watched the little drama. Some nodding assent along with Whitby and looking for the Governor's response. Parralt, in particular, smiled into his glass, enjoying the spectacle—with his hand inches from his sidearm.

But Talania just combed Eden's hair, trimming and measuring, watching Whitby's preening and posturing.

"Have you nothing to say for yourself?!" The political golem challenged.

Talania smiled. "I find fires tend to extinguish themselves when I don't give them any air."

"You don't deny it."

"I do not," she said. "And I would be a liar if I did. But while I was allying myself with criminals and monsters, you allied yourself with a particular criminal and a particular monster. And if you had stood at my side then...maybe Riley would be alive in an Imperial jail, rightfully deposed by his subordinates. But *you*...saw that wildfire burning and thought to yourself: 'maybe I can be Governor.'"

"I don't see how—"

"See that is your weakness," Talania challenged. "You don't see the connection. You never do. At least, not when it's inconvenient. The day Riley had me arrested, you stood right by his side, playing to the crowd. No one knew your name then. And we won't remember it when this is all over."

Bocho took a step, a thunderous punctuation that Talania could not have choreographed better. A handful of soldiers drew their weapons, and Whitby himself recoiled.

But Bocho simply huffed, a blast of hot air blustering Whitby's jacket, the smell burning nostrils and watering his eyes. And the Jergad drone marched away, dismissive.

The Queen had seen what she needed to see here. The humans were not so unified or placid. Even among those she sheltered, there were those sharpening blades for familiar necks.

She was disappointed.

Whitby scoffed at is retreating back. "Criminals and *monsters...*"

Eden stood up, the new long bob cut of her hair draping about her shoulders. She swiped her bangs back to the side—and they obeyed! Still oily and matted, but light and full.

She marched up to Whitby, her voice soft. "Speaking as one of the criminals: I can't make you understand. I'm just sad you don't."

CHAPTER
TWENTY-SIX
DECKARD

DECKARD'S INFORMANT had been illuminating. The charts of the interior of the Hive—a silent volcano's old magma chamber—were comprehensive. The naturally-occurring space had been drawn out further, excavated. The informant transmitted extensive details about the dimensions and materials used, and highlighting the importance of the three support pillars. These structures were not decoration.

The creatures secreted a kind of natural concrete that was both malleable and strong. Typical blasting agents wouldn't suffice. The material would more than likely absorb most of the force. This didn't need a detonation; rather, a decapitation.

Two pillars removed, and the old magma chamber would collapse under the weight of the mountain.

Echomapping by thumpers proved inconsistent, so Deckard had approved scanning by small-scale UAVs. Smaller than a housefly, they flew down into the mountains along the Pierson Corridor searching for a pathway to the Hive, embedding themselves in the pumice tunnel walls to act as relays and scanners.

They were destroyed within hours. Not because of detection— the Jergad simply buried them, digging out new tunnels. The labyrinth was always changing. Such was life for subterranean beasts of burden: they built and destroyed tunnels as needed.

Any strike team would have to go in blind, find the Hive, and destroy the pillars.

So what would be the course? Take one of the pillars and demand Aaron's surrender one last time? Or were they past all other recourse?

Aaron's words clung to the inside of his skull like leeches. He fought because people kept fighting him. Would the Capital really lay down arms? Conventional wisdom dictated that the first person to disarm always loses, words that Aaron himself would likely not dispute.

So why did this feel so different?

Caldwell sent Deckard out to put Aaron in his place: six feet under. Of course, Aaron pushed back again. What would the rebel do if instead Deckard let him get up? Maybe yet he could end this without more bloodshed? Offer the Capital his hand rather than a headsman's axe?

His door chimed and the AI Commandant's voice spoke up: "At this time, Captain Wolcott wishes to speak with you, Admiral."

Deckard sighed, rubbing out the stress and the fatigue in his face. "Send him in."

The door slid open.

The boy's face was blanched, his eyes wide and lips slightly parted. He wore his Naval Dress Gray, a curious thing to see outside of port or holiday. And the uniform had received some modifications: his shoulders were patched with cord and badges relative to his new station, a command orchid fixed to his flat cap—he was Captain of a ship in war stance, after all.

But the boy had lived in his utility dress. Why the formal attire?

Two Regulars flanked him on either side, stiff as stone. This couldn't be good.

"Admiral," the boy said with a hushed hollow tone.

No use beating around this. "Welcome back to the *Tartarus*, Captain. How's the Minister?"

Wolcott's eyes fluttered, his starched stance loosening as his brow furrowed. The formal attire had been a dead giveaway. "He's... concerned with our progress."

"Teacher's pet."

The soldiers tightened at that insult. Curious. It's almost like they owed their loyalty to the subordinate officer.

Deckard knew what was about to happen here.

Wolcott licked at his dry lips. Nervous. "The Minister of Defense asked me a direct question. I am obliged to answer it."

"The captain of a ship," Deckard snapped, "is answerable to his crew and to his admiral. The *admiral* is responsible to the Minister. If Caldwell wanted something done, you tell him to speak to *me*. That is not out of pride. That is for your protection, to insulate the soldier from the politics."

"Yes, sir." Wolcott did not seem to disagree on any particular point.

Deckard sighed, turning to consider the blank wall and his memory of the Hive that had projected upon the surface. "What has he instructed, Captain?"

The boy's eyes started to water, his voice shaking. "I have to say now, Admiral, I'm...in uncharted terrain."

What had happened to the haughty new Captain of twelve hours ago? Had he ultimately encountered the responsibility and causality that the role brings? And most especially, had the devil come to collect on his end of the bargain—only for the young officer to find himself woefully light in his pockets?

"What does he want?" Deckard asked, soft.

"He..." Wolcott stopped, no breath with which to speak. Deckard let him gather himself. The boy glanced at the soldiers on either side of him. Like they had their weapons pressed into him.

Finally, he drew himself up tall. "Admiral Deckard Tiberiet, under the authority of Article Seven, Sec-Section Nineteen of the Uniform Code...I am to relieve you...a-and assume command of the Vanguard theater."

Chapter and Verse. Deckard stood accused of insubordination. Caldwell had grown impatient, and hand selected a scapegoat to do his bidding—and take the blame.

Little did Wolcott know that Admiral Deckard Tiberiet was *not* the scapegoat.

One Regular stepped forward with cuffs. It was like the sight of the iron manacles set something off in the young naval officer. Wolcott objected, "No."

The Regular froze, glancing back at his commander, confused. They came here to depose the Admiral; why wouldn't they?

"Step outside and wait for my call," Wolcott ordered, shaky.

The two Regulars exchanged glances, before stepping outside. Wolcott waited for the doors to hush closed before glancing back at Deckard. "What's going to happen to you?"

"You're in command now, boy. You tell me."

Wolcott looked about the cabin, sniffing. "You'll be...confined to your cabin. Until further notice."

"Yes, sir," Deckard said, soft and even.

Wolcott's whole body shivered at that designation and his head just started shaking of its own accord, trying to deny everything that was happening. "I'm scared, Admiral," the boy whimpered. "What will he do to you?"

There was no sugar coating this. "In all likelihood, he'll reinstate me...after you fail. You should ask what he's going to do to you."

Wolcott set his cap down on the corner of a dresser, studying the silver orchid on the brim. He considered it for a long moment...

Before rushing to Deckard's side, slinging his arms around his mentor.

He felt the boy twitching and sobbing against his chest. Slowly, he draped his arms around Wolcott, tapping him lightly on the back, as though afraid he might somehow further upset him. "It's alright," Deckard said. "It's okay. It's just you and me."

"You've got to help me," the boy wept. "Please. I don't know what to do."

Neither did he. A graduate of the Academie Bellator was breaking down into salty fluids in his arms. Deckard had been smeared with blood before, but tears...he didn't know what to do with this.

The river seemed to stymie itself, drying up, but Wolcott's agony hadn't gone anywhere. Deckard could feel it in his hitched breaths, in the pounding heart that thrummed against his own and backwards against his hands.

Should he say something calm, something direct? Remind him he's a soldier? Tell him to 'man up?' Should he say anything at all? Not every nail needs a strike from the hammer. Maybe the boy just needed to blow off steam, and would gather himself up. Wouldn't that be so easy, to let Wolcott collect his own broken self?

No. He'd failed this test before and lost his son. Wolcott needed Deckard right now. He needed a father.

The aging lion laid a hand across the boy's shoulders, a gentle infusion of courage. "What you're feeling...is normal. Doubt helps keep you centered."

"He wants Aaron dead," Wolcott said, in between sobs and heaving breaths. "'Glass the planet. Every inch of it.'"

Would send a helluva message. And leave a lasting scar. Caldwell's ego couldn't withstand a Colonial Duster—a Capital at that—weathering his wrath. Now, there had to be an object lesson.

Deckard couldn't give him orders anymore. He only hoped that Wolcott had listened to him this past year, had learned.

Wolcott stepped away from Deckard, wiping his face on his sleeve and then the other, as though he could erase that canvas so easily. His eyes were red, tears staining his cheeks with cool rivers, and his voice croaked with the strain. "We practiced this at Academie. We ran simulations, war games...Why can't I do it?"

That was what distressed him?!

Deckard blinked. No answer for that. He had a conscience, despite all programming to the contrary.

Wolcott sniffed hard, looking back. "You think I should?"

He wanted permission. He wanted an excuse to settle that voice screaming in his ear: this is wrong.

A conscience is what kept a commander on the ground. Death *must* weigh heavily on them, or there would be no reservation at all to ride into battle, sword and banner high. There would be no qualms over torching fields or razing homesteads.

It *had* to mean something. Or none of it did.

Wolcott's conscience knew this was wrong. He just had to listen to it.

Deckard palmed open his file on the Hive, his spy, and all of the available intel. He pawed through the holographic folder, letting Wolcott see the pages upon pages of material. Then, he balled it up and threw it to Wolcott's wrist computer.

"Gather all available information, and choose the best tactical option...Captain."

Wolcott peered at his wrist, and then back at Deckard, trying to parse out the meaning. He had likely come in asking for an order, something he could follow explicitly. But he was in command now, and being in command meant forging your own way, composing your own verse for the Gospel.

Deckard could only hope he'd taught the boy well.

"I'll uh..." Wolcott began, "I should get back to the *Pompeii*."

That's a terrible signal to send. "*Tartarus* is your ship now. You lead from here."

Wolcott shook his head. "It wouldn't feel right. Not yet." A long pause between them, as Wolcott hung his head. A few deep breaths, then a curt dismissal: "Thank you, Admiral."

Wolcott left and the door shut hard, like it was welded closed, locking Deckard in. He settled back into his chair, feeling the hard cushion dig into his back. Lumbar support didn't feel all that kind right now.

He glanced at the shelf, the picture of his son. The face said smile but the eyes...cutting, judgmental.

He fished in his desk drawer for a long pine box, cracking it open to reveal the reeds of incense. His nose was instantly flushed with cinnamon and vanilla, amber and lavender, fresh cut grass. He plucked one from the sleeve—didn't much care which one at this point—and slipped it into the socket on his desktop. The contact strike instantly lit, spilling smoke across the surface and down into his lap.

He waited, breathing in the lovely warming spices: nutmeg, ginger. It smelled like a cup of cider in front of a roaring fire, his feet up and a blanket about his waist while snow drifted down from the sky like powdered sugar.

But to no avail. His heart still pounded and his fingers still twitched. His cabin, once a place of quiet meditation was now a jail cell.

Wolcott had been an exemplary student, almost too good. And given a normal tour of service, he'd have learned how to lead, would have proven an exceptional commander with humility, emotional intelligence, strength metered with kindness.

Instead, Caldwell had used the flag lieutenant as a puppet. Wolcott would go down in history a failure, weak and impulsive, a slave to his betters because he didn't know that defiance was an available option.

Like Marcus Riley had, just another angry young man.

Deckard wouldn't have it.

A few key strokes sent out the call, and he threw the picture display up to the wall. He was amazed it connected at all—the kid might have revoked his command, but apparently not his log-in privileges. A connection signal relayed from their satellites to the hull and beamed back to the Jump Point where it cascaded across the universe all the way back home.

To Minister Caldwell.

He might not be able to speak with the coward from so far away, but he could still engage with him.

A green light on his bracer indicated a secure link. The Minister might have ordered Deckard's arrest, but he was still taking his calls.

Deckard's cheek twitched, the flash of a smile before business took over.

As he spoke, white text scrawled across the projection. Deckard consulted the clock on his desk. "Minister, I'm surprised. It's three o'clock in the morning for you. Were you expecting my call? Kind of you to answer at all, really."

Somewhere on Earth, in a nondescript office building there was a nondescript office with a nondescript man. Deckard had visited Caldwell's office twice before and had not been impressed either time. The walls were blank eggshell white, absent any ornamentation, pictures, or art. His black geometric shelves lay empty and his minimalist cube of a desk stood barren.

Caldwell himself however, he stood in full regalia at all times, wearing the formal robes of his station to a night at Dunsweir manor and to his favorite steakhouse. Ribbons and medals from his service hung off his shoulder, enough to pull the man slightly off-balance. And his hair was cut high, the blonde length slicked back and combed to a precise stripe atop his head.

Caldwell didn't want to distract you or impress you. He wanted your attention. Deckard knew it for what it really was—vanity.

Somewhere in that office, Caldwell now sat. Perhaps he was sipping fine scotch and smugly reading Deckard's message. Perhaps he was fuming that Deckard was allowed privileges at all.

But the text soon wrote back, as the message bounced the six Jump Points to the *Tartarus*, white letters etching themselves on the wall.

Caldwell wrote: "I reserve time for things of import."

Deckard scoffed at that. Not enough time to come out to Vanguard personally.

"He's a perfectly good officer, Alvin," Deckard stated. "Don't do this to him."

"Speak plainly, Citizen Deckard."

Citizen. Not Admiral.

Deckard took a breath, composing himself. "Captain Wolcott...

has been directed to commit heinous and reprehensible actions. He doesn't know that he even *can* refuse those orders."

Caldwell had little to say in response. "Captain Wolcott is a loyal officer."

"Loyalty is not competency," Deckard said.

"No, but it is quite predictable."

Deckard's eyes narrowed. "You never gave the order. You gave an expectation. And the boy filled in the blanks himself."

He could almost smell Caldwell's smug satisfaction through the text. "I cannot be hung for an order I did not give."

The Minister had drawn restrictions on the boy, boxed him in, and let the young upstart fillet himself. He'd commit war crimes in the name of the Empire—and the Empire would see him drawn and quartered for it.

Loyalty.

Caldwell wrote: "You are no longer burdened with command, Deckard, and I hope you will enjoy your retirement upon return to Sol. But I do so hope that you'll remain ready to assume your station, in the event the Consul asks you to serve again."

Deckard had been outplayed. And Wolcott would suffer for it.

"My service is to the People, Minister."

CHAPTER
TWENTY-SEVEN
AARON

SOMEHOW, the luminescent moss knew what time of day it was. Perhaps it had its own internal clock, but the lights in the cavern dimmed at the appropriate hour, only flickering like candles at midnight. Taking the cue, the humans extinguished their lights and tried to sleep.

Aaron tucked himself in his little pocket in the wall of the cavern. Scar curled up just outside, the dull hum of its breathing a kind of comforting metronome. The big guy was actually snoring. They might be a unified consciousness, but mutations made certain each beastie was unique.

And Scar snored. Heh.

Aaron awoke with a start. No nightmare clinging to the edge of memory, no groggy fog to sift through. He was alert and precise, almost as though he'd never actually slept.

But the Queen stood at the edge of the light, an indistinct human form. A pair of solid blue eyes peeking out of the dark.

"They have come."

He didn't need to hear another word. He pulled himself out of his alcove, snagging his rig and rifle.

He tried to shout, to sound the alarm. But it was buried under the war cry of the Jergad—a hundred howling, chittering cries that seemed to come from the very walls.

And every human being everywhere was awake now!

Something slammed into him, an arm cupping his waist and hurling him to the ground. He skidded along the ground, his back finding every imperfection in the stone. It had been a good while since he'd been hit. He almost forgot the numbing vibrations that echoed up from shoulder to sternum and down his leg.

Graccus crouched over him, his laser rifle tucked hard into his shoulder. "They're here for *you*, Aaron."

"Did you have to throw me?!"

"Yes," the Oskie said, simply. "You were out in the open."

Troops started gathering around them, injured and not. Some lingered at the edges, barely able to stand. Others pushed to the front as they strapped on their gear. Nora adjusted Solomon's rig, trying to lift weight off of his gut wound. Eden hobbled over on her cane—

Her hair hung loose around her shoulders, framing her hardened face and stiff jaw.

A pair of gloved hands heaved him to his feet, seasoned and harsh callouses he could feel clean through the leather. Sergeant Bray spun him about, pulling him close with a palm to Aaron's neck. "This is it, shortstack. You ready for the apocalypse?"

"Are you?"

Bray smiled, the war-forged elemental in his gut reignited. "Tell 'em what you want."

What you want. He was in command. Give the orders. Be the soldier they all think you are.

"Graccus..." Aaron paused, thinking. The Oskie was fast, stealthy, and had already demonstrated he could handle members of his own class. "Guerrilla work, in and out. Keep 'em off balance, and take care of anything too big."

The Oskie grinned. His skin shimmered and he vanished.

Aaron turned to the crowd surrounding him, the eyes of his

friends and colleagues alike. Many bowed their heads, unable to meet his gaze. Some steeled themselves, drawing strength from his gaze.

A voice from the crowd. "Are we going to die?"

It was like all other sound dropped away. No one wanted to admit who said it. They all felt it.

Bray's eyes panned over the group. A few dozen shooters, and twice as many wounded.

He grunted. "There is no other foxhole. Backs to the wall. You hold your corners, you shoot straight, and they will bounce right off us. They have come a long way to be disappointed. Huah!"

Heard. Understood. Acknowledged.

A muted refrain from the crowd. "Huah."

Aaron's heart sank in his chest. They were already beaten. They were facing career soldiers, elite and seasoned, with state-of-the-art gear. They were the faithful, the righteous, and they were just Dusters, dirt farmers in the Reaches.

It was over.

Aaron called out. "I can't hear you."

Confusion at first, then they responded. "Huah."

"Do you believe? Because I can't hear you!"

"Huah!"

"Legatus asked you a question!" Aaron shouted, invoking their name for him. "He asked you if you believed? He asked you if you came all this way to lie down in the dark. You disappoint him. Or do you have something to say? Do. You. Believe?!"

Talania floated to the edge of the crowd, head and shoulders over most people nearby. She studied him, and something about her look caused him to hitch, pause. Her eyes narrowed and the almost imperceptible tilt of her head, curl of her lip.

Was she actually disappointed in him?

She wanted him involved. This is what that looked like.

Aaron studied the soldiers circled around him. "Are you frightened?" Murmurs in the crowd. "Are you angry? Okay, how about furious?! We've bled for this. Our friends have died for this! They brought fire to *our* doorstep, to our homes."

He let that hang in the air, the crimes of the invaders. He felt the swell, the pressure building in the air like a bubble ready to burst, straining against itself.

Everyone nodded. Talania didn't.

"I'll ask you again. Are. You. Angry?" he asked again. A roll of thunder through the crowd, their rage building. "Then let *them* know it! Huah?!"

"HUAH!"

"Alright!" Bray bellowed. "Let's roll out the welcome wagon. Combat positions, interlocking fields. Only shoot at what you can hit. Grenadiers? Channel 'em into the box. Marksmen? Cut 'em up!"

The crowd dispersed to their positions, bounce in their step.

Solomon staggered up to Aaron, an animal snarl, baring his teeth. Ready, eager. He didn't say a thing, giving Aaron a curt nod before staggering away, Nora drifting along behind him.

Eden lingered, her eyes panning over Aaron. She was lost somewhere in a distant memory. Wistful.

"What?" Aaron asked, sharp and impetuous.

"Legatus..." She shook her head. "You don't...sound like you."

This again? "I'm doing what you all told me to do."

"You used to be quiet." Accused, indicted, and judged. He wasn't a small man trying to ameliorate his enemies anymore. He rose to the call.

She pilloried him for it in just five words. And it hurt to hear it. His stomach fell out from under him.

He had been. He used to be quiet. Background, kind, don't be noticed, don't be seen. Keep the fire close, but don't burn so bright. There had been a time when he had dreamed of a quiet life devoid of conflict.

Now he sought it out.

That's not true. No, it sought him. Riley had tortured him and had decimated a city. He was supposed to just watch? Deckard sent troops in to his home again and again. A young cop had pushed a gun into a teenage boy's chest.

That boy had simply responded the stimuli of a violent world.

No...Aaron wasn't here by accident, by chance. Providence didn't bring him here. He did. He signed up to be a soldier. He entered into this compact willfully. It had been such a long road, and somewhere back behind him...when had he become *this*?

Eden was right. She always was.

When Aaron broke from his reverie, Eden had turned away. The medical staff were being ushered to the back of the cavern, away from the fighting. She fell in with the group, laying her rifle down on the stone, before disappearing from sight.

Bray pushed a cumbersome scope into Aaron's hands. "Get some altitude and call out targets. You give the order, we'll light up whatever you say."

He didn't want to. He wanted to follow Eden.

Bray sensed his hesitation, grabbing Aaron behind the neck. "It's the big time, Capital. Focus up."

Direct fire, advise troops, and achieve your goals. He was to give orders to an army. Give the wrong one, people die. The right one, they might still. They trusted him with an awful lot.

That was the one true reality of command: they trusted him.

Be worthy of it.

"Scar!" Aaron called out. The Jergad galloped out of the darkness, as though summoned from thin air. He stepped on the back of Scar's claws, and the beast leveraged him up onto its back, a stallion of thick hide and blades. Anybody nearby got to see their high priest sit atop a battle mount of nightmares. And they bowed their heads.

Aaron didn't have to press into the Jergad's flanks or pat him on the head. He thought and Scar took off, screaming straight for the central column. Aaron adjusted his stance as the beast hit the stone and began its brutal ascent.

He hadn't even made the summit when the first shot cracked the air. Someone cried out and the proverbial dogs of war were subsequently loosed.

Scar cleared the top, dumping Aaron back onto the plateau—his old residence and the seat of the Queen. That eldritch shape crafted from pure shadow sat perched on the stone, almost gingerly, like a bird on a roost.

The multi-voice of the Queen echoed in his mind. "What do you intend to do, *ak'thun?*"

He didn't have a good answer for them. "Give me everything you've got."

For the first time ever, the distant black monster seemed to ripple into the *real*, settling on to the stone. It cracked under the weight and the vibration ran up right through his boots. It shook off a thousand years of idleness, its piercing blue eyes sinking into his flesh like fangs.

We will stand.

Aaron dropped to his knees on the edge of the platform, craning his neck to see below, as hot flashes of red light strobed the cavern. Plumes of dirt were tossed from explosions. Flickering tongues of muzzle flashes as the Capitals returned fire.

The light show was easy to follow. The Imperials pressed forward, slow and steady.

It was dark. When Aaron had first come, the Oskies had used night-vision augments. Had the Imperials brought similar gear?

"Oh, your highness?" Scar rumbled under him. "Can you get the lights?"

As if commanded, the bioluminescent moss flared, streaking shadows high across the stone walls. They glowed like iron forges, molten metal in crucibles. In an instant, it was as bright as day.

It was like the Imperial advance hiccupped. The pressure forward halted as soldiers pawed at their expensive gear, favoring their eyes.

Aaron snagged the radio on his belt. "Check-check, we've got gatecrashers. Four enemy teams. They're breaking wide, two left, two right. Keeping their backs to the wall."

Bray's voice crackled back to him. "Solid copy, Red Haven. Call for thunder on my target."

Aaron could see the tac-light on Bray's rifle flash on and off, aimed at a batch of Imperials furthest from the door. He wanted to punish them for their arrogance.

It would be his pleasure.

"Your Highness?" Aaron asked. "They're playing your song."

He felt hands laid on his shoulders, a tender touch, but he swore it felt like pure ice had been injected into his carotid. The voice whispered and shouted, in his ears and in his bones, something deeper than words, a single tone.

Clambering overhead, the Jergad swarmed. Dozens. Maybe a hundred, even! Inverted, their claws sunk deep into the stone, they climbed towards Bray's target. And as they came to hang over...they simply let go.

Two-tons of leather and blade, dozens of them, fell onto the Imperial soldiers. They stomped down, driving their scythe blades into the exposed backs of the Regulars—crushing them into gooey mortar under their taloned feet.

The Imperials broke away, trying to flee back to their friends and the exit—but the ground was not their ally, not on Vanguard. It gave way under their feet, swallowing them whole, as hidden beasts dragged them into early graves.

The words rose up, echoes and vibrations, resonating out from the ground.

This...is...our world!

The Jergad joined their voices as one, a choir issuing a communal roar. Defiance.

Aaron peeled his eyes off the spotting scope, eager to blink away the gore that had painted itself onto the backs of his eyelids. He shook his head, once, twice.

Nope, all of it still in there. Charming.

Down—far below, beneath Aaron's perch, someone was moving about. Who? All of the Capitals were on the line and the noncombatants had been ushered to the back, away from the fighting. Aaron drew the scope around, leaning out over the edge of the plateau to get a look.

Someone. They were guiding a large crate. Ammunition? No, it was sealed. They wore a Capital patch on their shoulder. He pulled something out of the crate: a conduit.

"Bray," Aaron radioed, "somebody's at the Eastern Pillar. One of yours?"

A brief pause. But no response.

A tracer round snapped off the rock next to the interloper's head. Bray and a few others had turned about and fired backward. The rogue fled around the pillar, the cable unspooling from the crate.

"The crate!" Aaron cried out. "He's got something—"

A flash of light, as a beam of energy snapped out from the side of the conduit. A guillotine that lashed through the stone. It was a breaching tool, used to cut through walls and even retrieve citizens from train wrecks.

For ten thousand years, men had been felling trees.

Nothing happened at first, but the roof above them creaked, an old house weary of its burdens. And the pillar shuddered, like it let loose a death rattle. Maybe it hadn't worked. Maybe it was indeed cut, but still resting on its sticking place, gravity and friction holding it together. Maybe, maybe...

And then it started to fall, sliding off its stump and showering boulders across the cavern floor. It ripped from the roof, a ball of dirt clinging to it like tree roots torn from the ground. The whole chamber shook as the tower slammed into the ground, its weight digging in.

The Jergad leapt from their aeries, scattering from the tower. One of them landed next to the saboteur. It growled, teeth gnashing. It raised a scythe—

The first shot slagged the beast's arm. The second removed its face. It slumped before him.

"We didn't want you to come here..." the Queen whispered. She sounded so far away, like she had to say it from another room or underwater.

The Tree Cutter turned his weapon left, slagging another alien—before Graccus materialized next to him, and turned the man's wrist around, snapping the bone. For all the resistance it gave him, it looked like there was a mystery joint somewhere in the middle of the man's forearm that conspicuously spewed blood. The traitor screamed, crumpling to the ground, where Graccus swiftly hog-tied him.

"Graccus!" Aaron cried out. "The tower!"

The tower leaned, drifted on its uneven footing. For a moment, Aaron had thought its weight had settled, that it had sunk itself deep enough to hold. But then it drifted, tipped, hanging like the headsman's axe in the air, like it didn't want to do this. Like it grieved for what must come next.

And then it fell...straight for the Capital fortifications.

"Bray, get out of there!"

The tower crumbled, snapping under its own weight as it bent further and further, a hailstorm of stone crashing down. The Capitals leapt from their foxholes, fleeing for safety. And the Imperials laid fire on them the whole way. Shot in the back running away, their clothes catching flame.

Bray lay behind his cover, pinned by gunfire, watching the tower descend upon him. Praying.

A streak of yellow tracers flashed into the foxhole. Graccus sped in, and yanked Bray by the collar—

As the stone collapsed atop them. Had they gotten out? Were they safely behind it? Or were they both now buried under hundreds of tons of unforgiving rock?

He expected the dust and the sound, but he somehow didn't expect the wind. A gust of air swept through the cavern, a gale that seemed hateful and angry. It carried with it the sounds of gunfire and screaming and the singed air from Imperial lasers. It smelled like meat on an open flame.

He could smell the people dying down there.

As the dust cleared, he could make out the Imperials proceeding unabated for the second tower. Confusion had been sowed.

All the technology, all the strategy, all the money—he could've sent killer robots or poison gas or blasted the planet from orbit. All of that...and Deckard had simply used their own people against them. He had taken away the home field advantage.

"Bray!" Aaron shouted in his radio. "Bray, if you can hear me, they're moving on the second pillar."

No response. The troops were closing in.

"Graccus? Are you alright? Nora? Somebody?!"

A hand came to rest on his shoulder. Slender fingers. They didn't pull on him. And he did not clamber up on to his feet. Rather, he floated up, settling softly on the stone. A hand turned his cheek.

Jensen's face—the Queen's burning blue eyes—stared back at him, soft but...tears streaking down. The voice should've quaked, sobbing through, but her voice was calm as the ocean. A soft buoy for his troubles, hiding the monster underneath the waves. "We're so sorry, *ak'thun*. There is no other way."

They hadn't lost yet. "What are you talking about?"

"You've lost so much. We are afraid you will lose more." The Queen scooped his face into both her hands, her palms supporting his head. And in that moment, he had no cares, no reservations. Weightless. "But you are not defined by your loss, or your pain. You can decide who you are. Be worthy of remembering."

"What do you need me to do?" Aaron asked.

"Heroes are just stories, Aaron." Jensen's alien eyes hardened and the glow of the eyes dimmed, like a candle burnt to the quick, smaller and smaller. "Now tell our story."

She was leaving.

"Don't go..."

"Before you, we had never said hello. We've never had to say goodbye before."

"Please, don't go. We can find a way. I'm not *done!*"

Far below, the Imperials wrapped the breaching cable about the pillar, ready to bring the cavern down around their ears. They were out of time.

The Queen shook her head, a knowing smile at Scar. "Take care of them. They will not understand."

"You can't! You *are* them! What are they without you?"

All sound dropped away, like there wasn't a war raging beneath them, like there wasn't even a heart to beat in his chest. The Queen's smile wavered and her chin shook. A tear grew in her eye, like a single drop of crystal. "They are your family now."

His? He couldn't handle the responsibility he had. He could barely take care of himself! How would he manage caring for...?

But he knew, somehow, he'd do it. He would find a way.

The Queen threw her head back and the black shadow behind her followed suit, a grotesque dissonant cry ripping through the cavern. Aaron clutched his ears and fell to his knees.

And yet, this was the safest place to be. Far below, it sounded somehow worse, coupled with the pained screams of suffering Jergad and terrified humans.

This was the banshee scream of an entire planet.

Her hands came alight, glowing with the same rich blue fury as her eyes. She rose, her feet lifting a few inches up and her hair billowed about her face, almost like a wind had plucked her from the ground.

And she melted away, fading, just a mirage on the plains. The titan, the shadow, the Queen itself crumbled, collapsing in on itself. And its blue eyes winked out before the enormity vanished from sight.

But her voice might shatter the mountain above their heads.

You want my home. You want my people.

Come and meet us.

CHAPTER
TWENTY-EIGHT
DECKARD

HE WAS HALFWAY through the bottle of schnapps, studying how the light hit the crystal decanter in different ways, through the curve of the bottleneck and the body full of thick liquor. It cast lines of white light across the wall, ethereal chords on an angel's harp waiting to be plucked.

He rubbed at his sore feet through his therapeutic socks. A thousand days out of dock, most of them standing over his deck officers, did terrible things to his joints and the artificial gravity somehow made it worse. The pressure-wrapped wool soothed the idle pains, but only so much.

Deckard shook his head, taking another stiff pull straight from the decanter. He set it down a touch too rough, holding his hands out to stabilize as it wobbled to-and-fro. He didn't need broken glass right now.

With any luck, Wolcott came to the correct conclusion. Loyalists within Aaron's regime could be supplied by dead drop, smuggled in with other recovered rebel materials. A strike team led by an Oskie detachment would pathfind their way to the Hive, whereupon the Loyalists could strike. With the body of rebel forces occupied, Loyalists hit the first pillar and bring it down.

Should Aaron still refuse to surrender—as was likely—the Imperials would fell the second support. The entire cavern would collapse. They'd mop up the survivors in under a week, identify Aaron within a month, and be on their way home.

A shame—but a dagger in the back was far cleaner than other options. Betrayed by his own comrades would undercut his strength on the galactic stage. And Wolcott might yet escape Caldwell's wrath.

The ship shuddered, the streaks of reflected light dancing across Deckard's cabin wall. An Eisenclad dreadnought did not move easily.

Oh, no. He was firing on the planet.

Deckard jumped to his feet, and the alcohol hit him, lifting his head further and further. He clamped a hand on to the desktop, as though he could keep himself grounded. Or from tipping over.

He straightened his jacket and marched to the door. It didn't budge.

"Commandant," Deckard bellowed. "Open the door."

"Apologies, Citizen Tiberiet," the AI responded. "At this time, your privileges have been restricted."

"Hey!" Deckard called out to the posted Regulars almost certainly guarding his luxuriant jail cell. "I know you're out there, what's—"

He was cut short, as the ship shuddered again, a vibration so severe it nearly numbed his feet.

Gravity engines would keep them anchored if the ship was making maneuvers, which it shouldn't be doing. And that was a bit hard for weapons fire. An impact?

"Sergeant!" Deckard shouted, pounding a fist on the doorframe. "What was that? Are we taking fire?"

"It's nothing, sir." The quiver, the almost choke in her voice told Deckard otherwise.

"Commandant? Report."

The AI held its tongue.

The Sergeant's voice quivered. "I'm sorry, Admiral."

Deckard cursed under his breath, waving a hand in the air to dismiss whatever apologies the AI had lined up.

A crash, splash, and tinkling of glass! The decanter crashed to the deck, shattering, shards skittering across the bulkhead floor. The liquor slid left and right, like ocean waves lapping at the beach.

"Sergeant, you have your orders, and I would not begrudge you following them. But I can't help this ship if I'm locked in here. Tell me what's going on."

A long pause, as the Naval Regular with almost ten years of infantry under her belt considered the options. "We don't know."

Deckard stooped low and snagged his boots, slipping them on his feet. "Open this door, Sergeant."

He couldn't make any threats. There was no way his old bones were going to break down the door. He had no tools, firearms, explosives. But somehow, he knew that by the time he had finished tying his laces, the Sergeant would have the door opened.

And the Sergeant did not disappoint, silhouetted by the flickering lights outside as another quake rolled through the ship.

Deckard drew himself up to his full height. The woman was young, already scarred from conflict, twin jagged lines drawn across her chin. Shrapnel skipped off her face.

"Mayfield, right?"

The Sergeant snapped off a quick salute. Deckard waved the woman's hand back down. "Salute the man in charge. Today, I'm just a loud voice. What do we know?"

She hesitated. "Not much, sir."

Deckard extended his hands to the Sergeant. Mayfield squinted at him, eyes flicking back and forth from his hands to his face.

Deckard sighed. "I'm a prisoner. Slap some cuffs on me or they'll pull your stripes when we're done here."

It took her precisely four seconds for the cold compress of metal to find his wrists. Without another word, gripping the chains in one hand, she led him to the bridge.

With Wolcott away on the *Pompeii*, who would hold the deck on

273

the *Tartarus*? Officially, at least, the Officer-of-the-Deck would be Ensign Alette or Esposito. They couldn't handle ship-to-ship refueling maneuvers. In practice, it'd be Warrant Officer Lindell and his magnificent beard.

In reality, he could not have dreamed up a worse outcome. The door opened, and the first thing he heard was someone wailing. Neither Ensign was anywhere to be seen, the Warrant Officers shouted all over each other...

...and the planet was far too big, looming up on the view screen, dominating it, an artificial bronze horizon to the *Tartarus*'s many spires. They had held a considerate distance from the planet, far enough to bombard with impunity.

They were now in atmospheric descent.

"Report!" Deckard bellowed over the din.

That silenced the chaos for a mere half second, before Weapons Officer Saubert stood up from his station. "Sir! Our orbit is failing, and shipboard systems are—"

Officer Lindell barked out. "Saubert, shut up! Sergeant Mayfield, get that man off the bridge!"

Mayfield's grip tightened but Saubert didn't stop. "We're in a rapid descent and retro-thrusters can't push hard enough. LADAR, weapons—"

Lindell did what most of his station did. He spoke louder, like that did a damn thing. Volume meant nothing if you had nothing to provide. "I gave you an order, Sergeant!"

"Where is the Officer of the Deck?" Deckard asked.

"On the *Pompeii*," Saubert said, scornful. "Esposito too."

They were following the new Captain around, begging for scraps from the table. Far from their stations.

Deckard turned his eyes to big mouth Lindell. "If you have no further objection, I'm assuming command of the *Tartarus*."

He might've, but he didn't say anything more, retreating to his seat. Deckard yanked on his cuffs, and Mayfield stripped them off like she had never properly locked them. Deckard settled into his command chair, powering up the displays.

The chair felt good.

Three holographic screens leapt up in front of him. He only had interest in the center: navigation telemetry. It was a simplistic vector-path of the massive ship's descent into the atmosphere.

At this rate, they'd crash-land into the surface.

Mayfield took her place at his arm. "What do you need, Admiral?"

"A prayer wouldn't go amiss," Deckard muttered, keying up the ship-wide PA system. "Situation One throughout the ship. Emergency crews to your stations."

"He's not an admiral anymore," the consummately unhelpful Lindell groaned.

"Sergeant, help the young man with his chair. He's having trouble with it."

"With pleasure," Mayfield said, marching over to the jackass. She only needed one hand to...guide him up away from his station. She walked Lindell off the bridge with her hand on her sidearm.

"Navigation," Deckard barked, "give me full burn, twenty degrees up."

"Sir, retro thrusters are ineffective!"

"We don't need the retro," Deckard snapped. "Give me main impulse." They were going down hard but he didn't need to counter that force. He just had to push them hard enough straight outward to get back on to their orbit. They were falling; so he could just throw them far enough off the line that they flat out missed the planet.

"Saubert, divert power from all non-essential systems. CATCC, status?"

The air traffic controller didn't dare look away from their console, but their hands were lifted into the air. The screen flickered like it was trying to mind-control him with a secret message. "Sir, I can't see anything out there, and nobody's answering calls."

Deckard pulled the LADAR screen forward as he asked the

question. "Combat, I'm not seeing the other ships. Do we have the *Pompeii?*"

"I have them, sir! *Pompeii* & *Hestia* both...no. No, check that. I lost them."

"Speak up. You *lost* them?"

The officer stared at his console, flummoxed. "They're in and out of scope. They're there and then they're not."

But what could...

It hit him all at once. The aliens communicated via magnetic field. Magnetic.

"The Queen..." Deckard's blood ran cold. She had yanked them in, and now they were just falling.

He consulted the navigation telemetry. They were going to cut this close. "Screw the life support, Saubert. Give me everything you've got. All hands, brace for atmospheric."

Everyone pulled collars over their heads, hard plastic domes sealing them into their uniforms. Any loss of cabin pressure, and they'd be fine.

Deckard keyed up a communication channel. "*Hestia*, *Pompeii*, this is *Tartarus* Actual. Turn for full impulse into orbital vector. Do *not* fight the descent. Repeat, do not fight the descent."

The room went dark and his screens evaporated. The ship lurched, and someone fell, cracking against the floor. Deckard's knees and back ached with the shudder.

The backups kicked in. The dim lighting lit the room in a ghostly white, a pale shine to a dozen dark computers.

In that flash of darkness, Deckard would swear under oath before a tribunal that he had seen two pure blue eyes. On a screen, perhaps? Floating in the air? Had anyone else seen them?

But when the lights came up, they were gone.

The ship rumbled underneath them, a roaring dragon trapped in the cellar. Somewhere, glass shattered. Mayfield had crumpled on the floor, dazed from the fall. Deckard popped out of his chair, bending over to help her to her feet.

"I've lost power!" "Navigation's off-line! We're in the blind!"

"Will this work?" Mayfield asked, a little wild in the eyes.

Deckard shrugged. "You ever skip rocks on a lake?"

"No."

Deckard cocked his head, unable to find another analogy. "It'll work."

Somewhere beneath them, the hull was stripping in the upper atmosphere, as it compressed the air in front of it and dragged against the steel, molecular claws scraping atomic chunks off. With each swipe, the *Tartarus* lost speed. Without power, the engines silenced, he could only pray that they had enough.

And so, he bowed his head. "Bless our burdens, for they weigh on our shoulders."

The ship lurched under him as something important sheared off. They were in a steel box, no view of the outside. But the tongues of golden flame that licked across the metal had to be miles across, pulling and ripping at the floating metropolis.

Mayfield joined him. Saubert too. It was all any of them could do now. Pray that the Pilgrim had turned his gaze to their plight. "Bless our feet, for our Road is long. Bless our hands, for our work is hard."

Another buck from the bronco, sending Mayfield and Deckard clattering face down onto the deck. A warm splash and muted crunch as Deckard felt his nose compress against the corrugated steel.

"And Bless our souls..."

The auxiliary power cut, plunging them all into black.

"For the day is dark." A single meek voice finished the prayer, almost in recognition of the irony.

They didn't dare move, like they'd stir the beast anew, rouse it from its slumber. Every officer held their breath, trying to still their very hearts. Deckard would not have been shocked if the bulkhead tore right underneath him, sending him and two dozen deck officers into free fall.

But then the lights flickered on, and the assuring stentorian voice of the Commandant boomed. "Main power restored at this time. Calculating new orbital vector."

Deckard smeared the blood onto his sleeve and pulled himself into the command chair. "Lock us into CentCom and reset our orbit."

"Sir!" Saubert wiped the sheet of sweat from his forehead, his words grave. "I've got the *Hestia* on scope."

There was a notable absence from that. Where was the *Pompeii*? Where was Wolcott?

Deckard swung the camera feed up in front of him. The computer locked on to the falling fireball and focused in, revealing the crumbling remains of the troop carrier. There were now three distinct fireballs, with small ones crumbling off as every second passed. The ship had split.

And it was plummeting straight for the surface.

"Get me Captain Wolcott," Deckard ordered.

"I can't cut through the atmo interference! It's too weak."

"Give it to me anyway!" Saubert tossed the feed to Deckard's screen. It was a read out of the falling ship, glowing flashes as the LADAR was blinded by the fiery descent. While the *Tartarus* was a floating city, a disc with spires rising from its edge, the troop carriers were large tubes, with modules off the center line making for a fat bottom and narrow top. A massive engine block provided the ship with blockade-running power.

That main engine block was gone, torn off in the fall. The central hull had split in an ugly diagonal, sheering off a helpless middle chunk of the ship. The largest piece was still the front end as it spiraled awkwardly, flares of fire lighting up as the motion exposed new pieces of hull to reentry forces.

"They're twenty kilometers from the surface and falling fast," Saubert said with a hush.

"Wolcott, I don't know if you can hear me, but you have to flatten out your descent." Nothing. Deckard grit his teeth. "You are going to crash, there's nothing we can do about that. But we can save you and your crew. You *have* to flatten your descent. Now!"

Static on the line, and it was like a breath of fresh air. A voice cut through. "How?!" It was Wolcott. He was still alive.

Deckard felt his heart skip a beat, like it hiccupped in his chest. "Wolcott, you don't have your engines, so we'll have to do this with some quirky physics. But maneuvering thrusters should still work."

"What do I do?"

"Roll over, get that fat belly above you, and then turn *into* the fall. Broad top, narrow bottom, you'll become a wing. The air pressure will give you some lift."

"I can't—I can't do it!"

Deckard nodded. "Yes, you can. And if you want any chance of *living* through this, you need to do exactly as I say."

He watched as the metal tube tumbled, flipping its bulbous bottom up, like a dead fish in the water. And then it tilted down.

The unnatural wobble actually stabilized. Not a lot—the *Pompeii* was hardly an atmospheric vehicle. They just had to get their airspeed down.

And now, they were gliding—as much as any spacecraft could.

"Ten kilometers from the surface," Saubert warned.

"Very good," Deckard said. "Now pull up with everything you've got."

"*That's* the entire plan?!"

"It's an order! Do it!"

The reentry fire had stopped, so Deckard had a great view of the scorched ends of the *Pompeii* streaking down over Vanguard's cracked desert clay.

"Five kilometers."

"Pull up, pull up..." Deckard whispered, urging, praying.

The first chunk of the *Pompeii* struck the ground, the impulse engine block splintering and instantly vanishing, a cloud of dirt kicked half a mile into the sky. Shrapnel the size of small buildings went careening through the air at nearly the speed of sound. They didn't need to hit anything to be deadly; the pressure wave from the impact would kill anything within six kilometers of it.

An artificial asteroid had just struck the planet. The after effects would be cataclysmic.

And it was immediately followed by a second, less theatrical, one as the thorax off the troop carrier pancaked into the earth. This was slightly hollower, less mass, so its explosion was dwarfed by its neighbor.

But the front half of the ship sailed off, still descending. It obviously wasn't joining its friends.

This was working.

"Air speed?" Deckard asked.

"Two hundred meters per second."

Too fast. "Wolcott, you have to cut speed. Deploy your solar panels. It'll buy you something."

The *Pompeii* cast off glittering dust behind it, as the solar panels instantly sheared off as they deployed from interior shells. Barely any resistance at that speed.

What else? What else could he do? These ships were never meant to be planet-side, never had the fuel or power to escape gravity. They were *built* in orbital shipyards.

There was nothing else. They simply weren't designed for this.

"I've done what I can, son," Deckard said, soft and quiet. "Brace for impact."

"I—"

Wolcott's signal cut off sharply, as the *Pompeii* dug into the earth. It scraped out a scar in the planet, a trench miles long and leaving debris along every inch. The great wyrm refused to stop, dragging further and further, curling slightly as it went.

Until it finally came to rest, leaning slightly on its frame, half submerged in the piled-up terrain.

Mayfield laid a hand on Deckard's chair. Perhaps she was weak-kneed at the sight? After all, he was glad to be seated for it. Or perhaps she wanted to give comfort, solace, but stopped short, remembering her station?

He'd have welcomed it.

He didn't dare call the boy's name. There was no way communications were still functional after that.

Deckard rose from the chair, creaking old bones. The officers turned to him, waiting to see if he'd say something, anything. Raise their spirits or whip them into shape.

He couldn't. It wasn't his ship anymore.

"Sergeant...I should return to my cell at this time. Saubert? You have the Conn." He presented his wrists to Mayfield, ready for his shackles.

Instead, she dropped them to the deck with a clang, her hand up in a crisp salute. "Your orders, Admiral?"

Slowly and in turn, each officer stood from their console and snapped off salutes to him.

He was disgraced, stripped of his command and his honor. And they still wanted to follow him. It was rebellion by any other name. They were electing to break the chain of command, defy the Minister and by extension, the Consul himself.

This was mutiny. It'd get them all thrown in prison.

"Arrest me, Sergeant," Deckard said.

"Is that an order?" Saubert chirped. Wiseass.

Deckard leered at the Warrant Officer. "You're the Officer of the Deck."

"And this officer warmly welcomes his admiral back to the *Tartarus*...sir. What are your orders?"

Little bastard was going to make him cry.

Deckard sighed, looking back at the command chair—a bunch of nano-processors and hard drives embedded in a block of metal shaped to support his body. It would alter its shape for whoever sat there next, twisting and adjusting the metals to best suit the officer it carried.

It was waiting for him.

He laid a hand on the backrest, like it could speak to him. "Commandant? Redeploy the Vanguard garrison to the crash site. Secure the area before support arrives to search the wreck."

The blue sphere formed in the air, vibrating as it spoke: "I'm sorry, Citizen Tiberiet. At this time, your privileges have been restricted."

"You haven't heard, Commandant?" Saubert said, as he typed in a command to his console. "Admiral's home."

The ball flickered. "Welcome back, Admiral."

But Deckard's eyes narrowed. "Set Condition Two throughout the fleet. I want damage reports from all hands within the hour. Tell the *Hestia* to maintain a four-klick distance from us, echelon formation. Set new high orbit, four hundred. And dispatch search and rescue, staggered deployment."

He always knew command meant people could die. But in thirty long years, he'd never known what his command meant to anybody but himself.

They wanted him here. They all did.

Even Wolcott.

Deckard was going to bring that boy home.

PART FOUR
LEGATUS

CHAPTER
TWENTY-NINE
EDEN

THE DUST HADN'T YET SETTLED, STILL hanging in the air and catching the glow off the moss, like amber snowfall. The crumbling stone cracked and creaked under its own weight, resettling. The pillar laid against the ground like a toppled memorial. Specks of blood along its length, where Jergad aeries had been crushed.

And there was that all too common ambience of weeping. Cries of pain. They echoed off the far side of the cavern, coming back to her all the more baleful.

Sixteen men. Sixteen Imperial officers did all of this. They could've invaded, crushed all resistance—they didn't want to. They wanted to send a message.

Eden looked around, taking it all in. Bocho staggered out of a nearby shadow, its chest heaving with exertion. And there was something...glassy in its stare, its head drifting off to one side before refocusing.

Eden laid a hand on its hide, fresh dents in the leather still warm where bullets had skipped off. It purred at her touch, leaning into the hand, nuzzling up to it.

"I'm sorry," she whispered. "This is our fault."

"Eden!"

She turned to see Sergeant Bray bounding out of a dust cloud. "Gunny!"

Bray stopped a few feet from her, hands on his hips and huffing for breath. She could've sworn he had stopped himself from wrapping her up in a big paternal hug. He looked her up and down, putting a check on his excitement, before assessing Bocho. "You got one too, huh?"

Eden shrugged. "He kinda found me."

"That seems to be how it goes," he snarked.

"Have you seen Nora?"

He nodded. "She's okay. And last we saw, Solomon was up in the tunnels."

She waved her hand. Say no more. The man had gone 'hunting' whatever stragglers had fled. She didn't need to hear any more about it.

"What about Aaron?" Bray asked.

Eden looked up at the central pillar, and the Queen's plateau high above them. "He hasn't come down?"

Bray shook his head. "How would we even get up?" Bocho chittered, offering a ride, but Bray recoiled. "Yeah, I'll be taking a hard pass on that."

"I'll be with the Medical team if you need me," Eden offered.

Bray nodded, jogging off to resume whatever he had been doing.

Bocho perked up, as if to sniff the wind, but its focus had locked in on something. Eden followed its gaze.

Imperials, about four, had been brought to their knees beside the collapsed pillar. Several Capitals sat with them—traitors.

A line of jittery rebels stood, weapons ready but low.

This couldn't be good. Eden started to hobble over, pausing only when she recognized the man at the front.

The Oskie—Graccus—the man without an agenda. He walked up and down the line of captives, assessing them with a disaffected stare. Abruptly, he paused, target lock.

A particularly large Capital sat bound, a mountain brought to his knees. His hand was twisted at an ungodly angle and bound tightly with cord.

The former Regular with a fantasy storybook physique, the tree cutter: Parralt. He was the saboteur.

Graccus inspected him with his ghostly gray eyes. "How's the hand?"

Parralt spat at him, unable to muster more than a dribble down his own chin. Graccus raised an eyebrow in appraisal. Crouching low, the Oskie spy got close enough that Parralt could bite him. But Eden felt the cold aura chilling the air around Graccus, and she was good twenty feet away.

Graccus didn't smile, didn't frown. He didn't have any expression at all, as though the flesh of his face were not his own. "Cynicism is often confused for courage. It resembles emotional control. It's not." Graccus sniffed sharply, as if a foul scent had caught the air. "You're...quite out of control, aren't you, Parralt?"

"Zu gloriam," was all the Regular had to say.

"There isn't going to be any glory," Graccus sighed, with a hint of regret. "Not for you."

Parralt shivered, his lip pouting in a show of disdain. As though Graccus gave the traitor's opinion an ounce of import. The firing line itched at their weapons, eager to do their part of this arrangement. And Parralt was urging them toward that.

This wasn't right.

"Graccus!" Eden called out.

"Not now, Doctor. I'm occupied," he dismissed her, almost politically smooth. He turned his head, like he might get a different angle into Parralt's head. "Who provided you with the breaching cutter?"

"Zu gloriam."

"Gloria? Who's Gloria?" He stood tall, his voice echoing off the walls, "Is there a 'Gloria' in the camp?"

A new body was shuffled over to join them: civilian clothes, with a frayed linen jacket and torn pants. The tips of his polished shoes dragged against the stone, as two Capitals all but tossed their charge into the line.

"Stefan Whitby." Graccus almost saluted the Statesman. "I could've won good money on you being a part of this charade."

Delirious and foggy, Whitby lifted himself up, blinking through the ringing in his ears. Blood stained his cheek.

Graccus leaned in close, whispering something to him. Whitby's head started to shake, denials upon denials, but no energy to speak.

Enough of this bullshit. "Graccus, get over—"

She hadn't yet finished the sentence when he flashed to her side, looming over her. He saw her face twist up and immediately took a step back, correcting his literal misstep. With a slight bow to his head, he addressed her formally and politely. "Ms. Neria, I'm in the middle of an interrogation. Is there any way I can attend to your request later?"

"Who approved this?" Eden pointed at Whitby.

His eyes scanned left and right, like he was looking for the hidden camera. "I...don't require approval to perform my basic function?"

"You arrested an elected official?"

"No," Graccus gingerly corrected with a pointed finger, "I arrested a terrorist."

"Oh, cool," Eden said with a drawl. She then pointed at the line of twitchy triggers. "This is not an arrest. This is a twenty-one-gun *war crime*."

He leaned in to her ear, conspiratorial, not unlike how he'd leaned in to Whitby. "It's just a bit of theatre. Okay?"

"And *way* out of bounds, you should know that. Did the Governor approve this? Did Aaron?"

Graccus bit his lip, conceding with a small nod. "I don't...particularly understand your point, but I also don't particularly object to it. I'll—quietly—tend to our guests while you collect Legatus. I'm sure he'd want to see this anyway."

Aaron would be at the top of the Hive with the Queen. That meant the organic tank needed to give her a lift.

"Bocho." The Jergad stepped up to her side.

Graccus stifled a laugh, almost snorting. "You named it 'Bocho?'"

"Really? Right now?" she snapped at him, amazed he'd take that tone.

He raised his hands in deference and flashed back over to his charges. He lingered by Parralt, but indeed left the Regular alone.

Parralt, on the other hand, leered at her. He was drenched with sweat, his brow tight with pain. But his eyes didn't reflect the same intensity in his face.

Gratitude.

Eden mounted Bocho and spurred her heels. The big guy lurched forward and up the central spire. She clung to its back and squeezed her eyes shut.

She always knew that Loyalists were among their number, those that bled patriotic blue & white. But they ate and drank next to rebels, knew their names and families, shared trial and tribulation. They fought on the Wall and trained in the sand together.

Politics, nations, families, clans—none if it made any sense to her. All she had were more patients. She didn't check their affiliations at the door; she checked their injuries. She listened to what they said and what they weren't saying. And above all else, she simply tried to make it better. This would be like her chief thoracic surgeon telling her to stop sewing up a wound because the patient spoke ill of the hospital.

She didn't give a damn if he did it in print, on television, or to her face. He was hurt. She could help. If there was an explanation for what made one neighbor comfortable with injuring another...it eluded her.

Bocho curled under her as it crested the lip of the pillar. She forced one eye open, then the next, followed by working her jaw left and right to pop her ears.

No black monster cloud hung over the precipice. Perhaps that should've alarmed her, but it didn't. It felt oddly relaxed, at peace.

Aaron sat crumpled to his knees at the edge of the plateau. He wasn't shivering or shaking. Almost...he was vibrating, like a tuning fork. He didn't make a sound, but tears fell down his face like mountain streams, cutting through the dirt pasted onto his face. His eyes locked, studying something...

"Aaron?"

He didn't respond, not at first. But he sniffed away his grief, wiping his nose on his sleeve. "Yeah?"

Did she dare ask? He didn't look like he was in any condition right now. "...They need you down there."

Aaron drew himself up to his feet, each motion heavy and slow. Tired, or burdened. "I'm sorry."

"For what?"

"I haven't...been who you needed me to be. I haven't been what *anybody* needed." He looked back at the ground, at whatever speck of dirt he'd been fixated on. His brow creased and his eyes glinted with tears swelling up anew.

He was looking at something she couldn't see. Something horrible.

She shook her head. "Never mind. I'll handle it."

His voice was tempered, an iron that did not fit his frame. "What is it?"

"It's not important. I'll handle it."

"You climbed all the way up here," he chided. "What is it?"

Eden folded her arms across her chest, looking away. Bocho's stare wasn't any less welcoming. The big guy had stooped low, almost laying his head on the ground, and he looked up at her, expectant. It almost looked like a dog sorry for something broken she hadn't yet found.

"Y'know," she started, "it was probably wrong of us to put so much on you. Try to drag you back into all this. Be the *leader*. You never wanted it. We...expected you to behave a certain way, and when you didn't...we forced it. We shouldn't have."

He didn't say anything, but draped his hand across the ground in front of him, tracing the invisible pattern that had clearly captivated his focus. But she knew he was listening.

"We didn't *need* you to be anything, Aaron." She shook her head. This is where they'd come to, she supposed. "We...*I* expected you to be something you weren't."

"You expected a hero. It's what you needed. And I'm just..." He leered back at her, brow taut and wrinkled nose. He might have been looking at her but he was a thousand miles away.

She'd seen the look many times, too many times. That wasn't anger, or rage. He wasn't biting or snapping. At least not at her. She'd seen that look as doctors draped sheets over their patients, and the family couldn't grasp what this feeling was that now wracked their bones. So they experienced all of them in an instant, and for hours, days, weeks...

Grief.

"Aaron, what happened?"

His eyes flicked back to the bare stone of the plateau. "Now *she* expects me to..."

Give him room. Let him come to it in his own time. She waited, holding her breath.

He started to speak, but swallowed it. After a sharp, ragged breath, "The Queen. She did something and...now she's gone."

"Gone?" Eden leered at Bocho. The Jergad was perfectly docile, looking up to her with a bit of slack to its bifurcated jaw and a lilt to its head. "...Then who's controlling the Hive?"

Aaron squared his shoulders and Bocho squared up in return. "I think *I* am."

Bocho chittered, and a hundred other trills joined the chorus from the darkness below.

———

Aaron and Eden stalked up to Graccus' charges, taking in the line-up of Imperials and traitors. Graccus positively swelled up, seeing the inertia in Aaron's walk. Like a boy seeing his father approach, belt wrapped tight in one hand. He was eager to see justice laid out on a sinful sibling.

It was psychotic.

Aaron scanned the group, not unlike how Graccus had. The Imperials sneered and the turncoats balked at him. None of them bought into 'Legatus' or his legend.

Aaron stopped in front of Parralt, the tree cutter who had done the brutal deed. He crouched down and peered at the man, like he was trying to commit every pore, every whisker, every eyelash to memory.

Or perhaps, a predator perusing his dinner.

Parralt shivered. His arm had truly swollen now, ugly blacks and yellows tinging his skin. He was likely in agony, but he didn't say a word, not a peep.

Aaron's eyes narrowed with a sigh, dissatisfied. He reached up, and Graccus pressed a pistol into his hand. With a swift jerk, Aaron charged the capacitor and swung the weapon to bear on Parralt's head.

Eden could've sworn she'd swallowed her tongue. She tried to call out, shout at him, object. But the swift, aggressive response from her friend had shocked her voice, condemned it to hide in some forgotten cave. She could only hear it now in the back of her mind, shrieking till raw. But all she could manage was a wisp of air, not a sound on its breeze.

Aaron considered the quivering man down the aperture, gauging his response. "You're not a brave man, Parralt."

Parralt's eyes shifted, dancing in his skull.

Aaron squinted. "I see it now. You've no love for anybody but yourself. There's nothing wrong with that on spec; you have to love yourself before you *can* love anyone else. But you were scared you'd die in a damp hole in the ground. Alone. And so, you made a bargain. They promised you so much and you ate it all up." He lowered the pistol, a slight shake to his head. "What you want...they won't give you."

Aaron's eyes slid over to Whitby, the trembling political golem having drawn himself up straight on his knees. He would take whatever came next with high-class dignity.

"Statesman Whitby, I don't believe we've met," Aaron said with a wry grin.

"Spare me your hackery, Capital," Whitby spat. "Let's be done with it."

Aaron turned to Graccus, who happily stepped up. "The good elected official provided our Imperial guests with Intelligence on the Hive, its construction, and our munitions—including our supply trains—that would allow for the smuggling of a certain dramatic breaching cable."

Eden cocked her head. A civilian, albeit an important one, didn't know squat about supply trains and the quartering of munitions. That didn't square up.

Maybe Aaron reached the same conclusion. But all he did was look at Whitby, his eyes hanging on the man's sculpted features for a moment, before speaking. "Yeah, it's not him."

Graccus blinked. "How do you—"

"Because I do," Aaron said, flipping the sidearm back to Graccus. "Whitby's an asshole, but he's an innocent one. Cut 'em all loose, kick 'em to the surface. They can walk home."

Now Graccus was getting animated, putting a hand on Aaron's shoulder. "They were personally—"

"Graccus," Aaron chided. "I don't care what they were. They're nothing *now*. Let them go."

It was hardly a kindness. It was a bit of a hike through the tunnels to the surface, all the while wondering if the Jergad would spring from the shadows to carve them to bits. Then, down a mountain side and into the Hammer Fields, which was brutal in its own right.

Aaron knew it well. He'd done it. He wasn't letting them off with a slap on the wrist. They might yet die—he just refused to kill them.

The disgruntled Capitals shuffled the prisoners away. Graccus pulled Whitby out of the line, slashing his bindings off with a quick knife. For all intents and purposes, the knife teleported into his hand and back into its sheath before Whitby could so much as jump in surprise.

Graccus leaned in again, cold whispers of sinister imaginings. The statesman nodded and ran off.

Eden raised an eyebrow.

"What did you tell him?" Eden asked.

"Oh, I have a dramatic imagination." Graccus pursed his lips with an innocent smile. "You disapprove?"

She shrugged. "I stood up for him. Doesn't make him a nice person."

Graccus shook his head. "You all just...confound me. You don't interrogate, you don't kill your prisoners. You don't even ransom 'em back. That was literally material good that Aaron sent on walkabout."

That's because they had been prisoners once. They knew how it felt.

Maybe he saw the flicker in her eye or the stiffness in her stance, but Graccus let out a satisfied sigh. "Lesser people would've..."

"Excised their pound of flesh?"

He nodded, looking away. Oskies didn't show emotion they didn't intend to show, and this one especially so. He wasn't haunted by his guilt over past deeds over a long career—he was confessing to them.

He forced a smile. "Thank you, Eden Neria."

"For what?" she asked.

"For trusting me when you first met me, when you had every reason not to. I just hope I live up to it."

CHAPTER
THIRTY
AARON

HE FELT...ALIGHT. Like his skin was incandescent, his hair stood on end. It's not as if he was going to static shock anyone or that he glowed in the dark, but he *felt* like he did. It always felt like he was half a second away from snapping off a spark on every surface, every person he saw.

Closing his eyes didn't help much. On any other day, he'd squeeze his eyes shut, and it was like all the everything got six inches further away. Room to breathe.

Not anymore.

He could feel his breath in his chest, his ribs expanding, and the musty air warming his throat. He could feel the air on his skin: a humid eighty-one degrees, give or take. It made everything feel like a wet blanket clinging to his shoulders.

He walked the line of injured beds. Most of the soldiers had been tended to. Missing pieces. Bandages stained red. They winced and groaned as they tried to sleep, but the pain was too much.

One man stared into the vaulting stone overhead, as if waiting for it to come crashing down on him.

Anatoly. His left arm, a simple stub wrapped in gauze and dripping with medigel.

Kipling was curled up next to his bed, long since drifted off to sleep.

"'Toly," Aaron whispered, laying a hand on his bedside.

His eyes drifted over to Aaron, that dread in his stare still lingering. He was probably drugged, some morpha for that agony. Or perhaps he thought Aaron the Reaper, here to take him finally to the Sojourn, where he'd walk with the Pilgrim into starlight.

He was a big man, short and stout. But he was barely older than Aaron was. His olive skin had been stained with dirt and carbon, wrinkled and singed with more than his share of fire. A bandage covered the lower half of his jaw, but the concave dent certainly implied that it was not...all there anymore.

In a moment's flash, Aaron saw the moment. They had been heroes of the day, destroying not one, but two, Imperial dropships. Then a red-hot pain had lanced up from the floor. Like a snake biting over and over again, everywhere at once. And just as quickly, the pain had quieted, down to a smoldering coal fire, as the nerves in his arm had simply ceased to be.

He was lucky to be alive.

Kipling stirred in his sleep.

"Is he goin' to be okay?" Anatoly asked.

Aaron almost scoffed. The Regular had lost his arm, laid up to recover, and he was worried about scrawny Kipling.

That's true love there.

Aaron reached for Anatoly's hand, pausing just shy of touch. He waited a tender moment, for permission, for Anatoly to recoil, for Anatoly to reach back.

The soldier's lips parted, and his breath rattled. Trembling, he dragged his hand over, taking Aaron's hand in sausage fingers.

"Yeah. He's going to be okay," Aaron assured him.

The man struggled to breathe, but then he spoke. "How do you know?"

Aaron blinked. How did he know? He just did. He felt the churn of the air, the emotions, the same way he used to know his headaches and muscle pains. It was like the air had a texture and the sounds had a cadence. He couldn't explain it. He could...feel the moment.

He was certain of it.

Anatoly studied Aaron's face, waiting for a response. All he got was a stoic but soft smile, like a proud parent. And with one brief exhale, he closed his eyes. His chest rose and fell, rocked off to sleep at last.

"Nice trick, shortstack." Aaron looked over his shoulder. Solomon sat up in his alcove bed, one hand draped over his bandaged gut. "What else you got?"

"What?"

Solomon's eyes narrowed. "You're different."

"I like to think I wake up every day a new man, Sol," Aaron joked.

No laughter. Solomon shook his head, but his reptile eyes never strayed from Aaron. "I'm different too. Everybody says my wires are crossed." He hesitated, the words painful to compose. "Keira knew it. She took care of me."

"I don't need somebody to take care of me."

"Nah, you don't." Solomon eased himself out of his bed. The skin-patch was still taut across his wound, and everything inside likely didn't appreciate being stretched so soon in the healing. He'd probably needed to get it reset after the most recent battle. And there'd be more battles yet to come. But he made it over to Aaron, grabbing his leader by the shoulder a touch more firm than friendly. "You got us already."

Aaron laid a hand on Solomon's. The pale viper was so dim, so dark, no charge to his skin and no light in his eye. Everything he said seemed to echo more than everybody else, and the shadow he cast seemed shorter than it should be, murky and blurred.

Like he wasn't properly there.

"You've one foot in the grave, Solomon," Aaron cautioned him. "But you're not done here yet."

Solomon's eyes wavered, unsure of what to focus on. Aaron? Or his nightmares? "I don't know...I don't want it to..." He couldn't find the words, how to say it.

He'd never grieved before.

Jensen's permanent smile flashed across Aaron's mind, a bandage ripped free he wasn't quite prepared for. But it didn't sting quite as bad as he thought it would.

"It gets easier," Aaron promised. "But you don't forget them. They're never gone. You just stop bleedin'."

"Ain't nobody for me anymore," Solomon whispered. Lost. A child alone in the dark. On a precipice.

He'd lost the one thing keeping him grounded. Keeping him human.

Aaron raised two fingers, tapping them against the drum of Solomon's chest. "She's still right here. She always will be."

Solomon drew in a breath of that stale air, and he squared his shoulders like he'd drank from a cold refreshing spring. He closed his eyes, twitching and grimacing as he searched for her in the dark.

And then he opened them—and that reptile relaxed, his back curling, lowering him back down to Aaron's level again. He pulled on Aaron's shoulders, like he might touch his forehead to Aaron's, stopping just short. "We're both different men now."

Grief had hollowed them. But then something else had happened...

———

Talania had managed to find a cave set off the main Hive—or perhaps the Jergad had dug it out for her. It was twice as large as her office, a vaulted ceiling, with lighting strung around the perimeter. She even had a desk.

Add some art, and the whole thing would look on purpose.

Aaron walked into the space, taking it all in. Talania was finishing up a meeting, several folks in suits standing about—the Statesmen. "I'm not going to set a formal election while most of the voters are in a prison camp, Adé. And Whitby stands accused—until a Court rules, he's still a Statesman."

A wizened old man with a strong jaw answered. "A Statesman now marching down a mountainside!"

Talania pursed her lips, her head tilting like it was teetering on a shelf. It was a valid point the councilor was presenting.

"Without a Quorum, this body cannot function." Adé's eyes narrowed. "Leaving power resting solely in one place."

Talania stood her ground. "If you want my resignation, Adé, I'll happily give it, just say the word. But that leaves us with power in exactly no places. What kind of message does that send to the people out there?"

Something in her voice, the way she said 'people,' caught Aaron's attention. He studied her from afar, her stance, her hair, the oils in her skin. She was sweating. She stood tall and straight, seeking strength. Her hands were clasped in diplomatic display, but they were wrung tight.

What did she have to be so nervous about? Or sorry for?

She caught his eye, and her face crashed. Not the person she wanted to see. "Can you fine folk give me the room for a minute?"

They were about to object until they followed her eye line back to Aaron. He smiled, assessing the five politicians before him. A grifter without a game, a patriarch without a family, an empty suit following the wind, a mother of three who had disowned one, and a winsome woman with no stake.

He saw through their masks like they were glass.

The five departed in turn, avoiding his gaze. Like they knew that he knew. They drifted around him, careful not to get too close.

Satisfied that they were out of earshot, Talania dropped her hands to her sides. "I'm glad you're okay."

"Been a helluva time," Aaron said, pacing the outer edge of the office. He jerked his head at the door. "How's morale?"

"They're...jumpy."

"A lot of reason to be."

Talania hung her head. Again with the guilt. "I think I know what this is about."

Aaron peered at her, her shoulders slouched. Burdened. The skin on her nose wrinkled and her eyebrows furrowed.

Oh, Talania. Not you. Of everybody, why did it have to be you? He saw it like it was written on her clothes.

She was Deckard's spy. And she had no idea that he knew.

"Eden's really sweet," Talania rambled, "She's kind. She's hard-working, compassionate. She's short."

"Oh, that's a plus?" Aaron asked with a wry grin.

Talania blew right past his smartass comment. "Is this weird? 'Cause if it is, I'll back off."

"Weird?"

"I feel like it's weird. For you, I mean. You two were a thing and now—"

"Talania, everything's weird right now. Say what you want to say."

"I *like* her."

"You should. She's great."

Talania raised an eyebrow. "Really?"

He nodded. Time to let go. "I can't be what she needs me to be anyway."

"So..." Talania paused. "You're okay with it?"

She's off-balance. Hit her now. "Talania, I need to know why you did it."

She rocked back on her heels, confused by the sudden twist in tone. "Did what? I thought we were—"

"You know what I'm talkin' about." He didn't say it. But he wanted to.

Traitor.

She picked up what he was throwing out. She took a few cautious steps forward, lowering her voice. "Aaron, I had to."

"How long?"

"Aaron, if I didn't—"

"How long have you been feeding Deckard information on us?"

Talania took the accusation like a gut punch. But she didn't deny it. Because she wanted to be found out, she wanted to stop. She just never had the strength to do it. "A week before landfall. I'm the one who smuggled the bomber past harbor security. Whitby was a good fall guy, and he happened to be in charge of the very dock I was breaching."

"That *faux pas* with the press conference," Aaron said, "the recording of you—that was a misdirect. Sets him up as hating you."

She nodded, hanging her head like a sullen child. "How did you figure it out?"

"Whitby's a slug," Aaron said, "and a natural ally for the Imperials, so everyone did rush right to him. But he doesn't have access to our military schedule. *You* approve every single one of them, even if it's just a signature. You read so fast it's like you're looking at pictures. You knew how to smuggle material in. You knew how to get a secure line no one would listen to. You brought it up to the surface yourself yesterday. The day Keeper gave his life for his friends, you were getting him killed. You've been feeding Deckard intelligence from the beginning!"

Something about his stare, his voice, his manner. She recoiled. "Aaron...if that's really you in there—"

He cut her off. "It's me. There is no Queen anymore. I'm all there is now." He let that notion hang. All the power, all the Will...was his to command. He took a sharp breath. "Do you have any idea how many people are dead because of you?"

She had found her footing now. "Do you have any idea how many people are *alive* because of me?!" she hissed. "If the Imperials thought they couldn't capture you—if they thought for a single second that this was a waste of their time, they'd *glass* the planet in a heartbeat! Fifty-two thousand people...I bought us *time!*"

"The people out there buried under four hundred tons of rock— my friends, your *people*," Aaron snapped, "...they didn't know they were being sold."

He marched up to her, craning his neck to look up at her. She was almost drooping down to his level, wilting under the heat. "And you want *me* to go along with this thing, you and Eden? Are you out of your mind? I mean it, have you completely cut off oxygen to your brain?!"

The entire cave seemed to shudder, as a thousand Jergad echoed Aaron's fervor. It probably gave everybody in the Hive a good jump scare.

Talania shuddered, rubbing the prickling on her arms. "I don't know what to do," she murmured.

Aaron let her stew in that for a moment. He considered cuffing her, or just walking outside and pronouncing with religious fervor that Talania had betrayed them all. But instead, he just let her cook in it.

She didn't cry. She never did. But he recognized the look in her eyes. He'd seen it before, in a prison cell, a beaten and tormented young woman.

"I did what I thought was right. And you have every reason to be..." She waggled her hand in the air. Every right to be whatever the Hell he was.

"I shouldn't have yelled," he conceded. "For...a lot of good reasons." He quietly hoped he hadn't just driven a Jergad outside to kill someone.

"So...you're the new 'Queen?'" she asked, eyes poring over him. Maybe she was looking for alien scales to be sprouting from his skin.

He almost wished it were that simple. "Yeah..."

"Well...Legatus." She hung on the title for second, rolling it off her tongue. "Sounds like you really earned your title, now."

Legatus—diplomat. The human who commanded an alien horde. He had been a court clerk. Now look at him...

"How can I help?" Talania asked. "I wanted to save lives, and I did what I thought was right. I still want to. Tell me what I can do."

Earnest eyes, raised eyebrows. Hands still. Her jaw slackened.

This new Sense was going to take some getting used to. He was so hypersensitive to these details. He could tell when someone was walking up behind him. He could feel Graccus darting around the Hive outside.

He could feel Deckard in orbit, all concentrated mania, the devotion of his crew. And he could feel the survivors lurking on the crashed ship.

"You can come back home," Aaron said. "What have you learned from *them?*"

"Not much. Deckard's got a close grip. Why?"

"Because I'm done running from these guys."

CHAPTER
THIRTY-ONE
EDEN

IT WASN'T every day Eden got to attend a war council. She'd only just shed her cane and splint, all patched up and ready to go, when Aaron had summoned them to Talania's office—it was the only truly private space in the Hive. The whole room was all but filled with the scale hologram model of a crashed Imperial troop carrier. There was a word painted on its side, upside down and half-buried: *Pompeii.*

Solomon and Nora lingered on the wall, preferring shadows and distance. Bray and Graccus circled the hologram like it was wounded prey, while Aaron and Talania stood stock still, having already done all of the studying they wanted to do.

Eden was too busy watching Aaron. He'd never been the most animated of men, but something bothered her. It was...he more resembled a sculpture or painting of himself.

It turned her stomach.

"The Queen used the magnetic fields of the planet to communicate with the rest of the Jergad." Aaron's voice was like granite. Solid, unfeeling. But there were all kinds of cracks. "She used everything she had in her. Killed herself...and pulled a thousand-ton monster right out of orbit."

"Survivors?" Bray asked as he paced around it, studying every facet.

Nora waved her arm at the enormity of the crash. "Nobody survives something like that."

Graccus picked at something itching on his face. "There's too much valuable hardware, intelligence, troop movements. Confidential crypto. They can't risk it falling into our hands."

"So why haven't they blown it yet?" Aaron asked, implying the answer. "You've got two more ships in orbit, guns ready. A reactor you can overload. What's stopping 'em? Unless they need to get something off it before they do."

"You could've just said 'I see survivors with my new superpowers,'" Nora sniped.

Aaron squinted at her, mocking her behind his teeth. Eden let out a sigh. Yeah, there was the Aaron she remembered.

"They've repositioned most of the city garrison," Talania said. "Pulling troops, armor, and indirect fire to support the crash site."

"And whatever's not on the ground, can fall to ground in just under twenty minutes," Graccus cautioned. "You're talking about taking on the entire invasion force in one go. I assume you have an idea of what you want to achieve?"

"Said it yourself, Graccus," Aaron countered. "Playing defense, I was only ever going to get hit. It's time to hit back."

Talania poked at the hologram, spinning the ship to give the audience a better view. "The *Pompeii* is a Barrachiel-class transport with minimal armaments. It's meant to have escorts, but they spend most of their time in orbit over hostile planets. So what they do have is armor plating, shields, and a few—"

"Ventral cannons." It hit Graccus like a fond memory of childhood, his face positively lighting up. "They use 'em for deploying ground troops or heavy ordinance to clear a landing zone." Graccus reached out and flipped the image of the *Pompeii* over. "And she crash-landed upside down."

"Her cannons are aimed up?" Bray asked, incredulous.

Aaron nodded. "Right at the orbiting fleet. The Queen didn't just kill an Imperial ship. She gave us a gun battery."

"We can shoot back..." Eden whispered, locking eyes with Aaron. He nodded.

This couldn't end cleanly. They'd have to take the ship, deliver a crushing riposte to the orbiting vessels—one of which was an Eisen-clad dreadnought, more than a match for their little turret.

"Once we become too much of a nuisance," Talania cautioned, "they'll burn the planet and salt the earth. Nothing will live here for a thousand years after they're done."

"Unless," Aaron said, taking the baton like they'd rehearsed it, "we get whatever they won't destroy."

"You think it's a person," Eden said.

"I know it is."

"Who?"

Aaron shrugged. "I don't have his personnel file. I know he's on that ship."

Solomon leaned back, thunking his head against the rock wall. No one wanted to say it, but they all knew. This was scaling things up. Even if they pulled this off, not everyone was coming home from this.

"So have the Jergad bury it," Bray said. "They sank a whole building before."

"This is a *bit* bigger than a building," Aaron remarked with a raised eyebrow. "They'll drop Thumpers before the Jergad could finish their work. But don't worry: they're not going to sit this one out."

Graccus pieced out the beginnings of a plan in his head. "Two teams. A battle force engages the main body of the defenses, draws them out from the crash."

"We won't last," Bray objected.

Aaron stepped up, almost into the hologram, the illumination tinting his face with a golden hue. "We don't have to win. We just have to not lose."

On that contradiction in terms, Bray's brain turned to mush and slid out of both ears. "I'm sorry, how does *that* work?"

"So when a man and a woman love each other very, very much..." Graccus whispered to him, eliciting a glare.

"Once we draw them out," Aaron said, "we can break up the army into bite size portions. Deal with the groups one at a time."

"Aaron..." Nora started, "*we*? You're suiting up for this?"

The whole group turned to look at him, but Aaron kept her stare. "I've led from behind. I don't like the taste of it."

Eden snorted. Aaron was letting his guilt decide what he did next. Fine, let him see what was out there. He'd change his tune.

But the group was in an uproar. Bray marched right up to Aaron. "There is no way I'm letting you personally lead an *infantry charge*. Full stop."

Aaron clapped a hand on the old man's lean, meaty hock of a shoulder. "S'alright, Gunny, you can babysit me."

Graccus stepped up. "I'm inclined to agree. Aaron, you're too valuable."

"And they're not?" Aaron snapped, waving at the rest of the room. "This whole fight's been going on because of me. It wouldn't have happened if I...and now you ask me to take a seat? I took one, look what happened! I can't lead from the backseat, Bray. And I won't ask these people to do something I wouldn't."

"And so shortstack is going to win the war all by himself?" Nora was rather incredulous.

Aaron looked at her—and that flash of blue went across his eyes, drowning his pupils and filling every corner. And just as fast, it was gone. "I'm not just *me* anymore."

Nora snapped her fingers, pointing two finger guns at Aaron. "That was super creepy. Thanks."

"The Jergad'll dig out tunnels," Graccus conceded. "They can cut up the battlefield, screw up the terrain. That'll create cover, safe passage. Obstruct infantry, armor—and yeah, even the Oskies'll have to do some footwork around their traps. But what about air power?

The Locust and the CAP will need to be handled or you'll be mince-meat in minutes."

"That's where you come in, thanks for volunteering. Team two," Aaron said, pointing to the ship, "with a Jergad drilling the way, a small strike force penetrates the ship. They disable the air power, and take control of the ventral cannons."

"What's the signal to open fire?" Nora asked, already picturing the fireworks.

Aaron smiled. "Fire at will. The battle outside is just buying you breathing room to do your thing."

"What makes you think I'm going with the strike team?" she said with a smirk.

"You're not that hard to read."

"I'm going too," Eden said.

"No!" Aaron and Talania both said it in unison, and were both surprised at their harmony. Talania winced, trying to hide the flush to her cheeks.

Eden raised a hand. "Uh...I *am* going and you can't stop me. But...what the *Hell* was that?"

Bray and Graccus exchanged a look, the two older men immediately making a pact of silence. They might not have figured out whatever was going on, but they each decided they didn't want a piece of it.

"We need every medic we've got on the frontline," Aaron quickly covered.

"I'm a Capital, Aaron, same as you. I'm not just a sewing kit. Nora's going in? I'm going too."

"It's the single most dangerous part of the mission." Talania seemed to be pleading.

But Eden was hearing none of it. "Then all the more reason they're going to need me along."

Aaron clapped his hands together, cutting any further argument off. "Alright. Bray, you're with me. We'll take the ground offensive.

Everybody else—good hunting. You're the entire ballgame. Get it done."

Solomon and Nora popped off the wall, positively bouncing out of the room like they had a song in their hearts. Solomon had a goddamn bullet lodged in his back, and a hole in his gut with a silicate patch job, but he moved like a school boy headed to recess. The two Capitals gave each other fist bumps before splitting to go opposite directions outside.

Graccus slid up to Aaron's side. "I'll bring her back out again."

Oh, great. She was going to have a chaperone.

Aaron paused, locking eyes with her. Eyebrows raised and frowning—it was like he was saying a goodbye. But he said, "Bring 'em all back out. We're going to make medals for y'all. Big chunky ones."

Graccus raised an eyebrow, mock excited at the prospect.

Talania marched on over, obstructing her view of Aaron. "Can I just say this—"

"Nope," Eden cut her off. "Governor, you've said plenty."

Talania laid a hand on Eden's shoulder, and the touch sent a chill down her spine to her toes and back up again. "There's a lot of good you can do elsewhere."

"I've done my share," Eden said, dismissing the idea. "But it's high time I be the person they need me to be."

Aaron's lips drew tight and thin, wincing at the phrase. Good.

CHAPTER
THIRTY-TWO
AARON

THE SKY HAD TAKEN on a jewel tone hue, like a ruby somehow set aflame. Thousands upon thousands of pounds of dirt and dust had been kicked into the air by the crash.

The roasted hulk of the *Pompeii* sat perched in the dirt, listing slightly to one side under its weight. The scar carved by the crash had to be ten kilometers long, and debris was scattered all along its wake. The dirt still fluttered in the air, filling the sky with the orange hue of a distant fire. It would be weeks, if not months, before all of that came back to rest again.

The sun cooked behind their heads, searing their necks—and blinding the enemy. He'd take every advantage he could get, even if one of them was just plainly a star on the horizon.

Aaron couldn't see them, but he felt them out there. Almost a thousand men, squinting against the sun, scanning for the rebel threat. They were on edge, confused and frightened. They had no explanation for how the massive carrier had been brought to ground —and they didn't know what else they could expect.

Aaron had never tasted fear before. He knew that dogs, horses, all manner of animals could smell it. He didn't expect it to taste tart, almost sour.

Bray checked the chamber on his service rifle. "I hate this thing."

"Awkward magwell, chemical propellant, and a tendency to stovepipe?" Aaron remembered from the speech that Bray had once given a battalion of green Capital militia. "What's not to love?"

Aaron could feel the Capitals behind him, sweat radiating off of their skin like a mid-morning fog. Their clammy hands gripped on stocks, working out the stress in their fingers and popping their knuckles in. Somebody would not stop rolling out their shoulder, a revolting double-click with each rotation. Heavy breaths, like they'd already run a mile.

Being this close to everyone was like breathing in a sauna, all heavy and choking him.

"You know how I was sorry for ever doubting you?" Bray said.

Aaron chuckled, nervous. "Having second thoughts?"

"Fourth and fifth, really."

Despite all of the complaining, Gunny wasn't going anywhere. Bray showed his teeth out of love.

Aaron pinched the pads resting on his neck, triggering the mic. "Fingers light, heads down. We're knocking on the door."

A quiet chorus behind him: "Huah." And the whole battalion moved out, breaking into a somber jog.

There wasn't a lot of natural cover. Even grass had difficulty finding root in the cracked clay. But it did make the soil loose, perfect for the Jergad that burrowed under Aaron's feet. He felt the mild shake of hundreds of claws cleaving through the soil.

The Imperials would feel it too, and the fleet above would tag the advancing infantry the moment they left their spider holes.

But Graccus had briefed them well. Anybody's naked eye could see the puffs of smoke from the crash site as dozens of mortars sent their payloads. Aaron held his pace, counting in his head. Three, four, five...

"Tortoise!" Aaron called out. The Capitals bunched up, clumping into groups of five or six a piece.

The mortars streaked in, lawn darts sinking into the ground

around their advance. The shells cracked, revealing the focusing lens inside, ready to cut out their legs. Aaron sucked in a breath. In a past life, he might've taken that moment to pray. It wasn't unlike that, words and intention whispered into the dark.

But now, something answered.

Stone slabs leapt from the ground around them, tiny bunkers almost two feet thick, ensconcing the pockets of humans in armor. The two-stage mortars first scorched the stone in vain, searing carbon scars in the red sandstone. Then, the mortars all popped, hurling steel shrapnel. The chunks battered against the stone.

Aaron could feel pain, agony. A few people had been hit. Maybe they hadn't gotten to cover, or the cover had ruptured under the intense pressure.

One bunker exploded outward, stone tossed into the air like confetti, along with wet red ribbons. A mortar hand landed inside.

No time. Keep pushing. "Fangs out!"

The rock bunkers sank back down into the ground—and the Capitals began to sprint forward. Thankfully, few had seen what had happened to their comrades. Rather, they were emboldened by their newfound allies.

They were no longer so vulnerable.

The Capitals leap-frogged forward, hunkering down as new volleys sailed in, only to charge anew after the ineffective ordinance failed time and again. It must've been frustrating the charts and darts boys. They weren't off target and the payload was going off—why weren't the Capitals routing?

Because their ally was the planet itself, hundreds of aliens bending the ground to their will.

The next hurdle, glittering dust in the sky: the Locust descended. There were not enough bullets in three systems to shoot them down.

Ten thousand autonomous blades fell upon the Capital advance.

"Dive! Dive!" Aaron called out.

The Capitals clutched their gear close. They didn't want to lose track of it—as the Jergad Drones reached up through the earth. The ground that had supported Aaron's entire weight receded before the Jergad like it was a mere suggestion. Claws draped around his torso, pulling Aaron and the entire attack force down into the safety of the dark.

Coughing, hacking, wheezing—and the buzzing of the swarm somewhere above their heads.

Lights flicked on, as Capitals tried to connect with what just happened and where they were. They saw their fellows and breathed easy—and then they saw the Jergad Drones, hunched low to fit in the tunnel, like a panther coiled up to pounce. Rows upon rows of them, back and away into darkness.

Cursing ensued.

They'd all known this would happen. All part of the plan. But that didn't make it any less distressing. The Jergad cooed and chittered, making the most relaxing noises they could.

The Capitals were trigger happy enough. Friendly fire from a rude introduction wasn't going to make anyone happier.

They had less than a minute before the Imperials realized what had happened.

Aaron stepped up to the Jergad Drones. Scar purred at his approach, nuzzling his hand. "Pave the road," Aaron ordered, and Scar chittered back.

The Jergad turned, hacking away at the stone wall. Propaganda art had depicted the act in excruciating horrific detail. They'd analyzed corpses and determined that the creatures must've chunked the stone, melted it into paste with acidic leavings. All properly horrible.

But now that he saw it himself, it was downright adorable. They worked like a little team, chunking the stone in their way and passing it backwards with kicks of their feet. The Jergad in back proceeded to work the stone backward before the last ones packed it back into the walls. The clay and sandstone were malleable, compressing with ease.

They weren't digging it out, not really. They were just moving it.

It's why the Thumpers had been so effective at collapsing their tunnels—no reinforcements to keep it sturdy.

Aaron picked at the wall with a finger, feeling it crumble at his touch—and one of the Jergad barked at him, warning. Fair enough. Not exactly a moment for curiosity.

Wary, the Capitals advanced in the wake of the burrowing demons.

Aaron could feel the frigate looming over them. The people scampering inside. They could feel the advancing horde. They knew what was coming.

No—they weren't going to expect this.

"Pop, pop," Aaron whispered into his radio.

The Capitals racked the bolts on their rifles, a drum line of steel receivers singing. Scar leered back at Aaron, eager.

Aaron smirked. "Boom."

Scar snarled. And the Jergad line cut up.

The rock collapsed down, separating the Jergad from the Capitals, dropping a ramp.

Aaron charged up, Bray and the Capitals hot on his heels.

He felt the man before he saw him. A Naval Regular, seasoned. Two combat tours. No real patriot flare, just a paycheck in a uniform. As the glare of the sunlight faded away, Aaron saw him turning, raising his rifle...

Aaron swiped the weapon aside with his free hand, planting a shot into the Regular's bad knee, spraying bone and muscle out the back of his leg. As the man crumpled, Aaron drove his own knee up, slamming the man in the face. A spurt of red as his nose crunched.

He'd live. He didn't deserve to die because he was standing in the wrong spot.

The corpse of the *Pompeii* loomed high overhead, so much bigger in person. It was as tall as any skyscraper in Vanguard, but its scorched and molted exterior was haunting, like standing outside an abandoned hospital or sanitarium that had burned down in years past —now only filled with the haunted ghosts of its former residents.

Given a choice, Aaron wildly preferred being outside. He hoped Eden and the others were okay.

They'd emerged behind a barricade, steel blocks seated hard into the ground. Regulars had been posted up behind it, but most had started to scatter as the Jergad burrowed underneath. Twin Thumper towers had been primed, but not dropped, giant concrete cylinders raised high on thick chains.

They'd been preparing for the aliens, that ominous earthquake sounding their arrival. But the Imperials had lost their footing to deal with other humans.

Aaron snapped off two shots, the rounds skipping off the Thumper towers. The operators abandoned their post, diving away for cover.

And gunfire erupted from every corner around him, the stench of gunpowder blending with the acrid tingle of mag-pulse rounds ripping through the air.

A maelstrom of emotion. Rage, fear, adrenaline. Hot air blasting his face.

Aaron had seen battle. He'd killed. It always felt numbing, painfully so. It had weighed him down, giving each strike, each step a cosmic gravity. This was the opposite, like fire injected in his veins. He felt lighter on his feet, but each step was thorns pulling out of his flesh.

Bray snapped off shots with frightening precision, walking across the field with an even pace, selecting targets with calm reserve. He kept a steady platform, even as bullets screeched past his ears.

Then one trigger pull didn't make the bang sound. He tilted the rifle to see a brass cartridge jammed in the action. "Stupid piece of—"

He dropped behind a crate, angry shots meant for him carving out channels in the pot metal. He grimaced, reaching up into the box. And his eyes lit up, drawing back a sleek new model rifle. "Now this is what I'm talkin' about!"

"What?!" Aaron shouted at him.

Bray was giddy as a school boy. "Hogan Arms Model 62. Gauss-fed rifle in forty-forty! Real beast!"

He was comparing industry specs? *Right now?* "Very nice! Now shoot it at them!"

"My pleasure." Bray fished a live magazine out of the crate, checked the feed, and popped the breach shut. He twisted around, getting a good base on his knees before tilting out from behind his cover.

The JP-36 assault rifle made a deafening crack as a controlled explosion propelled a small piece of metal down a rifled barrel. It went bang, boom, sometimes pop. Always loud enough to hurt. The HAM-62 used magnets. It was quieter, but still disorientingly loud. And it hummed to life before a nauseating 'thwump.'

Aaron had no idea if he hit what he was aiming at, but Bray's giddy morbid laugh was enough information.

Reinforcements would be on them in minutes. There were far too few of them to take on the entire Imperial army.

Aaron closed his eyes, feeling out for the Jergad underneath them. And the Jergad heard his call.

Aaron never saw the shooter step up on him, square down on him. And the shooter never saw the Jergad claw that snagged him about the waist, pulling him into the unhappy depths.

When Aaron opened his eyes, he could see columns of dirt flying into the sky, as jagged lines were cut in the soil. Ten, fifteen feet deep —and in the darkness, demons lay.

The army was bisected, one group cut off from the other. More plumes, and more cuts, further separated the army again and again.

He'd clear this sector, move on to the next.

"Armor!" someone called out.

The Imperials had brought more than just men with guns, and men with bigger guns. They knew they had the alien threat to contend with. A tank rolled into view, emerging from the shadow of the *Pompeii*. A powerful maglev unit kept the enormous block hovering a good six inches aboveground, making rough terrain a non-issue. And three separate turrets—two front and one aft—offered a repeating 40mm response to any foolish enough to question Imperial authority.

Bray popped out of his cover, and slammed three shots from his new toy into the turret. It barely scuffed the paint.

Nothing they had was piercing that.

The turret snapped over to Bray, fast enough to make Aaron's neck crack just watching. There was an empathic part of his brain that kicked, hoping there wasn't a person inside that turret taking the whiplash ride of their life. More likely, it was all automated, maybe a driver buried in the hull somewhere.

It gave no warning, breathing dragon fire—

Neither did Scar, as the Jergad emerged under the tank, reaching a claw up the foot-and-a-half distance to the underbelly and jamming the tank into the air. The 40mm gun sunk its shot well short of Bray, spraying the old vet with half a ton of dirt and more than a little shrapnel.

The tank hung for a second at the peak of its flight, cartoonishly wondering how it got into this position...before the maglev engine caught its fall, cushioning. But not before the underbelly scuffed against the uneven ground, and jostling whoever was inside.

Scar glanced over at Bray, a strand of spittle dragging in the air like spider silk. Had to check its work, make sure Bray had survived. Gunny coughed from behind his cover, before throwing the big guy a thumb's up.

Satisfied, Scar turned back to the tank, as the Defense Ministry's latest toy twirled around to get both main guns on target. Aaron closed his eyes...

...and he saw the tank through Scar, how it tilted forward on the uneven ground, how it leaned before gaining speed, how the turrets seemed to twitch left and right before acquiring their target.

Scar hissed. And Aaron murmured to himself, "My turn."

He wasn't telling Scar what to do any more than Scar was

following orders. Aaron never told his hand how to grip or throw or squeeze. Just think, feel, and respond.

Scar roared, digging both claws into the dirt, squeezing.

The tank fired—and Scar lifted a chunk of dirt the size of a car into the air. The rounds detonated the slab, sending stone darts all over the field.

But Scar used the impromptu smoke screen, sliding around to the left. For being a ton-and-a-half of muscle and fiber, the Jergad were surprisingly nimble. And it's not like the tank driver was going to hear the stomping over gunfire.

A turret saw Scar, snapping over. But Scar stooped low, the shot sailing harmlessly over his shoulder.

It was a bit like opening canned food. Scar drove its claws into the side of the tank, only a few inches at first. The turret vainly peppered more shots in Scar's direction, but it couldn't quite line up, canisters launching over Scar's back. And with each passing second, Scar pushed the claws deeper and deeper into the steel.

Rifle shots, Gaussian small arms peppered Scar from the back, drawing spurts of blood. Scar roared.

Aaron opened his eyes. "Bray! Two o'clock, drop 'em!"

Bray nodded, peeking from cover. Three Regulars had stopped gaping at the display to actually shoot at Scar. Three 'thwumps' later and they were draped over their barricade.

Grateful to Bray, but hurt and pissed, Scar turned back to the tank. It pressed its face against the small hole it had carved, roaring and spitting inside.

A pull to the left, a pull to the right, and now Scar could stick his whole head into the torn armor. A pop-pop-pop as the tank driver pulled his sidearm on the beast. Scar took the hits to its forehead, twitching with each one. When one magazine didn't do the job, the driver snapped a fresh one in and emptied that one too.

Scar simply salivated, dripping thick viscous webs into the tank interior.

That sidearm might pock the Jergad's hide, but that skull fan was too tough. Aaron had learned that the hard way when he first met Scar.

"INCOMING!"

Aaron tilted his head to the sky, searching for whatever horror was due next.

Drop pods. They'd had their twenty minutes.

The steel eggs slammed into the ground, thick fairings peeling off on impact.

The Oskies stepped clear, their Warcom exosuits already firing into the crowd, rainbow streaks in the air as their shields soaked incoming hits. And tiny flecks of gray filled the air above—as the Locust reformed.

Aaron was out of time.

THIRTY-THREE
EDEN

BOCHO HAD MADE short work of the hull, carving a wide cross pattern into the steel. Nora was up first, springing up off the big guy's shoulder. She swept her rifle, panning left and right. Satisfied, she reached back down in the hole. Eden snagged Nora's forearm, pulling herself up into the belly of the *Pompeii.*

Immediately, she was queasy—the doors were above her, hung along the roof like ornaments. The lights were under her feet, giving everyone that campfire scary story look. Writing and titles were inverted, like some strange alphabet.

Of course. The ship had crashed. The whole thing was upside down, dug into the dirt. Maybe even some residual something off the gravity engines was still mucking with her inner ear.

Solomon took Nora's help, clambering up into the interior. *"Gulaw zu tau mey..."*

"Hey, you could've been laid up in a bed!" Nora barked back. "Don't gripe at me."

Bocho slunk up through the hole, clinging to the ground. Eden patted the big guy on the head. He didn't like the feel of this place either. She looked down the seemingly endless hallway, as it gently curved away and out of sight. Back behind was all twisted metal. "Which way?"

Nora glanced back down the hole. "You comin' or what?"

Crunch, bang, and the whir of servos—and Graccus leapt up through the hole, the small hole scraping against the shoulders of his commandeered Warcom exosuit. He banged into the floor, shaking out the machine's shoulders and knees. He nearly filled the corridor, the top of the machine damn near scraping the roof—the floor—dammit, which was it?!

Graccus chuckled to himself as he worked out his wrists, the exosuit's alloy arms and hands following his every move. "Oh....kay, yeah, I forgot how good this felt."

"Glad to see you're enjoying yourself," Eden snarked.

Graccus cracked his neck. His eyes flickered yellow, candlelight at night, and he smirked. He pointed one big metal arm at some of the upside-down writing. "E-501-13, Engineering Galley."

Nora shrugged. "Everybody's gotta eat."

"The guns are in the kitchen?" Solomon sneered.

"Nah, Battery Control's back behind all that," Graccus said, waving at the impenetrable wall of twisted detritus behind them. "We'll cut through the galley and come at it from the other side."

"Probably faster than asking Bocho to dig another hole," Nora jeered. The Jergad chittered, choking back an objection. Nora gave the big guy a pat on the head as she walked past.

Graccus marched over to the galley double-doors. They were just broad enough for his exosuit to fit through—probably by design. But they also weren't opening without the right codes.

Graccus brought his own skeleton key. He cracked his knuckles, the big metal fingers binding and scraping as they mimicked the same action. It sounded like a car crash a few streets away.

And just like that, he reached up and pried the doors open, slamming them back into their sleeves in the wall. He bent low, stooping to fit the exosuit through the gap.

Eden looked at Nora and Solomon, all sharing a heavy sigh and shrug. Eden almost laughed, lips pulled tight and eyes wide, because she could've sworn Bocho did the same thing.

"What?" Nora asked, a wry curl to her lip.

"Nothing," Eden all but squeaked, as she hopped up into the galley. Bocho purred, clambering up so close behind her it almost ran her over. She pushed back. "Stay here, Bocho. Guard this spot."

As she turned to follow Graccus, Bocho followed in her steps. She chuckled, pausing again to turn an open palm at the Jergad drone. "No. Stay."

Bocho shivered, chittering, before finally coughing. And then it turned back to its tunnel, shuffling away.

"They're almost too cute," Nora chirped.

Solomon shook his head, grunting. "Yeah. Makes me sick."

The galley was somehow wide, large, and claustrophobic—like all the tables were too close together. It made for plenty of awkward obstacles for heads and shoulders. Some platters were tossed to the floor, measly gruel and meat substances splattered into modern arts masterpieces.

To make matters worse, the roof was just a bit too low. Strange, lifetimes in space tended to make for larger, slender people—lack of atmospheric pressure on your head your whole life. But this was like it was made for someone...well, *her* size.

It was a good fifty feet across to the other side.

"Let's move like we got a purpose," Graccus whispered, a reverential hush to his voice.

But then—creak, crash, bang, as his exosuit lumbered forward, swiping tables out of his way, ripping one of them from its roots and sending it crumpling to the floor. Nora couldn't hide her smirk, her eyes almost watering from contained laughter.

They followed in his wake, trying to avoid the dangling tables that might fall and crush them.

But before they could reach the other side, the opposite door whined open a few inches. A gun barrel poked through.

The shots gonged off her ears, a supersonic boom pressed down into the room with them. Nora and Solomon dove behind the fallen tables, trying to hide from the shooter. Eden dropped behind one metal leg of Graccus' Warcom. She could swear the shield tried to push back on her for a moment, surface tension of water, but then she was through to him.

Ripples with each impact, like the very air was refracting the light. Rainbow colors and the barest hint of a sparkle, the impacts of metal muted.

And Graccus just sighed, raising one arm. A hollow heavy sound: fump.

And the door blew backward, twin steel barricades six inches thick bending like foil. And there was a scorched ring of black etched on each half, along with a grotesque spatter, nothing but gooey red threads.

Graccus looked back at Eden, tucked behind his kneecap, blasé and unmoved. "Come on."

The others emerged from their cover, falling back into their marching order, adding a few feet of distance out of an overabundance of caution. But Solomon couldn't keep quiet. "Can I have one?"

Graccus smiled. "Warcom units are...a bit of a handful. There's a lot to manage."

"Doesn't look so hard," Solomon scoffed.

"So what happens if one of us hopped in?" Nora asked, wary of the answer.

"You'd probably squish yourself," Graccus said with contrary cheer. "It'd be weeks before we got your stain out of the upholstery."

Graccus hopped up and through the blasted door, checking right and left—another metal titan slammed into him from the left, sparks and grinding metal. Another Warcom, another Oskie.

Twin scars up the neck and cheek.

She knew him. He'd killed Keira.

323

The big bastard didn't even look, extending a hand into the galley. They'd just seen this trick, so everyone ducked as a chunky cannon went off. The muzzle burst was enough to make Eden's ears bleed, but the round skipped off into the back of the galley.

The kill radius on a grenade was thirty feet from concussion alone, not counting any shrapnel or fire. She should be several different kinds of dead. When she glanced back, she was grateful to see the round had enough velocity that it had punched through the opposite wall, detonating in the outer hallway. Shoddy bulkhead or superior firepower?

Rainbow waves rocked the hostile Warcom, as it absorbed a barrage from Graccus. He even lifted a thick steel arm to shield the driver seat—just in time too. The shield broke down, a white flash across the dome, as too many hits finally overwhelmed the generator. Sparks erupted, as high caliber rounds peppered the frame.

Graccus came roaring back, kicking the Warcom out of sight. The Oskie bellowed at them. "Go! I've got this!"

Eden scrambled to her feet. Her legs objected, of course. She was running *towards* the awful explosions. But she had to. Out, right, and back towards the Battery Control.

The moment she cleared the threshold, she wished she hadn't. There might have only been two fighters, both units filling the hallway with their giant frames, but there might as well have been an entire platoon. They spat flames at each other, rapid fire guns, the rhythmic patter of heavy steel slugs.

As his attacker stuck a weapon out, Graccus would reach a steel hand up and slam it aside. Gouts of flame rolled off the shields, making for perfect domes of glowing embers. She even heard the crackling hum of a Tesla unit touching off the metal walls and snapping against the exosuits.

What was worse, was the shield wasn't stopping the bullets. It was deflecting them. She had no idea how big they were, but they were hitting and skipping all around her, carving out troughs in the steel like it was clay.

Solomon shouldered his rifle, but Nora swung an arm around his shoulders. "Don't! Just run!"

Solomon, Nora, and Eden took off down the corridor, ordinance ripping off all around them. They'd lost their guide—arguably to a more important assignment. But now they had no way of knowing where to go.

They were close, they had to be.

They rounded a corner, another, and then—

"Drop your weapons!" The starched voice of an Imperial Regular, shouted from down a gun barrel. He leaned against a door frame, all the pressure off of one bandaged leg.

Solomon assessed him. Shaking hands, sweaty brow. Panicked expression.

He wasted no time, marching right up on the Regular and swatting the gun out of his hand, the polymer and metal clattering to the ground. He grabbed the Regular by his shirt collar, pulling him close.

Reaching for his quick knife.

"Sol," Eden said, shaking her head, "he's just a kid."

Solomon never looked away, glaring into the Imperial's watery eyes. He studied the boy, memorizing his features, and arguing with himself. No doubt remembering Keira's words, her heavy laugh, her broad shoulders—what she sounded like hitting the ground.

Nora looked back towards the sounds of battle behind them, nervous and twitchy. Her grip on her rifle tightened, her finger slipping into the trigger well.

They didn't have time to linger.

Suddenly, Solomon shoved the boy backward into the bulkhead. He bounced off, catching himself—his bad leg immediately giving out. He collapsed onto his knees in front of Solomon.

The rabid killer leaned down. "Crawl out of here...while you still can."

The boy nodded, jittery and fast. Pressing himself back to his feet, the Regular hobbled away. Solomon watched him, tracking as the kid left his rifle where it lay.

Solomon sighed—satisfied? Frustrated? No. Disappointed. He wanted the kid to go for it, try and be a hero.

Give him a reason to kill.

Nora sauntered up to the doorway. "He wasn't sitting here enjoying the sights. Let's crack it open."

No power to the door. But no power meant the only thing resisting was friction. They jammed open a crack, and from there, they levered the door inch by inch, enough to slip through.

She didn't know what she expected. Eden thought there'd be rows of computers or a dais for a commander, some pedestal for him to hurl orders from like an orchestra conductor.

What she found was far more industrial. It was a small space, barely enough for two people to hold outstretched hands. Opposing computers were set into the walls, with a massive databank standing tall and silent.

Predictably, they had another problem. "How are we going to fire the guns without power?" Eden puzzled.

Solomon didn't say a word. He pulled himself up, hanging off the suspended operator chair, and began to dig underneath a computer. He yanked a panel off—stripping screws and sending small bits of metal dancing around the room.

"Uh, Solomon?" Nora asked. "What're you doing?"

He didn't answer her, pulling a braid of cables out from the computer's innards. He pulled his quick knife, sawing through the insulation with care. Free and easily, he licked his thumb and forefinger, proceeding to grab each exposed lead.

He was looking for power. He squeezed one, then the next.

"Somehow, I don't think this'll run on whatever juice's left over in the pipe," Nora quipped.

"It doesn't work like that," Solomon said.

"How would you know?"

Eden's breath hitched. Keira had been a member of a bank heist team. She'd been a lineman—an informal electrician, really, something of a safecracker. Why bother trying to beat AI at a hacking game when you can simply move the electrons directly?

"Keira taught you, didn't she?" Solomon looked up at her, but quickly looked away, afraid she'd catch a glimpse of the soul flickering in the back of his eye. Eden smiled, warm. "You find the hot line. You find where there's power still running. Backup generators, track lighting, anything at all."

"And I just need enough." Solomon twitched, banging his head on the frame. "That'll do."

"That *can't* be the safe way to do that," Nora said.

Whatever Solomon did made the one console beep-burp-boop to life. He dropped down to the floor, wincing and favoring his wounded gut. Eden almost reached in to check the bandage, check if he'd torn off the adhesive or lost the skin patch—but he shouldered her off.

With a wave of his hand, he conjured the glowing holographic keyboard into the air, spinning it down to meet his orientation. He craned his neck to look at the screen as he typed.

A sleeping beast awoke somewhere in the hull. Machines whirred to life, grinding on them.

Nora tilted her head upside down to read the screen. "Five out of nine cannons are...what is 'N/A?'"

"They're on the other half of the ship," Eden grunted. "The part that's three miles away."

Nora frowned, but bobbed her head. Frustrating, but it made sense. And they still had their four guns.

Solomon moaned again, this time rolling out his shoulder. Blood seeped through his uniform, the cloth wet and sticky. Eden had to say something. "Solomon, let me help you."

"You want to help?" Solomon pointed a gangly finger toward the door. "Make sure I'm not distracted."

"Can do," Nora said, bounding over to the door. She paused, waving Eden to follow. "He'll be fine. He's a big boy."

Eden lingered, waiting for Solomon to turn and look. She wouldn't leave him, not yet. She needed to hear the words.

He didn't look up, typing away. And the great beast around them was stirring. Someone would be coming to see what all the fuss was about.

CHAPTER
THIRTY-FOUR
AARON

THE WARCOM SHOOK off the landing, a shiver from head to toe. It looked like a dog shaking out water from the bath. But it was more likely a supersonic diagnostic, to ensure that every system responded to input.

The Oskie pilot sneered, the Locust swarm poised behind him. "Cut 'em up."

Aaron glanced up at the thousands of autonomous blades glinting in the sunlight. But they sat idle, hovering in the air.

No response.

They'd done it. They'd gotten to the weapons systems. This was going to work!

Aaron smiled, popping a small exhausted shrug. "Didn't say the magic word?"

The Oskie snarled, and the hum of batteries and buzz of ionic charges suddenly rose up around the battlefield as dozens of Warcoms began their work. That hollow percussion of deflector shields soaking ballistic fire, like it was being heard far away.

Orbital didn't need a cloud of robots to win this fight.

The Oskie tongued his cheek. And without another word, four

heinous and violent gun barrels craned up off the Warcom's frame, aiming all around—one cannon trained right at Aaron's head.

Aaron's whole world flashed that alien blue, like a pulse echoing up to the mountains and rippling back again.

And an uncountable amount of claws surged from the ground, scraping, grabbing, piercing into the Warcom's lower half. The rainbow shield rippled at their passing, but it was keyed to stop fast moving projectiles—not someone walking through it.

All four weapon systems snapped straight downward, spraying lead, plasma, and fire. But the gnashing whirlpool of bone and leather could not be dissuaded. It pulled him down, further and further, until grinding steel began crunching, bending, and snapping.

The Oskie unlatched himself from the exosuit so fast it was like he was never belted in at all. He popped off his metal skeleton, tumbling to the ground. He rolled to his feet, with a cocky smirk.

Amusing. He thought himself free.

But the ground was not his friend here. Every step found new claws surging up to swipe at his legs. The Oskie pirouetted his way across the clay, acrobatically springing away from each new strike. He was moving so fast, Aaron wasn't sure he was even touching the ground.

And with each passing moment, the implants grew hotter and hotter, streaks of orange and yellow flashing in the air.

Until he came to rest at Aaron's feet, gasping for breath, steam rising off his forehead and shoulders, his uniform singed from the overheating implants.

Aaron looked the man up and down—he couldn't have been older than sixteen, his frame still too narrow at the shoulders, not quite filled in. The tendons in his neck were drawn taut, strained. The Oskie's eyes flickered yellow, scanning Aaron's face. Perhaps receiving orders, or isolating Aaron's vital signs. Aaron never saw the gun draw. He was so fast, it was just suddenly in the boy's hand.

Perhaps the boy could feel the vibrations in the ground. Who knew what kind of talents these cyborgs had? But the kid suddenly spun about, tapping three lasers into the various Jergad emerging from the clay. He dropped them like they were steel targets at the range—

And Aaron held out his knife, letting the Oskie spin back and directly on to the tip of the blade. The Oskie reached down, gripping Aaron's wrist as it sunk into his midsection. He twisted, blade and owner both, leveraging Aaron clean off his feet and slamming him shoulder first into the dirt. It was like Aaron had been attached to a wheel, and the Oskie simply spun him.

"Clever," the Oskie grunted, pulling the quick knife from his abdomen, "but you're still just a Capital."

Just a Capital. Something lesser. Something inferior.

"Oh yeah?" Aaron said, weary and pained. "Then what are they?"

The ground fell away. Nothing to kick against, nothing to push off of. Physics was a bitch.

A sinkhole swallowed the Oskie like a great maw. No amount of speed or dexterity could help a man in free fall. He spun and twisted, almost like a cat able to right itself midair. But he was helpless.

And the Jergad raised their claws to greet him—impaling him on three separate sets of spikes.

Aaron elected to not watch whatever horrible thing happened next and the gushing sounds were buried under the war raging around them.

He tucked himself up against a supply crate, scanning the chaos around him. "Bray?!"

The Gunny slid up to his side, joining him under cover. Only he made the mistake of looking into the hole. Bray gagged. "Oh, sweet —guh..."

Aaron looked on to the raging battle. The Oskies were chewing up the Capital infantry wherever they were found. The Jergad roared, and gunfire joined the chorus. Deafening explosions and crashing metal and fires burning and cries of pain and shields resonating...

They were getting torn apart.

Aaron shook his head. "We can't keep this up."

Bray nodded. "Any sign of your VIP?"

Aaron squinted, reaching out. There was *a lot* going on. It was like trying to feel his way down a hallway in absolute dark, but instead he was blinded by far too much light, so much he couldn't bear to look at it. It was like staring directly into a sun and being asked to write your name at the same time.

"I can't..." Aaron gasped. "He's here, but I can't—"

A shot whistled past him, crunching into the stone. Bray sat back on one foot, improvising a tripod with his arm and opposite knee. He squeezed off a few shots, and that glaring light got just a shade dimmer, all of the strobing lives losing a few of their number.

More shots, and more Bray shooting back. And still Aaron could not find this person. There was just too much glare, too much to hide in.

Needle in a *gulaw* haystack.

"I can't nail him down!" Aaron opened his eyes—and gasped.

Bray sheltered under the wrecked Warcom, now half submerged in the soil and dead Jergad. He was clutching at his bloody chest. His breathing slow and shallow.

His light so dim.

"Bray!" Aaron stood to rush over, but was rewarded with sparks and a spattering of metal across his arm, a shot narrowly falling short and shattering against his cover. He ducked back down, hugging tight against the crate.

Bray waved a bloody hand at him, get back and stay back. He left a perfect red handprint on the side of the exoskeleton. But he lifted two fingers, pointing high and right, up toward the hulk of the *Pompeii* looming over the field.

Of course—the ship was still plenty occupied, offering height advantage to a variety of shooters. Aaron could see them scrambling around the exposed innards of the ship like ants on a carcass.

There. There he was, plain and obvious, like he was tagged. Aaron was certain of it. Fifth deck, with a team of snipers.

Deckard's prize.

Stop this right now—with just one man.

"I'll be right back," Aaron shouted to Bray. "Don't die on me!"

"Sure!" Bray responded with a thumbs up, his arm wavering in the air.

Aaron coiled up, closing his eyes. Reaching out for his ol' buddy. And he felt the old faithful respond, sweeping into position.

And Aaron took off running.

The snipers saw, peppering shots at him. But up popped Scar, lifting out of the clay like he was slipping out of water, a great shark emerging from the ocean's waves. He lumbered forward, his skull crest shielding Aaron from the shots. Bits chunked and chipped, Scar whimpering with each hit.

Aaron reached over, grabbing on and slinging a leg over Scar's abdomen. He squeezed hard around Scar's shoulders.

The big guy knew what to do next.

The Jergad hit the hull of the cruiser, claws biting into the metal. Hand over hand, it sailed up the side. Aaron spared a glance down, seeing dozens of Jergad start to scale the steel mountain behind him.

Imperials and Oskies aimed up, trying to scrape the critters off the wreck. Bullets rained in, the occasional lobbed ordinance from a Warcom exploding against the hull.

Alien squeals and cries ripped into Aaron's ears, as some Jergad were cooked in fire. Others still lost their grip and fell thirty feet to the ground. Injured and weak, they tried to turn into the fall, catch themselves. Most could do it, absorbing the impact with their strong legs.

Some didn't. Maybe they were wounded, tired, or simply couldn't turn into it, crumpling into the clay like they were discarded pieces from an old and rusted machine. He felt their lights fade, their unique signature erased. The night grew darker and the day paler, as if a hint of color had been drained from the air, forgotten, lost.

He could feel Bray down there, a flickering candle in the hurricane. Darts of molten metal lancing past him. In this quiet moment, evanescent and tenuous, he twisted up into a ball, knees to his chest.

He wasn't ready to go just yet. He didn't want to die.

Aaron counted the distance in his head. "Now!"

Scar bellowed, bashing its head into the side of the hull once, twice. Then it kicked in its feet, burying the talons in for a good solid support on the steel. It leaned back, and for the briefest of moments, Aaron thought they might teeter backwards off the ship.

Scar sunk its blades into the dent, the weakened spot surrendering under the force. Aaron pulled his weapon close...

...And Scar ripped a hole open.

Aaron rolled forward, tumbling over Scar's shoulder and inside the *Pompeii*.

Three technicians: they were working on consoles suspended on the ceiling. They reached for sidearms.

But Aaron's weapon was ready, tucked in his shoulder. He snapped two shots dropping two of the technicians. They flopped backwards, moaning and spasming in pain. He hadn't killed them outright, though that might not have been the kindest thing to do.

The third technician stopped, slowly raising her hands into the air. A crop of black hair, brown eyes wide. Her mother was a teacher, her father an architect with some shady accounting practices. She enlisted for the career training.

It was too much, overwhelming, nauseating. How had the Queen stayed sane? Why couldn't she have stayed, or at least trained him some? His brain was going to collapse under this load.

"Blaylock, right?" Aaron asked.

"How..." The technician blubbered, a thousand rumors proven true by just two words. "How'd you know my name?"

"It's...stitched on your uniform," Aaron admitted. "Get your energetic friends somewhere safe. It's about to get noisy."

Clang, bang—as Scar widened the hole, slipping its massive frame through on to the deck.

The technician nodded like she'd lost control of her head, before stooping to help her friends. Aaron patted Scar on the head, before turning to march astern.

The sniper that took Bray was so close. One hundred meters. There, Aaron would find this mystery person.

Imperials were taking up positions ahead of him. They thought they could hide from him, the dim light and echoing interior masking their movements. They posted up behind door frames and around corners, laying traps.

But he could see the waves of their passing in the air. He could feel their panicked breathing, the hunger rumbling in their guts, and the pulse ripping through their veins. Their scent clung to his nose, the musk of a dozen men and women on their breaking point, a collective insanity.

Yet all his eyes could see was a wide doorframe, the sliding steel long since pushed aside. The hallway beyond a stale gray, sanitized of life, curling off and out of sight.

It looked empty. He knew better.

"Fetch," Aaron ordered.

Scar lumbered forward, sticking his claws up around the doorframe. The wet slick of the blades stabbing into flesh.

Aaron slid up to the doorframe, kneeling to peek around. He slipped his barrel between the legs of Scar's victim, angling on the three other shooters stacked up.

They were all too busy being surprised by Scar's dramatic entrance to notice Aaron down low. The way their lights went out, they didn't feel a thing.

Bray was counting on him. Everyone was. He wouldn't disappoint.

Scar entered the hallway, lowering his jaw to the ground, filling the space with his skull fan. Shielded by his friendly biological tank, Aaron swapped the magazine on his rifle, taking care to check that the bolt had cycled all the way forward.

Fifty meters.

He saw an Imperial's meaty bicep coil. He saw it extend, something released from the hand. But it was the clinking sound that betrayed what had happened: grenade. It was a good throw, bouncing it off the opposite bulkhead, not letting it come to rest.

He'd ensured that Aaron didn't have a chance to do anything, give any orders. But Scar knew what a grenade was.

The big guy screeched and fell backwards onto Aaron, pinning him to the ground. Shielding him.

No!

Aaron heard the thud of the concussion, felt the wave of heat wash over him, and Scar chittered on top of him, full of pain and sizzling flesh.

He felt the Imperials advancing to check their work, confirm that the big creature was dead. Was the beast, with its leathery carapace now carbon scored and flecked with metal shards, actually finished?

Better shoot it again.

Scar opened his one good eye, peering at Aaron. The lid heavy and twitching.

Aaron pushed up on Scar's arm, sliding his rifle out. The soldiers broke for cover, but only a few made it. Scar cried out as the rifle went off right next to its head, but Aaron couldn't afford to stop. He squeezed the trigger again and again.

He had to get away from Scar or they'd simply frag him again. Scar was in a bad way and couldn't take another hit like that.

Aaron wormed out from under Scar's heavy frame, dropping his rifle. No time to fish it out too. He drew his sidearm and checked the chamber, the glint of the brass casing assuring him.

The Regulars posted up, ready to ambush him. They hung from the walls and ceiling, magnetic units allowing them to cling to all surfaces—neat trick. It might even throw off a shipboard assault team only looking for targets on the ground.

Aaron had a pistol—and the Sense.

He strafed across for the opposite side of the doorframe, popping two rounds into the chest of the closest soldier. The soldiers opened fire, filling the whole gap, but Aaron was gone before they could pin him down.

The wounded man slumped, fading, dangling from his boots.

The soldiers paused, considering, holding their positions. Wary. There was no way one man was getting by them.

Right? Their fears, their doubts, leaked like oil. Their feelings were as loud to Aaron as any spoken word. Their whole lives were as plain as any neon light. Two Ensigns, competing officers. Deeply competing.

They were open books.

"Ensign Alette!" Aaron called out to the hallway. "You going to let Esposito get away with it?"

"Get away with what?" The question wasn't at him, but accusing the person across from them. Everyone was distracted for half a second, their eyes drifting off target.

Aaron lurched out, planting a third shot into the dangling man to be sure of his work, before turning to the hallway.

He might not be fast like an Oskie or armed to the teeth, but he could...*feel*...them take aim, when they found him in their sights, when they squeezed.

It must've been like fighting a ghost, who could drift away before they could pin him down. And the ghost was shooting back.

Aaron worked his way down the hallway, killing as he could, and using the hanging dead as cover. The Gaussian rounds punched right through the armor and flesh, but their silhouettes helped to hide his movements, where he was going next.

A round found its target, slipping through his shoulder, skipping off something in Aaron's back as it exited. Blood sprayed across the wall. He cried out—and he heard every Jergad scream in unison.

Aaron took two strong steps, dropping on to his side and sliding along the floor. The sudden blitz was unexpected and the shooter couldn't swing his long rifle around fast enough. Aaron swiped the barrel aside, and pressed his pistol into the man's gut—squeezing two shots.

The Regular crumpled against him, like a sleeping child draping across a parent, limp and vulnerable.

No...that was what he was remembering! The dying man had no voice left, but cried out just the same, cried out for someone to hold him one last time. A child in the dark weeping against his mother's shoulder...

This Sense—it was torture.

Aaron turned back to his handiwork, at what he had wrought, at the absence where once there had been life.

They'd have killed him, without a second thought. But Aaron...he felt every death.

Ten meters.

Aaron turned to the door that the firing line had been protecting. There was no way that his target hadn't heard the gunfight that had gone on just outside his perch. He could see the life inside: three people. One of them glittering like a diamond, catching and reflecting and refracting everything near it.

His name was Ulrich Wolcott, Captain of the *Pompeii*, Master & Commander of Local Allied Forces. He was barely fit to command himself, still so uncertain. He projected strength, extending his borders to protect nothing, so that one day he might fill that void with something solid.

His father had expected so much of him. And still, so disappointed.

Interesting—what was that there? Was that esteem, admiration, with a soupçon of respect?

Deckard. Maybe not the boy's actual father, but he might as well have been. The Admiral would never let harm befall this young man, whom he loved like a son.

The door still had power, perhaps restored by technicians. But Aaron was able to key it. The steel doors parted for him.

The room had once been a command center, the small beating heart of a ship sunk deep in its center, but the crash had torn up quite a bit, removing an entire third of the room—making for an excellent sniper nest. The Vanguard day streamed ambient light inside, warming the cold grays, and catching on every floating bit of dust.

A sniper rifle trained on him, long barrel hanging in space, trigger squeezing. The thrum as the magnets inside reciprocated the slug of metal down the barrel's length, building and building and building...

Aaron leaned to the right, letting the supersonic bullet snap harmlessly down the hallway. The sniper went to chamber a new round.

"Don't," Aaron ordered, with a shake of his head, blood still leaking from his shoulder.

The sniper looked at Wolcott, waiting for confirmation. The other officer had his pistol half out of his retention holster, swallowing hard.

They all knew who this specter was, caked in blood and carbon and fire.

And Wolcott's jaw worked, no words left. Perhaps he knew this was his fate. But he was not ready yet to meet it. This wasn't right or proper. This wasn't fair!

The floor shuddered and the air thundered again and again. The ventral cannons ripped the sky, searching for the ships in orbit above.

Aaron sighed. "Captain Ulrich Wolcott...not sure I really need to say it, but you're coming with me."

CHAPTER
THIRTY-FIVE
DECKARD

"LOCUST PROTOCOL NOT RESPONDING!" "Icarus facing heavy ground resistance!" "They're coming out of the *goddamn* ground!"

The chatter on the Jump Deck was its usual chaos, as multiple officers barked reports on top of each other. The Commandant sorted out the data into text for Deckard's displays, critical updates and biometric reports from the surface. He could at a glance survey the beating hearts of every allied soldier in a simple bar graph. Watching it dwindle.

He was losing approximately thirty-two men every single minute. He had to assume the rebel losses were two-to-one.

"*Pompeii* is reporting boarding action!" Saubert shouted.

Well, that couldn't be tolerated. "Redirect Icarus teams to the interior," Deckard ordered. "Protect and extract all high value targets."

The lift doors opened, and the starched steps of Officer Lindell stepped forth. He turned, presenting a crisp salute to Deckard.

"Stand at ease, son."

Lindell nodded, dropping his arms to parade rest. "Sir, you called me?"

"Your station sits empty, Lindell."

The boy's jaw dropped for a split second before he snapped it shut. He sorted the variety of contradicting things going on in his head before speaking. "Sir, I disobeyed you on the Jump Deck..."

"Quite the opposite, Officer," Deckard said. "I wasn't your admiral when you disobeyed me. In fact, you followed the chain of command to the letter. I'd be a very petty man to punish that behavior."

Lindell scanned the deck crew, looking for dissent in the other officers. But they were all far too busy with the battle below, none even looking up at him.

Deckard nodded to the empty seat nearby. "Your station is right over there, Officer."

Lindell saluted, exhaling the heavy gratitude he couldn't yet form into words.

"Welcome back, Lindell!" Mayfield teased. He glanced back at the big woman, wary, immediately checking to see if her sidearm was still stowed in its holster.

Deckard watched the deck officer slide into his seat like it had iron needles sewn into the back. He settled into it, working out his shoulders, before swiping his monitor up. He drew his augment cable out of his wrist, sliding the data jack into the machine—his eyes glazing over for half a second.

"What do you see?" Deckard prompted.

"Multiple incursions on the *Pompeii*," Lindell said. "Air support is off-line. Rerouting connection."

"Sir!" Saubert called out, "Priority message, Ministry directive."

That's just what Deckard needed: Caldwell.

"Throw it to me, Saubert. You have the conn," Deckard ordered, catching the display and widening it with thumb and forefinger. Caldwell's grim photo filled the left half of the image.

"*Tartarus* Actual, the Vanguard scenario has exhausted our patience. Report."

He thought he was speaking to Wolcott. He'd be in for quite a surprise when Deckard's image popped up for him!

"Minister Caldwell," Deckard began, "we're currently engaged with rebel forces at this time. May I speak with you about this later?"

Saubert was doing his level best to field command directives from the others, but by the way he was clutching his head, he looked ready to unscrew it off his neck.

Something was very wrong.

Caldwell wrote back: "Citizen Deckard, return to your cabin and relinquish command of the *Tartarus* to Captain Wolcott, effective immediately."

Aww. He thought that the boy simply hadn't gone through with his order to remove the admiral. How positively quaint.

"Captain Wolcott has gone to ground, along with his crew, his ship, and crucial military assets, Minister. Our engagement is a recovery operation. As soon as I have retrieved him, I will present him for your personal debriefing."

A long pause. Far too long.

There was no way the Minister had missed Deckard's euphemistic declaration. The *ship* was planet-side?

Code streamed across the screen, a blur of letters and numbers. This wasn't meant for Deckard.

It was meant for the Commandant AI.

The blue ball slipped up from the floor, materializing one pixel block at a time in front of Deckard's face, a touch too close to be friendly. The soft and calming color had darkened to an icy tone. "Sergeant Mayfield. You are ordered at this time to escort Capital Tiberiet to the brig."

All chatter stopped. All updates ceased. Every eye turned to Deckard, gauging his response. They stared at him, heads tucked low, like they might have to hide from the inevitable explosion.

Deckard sighed. 'Capital Tiberiet.'

The name was additional spice. Soon, Deckard would be given a number—his name lost deep in the records vault. He would be the only one alive who cared what his name had been. As far as the Empire was concerned, Deckard had taken more than could be repaid.

Now, his life would be the payment, every breath set to labor for the glory of the Empire. And when he finally succumbed, his last punishment would banish him from the Sojourn. He would remain bound to the soil he toiled, never to walk the Path with the Pilgrim.

A Capital. He was just like Aaron now.

"Sergeant," Deckard said. "Do your duty."

Mayfield didn't budge, her lips moving in a silent prayer. She didn't want to do this. But if she froze up, if she betrayed the law, all she'd do was join him. Failing to act *was* an act.

But it was nothing like Saubert, who dove under his console.

"Saubert, stand down," Deckard ordered.

The Commandant whisked over to Saubert's station, looming over the Warrant Officer. "Officer Saubert, resume your battle station at this time."

Saubert leered at the big ball of blue light. "You can't take him."

Deckard's console flashed with a red and yellow icon, purpose built to grab all of his attention.

It got the entire Deck Crew's too. Lindell damn near leapt out of his seat. "Radiological alarm! Ballistic salvo, constant bearing."

A nuclear weapon?! Where had the little Dusters gotten a—the *Pompeii*. They weren't after Wolcott. They were after the goddamn ventral guns.

"Where?!"

"Exiting atmo now, two minutes to impact."

Made sense. The electromagnetic shell of the planet would've hidden the signature. Once it was clear of that...

Deckard cursed himself for being so blind. He valued the boy. That didn't mean the rebels did. Goddamn it all! "Evasive action, full reverse! Tell the *Hestia* to break formation!"

It was a ballistic weapon, fixed trajectory. They just had to break free, get out of the way.

But the Commandant had a few objections. "Capital Tiberiet, at this time—"

"Oh, shut up!" Mayfield shouted at the AI.

The Commandant pushed in on her, the blue glow painting her face. It made the big woman look half-dead. "Insubordination to Ministry authority is punishable by—"

Saubert was happy for the distraction. He bounced back into his station and tapped furiously. He cursed to himself, striking out a typo before confirming the order.

And the Commandant winked out of existence.

Lindell gawked at his comrade. "What did you *do?!*"

"Just a power cycle," Saubert snipped back. "He'll wake up from his last save state like nothing happened."

Deckard pursed his lips. The AI would forget probably the last twenty minutes of exchange. As far as the computer was concerned, he was still Admiral.

But everyone onboard were Capitals now. Something that was settling into poor Lindell's bones, fracturing the young officer's spine.

Saubert consulted his screens, and Deckard could see the incoming signatures on his own. The massive *Tartarus* was slowing, but there was a lot of mass behind an Eisenclad's chassis, and it did not move anywhere quickly. Four streaks of red reached up from the planet's surface.

And one of the shells was still on target.

"All hands," Deckard bellowed into the PA, "brace for impact!"

Every time he called that, it always took longer than he thought. As officers clung to their harnesses, and engineers wrapped themselves around support beams, everyone waited for the worst. And they waited, and waited...

Perhaps the machines were wrong. Perhaps the Commandant took telemetry offline with it.

But then it struck. The nuclear-tipped shell would've been almost three feet across. It struck the energy shield that wrapped the exterior of the *Tartarus*, transmitting millions of pounds of force.

The resulting explosion was designed to decimate ground forces. It wasn't meant for ship-to-ship combat, but a lead slug was a lead slug. Their shield was built to take gunfire, sure enough. But all armor plating still cracks under enough pressure.

The rainbow field around the Tartarus glowed bright, an effervescent aurora that suddenly snapped dark.

There might not be a concussive wave in space—no medium to translate it—but there was still plenty of shrapnel flying at relativistic speeds now inside the shield barrier. Somewhere below his feet, Deckard knew that metal shards longer than a car were punching through the bulkheads, ripping open channels to outer space. Soldiers were thrown back from the initial blast, only to be yanked the other direction as the vacuum sucked them out.

The Jump Deck lurched, lifting Mayfield a good four feet in the air before slamming her down to the deck. Her knee crumpled and Deckard heard something pop!

Deckard unbuckled from his seat, rushing to her side. He called out to the Officers. "Report!"

"Pressure drops on aft decks Foxtrot through Charlie," Lindell said. "Fires on Bravo. Secondary air bursts on Delta, aft."

Mayfield tried to stand, but yelped in pain. Her lower left leg was unnaturally crooked, the knee drifting out of its socket. Deckard stooped, helping her up. "Medic!"

"Teams are dispatched, sir!"

"Another salvo inbound!" Saubert reported. "Tubes are locked and loaded, sir!"

Wolcott was still down there!

"Negative," Deckard barked. "Break orbit. Get us away from the planet! Status on the *Hestia*?"

Lindell squinted at his screen before the realization hit him. "They're refusing hails, sir."

Caldwell.

They'd decided that the *Tartarus* had gone rogue. And they had a mission still to complete.

And their cannons were primed.

"No..." Deckard whispered.

The tactical calculus was clear. All assets in theater were expendable compared to removing ground-based cannons. They couldn't afford yet *another* crash.

Over the back of his command chair, Deckard saw the display, the holographic image of the *Hestia* tilting just so, like it was rearing back. And it spat a full battery of nine shots in response.

Start the clock.

CHAPTER
THIRTY-SIX
EDEN

THE BOLT CARRIER on Eden's rifle clacked open, shedding its last brass casing into the air. The round dug into the armored helmet of a Regular, and based on how his head bobbled, the round likely skipped around the inside of his skull, swirling the grey matter into mashed potato, before he slumped to the floor.

At least he didn't feel it happen.

"Solomon," Eden shouted. "It's dinner time. Let's go!"

"Almost done!"

Nora dropped her magazine, ripping the last one from her vest. "Almost ain't good enough, Sol!"

The ground rumbled underneath her—no, around her. Now, the gigantic Gaussian cannons built into the hull rippled from top to bottom, roaring off of the roof. Not like this. No, this...came from nearby.

"Nora?"

"Yeah, I felt it too."

Silence. Nothing. Even the war outside seemed more distant than before.

"Solomon," Nora hissed, "drop whatever you're doing and get—"

ALLEN IVERS

The bulkhead next to Nora exploded outward. Reflexively, she threw herself to the ground.

Eden whirled about to see two Warcom units tangled in each other: Graccus and his friend. The Imperial had a hand tangled up inside Graccus' pilot cage, stuck there. Graccus's suit had lost most of its guns, ripped off and dangling cables. One of them was slagged into a cold puddle now frozen onto the arm.

Graccus looked over at them. "Oh, hey guys."

The Imperial followed his gaze, teeth bared and blood dripping off his forehead. His eyes caught the light, searing umber reflected within.

Graccus nodded to Eden. "Little help?"

And do what? Wave at him?

With no better ideas, Eden shouldered her rifle, pelting the Warcom with shots. The slugs slipped off the rainbow bubble, slapping into the walls around it. No effect. There didn't even seem to be any push on the power armor.

"You chose your allies poorly, Graccus," the Oskie sneered.

"Eh. There's potential." Graccus slipped a hand up, unhooking his harness. And pressing his big robot hand to the deck.

When he squeezed, the metal fingers pulled up the grating like it was bread dough. The ground creaked under their combined weight.

The Oskie tried to jump back, but his hand was bound up in Graccus' suit.

And Graccus gave the ground a good thwack! The ground caved in, sucking both exosuits down into the dark.

Eden tossed her empty rifle, sliding over to the edge of the pit. She didn't necessarily reach for him, but she suddenly found Graccus dangling from her hand, nearly pulling her over into the hole.

Halfway falling in herself, she got a good look at the damage. Both suits tumbled three whole stories, smashing through roof and floor down, down away...

"Friend o' yours?" Eden asked.

348

Graccus's smug veneer slipped off, his feet kicking in the air. "Pull me up. Right now. Right now!"

Nora was quickly at Eden's side, helping to heft the Oskie back up through the hole. As soon as he had a foot on the terrain, the phantom was on his own two feet and behind them.

The sudden loss of counter-weight nearly sent the two girls onto their butts.

Graccus bounced from foot to foot, a runner in the blocks. "Did you get it done?"

Solomon slipped out of the gunnery chamber. Eden blanched, seeing the blood painting his gut and down his leg. Curiously, he looked no more pale than usual.

Graccus shook his head. "Damn, Solomon, you look like modern art."

"We got it done," Solomon said, breathless, ragged.

"Good," Graccus said, looking back toward Eden and Nora, "because two salvos of intermediate payload kinetics are en route to this ship right now."

Eden saw what just one of the things did to the Hammer Fields. A clean nuclear detonation, combined with the raw kinetic force of an orbital weapon, would atomize the *Pompeii* and anything within two miles of it.

There were eighteen of the damn things inbound.

"How do you know that?" Nora asked, skeptical.

Graccus tapped his forehead. "Warcom IFF wasn't updated. It gave me and my classmate the same breaking news at the same time."

"Can we even get away on foot?" Eden asked, gravely. She still remembered the concussion from the last blast. That sound, like a hateful dragon...

Graccus shook his head. "Not...conventionally. But you guys happen to be friends with some pretty serious diggers."

Nora's jaw dropped. "A hit like that will make the Thumpers look like chew toys. It'll shatter every tunnel in the field!"

"Yes," Graccus said. "Might even crush us to death. But it's our only shot. Spend a little bit of time underground, get dug out...or die in a cosmic hellfire."

The ground rumbled again. The war outside must be picking up. Maybe they also heard the news?

Solomon staggered over to the hole the exosuits fell through, inspecting the damage with a raised eyebrow. With all of the venom he had left, he hocked a wad of spit down the hole.

Good riddance.

"Okay, so we get back to Bocho and the tunnel," Nora summarized, "and just start digging and—"

A steel hand reached up through the hole, snagging Solomon about the waist and wrenching him down into darkness.

"Sol!" Nora shouted.

Eden felt her hair bluster at her ear, the squeal of rubber on steel, and a flash of yellow light. Implants aglow, Graccus tore off after Solomon, leaping down into the hole.

Nora and Eden staggered up to the edge, looking down. They could hear metal, scuffling, screams—but Eden did notice that one of the Warcom suits was missing.

That bastard was still alive.

Nora tugged on her shoulder. "We have to go."

The floor erupted behind them, spitting red light and slagging steel. The Warcom was bothered by the ten-inch steel about as much as Eden was by spider web. There might as well not have been a wall, or floor, or roof.

And Solomon came rocketing up through the new hole, banging, skipping off the ceiling, and crumpling at their feet. Eden rushed to his side. Blood leaked from his mouth—not terribly surprising, given the ride he just had.

Still breathing, somehow. But he wasn't walking anywhere.

How would they get out now? Leave him? No.

Nora settled next to her, rifle tucked into her shoulder. Fat lot of good it would do her.

Something tore through the wall, scoring the metal, rending it—

and Eden was never happier to see the hideous visage of a Jergad drone.

"Bocho!" Eden shouted. "You beautiful thing."

The beast stuck its head through the torn metal wall, catching sight of her. The big leathery beast chittered, tilting its head like a cocker spaniel.

"We're going with 'beautiful?'" Nora cracked.

"Help me!" Eden lifted Solomon up, dragging him over to Bocho. The beast tore the hole open a bit further, allowing the Capitals to ease their wounded charge through the space.

Eden looked back towards the damage, hoping to see Graccus standing there with humor and a limp. But nothing, just more rumbles from below deck.

Graccus—if he was still alive—was on his own.

It felt like a crime to say it out loud. "Let's go."

Everyone grabbed ahold, and Bocho stomped off. The creature lumbered up through doorways. She could feel the Jergad huff and puff, not used to carrying three extra loads. But there were no complaints.

They lumbered through the galley and back out into the hallway.

Eden had spent nearly a day underground after the siege. She'd then sat in the Hive for another. Underground was becoming her new way of life. Who needs sunlight anyway?

She could see Bocho's tunnel. They just had to—

Something hit them, and Bocho screeched. Eden, Nora, and Solomon all tumbled to the ground, rolling, sliding along the steel bulkhead. Eden looked back.

A steel fist had ripped through the ceiling above and snagged Bocho by the shoulder. How had it gotten in front of them? Let alone, *above* them?!

She could see blood where the hide had torn under the steel fingers. The Warcom had punched right down at them and broken Bocho's arm, squeezing and squeezing...

Bocho roared, reaching back with its free claw—and severed its own *gulaw* arm! Eden gasped, seeing the blood spurt across the floor.

The Warcom's hand retreated up into the ceiling. Bocho staggered back, squaring up on the threat as best as it could. It opened its maw and roared at the unseen threat, twin bifurcated jaws shaking.

"Bocho, you have to go," Eden whispered. "Now."

The creature coughed, dismissing the idea.

"Bocho! You need to start digging right now!"

The Jergad mewed, a high-pitched whine somewhere in its throat. Its blue eyes searched for another way. But Eden just shook her head.

Another cough, and the Jergad slumped, retreating into the hole.

Nora picked herself up, dusting off her uniform and swiping her hair out of her face. "Got a trick I don't know about?"

"No," Eden said, out of breath. "You?"

"Oh, a million," she said, "just...none of 'em work for this."

The wall leapt out at Eden, launching her. She bounced off the roof before banging into the opposite wall. Her shoulder dislodged, popping out of alignment, screaming. Eden curled up, trying to support the arm with her knees and take the weight off it.

Where did that come from? She thought the Warcom was above them! But the steel wall nearby had a nice Warcom-shaped dent in it where the big bastard had jumped out at her.

He was circling them. Penning them in.

"You can't hide from me, Capitals," the voice called out, echoing from below, above, all around. "I can see your hearts beating!"

A bloody hand clasped over Eden's mouth, the scent of iron and salt filling her nostrils. She went to scream, before she saw the skin and clothes materialize into the air, unfolding from some alternate reality like a mirage on the sand.

Graccus—looking quite a bit worse for wear. His hand was drenched in blood from the gash to his shoulder, one eye swollen shut and blood dripping down his face.

He pressed two fingers to his lips, urging her silence. Nora saw it too, and nodded.

"It's over, Dusters," the Imperial below pontificated. "You've nowhere you can hide now."

Graccus eased away from the wall, leaving Eden to nurse her wound. He slid his feet along the steel, padded boots making no noise as he took each careful inch. And as he moved, he listened.

Yes. Even she could hear it—the Oskie's big Warcom stomped around them, a circling shark that clomped with each step. The Warcom knew it was hardly quiet, instead trying to mask its steps with the battle noise outside.

"I'll kill you all," the Imperial called out, "just like I killed that other bitch."

Solomon blinked awake, shaking off his pain, grunting.

Graccus waved him back down. "Hey, Callum! You missed a spot."

The metal hand tore through the wall, reaching for Graccus—but Graccus moved so fast, the clawing fingers might as well have passed right through him. Graccus swooped underneath the grab and stood back up, eying the dark hole in the bulkhead.

"You're so wrapped up with these Dusters," Graccus shouted, hearing his voice bounce off the walls, "I almost thought you'd forgotten about me."

What was he doing? Stalling? They were running very short on time to be—no, he was playing the same game: echolocation. Listening for the Warcom's movements, the pilot's response.

"Tsk, tsk, tsk," Graccus teased, "Callum? Don't pack up now. We've got so much reminiscing to do!" A metal clank—Graccus turned, but his eyes went wide.

As the whole Warcom unit lurched through the wall, sending steel beams and shards of metal exploding out like a bomb had gone off. The big suit had lost an entire weaponized forearm, likely still stuck back in Graccus' wrecked suit. Now exposed, showing the Oskie's bare knuckles, clenched tight.

Graccus moved like water vapor, melting away from sight to slink along the floor. He danced around the titan. It was like watching a god swing at a ghost. Every swipe, Graccus would vanish, reappearing nearby to pick at the metal armor.

But Callum was an Oskie too. One swipe set Graccus up and Callum predicted the reaction. He kicked, catching Graccus in the midsection and sending the Oskie hurtling through the air.

No sooner had Graccus slammed into the wall—leaving a small man-shaped dent—he was back on his feet.

But he was still mortal, still flesh. And the hit had taken more than he had expected. His left leg buckled underneath him, and Callum seized the moment. The big exosuit lurched forward, wrapping Graccus up in its one good hand, giant metal fingers wrapping about his shoulders and around his waist.

Callum leaned forward, a dragon's toothy grin practically dripping spittle onto Graccus' face. "No more hiding, little shadow."

Graccus flailed, trying to get a leg or a fist close enough to land a blow, but nothing. He raised a hand—a flash erupting from his palm, but Callum simply slammed Graccus into the wall, stopping that little stunt.

All that was left was to finish up, and then hose the blood off the unit. Callum was going to squish him into chili paste right then and there.

Nora raised her rifle, popping a shot at the pilot. The precise spot of the rainbow refraction on the shield looked like it would've been a clean kill. But it didn't even shove the great machine. Callum drew his eyes up to her, pursing his lips with an almost matronly amusement.

He pointed over at her with the suit's broken arm, a single bare finger reaching out. "Watch close now. Because you're next."

Nora spat on the ground, rolling out her neck. Like she'd have any chance in a fist fight with a Warcom. If Graccus couldn't do it...

She looked at the hole Bocho had carved, the trail of Jergad blood leading down and away to safety. She could make it, maybe even drag

Solomon inside. Nora was healthy, fit, able to outrun the big mech—at least, while it was occupied.

But Graccus would never make it.

The Oskie grit his teeth, throwing Eden a look. Permission. *Fucking go.* This wasn't her fight, not her time. He knew what he was doing.

But necessity was not desire. He didn't want to die. He didn't want to end. She wouldn't leave him, not without hearing those words. She needed him to say it.

And he couldn't speak, not with a three-ton metal titan squeezing his ribcage. Augmented or not, he was still a bag of juices and meat. There was no DNR to respect, no living Will to refer to. Until he told her otherwise, she was going to do everything in her power.

What would Aaron do?

Eden dropped her rifle, and pulled her quick knife from its drop sheath on her shoulder. She'd used it to cut lengths of IV tubing, peel an apple, and strip barbecued ribs.

She'd never once used it to kill.

Callum's eyes drifted over to her, hearing the rifle clatter. He raised an eyebrow at her. What exactly was going through her little Duster brain? His eyes flashed: a ludicrous amount of data flashing across a display socketed in his skull. Perhaps it pulled her prison file, her name and history, intelligence gathered.

Whatever he saw made his lip curl with delight.

Well, he wasn't going to like this very much.

"Eden, don't—" Graccus tried to sputter, but Callum gripped a little tighter, and she could hear something snap.

Eden charged the Warcom, feet pounding. Somewhere below her, she heard Bocho echo her intention with a battle cry—

Because the big brute came surging past her, attuned to her emotions and her will. Maybe it followed her suit, or felt her desire, or she'd issued some command?

The wounded beast slammed into the Warcom, knocking it over onto its back. Jaws snapping, claw swiping, Bocho perched over the machine, begging for a taste of Imperial. Its feet sunk into the exoskeleton, rending talons inches away from the flesh inside.

Callum swept his suit's good hand up, grabbing Bocho about the jaw—and quite simply removed it, like the tendons and muscle were of no resistance at all.

Eden's heart sank, like the breath had been stolen from her chest. She dropped to her knees, her momentum carrying her into a slide. It was like someone had reached inside of her and pulled one of her lungs out.

She gasped and heaved, her free hand clutching at the front of her rig, trying to pull it loose, give her room to breathe.

Callum shoved the Jergad off of him, and pressed the suit to standing. A fresh wound crisscrossed his face where Bocho's claw had ripped open his forehead and down into his eye, revealing the pulpy, clear jelly inside.

Graccus cupped Eden about the waist, all but hurling her back toward the tunnel, to safety. "Go!"

What? Was he talking to her?

She could see him, arm draped about her shoulders, like she was somehow far away from herself...

...looking back at herself...

She was seeing herself through Bocho's eyes...as the Warcom stepped forward, hiding herself from her own sight.

How was that possible? She wasn't Aaron, Legatus; she wasn't tagged into their collective consciousness! But she had to be, because she could see the Warcom marching closer to her.

Without the Queen, the Jergad had sought new connections. And Bocho had found her...

...Bocho went slack, its head clicking against the floor.

Nora ran to Solomon's side, all but dragging the wounded psycho to the safety of the tunnel.

Graccus gave her a good shove towards the tunnel.

Her center of gravity tilted, shifted, ripping her back into her own body. She blinked, rapid-fire, hoping to wipe away the vertigo as she crumpled to the deck.

Someone called her name. She heard it, so far away. Graccus? He was in the tunnel, looking back at her. His eyes wild, panicked. Someone restrained him.

And Eden was back in her own skin. Steel under her hands, against her cheek. Her dislocated shoulder lodged its complaints. Sticky hair draped across her forehead, thick with oil and blood.

She scrambled to her feet, reaching for the tunnel, for safety and escape.

When she felt the steel claws of the Warcom wrap about her legs, squeezing her knees together so hard they clacked off each other.

"Eden!" Graccus shouted before Nora pulled him down and out of sight.

The world turned upside down, as the Warcom lifted Eden up like a prize fish. Scarred and maimed, the hateful Callum assessed his catch.

"317-YT," Callum said, citing her Capital number.

"...That eye looks infected." Eden asked, "Do they dock your pay for that?"

Callum's lip twitched. Likely just the considerable agony he was in. "They'll take it out of your hide."

Eden shook her head. "Like either of us are getting out of this wreck!"

"Oh, you mean the kinetics?" Callum sneered, pulling her in a bit closer. "Do you really think I chased little ol' you out of misplaced pride, some kind of patriotic martyrdom?"

Her brow furrowed. There were eighteen kinetic slugs with thermonuclear tips falling towards them right now. One little exosuit was not going to live through that!

Callum pulled his arms out of the exosuit's harness, leaving her dangling in space. With both hands he reached up to a console over his head and thumbed two switches. "Get ready for the light show. It's a helluva thing."

The invisible bubble, the energy shield of rainbow colors that erupted any time he was struck, suddenly solidified around him. It blocked out the husk of the *Pompeii* strung up around them behind an aurora of shifting blues and greens, like they were encased in liquid gemstone.

Callum propped his hands on his hips for a long moment, craning his neck to listen.

"What are you doing?" Eden asked.

He raised a hand, shushing her.

And there it was, like distant thunder. The shield glowed bright, the blues snapping through the entire spectrum, fixing on a yellow so hot it was almost white. She squeezed her eyes shut, but the light was so bright, so hot, it seared right through her eyelids.

Callum sighed, admiration, like he was taking in a beautiful vista. She felt his fingers slide across her scalp, balling up her hair in one hand and yanking it sharply.

"What's the matter, Duster? First time inside a nuclear blast?" Callum chuckled. "Don't you worry. You're perfectly safe. For now."

CHAPTER
THIRTY-SEVEN

AARON

THERE WAS nothing left but a series of craters. Salvage and rescue teams had only been at work for a couple of hours. But they had found a single Warcom unit, badly damaged but intact.

No pilot, long gone...

She was alive. She had to be.

The smoke cloud still hung over the field, almost six hours later. Just a bank of ominous shadows that clung to the air like a stain. Radiological readings said it had been a good strike, no misfires or lingering radiation. A cleaner bomb did not exist.

Aaron had seized an advantage and Deckard had promptly removed it.

But then, the fleet had scattered, departed. Tactically, it made very little sense to those missing the critical pieces. Deckard had just removed Aaron's only ability to offer real resistance. Why back off?

Because Aaron had taken something of real value. Captain Ulrich Wolcott hadn't said two words beyond his name and rank. But he'd done so with a quake in his voice.

Aaron didn't need him to say anything at all. He looked up to Deckard. More of a father than his biological one had ever been, more present and attentive. Stricter perhaps, but neglect was a particularly banal form of cruelty. He'd been *important* to Deckard, worthy of time and focus.

Wolcott took that revelation like he'd heard the voice of the Pilgrim echoing back from the distant stars. But still, he said nothing.

Now, Aaron had some leverage. But of course, so did Deckard Tiberiet. This wasn't a shooting war. Not anymore...

Shuttle craft could be seen departing Vanguard's harbor every few minutes, streaking into the sky. Perhaps they were hoping to catch up with the rapidly retreating fleet as it made its way back to the Jump Point.

Aaron never thought he'd ever see this room again: Riley's old office. *His* old office.

The tiny window had been shattered, likely by the supersonic flybys from hundreds of aircraft. The whole room had a tilt to it now, the foundation listing underneath. And with the power out, it had a very stark and stale look, lit only by the tiny glimmer of sunlight that peeked through the open window.

It wasn't technically safe to be in the Aurora building right now, liable to collapse at any moment, but...but Aaron had to say some goodbyes.

He stepped into the office, swiping the layer of debris and dust off of his desk. He picked up the chair, setting it upright again.

But...something. It felt wrong to sit in it.

A knock at the door. Graccus stood there, tentative. His arm slung and stitches over his eye.

"You should be in bed," Aaron said.

"I *should* have a dirt blanket six feet thick. But I don't." Graccus hung in the doorframe, picking his fingernail at the peeling paint. "Bray says hi."

"Is that *how* Bray said it?"

"No," Graccus said. "But it's the thought that counts."

Aaron would've joined Graccus in the little chuckle, but there was more than physical pain being masked with that humor. Aaron's eyes narrowed. "This keeps happening to you, doesn't it?"

Graccus sighed, spooling up for what was coming his way. Yearning for this, the recognition, the release.

"You go out on a mission. Not everybody comes back. You keep blaming yourself. You're supposed to be more...and it just keeps happening. Is that why you defected? One too many missions go sideways on you?"

Aaron knew the gist of it. How his intelligence gathering had been misled, faulty, gotten close friends and colleagues killed. How he hadn't been blamed, hadn't been reprimanded. In fact, it went onto a balance sheet instead—cost of doing business. Death and mayhem were factored in. He couldn't live with that, that mindset, that casual disposal of life.

It'd be healthy for Graccus to say it out loud to someone. But right now? Graccus couldn't even meet his gaze.

"You've gotten...exceptionally strange," the Oskie deflected.

"That's not a 'no.'"

Graccus cleared his throat, staring at the ground, the rivets in the steel. Maybe he was measuring how far from level the building was, with how intent he was to study the floor. Suddenly, a sharp intake of breath, and a sniffle.

He smiled, looking up at Aaron. "I'm sorry." Those two words were hard. They came out of him like barbs from his skin.

"You got the job done. Won the day."

"That wasn't my job. My *job* was—"

Aaron cut him off. "And you damn near lost yourself doing it. You don't owe me anything."

Graccus' voice cracked. "I said I'd bring her out."

"You said you'd bring her back alive," Aaron corrected. "You still can."

Graccus looked out at the cloud and the crater where the *Pompeii*'s scattered remains had once laid. "We'll find her, Aaron. I promise."

"I know we will." Aaron tilted his gaze up.

The recessed track lighting was cracked and loose. And beyond that was the Statesmen's offices and the Governor's chambers, up and out to the sky and the retreating fleet of ships...

A glow cast up from his desk. The computer still had power and there was a pending call.

Graccus caught his eye. There was a kind of pull to it, a gravity. He wanted to see but not be seen, draw closer but also run away.

It was Deckard. It had to be.

Aaron pressed down on the light, popping the spring-loaded monitor up and swiping to confirm. Sure enough, the grizzled face of Admiral Deckard Tiberiet sneered back at him. Sweat painted his forehead, an open crack across the bridge of his nose, with a stream of blood. There was an anima to him, a kind of idle sway, like a reed of grass in a soft wind.

The greeting was a nod and one word: "Aaron."

"Due respect, Admiral, you look like shit," Aaron said.

"Capital. I'm a Capital now, Aaron."

Aaron threw a glance up at Graccus, watching the Oskie spy blanche at that correction. "Well, you had a *bad* day at the office. Disobeyed a direct order in war time, did we?"

"If I had obeyed it, you and everyone on that little rock would be screaming in agony."

"Plenty of Imperials would be too," Aaron noted.

A picture flashed on the screen, and Aaron's breath hitched.

Eden dangled from her wrists, the manacles cutting into the skin. Her head hung loose, unconscious. Her eyes closed, a cut across her brow. Her cheeks puffy and yellow, bruising just starting to show.

They'd beaten her.

"She is a Capital criminal," Deckard declared.

Aaron's voice was cold, threatening. "So are you now. Means your big friends won't be so keen to help you."

"The Minister will find that I have friends in corners so dark he never knew they existed." Deckard's voice was so cold it could wake the dead. "I will not be so easily discarded."

Don't let up. Hit him again. "You're used up, Admiral. Your value has been spent. Weighed and measured."

"Taunting me," Deckard hissed, "will not have the desired effect, Capital."

"This isn't a social call. What do you want?" Aaron asked, fists tight at his side.

One word pushed past tight lips. "You."

"So Captain Wolcott is...disposable then?"

Deckard took a sharp breath, refilling the tank on his thinning patience. "Your treatment of Imperial prisoners will only invoke my wrath. But I don't need bombs or armies to beat you, Aaron Havenes."

"You won't risk harming him."

"And you—" Deckard lurched forward in his seat, but stopped himself, lowering his voice to a whisper. "You shouldn't tempt me."

Aaron nodded, a silent contrition.

Deckard settled back in his seat, looking towards his own display of Eden. "You will surrender yourself, or she will carry your weight, Aaron Havenes. And let me assure you, modern medicine is a marvel. She is alive because I allow it. And she will die when I say."

———

Aaron sat on the plateau overlooking the basin, the colony below, felt the cold stone against his legs. The dust had only just begun to clear, filtering the view with a brown melancholy.

There was a quiet part of him that hoped he'd feel the Queen's presence here, some lingering vestige of them that might offer wisdom.

It was hardly the same quiet place of meditation now. The colonists were still retrieving their gear from the Hive below, using his plateau as a staging ground. Crates would get catalogued, loaded onto transports, and ferried back to Vanguard. Workers scurried about, barking orders at each other and groaning.

Some Jergad were helping, heaving particularly heavy crates up to the surface. He caught more than a few of the workers teasing the big guys, laughing as they exchanged pats on the head for the latest shipment. The Jergad chittered and purred, before retreating down the tunnels.

The Hive belonged to the Jergad. It was their home, and it should return to that. Just because humans were welcome during a crisis doesn't mean they should set up shop. But at least the constant fear had been smoothed over.

He couldn't go after Eden. Too much was at stake, too many lives. He'd made that gambit once already, and it had a human cost—and he still hadn't saved her. She'd saved herself.

He had other moral obligations.

"Thought I'd find you up here."

Talania walked up behind him, and for the briefest flicker of joy, Aaron thought he saw the Queen's awkward formal smile and blue eyes. No—just Talania's apologetic shrug, hands jammed into her belt loops.

She looked back at the plateau, taking in all the activity. "Not exactly like it used to be, huh?"

"You think I should go after her," Aaron stated.

Talania flung her hands into the air, fed up. "You know, now that you have this super-sense, it's really hard to build diplomatic momentum."

"I want her back too."

"So go get her!"

"Tal, I'd be committing an entire rebellion to follow me on a massive suicide mission deep into Imperial space, chasing a rogue Naval Admiral, in the hopes of saving just one person. She's..."

He paused. What was she? Did he love her? He cared about her, sure. Cared about her a lot. But in over a year, he hadn't really had time to sit down and think about them, who they had once hoped to be, the quiet life they had dreamed up.

Eighteen years old, and Aaron somehow felt so very old now. "I have bigger responsibilities."

Talania sighed, settling down next to him. "Y'know...I had bigger responsibilities. I'm Governor of an Imperial Colony, duly elected by its citizens, swore an oath to their service. I lead the Statesmen as best I could. Then, I went behind their backs, your back—everybody's back. I-I was trying to save people too. But it didn't work. I still got a lot of people killed."

She leered at him, studying the curve of his back, the weight in his shoulders. The weight on him. "You tried to save her. It didn't work. That doesn't mean you stop trying! And you *do* have a bigger responsibility than just the calculus."

She turned, waving one long arm at the dock workers behind her. "These people believe that if they can do their jobs, if every person pools their skills—the sum total of everybody, together—they can *warp reality!* They saw something they didn't like, so they decided to do something about it. They did that...because *you* showed them they could! Just stand up, be heard."

Were it only so simple. He hung his head, drawing his knees into his chest, tracing the seams on his pants with his fingers.

"Aaron," Talania huffed. "The Navy came and went...and you're still alive!"

"Count up the people who aren't." Keira, Keeper—the Queen. An entire species was irrevocably altered because of his selfishness.

He couldn't let himself break again.

Talania looked down into the fields, taking in that view: the battle damage, the still smoldering city, and the lingering clouds. "You don't get credit for doing the right thing. A lot of times, you just get hit for it. But you still do it."

Aaron stiffened. "You're really going to give me Riley's speech?"

"Yeah," Talania said. "Because Eden's not here to do it herself."

He looked up at the Governor, and she met his gaze. Her stare was like a furnace, a fire cooked white hot and eager to spit and snap.

She would rekindle his fire with a touch of her own. She'd lost her father to the Empire. She wasn't about to lose Eden, too.

He felt them assembling behind him, ready and waiting. It was enough to bring a tear to the eye.

"We won't be able to move an army," Aaron said.

"Who said anything about a whole army?" Talania asked, looking back over her shoulder. Aaron followed her gaze back to the crowd.

The Capitals stood ready: Nora tucked a pistol into her rig. Solomon cleaned his quick knife with a rag. Bray stood at a stiff parade rest, trying to hide his pained grimace. Graccus hung loose, aloof, off to the side with a smirk. And the young pilot, Aisling, glided over in her chair, her red ocular implant glinting in the mid-morning sun.

Nora gave Aisling some strong side-eye. "Didn't know you could lay down on the job."

"Y'know, my ship stops whining when you kill the engines, but you? It's all hours with you."

Bray stepped forward. "We're geared and Jump ready any time, Aaron. Just say the word."

Eden had touched each of their lives. And they were all ready to dive into Hell to get her back: the gutsy bartender, their resident psychopath, the vengeful spy, an aging warhorse, and a hotshot jockey.

Aaron could read every one of them, and they all had just one thing in mind: 'Let's go get her.'

They were waiting on him. Get in the game.

"Well," Aaron started, "first: we'll need a ship."

Talania nodded. "I've already set up the call."

EPILOGUE

FIONA MCCORTY

THAT LITTLE BRAT had her completely dialed in. When she had to go on the run from Imperial cruisers, hide in dark back alleys on backwater planets, the very first thing she missed was her *gulaw* brass band. It had set her back a pretty penny. And she had earned every credit.

That power, that privilege, she clawed for every inch of it. She was proud of that work.

And now? Dripping condensation from a metal roof to a concrete floor. A creaking hammock slung off two twisted bits of rebar. A few ships left, but fewer loyal men.

Master of the Boolean Edge. Heh. The Consul's Navy scattered her like she was dust building up on a shelf.

When her safe houses grew particularly dank, dark, and dreary, that was when her mind ran off without her. She often thought of taking up Osyen on his offer, falling in with his band of merry pirates traipsing about the galaxy. A romantic notion, stuck fast to the bridge of a little freighter, looking to carve her name into the stars...

No, she'd only bring fire on to their heads now. She had picked a fight with an armored bear and brought only a sharpened toothbrush. She was knocked on her face, bloody and bruised, and deserved every bit of it: The Empire's Most Wanted gangster and artisan of the shortest Civil War in modern history.

Which is why she never expected the call. But her console glowed now, silently pulsing the polite request.

The code beamed back at her: K29-RF. That was Keira Ladd!

She hadn't seen Keira in years, not since Charon. The good ol' days, those were. The scrappy days. The hot boxes had been some of the most miserable months of her life.

And Keira had been instrumental in seeing them end. No nonsense, no flash, just the unvarnished truth. Keira gave it as hard and blunt as a lead pipe to the face. Those five alphanumerics blinked back at her like the name of a favorite song from childhood, a thousand happy memories pulling a smile onto her face.

The two of them had met during a prison brawl over a stale biscuit. Tough woman, tougher criminal.

What did that goliath bank robber need that Fiona could give?

For an ugly moment, she considered closing the screen. Keira *was* a Capital again, stuck hard to an Imperial labor camp. It might be a trap. But then...that friendly face might be worth sticking out her head, even if it was between some wrought-iron teeth.

At least, she'd get to see an old friend before the Empire finally got around to breaking her neck.

She reached one hand up, swiping the holographic screen open. And she winced, seeing a male face look back at her. Handsome enough, and fit, with dark skin and cropped hair.

Damn.

"So the Empire's finally tracked down some of my old friends," Fiona said, accepting it. "Good of you to show some ingenuity."

The man threw a glance off-screen, then back to her. "You Fiona McCorty?"

She blinked. This guy didn't recognize her on sight. Her bright red hair and cybernetic arm were usually a dead giveaway. Did she look *that* bad?

"Master of the Boolean?" the man fished. "Pirate Lord?"

"You found her," Fiona said, eyes narrowing. "Who're you?"

"Aaron Havenes. I'm a friend of Keira Ladd, and I can't believe I'm making this call."

"Y'know, you're lucky I took it."

His squinted at her, studying her. He lingered for a moment, before letting out as sigh. It was like he got her whole life story from the tip of her nose. "I'm no friend of the Empire. And you look like you need a job."

Fiona chuffed at that. "I'm taking something of a sabbatical right now, Aaron, but I'm touched you thought of me."

"You come highly recommended," Aaron said. "Keira was bustin' down my door to get us together."

"She playin' matchmaker now?" Fiona mused. He was pretty enough...

"She's dead."

Her heart ran cold, and her shoulders hunched. How had she died? Torture finally break her? An accident in a mine shaft? Or was it so simple that another prisoner finally drove a shank into her belly?

Her lip curled, and her shoulders ˙shook, and her augmented hand squeezed on the bit of rebar, imprinting herself on the rusted metal.

"We're going after—"

"Shut up," Fiona pushed past her teeth. "Whatever you're planning...whoever did it to her...I'm in."

———

Aaron's story continues in
Command of the Blood Service

And meet Fiona McCorty in
The Gold Service
a Space Opera companion series
with 'big damn heroes' energy

AFTERWORD

So this was an achievement for me, my third book in a single year. This series has blossomed into one my favorite worlds, with characters I love, a full-blown space religion, and grounded military combat full of realistic tech—even if we take some liberties for Rule of Cool.

If you're enjoying the Capital Adventures, please leave a review. It really helps small authors like myself.

Signing up for the Newsletter keeps you on top of the latest news around the Capital-verse.

I also have a cat. I will likely be dropping pictures of her there regularly, as she is a consistent part of my office day. She is bad at being a cat, but she is fat and good and adorable. Sign up and see!

https://www.authorivers.com/

ACKNOWLEDGMENTS

I'd like to thank my wife for being a tireless supporter of my work, my writing, and craft. She helps me get the best version of this stuff out of my head and onto the page.

Evan Price for continuing to be my fight choreographer and armorer. Half of the gear in this book came out of our combined heads!

And Jack Allen for ensuring my medical care and diagnostics were up to par.

This book wouldn't be what it is without these wonderful people!

ABOUT THE AUTHOR

Allen Ivers started writing original stories at the ripe age of eleven, largely trying to figure out why the Disney villains on the television box were the way they were. Villains, monsters, and politicians have always fascinated him with their behavior. Twenty years later, he's still fascinated by bad people and the bad things they do.

After spending ten years in Los Angeles as a screenwriter & script consultant, Allen decided to make the leap into fiction, where he need not concern himself with budgets or broad appeal, but could make his stories as big—or narrow—as he desired.

Allen now lives in beautiful Juneau, AK, where he is somewhere at the bottom of the food chain. You can find his thoughts about writing, politics, and the odd cute cat on his Twitter.

ALSO BY ALLEN IVERS